I0633305

MIDNIGHT TEMPTATION

SHARI NICHOLS

CITY OWL
PRESS

This book is a work of fiction. Names, characters, places, and incidents either are products of the author's imagination or are used fictitiously. Any resemblance to actual events or locales or persons, living or dead, is entirely coincidental and not intended by the author.

MIDNIGHT TEMPTATION
Raven's Hollow Coven, Book 2

CITY OWL PRESS
www.cityowlpress.com

All Rights reserved. Except as permitted under the U.S. Copyright Act of 1976, no part of this publication may be reproduced, distributed, or transmitted in any form or by any means, or stored in a database or retrieval system, without the prior consent and permission of the publisher.

Copyright © 2020 by Shari Nichols.

Cover Design by Mibl Art. All stock photos licensed appropriately.

Edited by Heather McCorkle.

For information on subsidiary rights, please contact the publisher at info@cityowlpress.com.

Print Edition ISBN: 978-1-949090-64-2

Digital Edition ISBN: 978-1-949090-65-9

Printed in the United States of America

PRAISE FOR SHARI NICHOLS

"Great read and start to a new series. I'm excited to see more of as it comes out!" - *Book Junky Girls*

"An emotional, action packed, YUMMINESS ride!"
- *Carrie Book Fairy*

"I can't wait for what is next in the Ravens Hollow series. I give this book 5 Fangs!" - *Maria Suarez, Paranormal Romance and Authors that Rock.*

"Action packed steamy paranormal romance with a host of intriguing characters." - *Crystal's Many Reviewers*

"Her plot was solid, her characters were complex and her writing hooks the reader right from the start and never let's go! Think of a multiple loop, fast, curving, upside down roller coaster and you have an idea of what you are in for with this book."
- *Stephenee, Nerd Girl Official*

"The chemistry between the characters is awesome! You won't want this story to end. Looking forward to the next book by Shari Nichols." - *Chris Clemetson, Romance Author*

"Nichols is excellent in setting the stage. The reader is instantly transported into a believable, three-dimensional, magical world."
- *S. Wilk, Romance Author*

"A gripping, sexy read you won't be able to put down. Nichols manages to infuse her characters with life and love, making them jump off the page." - *M. Kate Quinn, Award-Winning Author of Romantic Fiction*

"I was hooked from page one! A titillating, fast-paced read, this edge-of-your-seat paranormal romance kept me guessing."

- Sky Purrington, Bestselling Author of Time Travel Romance

"Paranormal has never been my cup of tea. However, I am starting to rethink that notion." *- EJ Cohn, Romance Author*

This book is dedicated to my mom — your light still shines bright.

CHAPTER 1

*I*t only made sense that certain protocols needed to be followed when attending a supernatural speed dating event: like how long you could check someone out for it to be considered socially acceptable. Three seconds, maybe four—tops.

When Gillian Howe tried to imagine sounding clever to a complete stranger in the span of five minutes, her stomach twisted into knots. Of course, there was the drink rule to consider. How many should you consume? One probably wasn't enough to take the edge off. Two might loosen you up enough to keep from getting tongue-tied during the stretches of awkward silences. By the time you got to three and were well on your way to getting sloppy drunk, it wouldn't matter anyway.

Fortunately, she didn't have to worry too much about it or go through the paces of said mini-dates. But that didn't mean she couldn't do her part from the sidelines.

Tonight, her job was to match each of Hoboken's fourteen supernatural and human singles brave enough to attend this event with a card from her tarot deck. And for those lucky enough to find a match, they were eligible for a full couple's reading.

Her breath caught as she glanced around the W's hotel lobby, struck by the cool, modern décor. One wall was comprised entirely of glass and the other of sleek wood paneling. Enormous rectangular fixtures, shimmering with black and silver lights, hung like floating sentries from the ceiling. Black leather chairs and cushioned benches with red pillows were artfully displayed on top of a black marble floor.

The room started to fill up with human and demon males dressed in fine cut suits. The only trouble with the latter–hot as they were–was that most demons had egos even bigger than their hulking physiques.

The ladies looked chic decked out in little black dresses, while some wore glittery tops with leather pants and uber-high heels. One by one, they made their way over to the bar, and like the rest of the living room, it was blinged out in silver and black. Sinatra crooned from overhead speakers, setting the perfect mood for the evening.

Instinctively, Gillian tugged at the hem of her short, black lace dress, starting to feel a little self-conscious. She'd gotten a steal on it, even by H&M's standards. The deep V in the front was currently being held together by a safety pin and a prayer, but it was all she could afford at the moment.

"What constitutes as clever first date conversation anyway?"

Gillian recognized the soft, feminine voice. She turned toward her business partner and best friend Saje. They ran a small magick shop with a group of other witches from their coven.

She took a seat next to her on a red banquette. The familiar aroma of Saje's perfume filled the air. Even that didn't relax Gillian.

With damp hands and her heart racing, Gillian placed several tarot decks on one of the small lacquered tables and began to shuffle the cards. Magick, pure and bright, pulsed beneath her fingertips. Gillian looked up. "I think I'm the wrong person to ask, but I'm guessing, 'do I have spinach in my teeth' is probably a major no-no."

Saje chuckled, easing some of Gillian's tension away. Different colored strands of beads adorned Saje's neck. She wore a flowy print dress that complimented her petite frame and high wedges on her feet. Her outfit screamed Boho-chic, and perfect for cohosting a speed dating event. She opened a small cooler and unloaded a cocktail shaker and mason jars filled with pink colored liquid. A mischievous gleam flashed in her eyes.

"Trust me, anyone who drinks some of my special brew will be inclined to follow their deepest desires, and see hearts and flowers in their eyes, not spinach."

"I always wondered where the adage 'love is blind' comes from. Now I know." Gillian cut the decks and began arranging her cards face down in a diamond pattern.

"Don't let your cousin Brooke hear you say that. I'm sure it would be considered sacrilege in some dating ritual handbook." Saje shot her an evil grin as she pulled a hair tie from her wrist and swept her long, dark hair up in a messy bun.

"Funny, I didn't know there was one." But if anyone had a copy, it would be Brooke. Speed dating for charity was her baby. Coined matchmaker to the millennial crowd, Brooke believed everyone deserved love and that one perfect person was out there, once the stars aligned and timing collided with physical attraction in some cosmic way. Gillian, on the other hand, wasn't so sure.

"Brooke's the eternal optimist in the family. She got the gene I never inherited," Gillian said with a smirk. "Seriously though, what have you brewed up for us tonight? Nothing too potent I hope."

"It's a special blend of lavender, crushed rose petals, grapefruit juice, and a pinch of vodka." Saje gave her a reassuring smile. "Trust me, there's nothing to worry about. I used a spell for general romantic feelings to blossom for those who are already into each other. This will just give them a gentle push so they can see through the clouds of their self-doubt. Think of it as a way to make their potential match's clear. As long as we're on the subject of love, have you ever considered…"

Gillian shook her head, amused. "Hey, I thought Brooke was the official matchmaker for the night. Besides, I want tonight to be all about the charity." Now that everyone in their friend group seemed to be pairing up, her love life continued to be a hot topic amongst her coven mates. They'd been planning this night for months, selling tickets and posting the event on their websites and social media. The purpose was to raise funds for Gillian's charity, Hope Club, along with their corporate sponsor, Kurt Lawrence of The Lawrence Cancer Support Network. The cause was near and dear to Gillian's heart. Gillian knew what it was like to watch a loved one get sick and feel helpless. At least now she could do something proactive. Besides, this event would serve as a great promo for their magick shop, not to mention fodder for her weekly podcast–Eat, Tarot, Love.

After Gillian lit seven votive candles for luck, she spread some business cards and pens with the charity logos on the table. She glanced at her watch and then at Saje. "We'd better finish setting up. This party's about to go full gear any minute now. Let me help you."

When she bent down to pull a funnel from Saje's bag, her heel slipped off her foot.

"I love the outfit, especially the shoes." Saje pointed to Gillian's feet. "Although, they do seem a tad big."

"Sorry, I should've asked first, but they matched the dress." Gillian adjusted the strap on her borrowed stiletto. Saje was the only one in their coven whose feet were bigger than hers. That's what you did when you lived with a house full of women; you shared everything, nothing was off-limits, and closets were no exception.

Saje tilted her head to the side. "Are you okay? I'm picking up on some major stress vibes from you."

The question made Gillian's skin flush with a mist of nervous perspiration. The trouble with having a psychic for a best friend was you couldn't keep anything to yourself. "Sorry. I guess I'm a little off my game tonight."

This was the first time they'd done something like this, and Gillian was still uneasy about the whole thing. She'd stayed up half the night tossing and turning, not able to pinpoint exactly what was off. Now she felt like a total zombie. She'd used half a tube of concealer to cover the matching luggage under her eyes.

But that wasn't the only thing keeping her awake. She couldn't shake the sense of emptiness and longing that twisted inside her. Pushing her uneasiness to the back of her mind, she refused to venture into a dark place tonight.

"This is supposed to be fun, remember?" Saje unscrewed the tops of the mason jars, and together, they went to work filling wine glasses with her potion.

"You're right of course. At the risk of sounding like a walking contradiction, does anyone fall in love the old-fashioned way these days?" This said by a woman who had zero prospects of her own.

"What about Willow? She fell in love the old fashion way." Saje pointed out. Their mutual friend and former coven mate was about to tie the knot to her gorgeous special agent boyfriend.

Alex proposed to Willow a few months back. Now their engagement party was just a week away, and Gillian still didn't have a date. But Willow wasn't the only one who'd been brought to her knees by the L word. Saje had fallen ass over elbow in love with one of Alex's coworkers.

Gillian wasn't sure what was flowing through the water of Raven's Hollow these days. But it seemed like all of her friends were pairing off and blissfully happy. The click-clack of heels made her glance over her shoulder, catching the eye of the event hostess for the evening. "Almost ready to go?"

"I just need a minute." Brooke walked up to their table looking like the picture of class in a red sheath dress and matching Louboutin's. Her wavy blonde hair was pulled up in an elegant chignon. With her fresh face, blue eyes, and fair skin, Brooke was Gillian's polar opposite. Gillian embraced her olive skin, dark eyes, and wavy, brown hair, grateful she'd inherited something from her mom.

Her cousin set down her tote bag, then reached inside to pull out score sheets and name tags. "Since you two are speed dating virgins, I want to give you a quick run-through of what to expect," Brooke said with a bemused expression. "Once the guests have arrived, and the format is explained to them, each person will get a tarot card and a sample love potion—at which point they can embark on their dates."

Even if Gillian wasn't thrilled about the choice of tonight's venue, she still planned to benefit from the publicity this event would bring for the shop and her charity. Having a corporate sponsor would be a huge boon on both fronts.

As much as she loved working at the shop, she needed to branch out on her own. She'd become too dependent on her friends. It was time to spread her wings and fly. Her ultimate goal was to combine her communications background with her gift for the tarot and launch a weekly radio show, which was slowly turning into an all-out obsession. She loved helping people realize their potential in love, career, and relationships through her readings. And radio was a great medium to reach a large audience. Hopefully, tonight would help her take a step in that direction.

"Crap, I forgot the decorations," Brooke shouted, pulling Gillian out of her fog.

"I've got them right here." Saje set the plastic bag on the table. The sound of voices drifted over from the bar. People lined up and made their way toward the tables. Everyone looked excited, some a little terrified; not that Gillian could blame them.

"Let me get those for you. Why don't you greet the guests?" Gillian whispered to Brooke. With one hand full of streamers, Gillian reached inside the bag for the scissors and tape. After she climbed on top of a chair, she twisted the ends and taped them around a wooden pillar.

Suddenly, all the hairs on the back of her neck stood on end. Her whole body tensed. The chatter and music became muffled. Her eyes flickered across the lobby in search of who, or what, had caught her attention.

Then she saw *him.*

Six-feet-three inches of tall, dark, and brooding stood at the front desk. Detective Garrett Mulroney? What the hell was he doing here? Seeing him again after all these months sent a jolt of shock rippling through her.

His gaze locked with hers, and for a moment, she forgot to breathe. They both stood there, staring at each other. It was as though he could see beneath her armor, the kind she wore under the little black dress.

The word handsome didn't even begin to describe him. Mythological titans like Adonis and Poseidon came to mind, males so stunning, they couldn't possibly be real. But then she thought of other words too, like arrogant, brash…controlling…she could go on.

Mulroney crossed the lobby with a confidant gait, his long legs eating up the distance between them in a few easy strides. Her heart hammered in her chest with every step.

Every female head turned to catch a glimpse of the vampire. The closer he got, the more her body became hyperaware of his presence. He kept his thick head of dark hair short on the sides and longer in the front. The cut showed off the angles and hard lines of his face. Sexy stubble darkened a square jaw, and he looked every bit as dangerous as she remembered. Long, and lean, Gillian could make out the ripple of sinewy muscle beneath the jacket of his grey suit. In the past, she'd always been attracted to the artistic types. So, there was no good reason why she was drawn to this rough-hewn alpha.

But Goddess help her, he was magnificent.

Laughter drifted from the bar, and that's when she realized she was still standing on a chair, gawking at him like some lovesick schoolgirl. She went to step down and her foot slipped out from one of her strappy sandals. Before she could fall sideways onto the marble, two strong arms wrapped around her waist and caught her in midair.

When she looked up and into Mulroney's ice-blue eyes, her heart gave a little flutter. Apparently, the legends about vampires having preternatural speed and strength were real. But then, as his gaze filled with a kind of raw, primal desire, she had no doubt the steamy ones about them possessing a certain sexual allure also rang true.

"You're lucky you didn't break your neck," Mulroney whispered close to her ear and set her on her feet. "What are you doing here tonight, Miss Howe?" The deep rumble of his voice did funny things to her insides.

"I could ask you the same question." Gillian grabbed the scissors and scotch tape off the table, then shoved them in her black beaded bag. "If you must know, I'm working," Gillian snapped. Ever since the prickly detective had been assigned to investigate the robbery of one of her clients, a local antique dealer, their paths had collided on more than one occasion.

Mulroney's eyes did a slow sweep of her from the tips of her three-inch heels to the top of her head. Goosebumps instantly spread across her flesh. Gillian wanted to squirm from the flagrant perusal, but remained still, refusing to give him the satisfaction. Why would she? After all, he had tried to ruin her life. "Interesting work attire," he murmured.

Her hands clenched at her sides, fighting the urge to tug on her dress again. "I'm sure you didn't walk over here to comment on my choice of clothing. To what do I owe the unexpected *pleasure*?" she asked with a healthy dose of sarcasm.

"Trust me, this wasn't planned," he said in a gruff voice, refusing to look her in the eye.

Gillian couldn't help remembering the day he and his partner had showed up at the coven. Peppering her with questions and unwarranted accusations, they'd invaded her safe space, conjuring that too familiar lash of shame, and reminding her of the days when the neighbors used to call the cops to keep her parents from an all-out war.

He kept his hands stuffed in his pockets, his stance casual, but he wasn't fooling anyone. There was no mistaking the predatory way he kept checking out the people strolling by as only a cop would. She followed his gaze as it took in every detail, restless with intensity, before finally landing on their banner. "Is this a private fundraiser?"

She nodded, not in the mood to elaborate. "Are you here in an official capacity? What's the matter, no real criminals on the streets tonight?" Or maybe this was personal and he was meeting someone. He'd worked with

Alex on several cases, and according to Willow, he was a confirmed bachelor, not that she had inquired or anything.

"A quick word, please, Miss Howe. We need to talk." The object of her unhealthy obsession ignored her questions and reached for her elbow, pulling her off to the side. His touch seared through the thin material of her dress, leaving a hot flush along her skin. At five-foot-seven, she wasn't exactly short, but even in her heels, he towered over her.

"Hold on. I'm kind of busy right now. What's this about?" Gillian demanded, catching a whiff of his masculine scent, a blend of sandalwood and clean laundry. She fought the urge to sigh and glared at him instead.

"You shouldn't be here." Mulroney glanced over at the couple's tables scattered with rose petals, floating candles, bowls of heart-shaped chocolates, and the Lawrence Charity placards. He turned back to face her and scowled. "I want you to leave. Now."

"Excuse me?" His words knocked Gillian off-center and before she could process them, an attractive female vampire with dark hair pulled in a tight ponytail walked up to Mulroney and placed a hand on his arm.

"It's time. We need to go." A surge of irrational jealousy coursed through Gillian's veins like battery acid.

For a split second he hesitated, his gaze still fixed on Gillian, and she sensed some kind of inner battle raging inside him. Then he gave her a curt nod and walked away. Her heart sank.

Brooke approached and crossed her arms over her chest. "What was that all about?"

Not sure what to make of their twisted interaction, or of Mulroney's ominous words for that matter, Gillian sucked in a quivering breath and let it out. "No idea."

CHAPTER 2

One creepy proposition and five readings later, Gillian was ready to call it a night when Brooke plopped down in the chair across from her. A rapturous expression spread across her pretty face the moment she slipped off her shoes. While Brooke hit on the finer points of the evening, Gillian's gaze kept darting around the lobby in search of Mulroney, but there was no sign of him. His cryptic words still rang in her head and made her stomach clench. *You shouldn't be here.*

"Gillian? Did you hear a word I said?"

Her cheeks heated. "What? I'm sorry. I got a little distracted. Please continue."

"I was saying that overall, the night was a huge success." Brooke flipped through the pile of score sheets before looking up. "Whatever you and Saje did must've worked because we had five out of seven matches."

"I think your expertise may have helped." Gillian smiled and pulled out her phone, posting pictures from the night all over her social media. She connected the event with the two charities, the shop, and her weekly podcast. *#SpeedatingForCharity #LawrenceCancerSupportNetwork, #HopeClub, #Enchantments, #EatTarotLove.*

From the beginning, she'd gained quite a following from her podcast. It had taken a few years and a tremendous amount of hard work, but now she had over a million followers. In a matter of seconds, her phone began to ping nonstop. She hoped tonight had helped her on the road to radio. Gillian stuck her phone in her purse and gave Brooke her full attention.

"Now I just have to build up my contacts again, but I suppose that's a good problem to have." Brooke glanced around the lobby. "No sign of Mulroney. What's the deal between you two? There's some major sexual tension going on, and trust me, from a matchmaker's perspective, you know it when you see it. You get this look in your eyes when you talk about him."

Gillian flushed. "What look?"

Brooke chuckled. "You're doing it right now. Your pupils get big and dilated. It's a signal of sexual attraction. Do you happen to know his birthday? I wonder if you two would be a match."

"Don't go there, Brooke," Gillian warned.

"I get that he came to the coven to investigate those stolen antiques, but you can't hate him for doing his job. Besides, don't you think it's funny that you two ran into each other again? Maybe it's fate."

"More like bad luck." Gillian shot back. For some strange reason, the universe kept putting them in each other's paths. This must be her karma for some past misdeeds, she reasoned. "Look, I promise I'll explain why I don't like him, even give you every sordid detail, but not tonight. I don't want to kill my jam."

"Fair enough. Where's Saje?"

"She took off. She had a date with Nick." When Nick Hastings, the demon special agent, had been attacked while protecting Willow, he landed in the hospital. Saje went to visit him and the two have been together ever since. Up until a few months ago, Gillian and Saje had been partners in collecting an impressive list of assholes. Now happily ever after was in the cards for Saje, and Gillian couldn't be happier for her. Okay, so maybe she was a little jealous. "I thought we could share an Uber and head out. I'm exhausted." She was just about to pack up her decks when Brooke stopped her by holding up her hand.

"Not so fast, cuz. Let's see what the cards have to say. I'd love to know if there's anything in there about you and Mulroney."

Gillian hesitated with her hand on the deck. "Nice try, but I'd much rather focus on your love life. I'm sure it's a lot more interesting."

"Fair enough." Brooke smiled. "I know deflection when I see it. Go ahead, I'm always game for a reading."

Once she cut the deck, Gillian flipped a card and sucked in a breath. "The Vampire. I see him lurking in the background, but I can't tell if he's a friend or foe." As an intuitive, it was nearly impossible for Gillian to sugarcoat what she saw in the cards. Call it an uncanny ability to separate fact from fiction and get to the truth.

"Interesting." Brooke sat up straighter in her chair, her blue eyes wide. "Well, don't keep me in suspense." "What else do you see?" Her gift was in the realm of the zodiac, using astrology in her matchmaking business to set couples up. The look on her cousin's face made her want to keep going.

"One way to find out." Gillian flipped over another one and her hand stilled. "The Fool. In most cases, it signifies a free spirit and innocence. That's so you. But the reverse can mean getting taken advantage of."

Before Brooke could respond, a tall, good-looking vampire with jet black hair slicked back off his face walked up to the table and flashed a wide smile, showing the slightest hint of fangs. "Brooke? Is that you? You look gorgeous as always." His cultured voice held a hint of an English accent. Most vampires had some sort of accent since they migrated to the US from other parts of the world. She had yet to meet one that was born here. "It's great to see you."

"Hey, Kurt." Brooke stood on her tiptoes to hug him, and he kissed both her cheeks. "I didn't think you'd be here tonight. I want to introduce you to my cousin and the founder of Hope Club." She turned toward Gillian and angled her head in the vampire's direction. "Meet our corporate sponsor, Kurt Lawrence."

The vamp needed no introduction; just about everyone in the greater metropolitan area knew his name, unless they lived under a rock. Not only did he own and operate several businesses in the city from nightclubs to restaurants, but he was also a big time philanthropist. Despite being wealthy as sin, he still managed to give back by donating to numerous charities and sponsoring local events like this one. He'd been named one of New York's most eligible bachelors in some gossip rag.

"It's great to finally meet you, Gillian." When Kurt extended his hand to shake, a red signet ring on his pinky finger caught her eye. "I've heard a lot about you from Brooke."

"Oh? Then I promise none of its true," Gillian said ruefully. "How did you two meet?"

"I met Brooke on the charity circuit, and we realized pretty quickly that we had some mutual friends," Kurt explained. His warm bemused tone affected Gillian in the way she suspected it did most women. He had quite the bedroom voice. "I was thrilled when she reached out to me. I'm always glad to help."

From his crisp white shirt and conservative navy suit, Gillian could picture Kurt sitting at the head of a conference table with a bunch of blue bloods trying to figure out the best tax shelters for their millions. "I bet you haven't lent your name to anything as colorful as speed dating?"

"I admit, this is a first, but speed dating sounds a lot more interesting than most of the benefits I do." Kurt winked. "I'd love to hear more about it, and I'm sure some of my out of town colleagues would too. I'm headed up to the penthouse to meet some of them for a small get together. You two must join me. I can guarantee spectacular views of the skyline, a magnum of Cristal, and all the Beluga you can stand."

"How could we turn down an offer like that?" Brooke piped up.

As much as Gillian should be jumping at the opportunity to network with a room full of movers and shakers, there was something about Kurt Lawrence that rubbed her the wrong way. Sure, he was rich…handsome, not to mention charming, but a little too smooth. Her mind drifted to Mulroney once more. Was he trying to give her a warning?

"Gillian?" Her cousin arched one perfectly shaped brow at her in a silent plea.

Nothing like being put on the spot. "Thanks for the invite, Kurt, but it's getting late—"

"Nonsense. It's still early." Kurt pulled a key card from the inside of his designer suit jacket and placed it in Brooke's hand. "A private elevator gets you to the Wow Suite. I look forward to seeing both of you soon." He placed a kiss on the back of Brooke's hand and then disappeared in a blur of speed.

"Before you say no, think about the connections Kurt has. There will be people up there who you could pitch your demo tape to." A look of determination spread across Brooke's face —one Gillian knew from experience. At this point, there was no stopping her cousin.

"Look, I know what you're trying to do, and I appreciate it, but something about this doesn't feel right. I'm all about networking, but doing it in a hotel room at midnight…" Gillian shook her head. "Not so much."

She'd recently auditioned for a spot at a local radio station for her show, a mix of psychic readings and love advice. Prepping for months, she was sure she'd nailed the interview, and they seemed genuinely stoked by the number of her followers. Then, without so much as an explanation, the station manager sent her an abrupt email passing on both her and the show. But Gillian had a strong sense that *someone* had leaked her being at the center of a criminal investigation—that someone being Detective Garrett Mulroney. She continued to send out both her resume and demo tape, but no responses yet.

"I may have a personal stake in this. I've been waiting to get a meeting with Kurt Lawrence for months now. I read in *Fortune* that he took over some international dating service for elite singles, and let's just say I'd like to be the experienced matchmaker on his speed dial. Besides, there will probably be a room full of handsome, wealthy vampires up there. I'm not letting this opportunity pass me by, and neither should you." Brooke batted her eyelashes for effect.

"That's not the point." Gillian shook her head. "What do you know about this guy? I don't trust him."

"His reputation is pristine," Brooke argued. "Do you think he got to where he is today by being a creep?"

Gillian choked back her laugher. "Should I answer that with a straight face?"

"Jeeze, stop being paranoid." Brooke sat back down, slipped her heels on, and then stood. "I guess I'll just have to go solo."

"Brooke, please—"

"C'mon, Gillie, don't make me do this alone."

There was a note of vulnerability in Brooke's voice that tugged at Gillian's heart. "I can see there's no stopping you." Maybe she was being paranoid. "Fine, we stay for one glass of ridiculously overpriced champagne, and then we're out of there."

"Deal."

As promised, the view from the penthouse offered a breathtaking landscape of the New York City skyline. A cool autumn breeze brushed Gillian's shoulders, and she shivered, wishing she had remembered to bring a jacket. But then again she hadn't planned on hanging out on the penthouse balcony at midnight.

"I've always wondered how the undead live." Gillian sipped her champagne and then set the flute on the ledge. She pulled the thin strap of her evening bag across her body before glancing over at Brooke, who stood beside her with a dreamy expression on her face.

"I don't know about you, but I could seriously get used to this." Brooke took a sip from her flute and sighed. Everything was top shelf all the way, from the champagne to the caviar, which was being served by waitresses carrying gleaming silver trays along with chilled shots of Belvedere.

But there was something else going on that Gillian couldn't quite put her finger on, a sense of unease that pricked along her skin. Call it psychic intuition. She caught a glimpse of some of the women at the party through the sliding glass doors. They were all young and attractive—all paired off with vampires, not a human male or demon in sight. It was rumored that vampires preferred to stay within their elite circles, but Gillian had never actually witnessed it until now.

Kurt appeared and placed a hand at the small of Brooke's back. He whispered something in her ear that made her giggle. "I hope you two are enjoying yourselves. There are a few people I'd like to introduce you to, Damon Greystone being one of them. This is his party." Kurt motioned to the people milling inside the suite. "He's here somewhere." Despite his looks and impeccable manners, there was certain smugness about the guy that seeped from his pores. It gave Gillian a queasy feeling in the pit of her stomach, and yet, for some strange reason Brooke didn't seem to notice.

"Lead the way." Brooke trailed behind him. When Gillian didn't follow, she stopped midstride and called to her over her shoulder. "Are you coming? Think of it as fodder for your listeners."

Brooke turned back to Kurt and motioned in Gillian's direction. "Gillian has a podcast."

The vampire smiled wide. "All the more reason you should join us."

"That's okay." She decided to stay put, not able to ignore the prick of unease along the back of her neck. "You go ahead. I think I'll stay here and soak it all in." Gillian turned back around and leaned against the railing to admire the glittering monoliths that lit up the sky. Gusts of air whistled through the buildings and blew her hair in every direction.

Her gaze drifted to the street below filled with cars and taxis. The sidewalks bustled with people coming in and out of the hotel, even at this hour of the night. From up this high, they all appeared as colorful specs zooming by. Their problems seemed a world away like the static on an intercom. For a moment, she let herself feel insulated by the concrete and glass, wishing she could stay here inside this cocoon.

If only her mom was alive to see all of this. Her strength was what inspired Gillian to start her charity, the reason she was standing here staring at this opulent view in the first place. She hoped her mom would be proud of the work she was doing. Tomorrow would've been her mom's birthday, and tonight Gillian missed her so much her chest ached with physical pain. She breathed in a lungful of crisp air and let it out, forcing herself to stay grounded. She was just about to pull out her phone to snap a few pictures when she heard footsteps behind her.

"No matter how many times you look, the view never gets old. And believe me, after living for over a century, that's saying something." The unfamiliar male voice made Gillian's heart skip a beat.

She spun around. A tall vampire with light brown hair stood behind her and leaned against the railing. "I have to agree. It's stunning up here."

"But it's nothing compared to the beauty before me." *Smooth.* Clad in a designer suit, he was classically handsome, but not at all her type. Not that she had a type per se, although she did have a thing for males of the tall, dark, and brooding variety.

"I'm Damon." He extended his hand, and she noticed the same kind of signet ring like the one on Kurt's finger. She sensed it wasn't a coincidence. "I'll be your host for the evening."

"Gillian," she said simply.

"How come you're not mingling?" he asked and motioned to the women and vampires crowded inside the suite; then, he turned back to face her with a hungry gleam in his eyes.

She shrugged. "I just needed a moment to myself."

"I haven't seen you before." His gaze traveled the length of her and back again. "I would've remembered. Are you here alone?" The intimate undercurrent in his tone made her take a step back.

"I'm here with friends. I'm just about to go back inside and find them."

"Wait." He took a step closer and bowed over her, swiftly moving into her personal space. "You seem like you're looking for something you've yet to find. Tell me, Gillian, do you ever wish for that special someone to have a real connection with?"

"That's a loaded question and a very personal one, don't you think?" Her eyes flickered around the patio. It was empty, except for the two of them.

"I know the perfect way to get more personal." His dark eyes gleamed with flecks of gold. "We could blood bond."

Shock held her tongue for an instant before she snapped out of it. "Whoa, back off, Damon." Okay, what female with a pulse wouldn't be somewhat fascinated by the act of blood bonding? There were rumors of intense euphoria, along with a mental and emotional connection that allegedly took place after a vampire bit you, the downside—becoming a renewable feedbag. This guy was a total stranger and a creep to boot. "What would make you think that I'd bond with you?" Gillian took a step toward the sliding glass doors, eager to escape.

The lights on the patio dimmed. "Look at me, Gillian." And when she did, she couldn't pull her gaze away...literally. She tried to run, but she couldn't move her limbs. Her mind and body became disconnected somehow. A scream erupted from her lips, but no sound came out. When she tried to conjure her magick, it stayed frozen inside her body. Her fear reflected at her from the endless depths of his yellow eyes. They glowed in the shadows like burnished gold.

"We need a place where we can be alone." Damon started to drag her along, and all she could do was follow. She felt like a puppet, and he was the master pulling her strings.

"Come with me." Her mind screamed no, but she found herself nodding in agreement. It would be so easy to just capitulate and go along for the ride. For all she knew, it might even be pleasant. She'd heard the rumors that vampires could be possessive, overly jealous, and capable of mind control, but the post-bitten ecstasy supposedly made up for any misdeeds. *No,* her inner voice warned. *He's trying to turn you into his personal blood slave.*

"I promise it won't hurt at all." He grabbed her arms and held her in a vicelike grip, then pulled her further into a dark corner of the patio. "It's better if you don't fight me. If you do, your blood won't be as sweet. There's no need to worry about bite marks on that pristine skin. They won't show up for several hours, long after you're gone."

She focused every ounce of her magick into breaking his hold. When Gillian attempted to dig her heels into the tile, to fight against this mental roofie, one of her shoes slipped from her foot and she stumbled.

"This won't do. We can't leave any evidence behind." The vampire kneeled to slip her heel back on, releasing her from his hold. The drugged sensation fell away.

Desperate, her gaze darted around for a weapon, but there was nothing, nada, zilch. She fumbled through her purse in search of something…anything. But what could she use to defend herself against a vampire? A tampon? A lip gloss? She tried to think of a spell, but nothing came to her frantic mind.

When her fingers closed over the scissors, a surge of adrenaline rushed through her veins. In one quick motion, she grabbed him by the shirt collar and jabbed the point up and into the soft skin under his ribs, grateful for catching the last *Buffy the Vampire Slayer* marathon.

Shock flashed in his eyes. Damon tried to grab her, but she ducked out of the way. His grasping hands ripped the front panel of her dress instead. Blood spurted from his mouth and dripped onto his crisp white shirt. He cursed, fell to his knees and gaped at the scissors in his abdomen. "You staked me."

"Yeah, and you deserved it. Maybe you haven't heard, but karma can be a real bitch." Gillian didn't wait for him to respond. She slipped off her other shoe, flung it over her shoulder, and ran to the patio door.

With her chest heaving, she wrenched the slider open and stepped through. Magick sparking on her fingers, she flicked her hand and the slider slammed shut behind her, the lock clicking in place. Gillian scanned the crowd for Brooke, but there was no sign of her, only women standing close to their vampire companions with glazed looks in their eyes.

She needed to find her and get the hell out of there. Frantic, she ran barefoot through the hallway of the suite and stopped at the first door she came to. Her magick continued to spark on her fingertips as she waved her hand. The door flung open, but the room was empty.

By the time she came to the next one, her whole body shook from head to toe. Voices drifted out to the hallway, along with what sounded an awful lot like moaning. She flicked her wrist again, and the door flew open with a loud bang. What she saw in front of her didn't seem real.

Panic hit her square in the chest. Women lounged on couches and beds;

some were spread across the floor with blood splattered on their clothing. Male vampires drank from the veins of the women who moaned in ecstasy.

The scents of blood and cologne swirled through the air and made her stomach clench. She gulped, taking in the scene. And there, in the middle of it all was Brooke with Kurt hovered over her. "Brooke?"

Heads turned in her direction. "Please come in and shut the door." An enormous, dark-haired vampire called out. "There's plenty of room for more."

Gillian froze. "I...uh, was just here to get Brooke. We, um, came together. Why don't we get out of your lair, I mean hair, and let you get back to what you were doing?" Her heart pounded in her throat, in her ears, and she swore every vampire in the room turned at the sound.

"Join us. It's not a request," Kurt demanded, moving closer.

Trying to think on her bare feet, Gillian reached for her phone, and held it up like a weapon. "Between Instagram and Twitter, I'm sure my million followers would love to know what you've been up to. A single tweet would ruin you." She motioned around the room. "Funny, this whole operation doesn't seem all that philanthropic." Gillian took a step back and sucked in a harsh breath, bracing against his wrath.

The next moment, shouting filled the room. Cops and MBI agents barreled through the open doorway with their guns drawn.

Gillian nearly sunk to the floor with relief.

"Does trouble find you, Miss Howe, or do you chase after it for sport?"

The familiar male voice pricked along her skin like barbed wire. She tensed, turning slowly around, and came face to face with Mulroney. Anger blazed in his eyes.

Gillian didn't think this night could get any worse, but apparently, it could. Trying to gather what remained of her dignity, considering half her thigh was exposed and she was barefoot, she pushed her shoulders back and stared him down. "Whatever you do, don't you dare say I told you so."

CHAPTER 3

*G*arrett moved to the area of the suite where Gillian stood. Of all the women he expected to see here tonight, she was the last one on his list.

Up until a few hours ago, it had been months since he'd seen her in the flesh, and somehow, in the blink of an eye, she still managed to get under his skin. He exhaled, and the scent of expensive perfume, sweat, and fresh blood flared in his nostrils.

"This is some mess you've gotten yourself into." The spacious room was currently filled with vampires, EMTs, and a slew of young, attractive women getting interrogated by cops and Magickal Bureau of Investigations agents.

Gillian looked pale and shaken, not to mention shorter than she did in the lobby. "If you're asking if I planned on getting mind roofied, then the answer is no. I honestly had no clue," she said, her brown eyes shooting daggers at him.

Over the years, he'd been forced to question mobsters, drug smugglers, and cold-blooded killers. Somehow this brown-eyed firecracker, standing beside him, gave them all a run for their money. "You said you were 'mind roofied.' I'm assuming you mean a vampire tranced you?" If it were anyone else caught up in the middle of a vampire blood ring, he might've found her response amusing, but as his gaze darted around the room, taking in the blood-stained walls and comforters, not to mention the young woman being carried out on a stretcher, there was nothing even remotely funny about the situation. In the last week, there'd been an unsolved murder, a Jane Doe who'd been found with all the blood drained from her body. The RHPD had classified it as a vampire killing.

"It was like being under some kind of spell. This vampire approached me and said something about blood bonding with him." Determination flashed in those big brown eyes. "I made damn sure that wasn't going to happen."

Garrett drew his brows together, impressed. "By using your powers? I'm surprised you didn't send him flying over the balcony." It would've served the bastard right.

"I use telekinesis to move inanimate objects with my mind all the time, but I can assure you nothing as big or as powerful as a vampire," Gillian said with a sigh. "I'm more of a clairvoyant. I have visions and premonitions. I also read signs and symbols with my tarot cards to see both the past and the future. Every witch's power is different. When Damon Greystone tranced me, I didn't use my powers. I acted on instinct."

"Thinking on your feet might've just saved your life." In more ways than she could imagine. Not that it surprised him. This wasn't the first time she'd been in the wrong place at the wrong time. According to her file, there'd been an incident last winter with a dark fae responsible for murdering a string of witches from her coven. Gillian had been targeted and later abducted, yet somehow managed to get away. Despite her looks and graceful mien, Gillian Howe was as scrappy as they came. "Someone with your history should know better."

"Don't patronize me, Detective. I had no idea what I was walking into, but now I think it's pretty clear." She bit down on her lip, and Garrett had a sudden urge to do the same.

"The proper term is blood trafficking." Ever since Tristan Saint Claire, a demon kingpin, was killed and his former crime syndicate, the Shadow Cabal, dismantled, another fringe group made up of vampires emerged to mastermind a high-class blood ring. And from all appearances, Kurt Lawrence was now at the helm, but Garrett suspected he wasn't working alone. "Things could've turned out a whole lot differently. Consider yourself lucky."

His gaze zeroed in on Gillian's bare feet and red painted toenails.

Refusing to admit he found them sexy, he wondered what the hell had happened to her shoes. But there were more pressing matters to discuss than the state of her missing high heels. Although he did recall in vivid detail how they showed off her legs. "Do you have any idea how dangerous these people are?"

"Well, you didn't think it was important enough to give me more of a heads-up earlier." She curled that damnable mouth of hers into a smirk. "A real warning like, 'these are bad, bad people' would've been nice."

His anger flared. "A warning? I tried, but you ignored me. I was undercover, Miss Howe, and not at liberty to reveal what was about to go down. Besides, I would think you'd know the dangers of going up to a hotel room with a group of strangers, vampires no less." When he thought about what could've happened to her, his jaw clenched to the point of pain. But it was more than that. There was something eerily familiar about this case that didn't sit right. Could Kurt Lawrence be involved in the same operation that he'd been lured into over a hundred fifty years ago?

Turning her head, she searched the crowded room until her gaze finally landed on a young, attractive, blonde woman in a red dress, who was currently getting interrogated by some uniformed officers. "As much as I'd love to stand here and chat, I want to go check on my cousin to make sure she's okay."

"Davidson, please bring over the witness," Garrett said into his mic. After a moment, the uniformed officer walked over her cousin. The two women embraced.

"Are you sure you're okay, Brooke?" Gillian whispered as she looked at her cousin with concern in her eyes.

Brooke nodded. "I just want to go home."

"You and me both, honey." Gillian turned back to Garrett and exhaled. "Thank you, but you can't keep us here. We've done nothing wrong and I, for one, need to get out of this hotel room. Adrenaline's just not cutting it anymore."

"I get that it's been a long night for you, but like it or not, you're now witnesses in this case. We have a few more questions, then you're both free to go." Garrett motioned for the officer to take Brooke back to the area of the suite where he'd been questioning her, hoping it would jog her memory. After they walked away, he pulled a chair from the desk and motioned for Gillian to take a seat. "I'm happy to get you some food or water, maybe some coffee?"

Gillian gazed up at him through the fringe of her dark lashes. "Are you planning on interrogating me, Detective?"

"Considering the circumstances you find yourself in, I think that's a given." He drew closer to her and stared her down. "Will you cooperate?"

"Is it going to be like the last time? Are you planning to do your bad cop routine and get all rough with me?" She crossed her arms over her chest, revealing an ample swell of cleavage. He tried to look away, but she was making it difficult in that black scrap of lace she called a dress.

Putting her over his knee and spanking her shapely ass until it turned good and red might be one way to teach her a lesson to keep her out of harm's way. What was it about this woman that had such an effect on him? Maybe it was the fact that she had long, chestnut hair, the kind he imagined wrapping around his fist, and the warmest brown eyes he'd ever seen. And her body, hell, she could bring any red-blooded male to his knees.

"Detective?"

Her voice broke into his musings. He cleared his throat. "Why don't you start by telling me how you ended up here in the penthouse?" Garrett knew she didn't want to answer his questions, but he wasn't going to give her a hell of a lot of choice in the matter. Too many lives depended on it. Cops, along with two of his best friends—special agents from the MBI, Alex Denopoulos and Cayden Teague—buzzed around the room, snapping pictures of the scene and taking samples of blood. He muttered a curse. That blood could have been hers if Kurt Lawrence or one of his thugs had anything to say about it.

"My cousin's a matchmaker and Kurt Lawrence recently took over an international dating service. Brooke and I were invited up here for what we thought was a party, to unwind from a long day and do some networking—"

"Networking?" he cut in. "Is that what he's calling it these days?" Garrett let his eyes roam over the smooth, unblemished skin on her neck and let out a sigh of relief when he found it unmarred. His gaze roamed lower to the bloodstains on her dress, not sure how they got there, finally, to the sizeable rip up the side, showing an indecent glimpse of long, toned leg. "Are you injured?"

She glanced down at her dress before her eyes met his once more. "No. The blood isn't mine."

Before he could ask her whose it was, his new partner, Natalya Dubrosky, who appeared to be recording the scene, walked over to him. Dressed in a conservative navy pantsuit, she stuck out like a cop amongst the sea of scantily clad women. Her probing gaze drilled into his. "Sorry to interrupt, but I wanted to give you an update."

Garrett had been partnered with her a short time but, enjoyed working with his female counterpart. She hailed from one of the oldest and wealthiest vampire families in the country. Females of her stature were more apt to be planning society events than work in law enforcement. But you'd never know it. She'd taken to her new position like a pro and did a damn good job.

"Excuse me for a moment, and don't even think about going anywhere," he muttered to Gillian over his shoulder and walked a few steps away.

He glanced at Dubrosky and let out a deep breath. "What do you have so far?"

"I thought you'd be happy to know that a total of five vampires are in custody, including a very pissed off Kurt Lawrence. He's being interrogated by the MBI agents as we speak." Dubrosky smoothed her dark hair back into her ponytail, looking bewildered.

"Did they say where they're planning to take him and the others?"

"From what I overheard, they're taking them to MBI Headquarters, and then an appearance in front of the Council will follow. I almost forgot to show you this..." Dubrosky held up a photo on her iPad of an unconscious vampire who appeared to be bleeding all over the terrace with a set of kitchen shears buried in his stomach.

"The plot thickens. Who do we have here?" Garrett rubbed the back of his neck, his irritation mounting.

"According to his ID, his name is Damon Greystone. This is his penthouse. We're still trying to work out exactly what happened to him. The paramedics just took him away."

"He's unconscious?" Gillian approached them sounding wary.

Garrett turned his attention to her and searched her face. "You wouldn't happen to know anything about that would you, Miss Howe?"

"He attacked me first, well, not physically. We were led up here under false pretenses." Gillian ran a hand through her messy hair. "The vampire who's bleeding, will he make it?"

"Hard to say at this point," Dubrosky said matter-of-factly. "My guess is he'll probably need a transfusion."

"I don't feel so good." Gillian began to shake and swayed on her feet. Garrett rushed to her side in an instant. His hand reached out to steady her, torn between wanting to shake her for putting herself in harm's way and wrapping her in his arms.

"What's wrong?"

"I got dizzy for a minute. I don't know what's worse, the thought that I could've actually killed a vampire, or what he could've done to me if I hadn't. I guess thinking about it made me a little queasy." This close he could see the flecks of green in her eyes and the smattering of freckles across the bridge of her nose. Gillian Howe might be a royal pain in the ass, but she was a gorgeous one at that.

"Trust me, you made the right call." He'd known even before their eyes locked earlier that Gillian was near. He'd smelled her immediately. He was still trying to shake off the momentary panic of finding her up here with a sociopath like Kurt Lawrence. When he thought about what could've happened to her, his mouth went dry. He removed his jacket and draped it around her shoulders. The tempting blend of lavender and vanilla flared in his nostrils and made the front panel of his suit pants tight. His heightened senses picked up on her fear as well. Guilt slid in his belly. After what she'd been through tonight, the last thing she needed was the detective in charge checking her out.

He cleared his throat and pulled a pad and ballpoint pen from his back pocket. Unlike most of his colleagues who used iPads and recording apps, he preferred to do things the old-fashioned way. There was something personal about ink and paper that made him feel closer to the words and tied him to the case. "What's the connection between Miss Corey and Lawrence?"

"They met through the charity circuit," Gillian explained. "And tonight we hosted a charity speed dating event here at the hotel that the Lawrence foundation sponsored."

"Yes, I saw the sign," Garrett muttered and scribbled a note on his pad before looking up at her again. "Then you're telling me this is the first time you met him, and yet, you thought it wise to come up to the penthouse, two women alone?" He tried to keep the jealousy out of his voice and failed. He had no business chastising her on her whereabouts. But from the very first day he laid eyes on her, he couldn't get her out of his mind. This investigation had to be his number one priority. For the sake of the case, he'd keep things strictly professional and remain detached. If he let himself soften where she was concerned, he risked not finding the bastards behind this mess.

Her cheeks flamed red. "I don't make it a habit, if that's what you're implying."

Hell, the last thing he wanted to do was start throwing accusations around. From what Alex's fiancé, Willow, had told him, Gillian hated his guts. Why make things worse? Her opinion of him shouldn't matter, and yet somehow it did.

"He's 'a well-respected entrepreneur and philanthropist.' How was I supposed to know he's some kind of...?"

"Human trafficker? In a matter of speaking, yes. What exactly did you see when you walked into the suite?"

Vulnerability flickered in her eyes. "Carnage. At first, I thought it was some kind of vampire orgy, and then I realized it was, but with blood and not sex."

Her words hit too close to home. Now he feared she thought all vampires resembled the vile creatures depicted in horror films and graphic novels. "Believe it or not, all of us aren't monsters, Miss Howe."

"No, just the ones I run into." Gillian pulled the jacket across her body, and it dwarfed her slender frame.

"What else can you tell me about Lawrence? Even the smallest detail might be significant in some way. This is important. It could help us get ahead of the press, which could mean the difference between tipping off the suspects and catching them. Please, try and think."

"I don't know." She exhaled deeply. "He looked like a clean-cut businessman. I do remember he wore this red signet ring on his pinky, and now that I think of it, my attacker had on the same one. What do you think it means?"

Trying to block out the noise, Mulroney tuned in to the multiple conversations in the suite. "It could be some kind of brotherhood." A brotherhood Garrett suspected was responsible for turning innocent women into blood slaves. He'd been down this savage road before, many lifetimes ago, and it didn't end well.

"How long have you been investigating his operation?" she asked, pulling him from a dark place.

He debated answering the question, but he figured after everything she'd been through tonight, she had a right to know. "Long enough to find out that Lawrence and some of his associates would be up here in Damon Greystone's penthouse tonight, which is why we set up surveillance from the hotel room next door."

If all went according to plan and the Council voted to put this case on trial, Kurt Lawrence's sorry ass would be locked up in a high-security mage prison for a very long time. They didn't call it Hellios for the high thread count sheets. Over the years, he'd seen guys like Lawrence before, rich, entitled, pretty boys that thought they could throw some money at their high priced lawyers and skirt justice. The bastard would be doing hard time if Garrett had anything to say about it.

"What about the other girls, are these women all victims?" she whispered, glancing curiously around the room. "Do they know what they're getting involved in?"

"No, we don't believe they understand the full extent of what it means to have a permanent blood bond with a vampire. From what we've gathered, most are kidnapped, and some tranced much like yourself and your cousin."

Gillian tilted her head to the side. "I don't understand. If Lawrence had a room full of women up here, why invite Brooke and me to join?"

Garrett smiled at the question, admiring her tenacity. "Last I checked I'm the one who's supposed to be asking the questions, not the other way around. But if I had to guess, I'd say because he's a greedy bastard."

To Garrett the answer was obvious: Gillian was stunning, and Lawrence assumed he could auction her off like chattel to the highest bidder. As for Damon Greystone, the vampire appeared to have simply gone rogue. "After Lawrence demanded you come into the room and shut the door, did you say or do anything?"

Her face fell, and then she let out a long breath. "I might've threatened to expose him and his operation to my million followers on social media."

"Jesus, now you've made yourself vulnerable by poking a bear." Lawrence had too much to lose to let anyone get in the way of his operation. If Lawrence was indeed responsible for murdering the Jane Doe, then it would only stand to reason that he wouldn't hesitate to go after Gillian to get her out of the way. "We appreciate your cooperation, Miss Howe. We'll be in touch if we have any more questions for you. In the meantime, lay off the social media. The last thing you want to do right now is to draw attention to yourself or to Lawrence for that matter. A squad car will drive by your house, and Miss Corey's, to make sure you're safe."

When Gillian nodded, stress lines appeared at the corner of her mouth. "Do you think that's necessary if he's in the slammer?"

"We can't underestimate the scope of his connections. He's managed to establish quite the crime network. Our intel tells us he's got people working on the outside. We like to take extra precautions." Garrett's gaze narrowed. "Do you have any questions for me?"

She lifted her chin. "Yeah, when can I get my shoes back?"

CHAPTER 4

Sitting in the back of Mulroney's Jeep, Gillian rested her head against the leather seat and tried to relax. When his partner, Detective Dubrosky, had insisted on driving her and Brooke home, her first instinct was to decline, desperate for some space away from the arrogant vampire. Unfortunately, Brooke accepted, and Gillian was too exhausted to argue.

The car glided through traffic at a steady pace, and if it wasn't for the blare of horns, the squeal of tires, and the static from the police radio, she probably would've passed out cold. In the last two days, she'd gotten a total of six hours of sleep. She didn't think there was enough caffeine in the world that could remedy the situation.

"How are you holding up? Are you sure you're okay?" Brooke whispered from the seat beside her. "You're awfully quiet, which is unusual for you."

"I'm fine," she said with a shrug, anxious to put this whole ordeal behind her and get on with the rest of her day, after she caught up on about ten hours of sleep. "It's you I'm worried about." With everything that took place, Gillian hadn't gotten a chance to ask Brooke exactly what went down when she walked in on her and Kurt in that hotel room, but from the haunted look in her eyes, she guessed they shared a similar experience. "What happened back there?"

Pieces of her blonde hair spilled out of her chignon, and she couldn't seem to stop shivering. "Kurt was laying it on thick, saying that he was really into me. The rest of the night's pretty fuzzy. I don't feel like myself. I don't want to be alone right now. Will you come back to my place?"

"Of course." Gillian reached out to squeeze Brooke's hand and then glanced out the window at the colorful storefronts. People bustled along the sidewalks on their way to work, and the routine of it put her somewhat at ease. She turned back to face her and smiled. "Let's try and forget last night ever happened."

"I recommend that you tell only one person, the fewer people who know, the better," Mulroney murmured from the front seat. This was the first time he'd spoken since they'd gotten into his car. His pale blue eyes slid to hers in the rearview mirror, and her heart skipped a beat. "For everyone's safety."

Gillian reached into her purse for her phone and glanced at the screen. It exploded with likes and comments from her recent posts; if any of them only knew the half of it. She had a few texts from Saje, reminding her of tonight's Mabon Ritual. Luckily, today was her day off so she could go crash for a few and get her bearings before she went back to work.

"Don't worry. I don't plan on saying anything about this to the others. It's one of the few things we agree on." Ellen and the other girls had been through enough this past year. Things were finally getting back to normal around the coven. From what she'd overheard Detective Dubrosky say to Mulroney, all of the vampires involved in the blood ring were in custody. So why worry them unnecessarily?

"I guess there's a first for everything, even in this particular instance." Mulroney agreed, his tone brimming with sarcasm.

Her first instinct was to rattle off some flippant reply, but she figured it was best to keep her feelings to herself when sitting in the backseat of a detective car, especially when the detective in question distrusted her with a blatant intensity.

Gillian observed the vampire sitting in front of her, reluctantly admiring the way his long, tapered fingers covered the steering wheel and the confidant way he maneuvered the vehicle. While part of her couldn't stand him, he was nothing like the vampire who had tried to mind-roofie her. Mulroney lived by a code—a code that she suspected made him worthy of his badge.

She'd never forget the first time Mulroney showed up at the manor. She had assumed it was Belinda, one of the witches from her coven ringing the doorbell as she was notorious for losing her keys. Gillian had just stepped out of the shower, never expecting the plain-clothed detective—who came to accuse her and her coven mates of being linked to an organized crime syndicate—to be so good-looking. The whole thing had caught her completely off guard.

Mulroney pulled up to Brooke's apartment building on Hudson Street and cut the engine. "We're here," he announced, and the four of them got out of the car.

Detective Dubrosky turned to Brooke. "I'm going to check your place first to make sure no one's inside. What's your apartment number?"

Brooke reached into her purse and handed the detective a heart-shaped key ring with a small copper amulet dangling from the center. "I'm in fourteen C."

"I'll be right back." Detective Dubrosky walked up the block to the red brick building in a blur of speed.

A few minutes later, she came back and handed the keys to Brooke with an encouraging smile. "All clear. Hopefully, you can put this all behind you." She got back in the car and began typing on her phone.

Brooke turned to Gillian and covered a yawn. "I need to go crash before I pass out. I'll meet you inside." After she thanked Mulroney and his partner, she waved goodbye and walked up the block.

"There's one more thing to put to rest, Miss Howe." Mulroney took a step closer, and she caught another whiff of his cologne. The clean laundry scent made her head spin.

Gillian smirked. "Let me guess, you decided to arrest me after all?" Why did her voice sound provocative, almost flirty?

"Tempting, but no. Would you be able to identify the vampire who tranced you in a line-up?"

"I think so. I mean it was dark, but I have no doubt his face will be in my nightmares. What I still can't figure out is why. Was this all for a few moments of undiluted pleasure?"

"You think this is just about pleasure?" The way he said the word *pleasure* made anticipation curse through her veins in hot revolutions. "Some vampires have an addiction to blood in the same way humans do to drugs or alcohol. When a blood bond is made, those who have that predisposition become insatiable for the next fix and will do just about anything to satisfy the craving."

His words made her stomach clench. She tried not to think about what could've happened if he hadn't shown up. "That should help me sleep tonight."

"I'm not about to sugarcoat the facts. It's a good thing you won't be alone. Last night was a bizarre evening."

She sighed. "Yeah, that's certainly one way to describe it." She took in the dark street with its pale pools of light from the streetlamps, which now seemed too far apart. A shiver slid down her spine.

"Please, don't hesitate to call if either of you remember anything else." He closed the remaining distance between them and handed over his card. Their fingers touched, and a bolt of electricity shot up her arm like a live wire. Her eyes locked with his, and she wondered if he felt it too. If he did, he didn't show it—his expression remained blank.

After an awkward silence, she motioned to his Jeep. "I'll let you get back to work. Thanks for the ride, and well, for everything."

His ice-blue eyes stayed locked with hers, and she got the feeling he wanted to say more but shoved his hands in his pants pockets instead. "You're welcome."

Gillian turned and walked up the sidewalk, glad to be rid of the sexy vampire. She'd had more than her fill of creatures of the night to last a lifetime.

CHAPTER 5

*L*ate afternoon sunlight streamed in through the blinds. Gillian blinked and sat up, momentarily disoriented from waking in a strange bed. And then she remembered she'd crashed in Brooke's guest bedroom. She glanced at the clock. She'd slept for almost seven hours straight and felt oddly refreshed.

Her fingers trailed over Mulroney's suit jacket, spread out on the bed. For reasons she couldn't explain, she'd slept with it next to her pillow. Lifting the fabric to her nose, she inhaled his intoxicating male scent like some lovesick teenager. He'd ridden in as a kind of crazy-hot knight in shining armor—all self-important and judgy. It's not like she needed him to save her. She'd done that without his help, even before he arrived. Still...

She reached for his card tucked behind her phone, which sat charging on the nightstand, and turned it over. Her heart gave a little flutter when she saw his cell number written on the back. Debating what to do, she finally gave in and entered his digits into her contacts.

After she pushed this ridiculous attraction to the back of her mind, she moved the duvet aside and got out of bed. She went to the window, opened it, and caught a whiff of roasted coffee and fresh-baked bread from the bakery across the street. She loved this neighborhood. It still managed to maintain its kitschy feel while being only a quick train ride from the city.

She walked into the bathroom and pulled her hair up in a ponytail. After she brushed her teeth and washed her face, she added some of Delilah's homemade moisturizer they sold in the shop. In search of some clothing, she walked to the guest closet and found a pullover and sweats, then changed out of her borrowed PJ's.

Once she found a pair of Brooke's old sneakers, she slipped her feet into them and decided to go for a run to clear her head. Her heart thudded against her ribcage. What if one of Lawrence's thugs came after her? She took a deep breath and reminded herself that the vampires who'd attacked them were in custody. She would be safe. Besides, she wasn't about to let them dictate her life and scare her out of her routine. She swiped the hematite crystal off the nightstand just in case and shoved it in the front pocket of her hoodie.

The moment she made her way into the dimly lit hallway, her whole body tensed. She found Brooke curled up on the couch in the living room, pale and covered in sweat, clutching the amulet on her key ring.

"What's wrong?" Gillian put her hand on her forehead. "You're burning up."

"I don't know what's happening to me, Gillian. My body feels like it's on fire. I'm crawling out of my skin." When Brooke lifted her head, two red bite marks showed on her neck.

"Lawrence bit you?" Saying the words out loud made her stomach churn with revulsion. She swallowed the bile rising from the back of her throat. Gillian took the key chain from Brooke's hands and stuffed it in the front pocket of her hoodie. Then she replaced the amulet with the giant quartz off the coffee table to give her a surge of healing energy. "I'm calling Saje, There has to a potion that can bring you out of this. I'll be right back." She was headed to the guest room to grab her phone when all the hairs on the back of her neck stood on end.

The front door creaked open. Her heart pounded wildly in her chest. Immediately she sensed a vampire in the room. Gillian turned and caught sight of Kurt Lawrence, along with his bodyguard, the hulking vampire from the hotel room. She froze, too stunned to move.

"You need to invite me in, Brooke," Lawrence commanded.

Before Gillian could even utter a warning or protest, Brooke invited him in. Her voice sounded desperate, hollow. The vampire swooped over to where she lay on the couch in a blur. He bent his head to her neck.

"You're bonded to me now. You go where I go." When his fangs protruded from his lips and sunk into her neck, Brooke let out a blood-curdling scream.

Adrenaline surged through Gillian's veins and forced her into action. She focused her mind on the quartz. With a flick of her wrist, the crystal soared up in the air and smashed into the back of Lawrence's head.

When he turned around, his eyes narrowed into slits, filling with rage. "Don't bother trying to fight me, you'll never win."

Before Gillian could look away, his gaze locked on hers, and just like before, her mind and body went rigid. Her magick stalled inside her body, frozen like a cold engine.

"It's a shame because I found you charming, But let this be a warning: don't ever get in my way again, witch, or next time I won't be so nice."

"Let's go." Lawrence motioned to his bodyguard and then grabbed Brooke by the waist and led her out the door.

Gillian blinked and the mental and physical hold on her drained away. She ran to the nightstand and grabbed her phone. Her chest heaved as she searched through her contacts for Mulroney's number. When she found it, she pressed a button and inhaled.

Thankfully, he answered on the first ring. "M-mulroney?" Panting, she tried to catch her breath. "I...need your help."

"Miss Howe? Is everything okay?"

"No! Brooke's been bitten by Lawrence. He...he took her. The bastard tranced me. You need to send the police now!"

"You're still at her apartment?"

She bit back a sob, and her eyes filled with tears. "Y-yes."

"You need to get out of there. Now. Go to the Starbucks on Hudson Street."

The adrenaline coursing through her veins made it hard to think or speak. "You need to find her. What if he—"

"I'm sending back-up to Brooke's apartment as we speak. Maybe we can intersect him. I'll be in touch," he said, and the line went dead.

All Gillian could do was hope and pray that he wouldn't be too late.

CHAPTER 6

*S*haking from head to toe, Gillian got more than a few curious glances from the barista and the constant flow of customers lining up to get their drink orders. Too nervous to sit, she began shredding napkins and pacing back and forth—spilling the coffee she tried to drink all over the table. She probably looked like a crazy person. She tried not to think the worst, but it was impossible considering what she now knew about vampires. Brooke's fate rested in the hands of Kurt Lawrence, a total psycho with a personal bodyguard and unlimited funds at his disposal. What did it all mean for Brooke?

A sudden tremble in her limbs made her sit down at an empty stool. The ache in her chest intensified. She refused to stand back and do nothing. She lifted her phone from her pocket and began composing a tweet.

#KurtLawrence, #vampireentrepreneur arrested amid #humantrafficking scandal.

She posted it and then linked it to her Instagram account, praying the two would work in Brooke's favor. Before she could go over the whole ordeal again in her head, the front door blew open bringing a brisk autumn breeze with it. Mulroney walked in alone. Relief washed over her, and she had to force herself not to jump into his arms.

He towered over everyone else, a tall, brooding presence with an intense look in his light blue eyes that made her shiver. A few female heads turned to stare at him, but he appeared not to notice, his focus directed solely on her.

"Miss Howe?" His brows creased in concern when he spotted her through the crowd. He made his way over to her table, and her breaths came out too fast. "Are you okay?" he asked, his gaze darting to her neck. Despite having just been tranced and threatened by a vampire, the sound of his voice managed to chase some of the darkness away.

"I'm fine. What about Brooke?" she whispered. "Did you find her?" Tears burned her eyes and clogged in the back of her throat. To her horror, she let out a sniffle. The last thing she wanted to do was fall apart in front of Garrett Mulroney.

"Why don't we go somewhere private to have this discussion?" Mulroney motioned to the door.

A shudder rippled through her. "No, I'm not going anywhere until you tell me what's going on." Between his solemn expression and his rigid stance, she sensed whatever he had to say was bad. Her hands began to shake.

His gaze softened a fraction and then darted around the coffee shop before they met hers once more. He resumed his usual guarded expression, pulled out a chair, and sat down. When his jaw visibly clenched, she braced herself for the worst. "We combed through the apartment, but there was no sign of her. From what you told me on the phone, and by all appearances, we believe Brooke was kidnapped."

Hearing her suspicions confirmed made Gillian burst into tears. A mixture of fear and anger washed over her like a tidal wave.

"I'm so sorry. Hey, it's going to be okay. We're going to find her." When he reached across the table to squeeze her hand, a searing heat spread up her arm and burned through the thin material of her sweatshirt. He froze momentarily before he swiped his hand away. What was with her reaction to this guy? She tried to ignore it along with the knot of guilt in her belly.

His expression turned fierce as his eyes locked on hers. "This should never have happened."

"What about the cops?" Her voice bordered on hysterical, but at the moment, she didn't care. "I thought they were supposed to be keeping an eye on Brooke's place. How did Lawrence and his bodyguard slip past them?"

He frowned. "We sent a patrol car to drive by earlier, but they didn't see anything suspicious, so they left. I'm so sorry I wasn't there."

After a few minutes, when the tears finally subsided, she took a deep breath and tried to pull it together. It wouldn't do Brooke any good to have her falling apart. She needed to remain strong so she could help find her and bring her home. "Now what?"

"Good question. We have a team of special agents and police working on locating her as we speak. Let me get you some water." He walked to the counter and came back and handed her a glass bottle. He sat back down across from her and pulled a silk handkerchief from his pocket. He placed it in her hands, clearly uncomfortable.

Shock mingled with gratitude as she wiped her eyes and blew her nose in a very unladylike way. "Thank you." She glanced down at his initials embroidered across the front before looking up. "Who carries a handkerchief around anymore?" She wasn't sure why she was even talking about monogrammed handkerchiefs at a time like this. *I must be in shock.*

"Some of us still do," he clarified.

She supposed it was kind of sweet, in an old-fashioned way. "My grandfather used to carry a handkerchief," she said with another sniffle.

"It's nice to know I remind you of your grandfather. I'm guessing I'm probably much older than him."

He seemed like he wanted to smile, but from the haunted look in his eyes, she guessed he'd seen too much pain and suffering in his life. In a flash, the vulnerability was gone, evaporated like a fine mist. The image of Lawrence biting Brooke and taking her would never leave her mind. She guessed Mulroney must've seen a lot worse in his day. Maybe sarcasm and jokes were his way of not letting all the ugliness get the best of him.

"Why don't you start by telling me what happened?"

After she relayed the details to him, she took a sip of water and tried to calm her nerves. "If Lawrence was arrested and brought into custody how did he get out of jail? I thought he was going to Hellios where he belongs."

"He's got connections, not to mention a team of high-priced attorneys. They got him out on bail." His full lips pursed into a tight line. "The Council didn't even have a chance to vote."

For the first time since she met Mulroney the air of arrogance was gone, replaced with remorse. He ran a hand through his hair, and shadows appeared under his eyes. This case appeared to be taking a toll on him as well.

"I just found out. The officers parked outside of Miss Corey's apartment were supposed to warn both of you, but by the time they got inside, they said the place was empty."

"Yeah, well, I think they were a little late. How did Lawrence and his bodyguard slip past them?" she asked, exasperated. "I thought they were supposed to protect her from something like this happening."

"Unfortunately, the officers didn't see Lawrence or his bodyguard go into the building. Vampires can move quite fast when we want to." His eyes remained steely. "I'd like you to come back to Brooke's with me and then to the station to get your statement. It's a miracle you managed to get away from them." He got to his feet. "It seems as though luck is on your side, Miss Howe. You have more lives than a cat."

By the time they made it to the coven in Raven's Hollow, the sky had turned dark. After spending hours back at Brooke's apartment and the station, she gave Mulroney, Alex, and his partner Cayden, what they deemed an eyewitness account. After that, Mulroney had insisted on escorting her home.

Moonlight illuminated the stone path that led to the kitchen door. Mulroney instructed her to go in through the back of the manor in case someone was inside waiting to attack. The thought filled her with unease. A cool autumn breeze whipped through the air and blew loose strands of hair from her ponytail. The wind chimes clinked together, soothing the anxiety churning in her gut.

"Try to stay calm. I can smell the adrenaline pumping through your veins. If a vampire's here, you'll give yourself away," he whispered close to her ear. His breath fanned her cheek and sent a tingle down her spine.

"Was that supposed to put me at ease?" she whispered back. Taking a deep breath, she turned the handle on the old wooden door, and it slowly creaked open. Living in a hundred-year-old Victorian had its perks, as well as its fair share of challenges—like no one could ever remember to lock the numerous doors and windows around the house.

Mulroney brushed past her, and she followed him into the kitchen. "Stay put while I have a look around." The idea of Lawrence, or one of his thugs, waiting for her inside the house made her break out in a cold sweat. The place was unusually quiet. The only sounds came from the hum of the fridge and the pounding of her heart.

Fortunately, one of them was able to see in the dark. She stood there frozen while Mulroney roamed through the house. After several agonizing minutes, heavy footsteps scraped against the stone floor.

"We're all clear." His voice cut through the darkness and eased some of her fear. He flicked on the lights, and she covered her eyes from the sudden brightness. "You need to take proper precautions. A bunch of women living alone, leaving the back door open is a recipe for disaster." He took a step closer to her, and her eyes roamed over his tall, powerful frame. He was so big and broad, all six-foot-three inches of him filling the space.

"I'll talk to the other girls." Not that she tended to agree with him, but in this case, he was right. Besides, if a creature was powerful enough, they could break through the protective charms and spells throughout the house if they wanted to.

"Speaking of the women, where are they?" Mulroney asked, glancing around the empty kitchen. The scent of rosemary and thyme filled the air. Dried herbs from their solarium hung from the wooden beams above the island. "I'm not picking up on any conversations."

"A Mabon Ritual, for the autumn equinox." She wasn't sure what she was going to tell the other girls as to the reason she'd blown it off. They'd worry when she didn't show, but if she told them the truth, she'd ruin the ritual. For now, she needed to let them know she was okay.

She reached for her cell from her back pocket and sent a group text.

Sorry, I couldn't make it tonight. Something came up.

At least that part wasn't a total lie. After she shoved the phone back in her pocket, she glanced over at Mulroney and pointed to his cell which continued to beep. "You can actually hear other people's conversations? I thought that was a myth along with burning up in the sun."

His stance was rigid, his jaw locked tight. "There's always some hint of truth to all those legends, and while some of us can pick up on a dozen conversations at once, even from far away, we can't burn up in the sun. Although sunlight does slow down our speed and strength. As for some of the other myths, I prefer my meat cooked rare actually and not raw when I indulge. Any other questions, Miss Howe?"

"Yeah, do you have any idea where Lawrence could've taken Brooke?" Gillian's mind whirled in a million different directions, devising ways to keep the other girls out of harm's way. They'd have to use their collective magick to strengthen the spells and charms throughout the house.

He rubbed the back of his neck, and a crease appeared between his brows. "I've been on the phone with Alex and my partner and that seems to be the question of the evening. The MBI sent a forensics team to take hair and blood samples. The case is in their jurisdiction. Agents have been sent to Lawrence's last known address in the city, and they're searching his offices for any evidence that could lead us to her whereabouts. I'm afraid we don't have much to go on at this point. But we are pouring all our resources into it, I promise you." He motioned to the table. "Why don't I wait with you until the others get back? You shouldn't be left alone. I'm hoping a conversation might jog your memory."

His words filled her with a mixture of disappointment—and fear. Gillian wanted to try scrying for Brooke, but her powers were depleted after expending so much magick in the last twenty-four hours. "I'm willing to try if you think it might lead you to Brooke," she said over her shoulder as she walked to the fridge and took out a green juice. She offered one to Mulroney, but he made a face and held up his hand, taking a seat. "If you were doing surveillance on Lawrence, then you must know all about his operation." She unscrewed the cap off the Mason jar and took a sip.

"Our sources tell us he's not working alone," Mulroney explained, folding his arms across his broad chest. "We have reason to believe he's the frontmanfor a bigger, badder organization. A demon by the name of Tristan Saint Claire was the head of a crime syndicate known as the Shadow Cabal. When he was killed, his operation was dismantled, making room for a group of vampires who call themselves the Du Sang Brotherhood to take over the reins."

"The Du Sang Brotherhood?" she repeated. "I suppose it has a certain sinister ring to it."

"I suppose it does," he agreed, rubbing at the scruff along his chin, and she wondered if the man ever shaved. "It's French for blood. We have reason to believe they're now being led by Kurt Lawrence and his cronies.

The bastards have their hands in everything from human trafficking to money laundering."

"I don't understand," she said, shaking her head. "Kurt Lawrence is a mogul with a legit business. Why go into this life of debauchery? It can't be for the money." She walked to the table and sat down next to him in one of the wicker back chairs.

"He's been using the other business as a front for money laundering," Mulroney explained, resting his hands on the table. "Lawrence's empire is in trouble and has been for a while, mainly because of his gambling problem. He owes debts all over the place. He was vulnerable and a man with connections, which put him in a prime position to be recruited by this type of organization. But I believe someone else is running the show."

"What does this mean for Brooke? Are you officially calling this a kidnapping even though she invited him in?" she asked in a defensive tone and immediately regretted it. She wasn't angry at Mulroney but furious at the whole situation. She reached for a deck of her cards stacked on the table and began shuffling them, needing something to do with her hands.

"I'd say that's pretty much a given. She had no choice because of his sway over her. Once the bonding pheromones took over, Brooke became desperate for the next fix. In essence, Lawrence turned her into a blood slave. The penalty is an automatic death sentence. The Council doesn't take kindly to innocents being taken against their will. When we do find Lawrence, and I assure you we will, they'll vote for execution." Mulroney exhaled, and she picked up on his anxiety as it rolled off him in waves.

"What aren't you telling me?" She finished the last of her drink and started to feel more like herself. "Please, I have a right to know."

He ran a hand through his short, dark hair. "A week ago, a young woman was found in a ditch with all the blood drained from her body. She was last seen at one of Lawrence's events. The murder is what led us to beef up our investigation."

Her heart thudded painfully against her ribs. "Are you saying that Kurt Lawrence is a murderer?"

His ice-blue eyes softened a fraction when they gazed into hers. "It's sure starting to look that way. You threatened to expose one of the most influential vampires in the New York area as both a fraud and a human trafficker to a million of your followers. We've managed to keep all of this out of the mage news. But a single tweet could ruin him in no time flat.

And now that Brooke's been taken, you're our prime witness in her kidnapping, which I'm afraid puts you in terrible danger, Miss Howe. This isn't just a human you need protection from. Are you aware of a vampire's speed and strength?"

Gillian figured she must be suffering from shock because she couldn't fully wrap her brain around what he was saying. Seeing Lawrence take Brooke was bad enough, to think that the vampire could also be a killer was too much to process all at once. "I get it. I'm in danger." But she wasn't sure what she was supposed to do until Lawrence was found, except maybe hide out for a while. "There are protection spells and charms I can weave here."

"With all due respect, Miss Howe, you'll need more than a spell to protect you against a vampire." His words cut through the room and made her tense.

"How come you're not going after the vampire that Lawrence works for?" She got up and began to pace; then, she remembered Brooke's keys in the front pocket of her hoodie. They jingled with every step. "If he's the one pulling the strings, why not bust down his door and arrest him?"

"Trust me, it's not that simple." His tone filled with anger. "If it were, he'd been in custody. He knows how to keep his hands clean and let others do his dirty work."

"I refuse to stand here and do nothing while my cousin's out there. I'm going to try scrying her." Gillian pulled out Brooke's keychain from the front pocket of her hoodie and set it on the table. She took the map of Hudson County that they kept on a corkboard and spread it across the table; then, glanced over at Mulroney. "Do you have anything of Lawrence's that I can use, like a business card? I don't know, maybe a fang?"

His lips curled into a smile. "I think I might have something." He reached inside his jacket pocket and grabbed a business card. "You're in luck." When he handed it to her, their fingers touched, and she felt that same shock of electricity like a live wire.

She ignored it and placed the card on top of the map, along with the small hematite crystal from the inside of her bra. "Thanks." After she grabbed a lighter from a kitchen drawer, she lit a few sticks of incense and three white candles. She picked up a saltshaker and sprinkled a circle of protection around the table. "Here goes nothing," she whispered and reached for the keychain, holding it over the map. The moment she closed her eyes, she focused her mind and set her intention for her spell.

"Goddess of light give me the power to see,

To find this innocent and set her free.

This is my will, so mote it be."

Sparks of light filled her vision as the spell took shape. Magick, pure and bright, pulsed through her fingertips as the keychain swung back and forth. After a few minutes, it began to swing in a circle. Finally, the keychain landed on a spot on Route 3. "Mulroney? You need to see this."

"Did you pick up anything?" He moved to her side and ran his finger over the place on the map where the pendulum had landed. His arm brushed hers, and she tried to ignore the tingle along her skin. "This is somewhere in Lyndhurst. There's a stretch of motels along the highway." He grabbed his cell and took a picture of the spot before glancing over at her again. "I'm calling my boss."

For a moment, his words took Gillian by surprise. Not all cops were open to using psychics in their investigations, even in an unofficial capacity. Gillian could thank Willow for the shift. While working as a consultant for the MBI, her friend had helped solve a murder case. Gillian suspected even a hard-ass like Mulroney would be open to the idea after that. She supposed maybe he wasn't a complete jerk after all. "I just pray it leads us to Brooke."

CHAPTER 7

$\mathcal{M}$ ulroney found a corner of the kitchen next to a butcher block and took a seat at a stool. A leather-bound book sat open with splotches of candle wax of all over the pages. He took his cell, pushed a button, and his captain, Mark Matthews, answered right away.

"Where the hell are you?"

"Hello to you too. I'm at the coven." They'd been working together for almost a decade now, but rarely saw eye to eye. Right now he wasn't sure how to phrase what he was about to say without sounding like he'd lost his marbles, so he just dove in. "Miss Howe used magic to try to locate her cousin, and frankly, I think she may be onto something." After he filled him in on the location, he stole a glance at Gillian. She continued to pace back and forth with a shell-shocked look on her face. "I need a squad car to comb the area along the highway." There was dead silence on the other end of the phone line. "Sir?" he prompted.

"Still here. I guess I'm surprised that you're taking the word of a psychic into account, but then again this is Gillian Howe we're talking about." Some gossip had spread through the station that they shared a rather contentious relationship, and now, Garrett was the butt of some colorful ribbing. "Don't worry. I'll send a car."

"It's worth a shot. I'm copying Denopoulos and Teague on the area as well." He didn't typically rely on something as unscientific as the occult in police work, but over the years, he'd experienced his fair share of cold cases that eventually became reopened and solved using forensic psychics. Hell, he'd try anything at this point if it led them to Lawrence. "How about you? What do you have so far?"

"I've gone over all the interviews from the hotel room, and it's a major shitshow. I'm sending you the video to see if you can pick up on something I might've missed."

After a moment, his phone pinged. "Got it. You were saying?" Garrett asked, hoping to get something concrete.

"All of the women there, aside from the two witnesses, were sent by a business associate of Lawrence's. She goes by the name Rowena Cherry."

Garrett scratched his head. "Why do I know that name? Wait a minute; I busted a Rowena Cherry years ago. She was some Upper East Side socialite. The woman would have to be close to eighty by now. She can't still be doing the same thing. Could it be her daughter?"

"I've got her file right here." The sound of his captain pounding on his keyboard crackled through the phone line. "Trust me, it's her. I guess she figures she has a good thing going and it beats canasta. She's been busted in Brooklyn and Queens for pretty much the same thing. She's somehow managed to lure these women into the blood ring by promising them educational scholarships and fashion careers. But it's all just a ruse to groom them into becoming blood slaves. Nothing we can prove solidly enough to put her away, but you know how that goes."

"Let me get this straight, I want to make sure I get all the players right," Garrett said, shaking his head. "Lawrence pays Rowena Cherry for the women she sends over while he gets paid by the Brotherhood to find them a blood bond. They have quite the business model going on. Send me the client list and the forensics report on the Jane Doe found off Frank Sinatra Boulevard. It can't be a coincidence. The killer must've dumped the body there for a reason, either because they were sloppy or to frame it on someone from the Brotherhood."

"The Jane Doe's been identified as Serena Benson, age twenty-four, a grad student at Columbia. She was last seen at one of Lawrence's soirées two weeks ago. I think it's safe to say that whoever killed her was somehow connected to the Brotherhood, the question was how."

Garrett ran a hand over his mouth, and sighed, the realization making his throat tight. "Could she have threatened to expose their operation?"

"Lawrence is more or less a flunky," Matthews said. "He's not experienced enough to pull this off himself. Someone else is pulling the strings."

"Someone like Malcom Von Scrivner?" Garrett's jaw clenched. From all accounts, the vampire had reputed ties to human traffickers all over Europe before he came here to the states.

"We've done surveillance on him, and there have been multiple calls and text messages to Kurt Lawrence."

Garrett bit back a curse and ran a hand through his hair. Hearing the words fueled his anger even more. "What does that mean for the investigation?"

"We can use your connection to Von Scrivner to our advantage."

"What are you saying? What do you want me to do?"

"Protect the witness. If he discovers you're involved, it could draw him out," Matthews continued. "From now on, I want you glued to Gillian Howe's side as much as possible. Make sure she sticks to her normal routine to keep from arousing suspicion. You can take turns with Dubrosky keeping an eye on her at work. If memory serves, she owns some kind of head shop on Washington Street."

"It's called *Enchantments*," Garrett muttered, trying to sound nonchalant. He'd driven by the place more times than he could count, hoping to catch a glimpse of her. His boss didn't need to know he'd taken a personal interest in the witness, or he might pull him from the case.

"My guess is it's only a matter of time before Lawrence sends one of his thugs to keep her quiet. Your favorite witch has been tweeting about him, and we can use it to our advantage to lure him into the open."

He'd warned her about this very thing. "It sounds like you want to offer her up as bait." Garrett tried to keep the anger out of his voice and failed.

The captain's silence only confirmed his suspicions. "I wish I had something different to report. We'll send a uniform to stay parked outside the coven."

"Thanks for the update. I'll check in with you later," Garrett said, ending the call. When he made his way back to where Gillian stood, she turned to face him, looking pale and shaken. Even without a stitch of makeup on her natural beauty shone through. Loose tendrils of dark hair fell from her ponytail. She wore an oversized, grey NYU hoodie and a pair of jogging pants that hugged her ass and shaped her long legs. Everything about this damn woman was a distraction he didn't need.

He stood close to her, his boots almost touching her sneakers, absorbing her heat. "I just got off the line with my captain. He's putting the location out on the police scanner. A squad car will be sent to the area."

Gillian nodded, looking relieved. "Thank you. I guess it's a start." She walked around the kitchen, waving her hands, leaving a trail of magick sparks as she lowered the blinds on all the windows before turning to face him.

"There's still another matter to contend with. Have you been tweeting about Kurt Lawrence when I specifically told you not to? What could you be thinking?"

"Yes, but it was for the sole purpose of exposing him and his operation—"

He held up his hand. "No more. You're only adding kerosene to the fire." Tears swam in her eyes, and the sight burned any remnants of anger away.

"I didn't mean to. I was only trying to help."

"From now on, there will be no tweeting. It's too dangerous." He wanted to take her in his arms, rub her back, and run his fingers through her hair to ease her pain, but he stayed rooted to the spot. Guilt gnawed at him. He wished he could've given Brooke Corey a warning. The whole thing happened too damn fast.

She huffed out a breath. "Fine, I get it."

"I'll do everything in my power to find Brooke, uh, that is my partner and I will, along with the other agents," he clarified, not wanting Gillian to know that he'd taken a special interest in this case. She was a witness and the last person he should be thinking about in such a raw, sexual way.

He wondered if a frantic lover was waiting for her call. How come he wasn't racing over here to make sure she was okay? Maybe there wasn't one. The thought shouldn't have filled him with relief, but somehow it did.

"What happened to your other partner, the guy that came over to the coven with you?" Gillian grabbed a couple of glasses from the cupboard, filled them with filtered water from the fridge, and set them on the counter. She held the glass to her mouth and took a long pull. He tried to look away, he did, but his eyes, of their own accord, darted to the sexy tilt of her lips. "He was pleasant. Let me guess, you scared him away?"

Very funny. He didn't need to drink water as humans did, but why be rude? So he lifted the glass and chugged. When he finished, he set it back on the counter. "He took a transfer that had absolutely nothing to do with me." He didn't owe her an explanation. Derek Sorenson had been his partner and friend for the past five years up until his wife had their second child. He requested to be relocated to North Carolina, something about being close to relatives. Every time Garrett thought about Derek and his happy, little family, his chest grew tight. Living like a vampire for the better part of his adult life meant that being a parent and a husband was something he'd never fully understand, or have the good fortune to experience, but deep down, he envied the hell out of the guy.

"What now?" Gillian asked, interrupting his musings.

"I haven't checked your bedroom." Garrett angled his head toward the hall.

She visibly tensed. "You want to search my room?"

"I'm not letting you go in there alone. I won't take a chance with your life." From the skittish way she reacted, it became abundantly clear she didn't want him anywhere near her bedroom. The question was, why? "Is that a problem for you?"

"Nope, no problem at all. It's on the main floor, second door on the right," Gillian said and hurried out of the kitchen.

Mulroney followed her into the hallway and fell in step beside her. They passed dark wooden beams and archways, along with stained glass windows and doors. Tall trees in clay planters lined every corner.

They walked past the ritual room, and he remembered it from the last time he'd been there. Antique lanterns and redwood moldings matched the Victorian style of the house. He pointed to an area of unfinished molding, baseboards, and sheetrock. "It looks like your project never got finished."

"After the murders last year, we lost quite a few members and ran out of money." Gillian shrugged. "We've just never found someone to finish the job."

Now he had even more reason to assume she didn't have a boyfriend, at least not a handy one. His attention caught on the black and orange twinkle lights strung along the dark wooden beams. After they turned the corner, they passed the sun porch, and he let out a low hiss.

Hay stalks stood on either side of the screen door. Bright colored mums, pumpkins, and gourds sat on top of giant bales of hay. A life-sized plastic witch with a black pointed hat, crooked nose, and a cape dangled from a wire. Amusement shot through him at the artful display. At least these women could make fun of themselves. They certainly knew how to decorate for Halloween.

"Where do I go from here? Do you think Lawrence will come after me?"

"It's certainly a possibility. We're working on a way to offer you protection." He rubbed the back of his neck and decided to leave out the part about getting assigned to be her bodyguard. "I wish I had more to tell you at this point. You need to be patient a little longer while we figure out a plan."

She nodded, and a curious expression spread across her pretty face. "I've been thinking about the vampire that Lawrence works for, the head of this Du Sang brotherhood. Have you arrested him before? I mean, you seem to know a great deal about him."

He stopped in his tracks, and his hands clenched into fists at his sides. "I should. He's my sire."

When they reached Gillian's door, Garrett darted in front of her with one hand on his Glock. He needed to make sure no one was lurking in the hallway. He tried to tamp down the anger still coursing through his veins. How could he not want to go after the bastard himself? Sitting on the sidelines was going to kill him.

When they got to her bedroom, Garrett stood outside the door and remained rooted to the spot. He cleared his throat.

"What, aren't you coming in?" she asked, looking at him like he'd sprouted another head.

"You need to invite me first. There are laws in our world, Miss Howe."

Her brown eyes locked on his. "My apologies, your highness." She extended her hand and bowed.

"Are you always such a smartass?"

"Only around you. Please, come in. Forgive me, this is the first time I've ever had a vampire in my bedroom."

He crossed the threshold and scowled. The thought of any male going into her room filled him with irrational jealousy. "As long as we're on the subject, vampire blood rings aside, you need to be careful who you trust. If I told you the things I've seen in my life as a cop, you'd think twice about who you date." The last he'd inquired, which was several months back, Alex had confirmed Gillian was single. "Not that it's any of my business, but you do have a habit of putting yourself in dangerous situations." He couldn't keep the note of possessiveness out of his voice.

"I'm not sure what you're implying, but I don't make a habit of bringing strange men or vampires to my room. And like you said, it's none of your business."

"Agreed. I'll just have a look around." Her unique lavender scent flared in his nostrils and made him want to groan. He sniffed the air and caught the smell of an animal. "Do you have a cat?" He glanced around the spacious room, looking for anything suspicious.

"Yes. Salem's probably hiding somewhere. It takes a while for her to warm up to strangers. How much longer is this going to take?" she asked, sounding nervous. "If one of the girls comes home and sees you in my room at this hour of the night, they'll get the wrong idea."

"Maybe they'll think this is what you've wanted to do since the moment we met," he said, not able to resist goading her.

"Keep telling yourself that if it gets you through the day. Are you trying to get a rise out of me?"

"Sorry, but you walked into that one." He pursed his lips to keep from smiling. "I'm almost finished." A gossamer drape caught his eye and billowed around an open window. He walked over and pulled his gloves from inside his jacket pocket and slid them on. After he dusted for prints, he turned back to face her and gestured to the window. "Was this open when you left?"

"I don't remember, but no one could get in. We keep charms on the windows and doors," she explained, standing next to a desk cluttered with glass jars filled with herbs, and candles, along with piles of folded laundry.

"If a creature is powerful enough, especially a vampire, they could find a way to break through them." He turned to slam the window shut and click the lock in place. His gaze went from the window to the lush, green plants. He crouched to touch the soil. It was still damp, which meant someone had been in her room today. Turning his head, he glanced at the assorted pieces of clothing and shoes that left a trail from the door to the bathroom. Who knew she was a slob?

"Sorry, maid's day off," she said, reaching for a pair of jeans and a sweater off the floor. She pitched both in the hamper.

"No problem," he muttered, and his gaze rested on the carved, wooden headboard attached to her bed and the old-fashioned cream and navy comforter decorated with big, navy throw pillows. The room exuded a romantic, ethereal vibe, much like the lady herself. An antique rattan chair sat next to the bed, piled high with clothing. It felt intimate to be standing in Gillian's bedroom.

"Well, have you picked up on anything else that seems suspicious, Detective, aside from the fact that I haven't done my laundry in a while?" she asked, her tone dripping with sarcasm.

"Not so far. But you should make sure everything's in order." The statement was an oxymoron, considering her room was a mess. His gaze narrowed on the decks of tarot cards, candles, and spellbooks lining her shelves, curious how she learned to use them all.

Through the corner of his eye, he caught sight of a collage of photos of her as a young girl. He couldn't help but stop and stare. She posed alongside a very pretty woman with the same chestnut hair and goldish-brown eyes. From the resemblance, he guessed it must be her mom, and now, he knew where she'd inherited her looks. There were other pictures too, some of her with Brooke, and from the bright smiles on their faces, it was clear they shared a genuine affection for each other.

She picked up a laundry basket and began to fill it with the clothing from the floor. His gaze landed on something small, red, and lacy…a thong. Of course she wore sexy underwear. The realization made blood rush to his groin.

He moved behind the dresser, took off his suit jacket and folded it over his arm, hoping she wouldn't notice his erection. She must've caught him staring at the underwear because a lovely blush spread from her cheeks to her neck. There was a long stretch of silence, and the air became thick with sexual tension.

His reaction to her didn't surprise him. She'd made quite a lasting impression on him the first time he paid a visit to her coven. He'd made the mistake of going there first thing in the morning to question her and the other women about one of their clients who had been mixed up with some stolen antiques being fenced by the Shadow Cabal. Gillian had been the one to answer the door wearing a short silk robe that left absolutely nothing to the imagination. Stunned by her beauty, he had wanted to run his hands over every inch of her luscious body and lick all that creamy skin. He'd been forced to count backward from a hundred to keep his thoughts in check, a trick he'd learned at the academy. Fortunately, he had one hell of a poker face.

The next time he stopped by to tie up some loose ends that frankly could've been finished from his desk, he'd been rendered momentarily speechless. The sight of her soaked in sweat with her nipples poking through her sports bra still replayed over in his mind when he was alone in his room, his hand down the front of his boxer briefs.

He needed to do something about this infatuation. It would only lead to trouble. She was a witness—things could get messy, and if there was one thing Garrett avoided at all costs—it was messy.

After he did a final sweep of the room, his gaze darted to hers once more. "I'm going to ask you one last time, does anything look unusual or out of place to you?"

Mortified, Gillian gestured to the piles of clothing scattered all over her room. "Is that a real question?" she asked, heat suffusing her cheeks. Was he mocking her clutter?

"Fine. Let me rephrase that, more so than usual?"

"Aside from the usual mess, nothing looks strange." Gillian turned in a circle, and her eyes landed on a flash of white peeking out from the piles of folded clothes on her desk. "I didn't see this here before." She walked to her desk and lifted the clothing to find a large, white package tied with a red ribbon next to her laptop. "I would've remembered." She looked for a return address, but there was none, and her heart thumped against her ribs.

"Don't touch it." Mulroney crossed the room in a single stride to stand beside her. "It could be evidence."

"Let me see if I can pick up on what's inside." Gillian waved her hand over the box and sucked in a breath. "I detect a kind of dark, twisted energy surrounding it." She glanced at Mulroney, and a line appeared between his brows.

"If that's the case then I'm sure one of the other witches would've picked up on it immediately. They'd never deliver a dark object to your room." Garrett glanced toward the hall. "Was someone else here?"

"We have a plant service that comes every Saturday. There's a lady that's been coming here for years. She'll occasionally drop off packages if she's stopping by my room to water my plants."

"Are there any disgruntled customers from the shop who'd send you hate mail or weird objects? How about stalkers or ex-boyfriends out for revenge?"

Her heart began to pound. "Not that I can think of, but I guess anything's possible."

"All right then, please, take a step back." Mulroney pulled a small pocketknife from his keychain and cut a slit at the top of the box. She caught a pungent whiff of rotten meat. When he opened the top, blood seeped out and ran along the sides. "Jesus, turn around, Miss Howe."

"What's in there?" Gillian peeked inside to find the bloodied, mangled body of a white cat. Salem! Staggering back, she screamed and began to sob. "It's my cat."

"Fuck...I'm sorry." He picked up the note left in the box and read the chicken scrawl aloud.

"Keep your mouth shut. Stay out of our way, or you and your friends will be next. If you go to the cops, you will never see Brooke again."

Mulroney cursed and reached for his phone. "I'm calling for back up. I need to take the evidence to the station and have forensics run some tests. Grab your suitcase and your computer. You need to pack up your stuff. You're not staying here. You'll need to come with me."

Her stomach still felt queasy, and her head spun in a million different directions. "Where are we going?"

"Somewhere you'll be safe. I'm taking you to my place."

CHAPTER 8

*L*ifting her phone from the front pocket of her hoodie, Gillian stared at the screen, hoping and praying Brooke would text her to tell she was okay. But it was wishful thinking on her part. She didn't even have her phone on her, and she doubted Lawrence would let her use his. She exhaled and glanced out the window of Mulroney's Jeep. Streetlamps lit the sidewalks, but very few people wandered around the city at this hour of the night. "I don't get why you're taking me to your home."

If someone had asked her the day before to bet on the odds of getting invited to his place, she'd say the chances of winning the NJ lottery were probably much higher.

"The only one who can protect you against the threat of a vampire is another vampire," he murmured from the front seat. "We're the only ones strong enough or fast enough, except for a demon."

It surprised her when he pulled onto Garden Street. The treelined drive was one of the poshest neighborhoods in all of Hoboken. He parked in front of a turn of the century brownstone and cut the engine.

"Home Sweet Home," he said and popped the trunk. Before she could reach for the handle, he opened her door and wheeled her suitcase up the sidewalk. She got out of the car and followed him to a black wrought iron gate. He swung it open and extended his hand, motioning for her to go ahead of him.

The crisp fall air made her shiver. She looked up into a crescent moon and saw blood, a sure sign of trouble. Her mind drifted to Brooke and then to poor Salem, and a sharp pain sliced across her chest. This was turning out to be one of the worst nights of her life, and she'd had some doozies. She walked up the steps to an ornate black front door. Two black urns filled with yellow mums cut through the darkness.

Turning, she stared down at him, not able to hide her surprise. "Wow, this is your place? It's not at all what I expected." Crap did she say that out loud? She blamed it on the state of shock she was probably still in.

"Oh? What did you expect?" He walked up the stairs and his arm brushed hers, sending a tingle along her skin. After he pulled out a key, he opened the door. A buzzing noise sounded. They both walked into the hallway. He punched some numbers into a keypad, and the blaring stopped.

"Why would a vampire need a security system? Who would be foolish enough to break into your place?"

"You'd be surprised. I've put a lot of dangerous creatures behind bars." Mulroney shut the door and bolted the lock in place. His eyes grew dark, almost steely. "You might find it hard to imagine, but there's a lot of people I've managed to piss off over the years."

"With a personality like yours, I would've never believed it for a second," she said with mock sarcasm.

Mulroney flicked on the lights in the hallway, illuminating the earth-toned décor. Her gaze darted to the natural wood blinds and the wrought iron chandelier. A maple table with cream fabric-covered chairs added to the serene aesthetic. The place gleamed, and it was clear from the upscale décor that he spared no expense. She tried to keep her mouth from hanging open.

"You're staring."

"Sorry. I guess I didn't realize detectives lived like this." Her face heated. "That was rude. I shouldn't make assumptions."

"No, it's okay. It's certainly a valid point. Those of us who have lived for a very long time can acquire wealth over many lifetimes. I work in law enforcement because I choose to, not because I need the money."

She nodded her head in agreement. "It makes sense." And it was certainly admirable.

With a twinkle in his eye, he picked up a remote and pressed a button.

Jazz music piped in from overhead speakers. "Any more questions, Miss Howe?"

"No, I think I'm good for now," she murmured and took a few steps away from him to look around the rest of the place. She glanced up at the coffered ceilings, then her eyes moved lower to the crown moldings and ornate, white mantle on the fireplace.

"Tell me," he whispered from behind her. "What did you expect?"

His voice came out deep and sultry. She imagined he could seduce any female without even trying. "What? Oh." She turned to face him and shrugged. "I'm not sure." She didn't want him to know that she'd given the subject much thought. But there'd been more than one occasion where she laid awake, alone in her bed, imagining how Garrett Mulroney lived, and what he did on his off time. Nothing could've prepared her for this.

She couldn't shake the overwhelming feeling that she belonged here, and that none of this was a strange coincidence.

"I guess something much simpler." Her mind drifted to Brooke once more. She would've gone gah-gah over this place. As an avid decorator, she loved color and detail. They used to spend their off time eating take-out while binge-watching HGTV. "You said you've put away your fair share of dangerous criminals. What about the criminals that took my cousin? How do you plan on finding them and bringing her back?" She rubbed her temples, feeling the start of a mother of a headache coming on.

"I'm not at liberty to go over the details of a police investigation with you, but I can assure you we're doing everything in our power to find her. What about you? What happened back there would've sent anyone with a pulse into a tailspin. Are you sure you're okay?" he asked, his voice taking on a softer tone.

No. Not at all. "I'm fine," she lied. "My cousin was kidnapped and whoever did this killed my cat and stuffed her in a box. What makes you think something could be wrong?" Saying it all out loud made her stomach tighten into knots. She exhaled. "I apologize. It's not fair to take my anger out on you. I appreciate what you're doing, truly. I'm just freaking out right now."

His jaw visibly clenched. "It's understandable. Killing your cat was a cowardly thing to do. I'm sorry you had to see something like that." He took off his holster and set it on the hall table. "Lawrence was trying to send you a message to try and intimidate you."

The weight of his words boomeranged inside her head. "Well, I got it loud and clear." If he was willing to kill an innocent creature like Salem, what would he do to Brooke? She couldn't bear to let her mind go there.

Gillian reached into her pocket to touch Brooke's keychain. She closed her eyes and tried to tune into her, but all she could make out were grainy shadows. Frustrated, she opened her eyes, and glanced at Mulroney, hoping for some answers. "When can I go back to Brooke's place? I have a better chance of opening a psychic link with her if I'm near her things."

His gaze darkened. "I'm sorry, but no one can go there right now. It's still an official crime scene."

"Right. How could I forget?" Gillian tried to shrug it off, but a combination of fear and anxiety threatened to overwhelm her. She pointed to Mulroney's phone. "How long do you think it'll take to hear back from anyone about Brooke?"

He glanced at the screen and frowned. "Hopefully soon. Please, come in and make yourself at home. Can I get you something to eat or drink?"

"No thanks, I'm not very hungry." Restless, she leaned against a dining room chair but didn't sit. "Tell me more about the vampire pulling the strings in this blood ring. He's your sire?" She needed to do something to keep her mind off things.

"I've been keeping an eye on Malcom Von Scrivner for over a century, and he's doing the same thing now that he did over a hundred and fifty years ago when he turned me." His blue eyes glowed under the lights, and it made him look otherworldly.

She wasn't sure what surprised her the most—Mulroney admitting to this juicy tidbit or the fact that he was practically ancient. She contemplated this new information, not sure what to say after that.

"I know it's easier said than done, but you need to eat and rest to keep your strength up, for Brooke's sake as well as your own." He slipped off his suit jacket, hung it on a hook by the door, and loosened his tie.

His green dress shirt brought out the blue in his eyes. The fabric hugged tight to his broad shoulders and stretched over the sculpted muscles on his chest. After he unbuttoned his cuffs, he rolled up his shirt sleeves, revealing tan, golden skin, and brawny forearms. She never knew forearms could be sexy. The idea of checking out Mulroney when Brooke was missing filled her with guilt.

He arched his brows, turning his full attention on her. "Miss Howe?"

Busted. Her cheeks heated. She quickly looked away, pretending to fawn all over some statue of a guy resting his face in his hand. "I was just admiring your statue." She felt him behind her, edging closer. His heat and masculine scent permeated the air. Her body responded in kind. Her breasts grew heavy, and her nipples tightened into points. The guilt became tenfold, forcing her to take a few steps back. She turned to face him, cautious of his proximity.

"By all means, admire away." He angled his head to the bronze. "Socrates sought to gain knowledge rather than victory over his opponent."

Mulroney was wicked smart, not to mention crazy-hot, and completely different from the men she typically met. He quoted philosophers for one and made his living protecting the innocent for another. It was bad enough that she'd slept with his jacket on her bed, feeling somehow calmed and aroused all at the same time. His intoxicating smell was the only thing that had gotten her to go back to sleep after waking from a nightmare.

She turned back to face him and wrapped her arms around her body to stave off the chill in the room. "I still have your suit jacket. I planned to messenger it over to the station, but with everything going on, it sort of slipped my mind."

"It's understandable. Don't worry. I have plenty." He smiled wide, and it made her knees weak. Yup. She was suffering from some kind of PTSD.

"Do you typically bring your witnesses back to your home?" Granted she was grateful to him, but that didn't change anything. There was still the matter of his interference, which ended up costing her a job.

"This would be a first. It seems we're still in Q&A mode, and I believe it's my turn. I'm not letting you off the hook. You never answered my question, and I admit I'm curious." He walked to the thermostat and pressed a button to crank up the heat. "What did you expect my home to be like?"

Oh, that question. "In truth? I expected a Gothic building tucked away in a dark alley somewhere with black, velvet curtains and a coffin in the center of the floor." Not a curved wood staircase with a skylight above it and wide planked, wood floors with Aubusson rugs. The home was bright and airy, welcoming.

He laughed and her whole body responded to the sound. His blue eyes locked on hers. They were beautiful, and right now, devouring her, trying to delve beneath the surface. Although not an inch of her skin showed, she felt naked and vulnerable under his scrutiny. "Sounds scary. You have quite the imagination, not to mention one hell of a sense of humor, which is what's going to get you through this ordeal. Please let me know if I can get you anything."

"Thank you," she murmured, not used to him being nice to her. Mulroney's usual prickly demeanor she could handle. It made her one-sided crush easier to navigate, but this attentive and gracious host was a different story entirely. And now it seriously messed with her head. She decided to change the subject. "I understand you're not allowed to discuss the case with me, but can you give me any idea as to how you plan to find Brooke?"

He sighed and ran a hand through his dark hair. "I can't imagine what must be going through your head. I wish I had something to tell you to put your mind at ease, but so far, there's not much to go on." He pulled out his cell and glanced at the screen before his eyes met hers again. "A group of agents went over to Lawrence's residence. The place was empty. No surprise there."

"Now what? There must be some way to find out where he's taken her? Don't you have any solid leads?" she asked, trying to tamp down the sadness and fear threatening to overwhelm her.

"We plan on questioning your attacker Damon Greystone the second he's out of his coma. You can rest assured, if and when he does wake up, I'll be the first one he talks to. The hospital staff has been asked to notify me or Dubrosky immediately. I'm meeting with Alex, Cayden, and my partner first thing in the morning. We plan on going over all the interviews of the people at that party to see what we can come up with." His phone buzzed. "Excuse me for a moment."

Mulroney walked away, nodding his head, and she tried to listen to his conversation, but she couldn't pick up on anything.

After several agonizing minutes, she began to think the worst.

He soon came back and ran a hand along the stubble on his chin. "There might've been something to your keychain trick. That was Alex. A hotel manager from the La Quinta Inn on Route 3 in Clifton confirmed that a vampire and a young woman matching Brooke's description checked into the hotel yesterday. They checked out some time in the middle of the night. He paid by credit card with a name I didn't recognize. He's going straight to the Council and asking them to issue a search warrant to get the owner attached to the credit card."

To think Brooke could be this close right here in Clifton filled her with nervous energy. There had to be more she could do. "What now?"

"Our guys are at the hotel room, checking it for clues. They'll let us know the moment they discover anything." He glanced at her phone before his gaze met hers. "You should probably notify your friends and let them know you won't be coming home tonight, but you're not to tell them where you are. I'll explain why later. An unmarked car will be parked outside the coven from now on to keep them safe. But they don't need to know that."

She needed to give the girls a heads up to keep them protected, but it seemed Mulroney wouldn't let her get into all the sordid details about Brooke's kidnapping just yet. She picked up her phone and dialed Saje. She answered on the first ring.

"Gillian? Where are you? How come you never made it to the ritual?"

"I'm fine. I'll explain everything. How about the rest of the girls? Are they nearby?"

"Yeah, they're standing right next to me. We just got back. We're in the kitchen attacking the fridge. Why? I'm picking up on some serious tense vibes from you, girl."

Gillian let out a deep breath and continued, "Go somewhere quiet where no one can hear you." After she filled her in, she went on to explain the danger involved. "You need to put extra spells and charms on all the doors and windows. I'm staying at a friend's tonight."

"What's going on? Are you okay?" Saje whispered.

"I'm fine. I'll explain the rest in the morning. Promise me you will do what I say. Saje?"

"Fine, I promise."

She sighed with relief. "Thanks. I'm exhausted. Let's talk tomorrow."

Gillian ended the call, glanced over at Mulroney, and let out a deep sigh. "What happens tomorrow? What should I do?"

"You go about your routine. Do everything you normally would. You don't want to draw attention to yourself. I'll drop you off at work and pick you up. Someone will be there to protect you at all times from now on."

"What now?" she asked, praying the lead panned out and they found Brooke.

He frowned. "We wait."

"I had a feeling you were going to say something to that effect. My phone's about to die. Where can I plug in?" She walked to her suitcase and pulled out her charger.

Mulroney pointed to an outlet next to the dining room table. She bent to plug in her phone and her stomach growled loudly. Embarrassed, she tried to shrug it off. She always kept snacks in her purse, which should hold her over until morning.

"When was the last time you ate?"

"I don't remember. It's been such a crazy day." She glanced down at her leggings. All she wanted to do was take a shower, get into her PJ's, and collapse in bed.

He edged closer to her, and in her sneakers, she had to crane her neck to look up at his face. It was almost a crime for a male to be that good looking. "I can cook you something here."

Did he just say he could cook her something? In the seven months she'd dated her last boyfriend, the most he ever did was make her a PB and J. "I don't want you to go to any trouble on my account."

His brows shot up. "Let's face it, Miss Howe; you've been trouble since the day we met. I've grown to expect it by now." With a twinkle in his eye, he motioned to the kitchen. "I'm sure we can find something to eat here."

When he flicked on the lights, she stopped in her tracks and gaped. Oh boy. Don't even get her started on the oven. He had a friggin' Viking. From the subzero fridge to the enormous marble center island, and tall, white wood cabinets, she imagined Joanna and Chip Gaines would have a field day. White moldings and raised panel wainscoting decorated every wall. The exposed brick behind the stove added a casual elegance.

"This is quite the kitchen. Do you cook a lot?" she asked, desperate to take her mind off her pain.

She imagined he entertained his fair share of women here. What about his friends and co-workers?

"Not so much for myself anymore but for friends on occasion. Vampires don't need to eat to sustain themselves as humans do. I mostly eat for routine, and of course, for pleasure. Let me get you something to drink." Her breath caught from the intense look in his eyes. "Perhaps you'd like something from the wine fridge?"

"I could use something strong." She walked to the island and took a seat at a leather barstool.

"I have just the thing." He crossed into a sumptuous living room with a crème colored sectional sofa and two blue, silk-covered Chippendale chairs. Stacked with books, a glass coffee table was arranged in front of the couch.

After he walked to a wall of windows that led to a set of French doors, he checked the locks, glanced outside, and shut the blinds. "I don't believe we were followed."

She sighed and started to relax, trying hard to erase the bloody images of Salem from her mind. With his crazy driving, she would've been surprised—and kind of impressed—if anyone had been able to follow them. "Hmm, the first good news I've heard all day. Have you lived here long?" Everything looked so shiny and new, like he'd just moved in. But then again, in his line of work, he probably wasn't home much.

When he turned back to face her, he appeared more at ease. Maybe being in his home made him less guarded. "I bought this place just under a year ago and did most of the renovations myself," he said with a note of pride in his voice. "I lived in a much smaller apartment a few blocks away for years, but with gentrification, this area has changed a lot and become trendy. This place came on the market, and well, it held a certain intrigue. Before vampires came out in the open in the seventies, I was forced to move a lot. I wanted to finally make a home for myself."

"I can see how you would." She could relate. She'd been living at the coven since her mom died. While she considered it her home, it was high time to get a place of her own. "Did you decorate it yourself?" she asked, taking in the contemporary artwork and the tasteful knickknacks artfully displayed around the room.

"I have a decorator friend who put the place together for me." He walked to a liquor cart and poured amber-colored liquid from a crystal decanter into two snifters.

A male that looked like him probably had lots of female friends falling all over themselves to help him in a pinch. She might not live in a luxury townhouse, or have a decorator on hand, but the things she treasured most revolved around family, friends, and her cat. She swallowed hard, and it finally hit her—Salem was never coming home. An unexpected explosion of anger and sorrow ripped through her and made it hard to breathe.

"Miss Howe? Are you okay? You got pale all of a sudden." Before she could respond, he made his way back over to her and handed her a glass. "You should drink this. It's Glen Livet."

The liquid swirled in her shaking hands. "Thanks." She took a long, slow sip. The scotch burned the back of her throat, and then, warmth spread from her head to her toes. "This is smooth."

"It will help you sleep."

"I could probably drink the whole bottle and still have trouble sleeping." She prayed the images in her head wouldn't keep her awake. She felt like a walking disaster, a danger to everyone and everything around her. "I have no idea what I'm going to tell Brooke's family and friends."

Lifting the snifter to his lips, he leaned against the counter. The man had amazing lips, full and lush, perfect for kissing. Where did that come from? It had to be the stress. "You have to be very careful what you tell them," he murmured, breaking into her thoughts. "Are they local?"

"Her parents live in Philadelphia. Her younger brother lives here in Jersey. I'm sure he's going to freak out when he doesn't hear from her. They're very close."

"I would let them know what's going on, just make sure they keep it very quiet for their safety, as well as Brooke's. Feel free to give them my number. I'm sure they'll have questions." His gaze narrowed. "What about you? Is there anyone you need to call?"

Her fingers tightened around the glass. "I'm an only child. My dad's remarried to a younger woman. I don't see much of him these days. They live in the city, and you might say the new wife and I don't get along." She'd never forget the day he'd left, claiming he couldn't handle her mom's cancer like she'd chosen to get sick.

"No? I can't imagine you not getting along with someone," he said with a teasing smile.

"Hard to believe, right?" She shrugged and tried to play it off. "She's only a few years older than me, so it's kind of weird."

"I see. I bet that is weird. How about your mom?"

She avoided his searching gaze and took another sip from her glass. The scotch must be doing the trick because her hands shook a bit less. "She died a few years ago." She was surprised how easily the words fell from her lips. This was the first time she'd ever told Mulroney anything personal about herself. They didn't exactly have that kind of relationship. Even now, talking about it made her throat tight. Tears threatened to spill over again, and at that moment, she wondered if the pain would ever go away. Maybe time couldn't heal the wound but simply numbed the ache. She couldn't save her mom or Salem, but she could save Brooke. She'd make sure of it.

"I'm sorry. Hell...I didn't know," he said, sounding sincere as he loosened his tie.

"My mom's the reason I started my charity. Hope Club helps to raise money for families who aren't able to pay for medical bills not covered by insurance. We're not a huge deal yet, but we're getting there." This was so different than her typical interactions with him. She didn't know what to make of this new exchange, but she was surprised at how easily she could talk to him.

His gaze seared her with so much intensity, it made her breaths shallow. Right now, she'd give anything to have Willow's ability to read minds. For the first time since they met, she began to think this attraction might not be one-sided. But then why had he tried to ruin her reputation? "What?" She pushed her hair behind her ear, feeling self-conscious, and wished she could clear the heaviness in the air.

"Your charity sounds important, and the cause is certainly worthwhile." His praise caught her off-guard, and she couldn't mistake the note of admiration in his voice. As much as she hated to admit it, his words made her feel special. He bent his head so they were eye level. "I'm sure your mom would be very proud. If you put every bit of that moxie I see burning in your eyes into helping families in need, then I'd say they're lucky to have you on their side."

Her face flushed again, not used to receiving compliments from Mulroney of all people. "I appreciate that. Hold on, did you just say, 'moxie'?"

He straightened. "Yeah, why?"

"People don't talk like that anymore. They certainly don't use words like 'moxie,'" she said with a chuckle.

"What can I say, I've lived for over a hundred and fifty years, and sometimes I show my age." His deep, raspy voice tugged at her.

"I think you just did."

After that, neither of them said a word. If someone had told her she could have a conversation with him without throwing barbs, she would've called them a liar. She'd never been this close to him, and under the glow of the spotlights, she became transfixed by the color of his eyes. They reminded her of the Caribbean Ocean...seven shades of blue. The air snapped with sexual tension.

"Let's get you that food." After he finished the last of his scotch, he set his glass on the counter and turned to open the fridge. Picking up a couple of takeout cartons, he turned back around and rubbed the scruff along his jaw. "I've got some leftover steak and salad from yesterday's lunch. Or if you're in the mood for something lighter, I could make you a grilled cheese sandwich with tomato soup."

Who knew Mulroney was so domestic? "Thanks, I appreciate the offer, but I'm vegan. We all are at the coven. I keep it a rule not to eat anything with a face." The bloody image of Salem's mangled body flashed through her mind and her stomach churned. "You know what, on second thought I think I'd just like to crash."

Sympathy flashed in his eyes. "I'll show you to the guest room. I know this isn't an ideal situation for either of us, but I assure you it's the only way to keep you safe."

His words made it clear that he didn't want her here. Not that she could blame him. They weren't exactly buddy, buddy, but still...She must've misread the vibes he'd been giving off. Setting her glass on the counter, she got to her feet. She was just about to get her suitcase when Mulroney passed her and hauled it up the staircase.

She followed him, glancing at the black and white framed photos of different locales and ancient-looking maps along the wall. Traveling seemed to be one of his hobbies. From the photos, he'd been all over the world. Curious, she wanted to ask him about his travels but decided against it for now.

"Are you always such a gentleman, opening doors and carrying suitcases?" Her eyes moved to his broad shoulders and wide, muscled back, watching them flex as he walked up the stairs. Not that she was complaining. She also got a bird's eye view of his fine muscled ass.

He glanced at her over his shoulder with a wicked gleam in his eyes. "No. Not always," he murmured in a sultry voice, and there was no mistaking his innuendo. Every nerve ending in her body zinged to life. A delicious shiver danced along her skin. "But in matters such as this, yes. I'm old school. It comes from living a long time."

They stopped at the landing. Decorated in the same soft shades of green and creams as the lower level, modern artwork adorned the walls up here. She could only dream about owning a home like this someday.

He walked into the bathroom and turned on the lights, and her jaw dropped. It was massive, practically the size of her entire bedroom, and decked out exactly like the kitchen in white and grey marble. The ginormous glass-enclosed shower called to her.

"It's a rain shower," he said, following her gaze. "There's a soaking tub should you feel the need to indulge."

At least she didn't have to share a bathroom. She gulped and wondered if *he* indulged in long soaks with the women he brought here. Is that why he had the bathroom designed that way?

A white, terry cloth robe hung on a hook near the shower. How many female guests did he regularly entertain here? She wasn't sure where this was all coming from, so she redirected the train of her thoughts to what was important—resting so she could replenish her magick and help find Brooke. She took a step back, and a wave of dizziness hit her hard, forcing her to lean against the wall for support. Luckily, Mulroney didn't notice. Maybe the scotch and lack of food had been a bad idea.

"I'm glad you approve." Without another word, he walked out of the bathroom and down the hall. She followed him, and he pointed to the room to his left. "You'll be staying in here." He extended his hand for her to walk in front of him, and she decided she could get used to his old-fashioned manners. Sadly, none of the men she knew as of late could be coined as gentlemen.

She took another step and swayed. In an instant he appeared at her side, wrapping a strong arm around her waist. She wasn't sure what unnerved her most, his closeness, or his scent, dancing across her skin with a rush of unexpected tingles.

"What's wrong? Are you okay?"

"I got a little woozy for a second. I usually don't drink on an empty stomach. I'll be okay. I just need to sleep."

"I think this is becoming a habit of yours, Miss Howe. Do I make you swoon?" His voice turned husky and vibrated through every cell in her body.

She blinked, and the haze cleared. "Don't flatter yourself."

Embarrassed, she pulled away and walked on shaky legs into a gorgeous bedroom. Covered with a white and green duvet and some throw pillows, the queen-sized bed looked inviting. An oversized chair, the same colors as the comforter, looked perfect for curling up with a good book. And speaking of books, there were tons of them. Floor to ceiling shelves were stacked with leather-bound spines, and even some old, rare looking ones.

She walked to the bookcase and thumbed through his collection. Maybe reading might help her sleep. "I'm impressed. You have all the classics. You must read a lot."

"When I have the time. I've collected quite a few over the years." He wheeled her suitcase to the corner of the room and glanced at the shelves. "Please, help yourself. Losing yourself in a good book, in my opinion, is one of the greatest passions in life."

"I agree." She wondered what other things Mulroney was passionate about. What would it be like to be at the center of his passion?

When she came across the three volumes of *Pride and Prejudice*, her heart skipped a beat. She picked up one of the maroon, leather-bound books, flipped to the first page, and gasped. "This is a first edition?"

"It belonged to my sister. It's the only thing I still have of hers. I've held onto it all these years," he murmured with a faraway look in his eyes. "Are you an Austen fan?" The question made her nostalgic.

"My mom got an old, worn copy for me when I was a young girl. We moved after my parents divorced, and it got lost. The only thing that seemed to make the new place familiar was my books."

"How about now, are you still a big reader?" He checked the locks on the windows and then turned back to face her, studying her with a curious expression on his handsome face.

If he only knew the half of it. "I'm voracious actually. I try and read everything I can get my hands on. Cookbooks, books on philosophy, history, alchemy, love and relationships, spell books. Reading became the one thing that got me through the really hard nights at the hospital when my mom was dying."

His gaze filled with understanding. "That must've been very difficult for you."

She hadn't meant to say that last part aloud. She could blame it on the stress and the scotch. But his sensitive reaction took her by surprise. Tilting her head to the side, she gestured to the bookcase, hoping to lighten the mood. "It's important to be up on a lot of different subjects for my podcast."

"You have a podcast? That's cool."

Who was he kidding? He had to know that she auditioned for a spot on WRHL radio. She contemplated asking him flat-out if he had anything to do with leaking the investigation on the coven to the station manager since the two seemed to be buds but thought better of it. There were more important things at stake right now. Finding Brooke was the only thing that mattered. She'd put her differences with him aside because she needed his help. If she ticked him off, she wasn't sure if he'd keep her in the loop, let alone allow her to be involved.

"I can see how apprehensive you are about all this. The last twenty-four hours must have been quite traumatic for you. Perhaps you'd like to talk to someone? I'm sure my partner Natalya Dubrosky would be more than willing."

She tensed under his sober regard, hating the fact she was so transparent. It was clear he was uncomfortable, and she couldn't blame him. He was a handsome, eligible bachelor. He didn't need her cramping his style. No, this wouldn't do at all. She straightened and took a step away from him, needing some distance. "There's no need. I'm sorry for putting you out like this."

"It's my job, Miss Howe. I'm following protocol." Shutters clamped down on those ice-blue eyes, the warmth from a moment ago now gone.

The sudden shift in his demeanor made her chest grow tight. "Of course, protocol." It was high time to get any silly romantic fantasies about him out of her head. "I appreciate what you're doing...really I do, but hopefully, I'll be out of here tomorrow. Whatever's going on in my head is nothing for you to be concerned with. Finding Brooke and putting this maniac to justice is my main priority, my only priority, and should be yours."

He closed the distance between them in a blur. "You don't need to tell me how to do my job."

"I didn't mean—"

He placed a gentle finger on her lips. His touch seared her, leaving a trail of heat and raw need. He took a step away like he'd been burned.

"There's no need to explain yourself. Please let me know if there's anything you need." He glanced at the bed. "You're probably exhausted. You should get some sleep."

"Yeah, like that's going to happen," Gillian said under her breath. "I'd like to take a shower. I, um, also wanted to say I appreciate everything that you're doing." *Talk about awkward.*

His gaze bore into hers, hot and intense. "You're welcome. There are fresh towels in the bathroom. I sleep upstairs in the master suite but not while you're staying here. I'll use the room across the hall for the most part. I need to remain close to you at all times to make sure you're safe, especially tonight. They'll be looking for you."

Power and strength practically radiated from his pores. It made her feel safe and on edge at the same time.

She let out a nervous giggle. "Surely that's taking it a step too far."

"You threatened Lawrence's reputation, which is everything to him. It's how he built his empire. And now the truth has come out. It's all going to come crashing down. You're our prime witness in this investigation, which means he'll want you out of the way. Who knows who he'll send for you? I still don't believe we were followed, but that doesn't mean I can afford to get sloppy. I'm not taking any chances with your life." The fierce look in his eyes made her breath hitch. He pointed to the chair. "Granted, it's not ideal, but this will be my bed for the night."

Her whole body liquefied. At that moment she could have been knocked over with the brush of a feather. Just when she thought things couldn't get any more uncomfortable, the hits kept coming. She prayed for peaceful dreams, free of dead cats, blood rings, trancing, and tall, dark, brooding vampires for that matter.

CHAPTER 9

*W*alking into his bedroom on the third floor, Garrett placed his phone on the nightstand and peeled off his clothes, leaving a trail on his way to the shower. Yet another night he'd be taking a cold one. Not that it would do much to cool his ardor.

Hell, he'd been taking cold showers for months now. Having Gillian a breath away was going to be excruciating. He glanced down at the hard ridge of his erection. From the very beginning, his reaction to Gillian Howe had always been the same. His body had been on a heightened sense of alert all day long, since the moment he found her in Starbucks. Guilt made his gut clench. He had no business checking her out when she was vulnerable, in fear for her cousin's life.

He glanced at his phone, still nothing about Lawrence. This case beckoned him, and yet, his mind was too preoccupied with Gillian. He couldn't let this go on. She was occupying way too many of his thoughts as it was, which meant he needed to find another way to draw the head of the Brotherhood out ASAP. Endangering her life and using her as bait was a terrible option. The more time he spent with her, the more he realized she wasn't only beautiful, but caring and altruistic. How could he willingly put her in danger? Frankly, the captain's plan sucked. Despite his misgivings, he'd have to tell her the truth at some point. She'd been through hell and back tonight, no need to pile it on.

The downstairs shower turned on, and his whole body tightened in anticipation. It was like having an invisible string pulling at him twenty-four-seven.

All night long he had become painfully aware of her every move and her scent. Touching her casually ignited a simmering flame ready to blaze into an inferno. He wanted to do a hell of a lot more than touch. He wanted to taste her and explore every inch of her skin. He'd spread her legs and spend hours giving her unimaginable pleasure.

The last thing Garrett ever expected to do was bring her here in the middle of the night, but what choice did he have? Lawrence wouldn't stop pursuing her, and he wouldn't trust anyone else to protect her.

A part of him still couldn't believe *she* was in his apartment. He'd fantasized about it more times than he could count. A rope of excitement coiled down his spine. He'd been fantasizing about getting her alone for months. He wanted to talk to her, get to know her better...learn everything about her inside and out. Tonight, he'd gotten more than he bargained for.

Sex had always been fulfilling, but with Gillian he suspected, it would be exhilarating and addictive, the kind of connection any man or vampire would give his soul for. He groaned in frustration. No matter how hard he tried, he couldn't get her out of his mind.

Living under the same roof with her was going to be pure torture. He had to talk to one of the team to find out if they had any leads. He picked up his phone and shot out a group text to Alex, Cayden, and his partner. Then, he plugged his phone in the charger, not expecting to hear back until the morning.

After he went to his closet and gathered some dress shirts, slacks, jackets, and belts, he laid them on his bed. Muttering a curse, he walked to his dresser, and pulled out boxers, socks, and some pajama pants, enough to move into the downstairs guest room for a stretch.

By the time he made his way into the bathroom for his shaving kit, his thoughts spun in a thousand different directions. The water cut off downstairs, and after a few minutes, he heard the soft footfalls of Gillian headed back to her room. When the door shut, the sound of her quiet sobs pierced his chest like a knife.

He glanced at the clock on the wall. It was after three. Maybe he'd come up with a way to tell her about this new plan by the morning. He rubbed a hand over his face, and just maybe, he was kidding himself.

When he finished with his shower, Garrett tiptoed downstairs to the second floor, careful not to wake Gillian. He ducked into the guest room across the hall and booted up his desktop to check his email. His boss had sent him the client list from the Cherry woman. But how did it relate to Malcom? He'd been looking for the Ancient for over a century and had come up emptyhanded. The Du Sang Brotherhood had the vampire's name written all over it. His sire had to be close.

He typed his name into the RHPD database and waited. The Ancient vampire had all but disappeared like a wisp of smoke after he'd left Hungary.

His hands curled into fists when he found a link to a website for some type of elite singles dating service that both Lawrence and a Malcom Strauss were involved in. Somehow this was all tied together. He felt it deep in his gut.

Sadly, it wasn't in a neat little bow. He pulled out his cell and sent the info to the agents and his partner. For now, he'd just have to wait.

It wouldn't be a stretch to assume that Malcom had come to Hoboken or the neighboring town of Raven's Hollow because of Sybil's Cave. From what he'd gleaned over the many years of living here, the caves were excavated back in the nineteenth century and held a natural spring. When a vampire drank the water, their vitality became restored, especially for those who sucked the blood from the sick and the weak, much like his sire had done to him. Vampires had flocked here from all over the world to gain access to the water until it became a rare commodity. Now only those with connections to shady figures could get their hands on it. The cops and the MBI left the caves alone, never having enough resources to do a clean sweep of the place. Could Sybil's Cave be connected to the Brotherhood somehow?

Garrett contemplated all the possibilities as he tapped his fingers on his desk.

If Malcom was behind this trafficking ring, he'd make sure he paid. Thinking about his sire turned his mood dark. He leaned back in his chair and took deep breaths to calm the rage building in his gut.

After spending a few more hours researching the case, he finally logged off the computer. Drained, he got to his feet and stalked across the hall to the room Gillian was staying in. Even before he crossed the threshold, he could detect the steady sound of her breath and the soft flutter of her heart.

Moonlight spilled in from the window, illuminating her sleeping form. He walked to the bed and stood over her, mesmerized by the sight in front of him. She reminded him of a rare piece of art he got to admire for the first time. His chest grew tight when he saw her tear-streaked cheeks. Fighting the urge to wipe them away, he pushed his hands into his pockets. She'd been through hell tonight and held up remarkably well. Beams of moonlight licked across her skin. Her hair fanned her pillow like spun silk. The sight of her took his breath away. Her beauty tamed the beast within him. Women like her were the inspiration for sonnets and love songs—the downfall of kingdoms.

She murmured in her sleep and kicked off the covers, half expecting to see her in a scant piece of lingerie he'd spotted in her room, she wore a simple white tank top that emphasized the swell of her breasts and the outline of her nipples. He could almost make out their pink, dusky color. His cock instantly swelled.

"No, you can't," she whispered.

He realized she was having a nightmare. When he smelled her fear, he placed his hand on her shoulder. Her skin was even softer than he imagined. A gentle shake didn't wake her, but when she whimpered, he shook her again, a bit firmer this time. Finally, she stopped twisting about and moaned in her sleep, her face flushing as pink as her nipples. Her breaths grew shallow. Whatever she was dreaming about now, it wasn't a nightmare. He could smell her arousal.

"Garrett," she whispered.

Part of him wanted to rouse her awake, wrap her in his arms, and comfort her with deep kisses and soft caresses. The other part of him feared he was in over his head. She let out a breath, turned on her side, and fell back into a deeper sleep. At least now how he knew she didn't hate him.

Shaking with lust, and a possessiveness he couldn't explain, he took a step back and sank into the chair. With the tempting scent of her arousal surrounding him and the soft breathy sounds coming from her lips, he wondered if this longing would ever go away. His body was strung tight, hard as stone.

One thing became crystal clear, he needed to push aside his selfish desires and relinquish this foolish infatuation once and for all. As long as he stayed frozen in his immortal existence, he had nothing to offer Gillian. Worse, his ties to his sire would put her in even more danger.

He'd do everything in his power to make sure no harm came to her, even if that meant pushing her away.

CHAPTER 10

a ray of bright morning sunshine filtered in from the bedroom window and forced Gillian to shield her eyes. Momentarily disoriented from being in a strange bed, she remembered where she was and turned her head so fast she was surprised she didn't give herself whiplash.

Glancing over at the empty chair, she let out a sigh and sat up. Mulroney must've left his post at some point early in the morning. The idea of him watching her while she slept made her seriously self-conscious. Had he heard her snoring or caught her drooling? Goddess, she hoped not.

Fumbling around for her phone to see if anyone had contacted her, she realized she'd left it charging downstairs. What if Brooke had found a way to call? If only there was a way to know if she was okay.

Mulroney vowed that he'd do everything in his power to find her, and despite their differences, she believed him. If nothing else, he was a man of his word.

She had to try to find out more about where Brooke was being held. After she kicked off the covers, she walked to her suitcase and pulled out her tarot cards along with her crystals. She arranged both across the bed and tried to tune into Brooke's energy. At first, all she could make out were the same dark, grainy images from last night. She cleared her mind and concentrated harder. After a few deep breathes, Brooke appeared. She walked through a maze of sprawling green lawns.

Her heart thumped against her ribs. She was alive, but she could be anywhere.

She blinked, and the image disappeared. Frustrated, she got out of bed and reached for her robe, which she'd hung on the back of the door. She threw it on over her tank top and PJ shorts and then grabbed her toiletry case out of her suitcase. It made no sense to unpack; she wouldn't be staying long.

After she padded down the hall to the bathroom, she brushed her teeth and splashed cold water on her face. When she glanced in the mirror at her reflection, dark smears appeared under her eyes, and she had a serious case of bed head after sleeping on wet hair. She looked like death warmed over. She'd have to apply a boatload of concealer when she got ready for work. The idea of going about her day and acting natural when Brooke was still missing filled her stomach with nervous butterflies.

Mulroney said she needed to stick to her routine, and part of her morning routine involved meditation to replenish her magick and going for a run to clear her head. Nothing, except maybe a good orgasm, beat the endorphin release, and today, she could use both. But asking Mulroney to accompany her on her morning jog would be pushing it, although having him help her with the orgasm sounded tempting but completely out of the question.

The smell of coffee and cinnamon wafted through the hall, and her stomach growled in response. Once she made it to the bottom of the stairs, she froze, struck by the tantalizing image in front of her.

Mulroney stood in the kitchen clad in a simple navy blue, RHPD t-shirt. This was the first time she'd ever seen him in anything but a suit. The thin cotton clung to his sculpted chest and showed off his corded arms. He'd been hiding some serious guns under there. His biceps practically bulged out the sides. For a moment, she imagined what it would be like to have them wrapped around her body.

He moved to the stove and began flipping pancakes over a griddle like some kind of smoking hot master chef. He must've sensed her in the room because he looked up, and his gaze flew to her, taking in every inch of her from head to toe. His perusal lingered on her legs, and her breath caught in her throat. She fumbled with the tie at her waist, self-consciously pulling it closed.

"Good morning, Miss Howe. How did you sleep?" He stared at her as though trying to gauge her mood.

Her face flushed, and she prayed he hadn't caught her checking him out. "Better than I had a right to, considering the circumstances. I think it must've been the scotch and the fact that your bed is extremely comfortable. Uh, what I meant was your guest room bed is comfortable. Obviously, I didn't sleep in your bed, so I wouldn't know." She couldn't seem to stop rambling.

He chuckled, something she'd never heard him do, and the sound warmed something inside her, putting her at ease. "I can see how awkward this is for you. It doesn't have to be."

Nope, not awkward at all. She wasn't sure which was worse, the rambling or the blushing. She refocused her attention on what was important— Brooke. "I had a vision of Brooke outside in a garden. It could be a park, though. I'm just not sure."

"I'll make a note of it, but I'm afraid that doesn't give us much to go on," Mulroney said and turned off the griddle.

"Has there been any news about Brooke or Kurt Laurence's whereabouts?" she asked, sounding anxious.

"If I had to go with my gut, I'd say Lawrence took her away from the city while still close enough to keep his eyes on his empire. He violates the terms of his bail, if he crosses state lines." He lifted his mug to his lips, and tension rolled off him in waves. "There's another matter we need to discuss."

Anxiety clawed at her throat. "What aren't you telling me?"

"I'm sorry. I should've made it clear that this isn't about Brooke," he said in a soft voice. "By tweeting, you've given Lawrence a motive to keep you quiet and get you out of the way. My captain thinks you should stay here until he's behind bars."

Her chest pounded hard from the determination in his voice. "Stay here, with you?" She knew they were sexually attracted to each other, even if neither of them would admit it aloud, but now, he was asking something entirely different. "I don't think so. Don't get me wrong, I'm grateful for everything, but I've put you out enough."

His gaze roamed her face. "I'm sorry, Miss Howe, but this isn't up for discussion."

"Even if I exposed him, what makes you think he'd send someone after me? I'd think having the cops and the MBI chasing after him for kidnapping would be enough to keep him busy. And what he did to Salem..." She looked away, her gaze catching on the orange and pink ribbons of light streaming in from the dining room windows. Her cat used to love curling up in front of her windowsill to warm her little body. She squinted and glanced back at Mulroney, hoping her expression didn't reveal how lost she felt inside. "I assumed he did it to scare me. I get what you're saying, but there must be another option."

Mulroney lifted his mug to his lips and her eyes darted to his white-knuckled grip. He was nervous. The question was why. What wasn't he telling her?

"My guess is it's only a matter of time before he sends one of his thugs to keep you quiet. This may not be your ideal plan, but it's the one we're going with for now. We can use it in our favor to draw him out."

Their eyes locked in a battle of wills. "Are you planning to use me as some kind of bait to catch this maniac?"

His eyes softened. "I can assure you you'll be protected at all times. A uniformed officer will be keeping an eye on you this morning. My preference would be for it to me, but I have a meeting at the MBI offices right after I drop you off at work. I should know more then." After Mulroney scooped a heaping pile of pancakes in a casserole dish, he placed them in the warming tray. "That's right, I have no car here." She'd left her beat-up Camry parked at the coven. Luckily, she packed clothing for work today.

"It's safer if I take you from now on."

"I need to check my messages." She walked to the dining room where she left her phone charging and picked it up. Disappointment gripped her. No missed calls or texts from Brooke. She guessed it was wishful thinking on her part. She kept thinking she'd turn up and that this had all been a bad dream. There were a bunch of texts and missed calls from the other girls, but nothing jumped out of her.

"Everything okay?" he called, sounding genuinely concerned.

"No one suspects anything at this point." She slipped her cell in the pocket of her robe and walked back to the kitchen, resting her hand on the countertop. "What's the plan?"

"That's what I want to talk to you about. I thought we could have some breakfast and discuss the matter further. I sent a friend to the market to pick up a few things that I thought you could eat. I figured you'd be hungry."

Even with his hair sticking up in all directions and a days' worth of delicious scruff darkening his rugged jaw, he looked sexy as sin. "Starving, actually. I could use some coffee."

"Please help yourself." He pointed to a white ceramic mug on the counter, a sugar bowl, and a small container of almond milk.

"Hold on, did you say you sent someone to the grocery store for me?" There were many words to describe Garrett Mulroney, unrelenting, stubborn, sexy, but now she'd have to add thoughtful to the list.

He inclined his head to the side. "Part of keeping you safe means feeding you. It comes with the territory, and since you couldn't eat anything here, I didn't have much choice in the matter."

"Right, thanks." *He's just doing his job. This isn't personal*, she reminded herself.

"Is something wrong?" he asked, eyeing her skeptically.

"No, it's just I'm not used to anyone doing things for me." Aside from the high priestess, Gillian was the mother hen at the coven. She enjoyed taking care of the other girls, cooking for them, and helping out where she could. It made her feel needed. Maybe it was from being an only child and taking care of her mom. "It smells delicious."

"I've never made anything vegan before. I make no promises." He held up his hands in surrender. "Maybe you should taste it first."

"I think I'll take my chances," she shot back and walked to the fancy looking coffee maker and poured herself a steaming cup, enjoying their banter more than she should.

She turned back to face him, and her gaze roamed over the threadbare sweatpants he wore. They molded perfectly to his muscled thighs, and she wondered if his would be hairy or smooth. Everything about him was so big...so manly. Her gaze traveled lower still, and she could make out a sizeable bulge.

Apparently, there was absolutely nothing small about him. It was clear he was very well endowed. Now she understood why he was so damn cocky. He'd been seriously blessed in the looks department. The vamp was a cornucopia of good genes. She tried to look anywhere but at his crotch and forced her mind out of the gutter.

"Can I do anything to help?" she asked, taking a sip of coffee, holding the mug up to hide her expression. "Mmm, this is good. I'm impressed. Making good coffee takes skill." Nothing short of a caffeine IV drip would get her going this morning.

"And you doubted my skills, Miss Howe?" His eyes pierced hers in silent challenge, inviting her to test those other skills. When she just stood there gaping at him, he wiped his hands on a kitchen towel, and his lips twitched. "Why don't you grab the syrup in the fridge?"

"Will do." Good thing too. Maybe the cold air would help her from self-combusting on the spot. She opened the door, impressed at the lengths he went to for her, even if it was his job.

He kept the subzero stacked with fresh veggies, fruit, and bottles of Moet. He'd even picked up some tofu. And then a thought occurred to her, how long did he think she'd planned to stay? She reached for the syrup off the shelf, shut the door, and set it on the island.

He motioned for her to take a seat at the island where he'd set two place settings. He pulled the casserole dish out of the oven and rested it on the counter, next to a bowl of fresh fruit. "Bon Appetit."

"I appreciate all the trouble you went to, but it wasn't necessary. Thank you." She plopped down in a barstool and scooped a generous amount onto her plate. She could be one of those girls who pretended not to eat much and be dainty about it. But what was the point?

Trying to make a joke, she held up a forkful of pancake. "Tell me, Detective, are you trying to bribe your witness with food?" Despite their history, from all accounts, he was a great cop.

He arched his dark brows. "If that were the case, I'd use better ammunition like a fine port or Swiss chocolate perhaps."

Most of the men she dated waxed poetically about drinking beer from a glass versus a bottle and liked to eat Cheese Wiz straight from the can. They weren't cultured like Mulroney and knew nothing about port wine or Swiss chocolate for that matter. She glanced at the perfectly shaped silver dollars on her plate. It was probably safe to say he knew his way around in the kitchen, something she found incredibly sexy.

His phone buzzed on the counter. He held it up and glanced at the screen. "Sorry, it's Alex. I need to take this." He walked into the living room, and she tried to listen in, but he kept his voice to a whisper. After a few minutes, he came back to the breakfast bar. From his solemn expression, she sensed it wasn't good news.

"Anything about Brooke?" she asked, gripping her fork.

"Nothing yet, but there's a new development in the case we should discuss. Why don't you eat first? You can consider this a peace offering, he said, placing the griddle in the sink and rinsing it off. "You're under my protection now." There was a note of possessiveness in his tone that made fire spark low in her belly.

What would it be like to be possessed by Garrett Mulroney—and be at the center of his world? She imagined it would be everything, consuming and erotic. The memory of him outing her snapped her from her reverie. It lingered at the back of her mind like a dark cloud. Despite their electricity, she could never trust him.

"For how long?"

Before he could respond, the doorbell rang. They both glanced at each other, then he lifted his pant leg and reached for the gun in his ankle holster. She couldn't deny seeing him in action was hot.

"I thought bullets don't work on vampires."

"Normal ones don't." He moved to the door like smoke. "These are silver-tipped. I came prepared for the occasion. No one, and I mean no one, gets past me."

CHAPTER 11

Garrett moved behind the door until he stood flush against the wall. Drawing his Glock, he tried to pick up on the scent coming from the other side, not sure if it was vampire or human.

"If a vampire was after me, would he knock on the door? I mean, c'mon." Gillian followed him, curiosity seeming to overrule her fear.

"Our plan might be working. This would be one way to throw me off my guard," he whispered back and held a finger to his lips.

He moved closer still, and the scent of old books and flowery perfume flared in his nostrils. With a curse, he put the safety back on his gun and holstered it in his ankle strap. "It's my neighbor," he announced and opened the door.

"Good morning, Garrett." Annette Thornwood wore her dyed black hair in a sleek bob, which gave her an eccentric look. Now pushing eighty, with her bright, green eyes and porcelain complexion, she must've been stunning in her youth. "You left before I could give you the change for the groceries." She reached out her small, withered hand and tried to give him some cash.

"Please, keep it, Annette. I'm a little busy right now." He tried to block Gillian from her view, but it was too late. Her owl eyes darted to her and gave Gillian a once over.

"I'm sorry. I didn't realize you were entertaining a lady friend. Am I interrupting?" Annette asked with a wink.

Gillian stepped forward, and from the shocked expression on her face, she wasn't expecting to see a petite, older woman standing on the other side of the door in a silk kimono and house slippers. "No, not at all. I'm Gillian. It's nice to meet you."

"You too, Gillian. What a gorgeous young lady you are," Annette exclaimed. Garrett couldn't argue with her there. "Well, I'll leave you two young people. It's almost time for Good Day New York." She touched his face. "You're such a sweet boy, just like my Henry." His neighbor turned to Gillian and smiled. "You should stop by for a cup of tea."

"I'd love to. I bet you've got some great dirt on this one." Gillian flicked her thumb to Garrett, and he got the feeling she was enjoying the hell out of this.

"Don't let him fool you with his tough-guy act. This is a first, me picking up groceries for him. He takes care of all the seniors on the block. He checks in on me every day in fact—"

"We should let you get back to your show," Garrett interjected. "I'm sorry, but we've both got to get to work." He tried to escort her out the door without being rude.

"Sure. See you later. Have a great day, you two." Annette waved and walked out of his apartment.

Garrett shut the door and exhaled, not sure how Gillian would react. He did have a bad cop persona to uphold. "We should probably eat before the food gets cold." Garrett motioned to the breakfast bar. They walked back to the island and sat down. "Look, about those things Annette said, you can't believe everything you hear."

"Right, of course not," she nodded in agreement, and that damnable mouth of hers slanted into a smirk. "But I do like the nickname 'sweet boy'. It suits you, and you shouldn't be embarrassed about helping the people you care about."

After that, neither of them said a word. He broke the awkward silence by heaping some food on his plate. He wouldn't let her eat alone. "Getting back to our discussion, there's no one else that can protect you, but me. You'll have to make the best of a bad situation. It's the only way to keep you safe. Sunlight negatively impacts a vampire's speed so we should be okay during the day. I'll give you a key as well as the password to my security system."

"There must be some kind of mage witness protection program. If so, I'm all in as long as it doesn't involve driving a minivan."

He laughed. "I can assure you, that's not an option. For now, we stick to the plan. You will stay here with me."

"I can't keep this from my friends. Why not tell them the whole truth?"

He shook his head. "And have history repeat itself? I don't think so. The last time the ladies from your coven got involved in a police investigation it only complicated matters. They got in the way of authority. We need to keep them out of this for everyone's safety."

After she wiped her mouth on a napkin, she gazed over at him with an expectant look on her face. "For how long?"

"Hard to say at this point." Garrett wanted to be as upfront with her as he could. After he took a bite of his breakfast, he chewed and swallowed. "It could be a week, maybe more."

The pleading look in her eyes gutted him. "A week? There has to be another way. I can't take not knowing what's happening to her."

"You have to trust us. I can assure you, we're doing everything in our power to find her." He only wished they had more to go on. "Getting back to you, I should be aware of your schedule," he said, trying to redirect the conversation. "Do you have any prior engagements or appointments I should know about? If nothing's urgent, you might want to cancel everything."

"The shop's participating in a festival on Halloween at the Weehawken Waterfront Park. I'm not going to cancel. It's also a fundraiser for my charity. The proceeds go to kids with cancer. Is there any chance you can go with me?"

He nodded, taking a sip from his mug. "I'm familiar with the festival. It's for a great cause. I'll personally make sure we find a way to get you there." The more he got to know her, the more it became clear how much her charity work meant to her.

Relief and gratitude flashed in her eyes in equal measure. "Thanks. I appreciate it." She sat back in her chair, holding up her mug. "You were about to fill me in on anything that might lead you to Brooke."

"I made some inquiries and found a link to Lawrence's dating site. Of course, it was taken down, but from what I've researched, they prey on young, attractive women."

"What can I do? I can't just sit here and do nothing while Brooke is out there." She pushed her plate away.

"You have to act natural and stick to your routine. I'll drop you off at the shop and pick you up. It will help draw him out. From now on, I'll be taking the day shift until the case is wrapped. Can you switch your schedule so you work during the day?"

"I'll have to talk to the girls." She tilted her head. "It's going to be a challenge without telling them the truth."

"We've already discussed this." He met her gaze. "The last time they got in the way of authority, and it put all your lives in danger. No. It's too risky."

"How about a compromise?" she asked in a tentative voice.

"Fine, if you must tell one person, let it be someone who can keep a secret."

"Thank you. But what am I supposed to tell my friends as to the reason I decided to move in here with you, someone they think I dislike?" Her lips parted. "Sorry if that came out wrong."

"Not to worry. I've given this cover some thought, although I don't think you're going to like it very much."

"What does this cover entail?" Gillian crossed her arms over her chest, and her robe peaked open. He followed the movement with his eyes, not able to keep from gazing at her creamy skin.

He'd always been of the mindset to rip the band-aid off clean. "It's simple; we tell everyone that we've been secretly seeing each other. We tell them we're a couple."

Laughter bubbled up from the back of Gillian's throat. "You've got to be kidding me. They're psychic and intuitive, even if I managed to pull off this lie, they'd be able to see right through it by my breathing and body language."

"Not if it were true." Mulroney reached over and pushed her hair behind her ear. Goosebumps pebbled along her skin. "Like it or not, you're attracted to me. Well, at least physically anyway."

Maybe it was the warmth in his blue eyes or the huskiness in his voice, but Gillian couldn't help thinking that maybe the feeling was mutual. The abrupt shift in his demeanor made her head spin. "You're pretty sure of yourself, Detective," she whispered, not able to deny the stream of anticipation pulsing through her blood in hot revolutions.

"Forgive me for also pointing out that your heart rate speeds up whenever I come within five feet of you. I'm not saying this to sound arrogant. It's simply the truth and will assist in our cover. It shouldn't be too difficult to convince everyone we simply took our attraction to the next level." His words cut through her and cleared away any misconceptions she had about their relationship. She was good for one thing—to act as bait.

"Okay fine, so maybe my body might be, but it takes more than physical attraction to make a relationship, even a fake one. What about trust and compatibility? We have none of those things, and how about the fact that we barely tolerate each other?"

"Don't make this more complicated than it has to be," he said, finishing the last of his breakfast and pushing his plate away. "We should start by getting to know each other. What if we say that we started dating recently and kept in touch after the investigation on the coven? We convince everyone there were instant fireworks between us."

"Oh, there were fireworks alright." She wanted to throttle him.

"Not those kinds of fireworks." His expression grew serious. "Can I ask you a question?

"Why not?" She smirked. "We're a couple now."

"Last spring, during the investigation on the coven, you never told me why you took such a personal offense when I interrogated you."

She shrugged and ran a hand through her tangled hair. As much as she might be put off by staying here, he was risking his own life to keep her safe. At the very least, he deserved to know the truth. "When I was younger, my parents used to have some very heated arguments, mainly about my dad's gambling. I remember one night in particular. I was probably about seven at the time when the neighbors called the cops."

He knitted his brows together. "Please, go on."

"It had been a Sunday evening, and I'd just finished watching a cheesy family movie on TV. We were about to have dinner when the fight started. It got heated fast. I was ashamed when the cops came in and started questioning my parents. I remember I ran out of our apartment and hid in the hallway until they left. I guess having you come to the coven reminded me of that time in my life and it freaked me out."

"I'm sorry you had to go through something like that, or if it brought you back to a dark place." His words softened the crux of her anger. "It was never my intention."

There was still the matter of him ruining her chances at a job she'd been vying for, but this wasn't the time or the place to drag up the past. For now, they'd bury the hatchet for everyone's sake. Besides, once Brooke was found she'd probably only see Mulroney in passing. "Apology accepted." She got up from the table, rinsed her plate, and loaded it in the dishwasher. "Since you cooked, I'll do the dishes."

"Fair enough." He loaded the rest of the plates in the sink, cleaned off the counter, and put away the remaining food in the fridge. When he finished, he leaned his hip against the edge of the counter. "We should probably start by asking each other some questions."

"Okay, let's do this." She glanced at the clock on the microwave. "We have about thirty minutes to get to know each other before I have to get in the shower."

It didn't take long to learn where they'd both grown up, their favorite movies and TV shows. Who knew Mulroney loved *Impractical Jokers*? It was hard to believe he had a sense of humor. He always came across as such a tight-ass.

"Where did you go to college?" he asked. "Wait, I saw the NYU sweatshirt."

The subject filled her with regret. She finished the last of the dishes and refused to look him in the eye. Mulroney brushed past her to open a cabinet under the sink, and a shiver danced along her skin. He pulled out the dishwashing liquid and poured the soap in then pressed a button.

After she wiped her hands on a towel, she walked into the living room and sat on the couch. She tucked her legs beneath her. He followed and took a seat opposite her in one of the wing-backed chairs. "I never went to college. The sweatshirt belongs to Brooke. I had to take care of my mom. I went to work instead." She leaned back against the pillow. "Enough about me, how about you?"

Gillian braced for the worst, expecting him to look at her with pity in his eyes, something she wouldn't be able to handle. His gaze filled with compassion instead. "I went a few times actually, first in Europe, and then, to Fordham for criminal justice. It's never too late to go back and take some classes online you know. You can do anything you want to."

His encouragement surprised her. Warmth spread from her head to her toes and everywhere in between. "I have thought about it. Okay, back to the questions," she said, eager to change the subject. "Do you have any siblings? I mean, are any of them vampires?"

He gazed down at a spot on the coffee table before his eyes met hers once more. When he did, his expression became stormy, filled with a myriad of emotions. "No. They all died a very long time ago."

"I'm sorry. It must be difficult to live all this time alone."

He remained silent. She sensed there was a lot more to the story, but it wasn't her place to probe. "Okay, we might have enough to convince everyone if they ask us questions, but what about Willow and Alex's engagement party? It's in a few days. I hope we'll find her by then, but with Brooke missing, how can I plan on attending?"

"You must do what you normally would to not draw attention to yourself, or it might make the others suspicious. It's important to stick to your routine. I was invited to the party as well. We'll have to figure that part out later."

This was getting more difficult than she thought. She assumed she could keep their pretend relationship under wraps, claim they were having some crazy hot sex, and then, when Brooke was found, she could say things had simply fizzled out. The idea of trying to "fake it" in front of their friends was something she wasn't sure even she could pull off. She glanced at her phone. "We have a few more minutes left. Are there any deep, dark secrets to divulge?"

His eyes clouded. Perhaps she hit too close to home. "How about we focus on how we started dating."

Now came the part Gillian would have to pay extra close attention to, their story—the story of how they went from disliking each other to falling madly in love and moving in together. "Would you like to give it a shot?"

"A few months after the investigation wrapped up, I got your number from Alex and gave you a call. I asked you to meet me for coffee. At first, you thought this was related to the case and agreed. You were surprised when I showed up holding a single red rose."

"A rose? Isn't that a little corny?" *It was kind of sweet.*

"Okay, forget the rose. You were shocked when I showed up and told you that I couldn't stop thinking about you," he said in a husky voice.

Her heart pounded. Even if this was a ruse, just hearing him say the words made her a little giddy inside. "How did you convince me to give you a chance?"

"We shared coffee and some conversation. We took a walk and watched the sunset." He gestured to the sun shining brightly through the windows.

She reached for a couch pillow and placed it in front of her body. "Sounds romantic. It seems as though you've given this some thought."

"Undercover work makes me good at my job, Gillian." This was the first time he said her name, and it made her skin flush. "I think it's time we start calling each other by our first names."

"How did you get me on my good side, Garrett?" His name sounded funny on her lips, and the moment she said it, he visibly tensed. Damn, she'd give anything to find out what he was thinking.

"After I did some heavy-duty groveling for the way I treated you during the last investigation, you agreed to go out with me on a real date."

"I think I like the groveling part. Where was this alleged date?" she asked, curious at what he'd come up with.

"I took you to hear live music." Garrett smiled, showing a flash of straight white teeth and a hint of fangs. "I found out where your favorite band was playing, and then, we went to a vegan restaurant and talked for hours."

"I'm impressed by the level of your deceit," she said sarcastically.

"You were devastated by my charms and how attentive I was." He moved from the chair to the couch. His sexy male scent invaded her nostrils, and she forced herself not to sigh. "I couldn't keep my eyes off you." His gaze filled with heat. This is all a game, she reminded herself. "I was the perfect gentleman, which intrigued you even more." Lust gleamed in his blue eyes. "As a matter of fact, you told me late one evening when we were on the phone that when you went to bed you were aroused the whole night."

Heat shot to her core. "There's quite a level of detail to this story."

"We want it to be convincing, don't we?" He moved closer still.

"Is that you what you do, move in for the kill? No hesitation?"

"None," he said with conviction. "Especially when I see something I like, and when I do, I go after it full-on, no holds barred."

"What happened after this momentous date in which you swept me off my feet with your charm and good manners?" she murmured, swallowing hard.

"Don't forget attentiveness." His big body filled the small space between them. "I called you every night. I needed to hear the sweet sound of your voice."

Her breaths came out in short little puffs of air. She wondered when this had become real. Or was this still part of the charade? But the truth was, she wasn't sure anymore. She knew one thing—she didn't want it to end. "What about the second date?" she whispered, hanging on his every word.

"By then we were both pretty worked up, being so attracted to each other and denying ourselves." He glanced at her lips. "After all those late-night calls, we became desperate to see each other, but we were both busy and couldn't get together right away." His voice sounded pained now. "But I knew, as we both did, that once we gave in to our desires there'd be no turning back for either of us."

His words made her warm all over. "You assume a lot."

"I couldn't wait to be alone with you. Naturally, I invited you here so I could cook you dinner. I bought your favorite wine and cooked your favorite foods, and then, after a fabulous dinner—" He stopped and simply stared into her eyes, not saying a word. His hand moved to rest on the arm of the couch. He was so close now all she had to do was lean back and he'd be touching her.

She swallowed and wondered if he could hear the wild thump of her heart. "What happened after this fabulous dinner?"

"I explained the power of sex with a vampire and that it can be irresistible to some." He cocked his head to the side, as though trying to gauge her reaction, and she found herself falling deeper into his gaze.

"Do vampires ever just have sex without the blood bonding thing?" she whispered, and the air grew thick with sexual tension.

"Sure, some do, yes. Not all vampire blood's addictive. When the technology became available, I made sure to have mine tested and found out that it's not."

Gillian tried to collect her scattered thoughts. Everything was happening so fast. She could barely keep up. "Getting back to this fake relationship. How did things progress so quickly? I'm still not sure anyone will believe it."

"At first, we agreed to take things slow, but we couldn't resist each other anymore. So, after we peeled each other's clothes off and made love until the sun came up, I couldn't bear to be away from you a moment longer. I asked you to move in with me."

"And I agreed just like that?" Gillian asked in disbelief. "This cover you've created makes you sound a little possessive and impulsive. Do you honestly think anyone will buy it?"

"What if you said you've always secretly fantasized about getting swept off your feet? You and I both wanted to explore this thing between us and give it a real chance, so you moved in, end of story." His face changed back to normal, the heat now gone from his eyes. He moved in a flash of light, to a chair at the dining room table and booted up his laptop. "Do we need to go over this again?" he asked, not bothering to look her way. This little game seemed to have had zero effect on him.

Her face flushed. "You're one hell of a storyteller, but do you really think my friends will believe that after a couple of dates, and some good sex, I moved in with you?"

"It could never be just good between us, Gillian—exceptional, mind-blowing, yes." He looked up and his eyes turned dark, almost molten.

The conviction in his words made her nipples tighten into points and heat pool to her inner thighs. His confidence bordered on cocky. She wanted to deny it, but the words got sucked back in her throat, along with all the air in the room. "Even still, I've never been flighty." Okay, maybe she was, but he didn't need to know that. Ever since a dark fae tried to abduct her and turn her into fish bait, she'd made an oath to live life to the fullest every day.

"It's your job to convince them for their safety as well yours, but I'll be right there with you every step of the way." The warmth in his voice made her melt.

She shook her head from the sexual haze. "This all seems so out of character, even for me."

He pinned her with his gaze, as though trying to delve beneath the surface. "Yes, but when it comes to love and passion all bets are off. Don't you agree, Gillian?" Her name sounded decadent on his lips like warm chocolate.

She nodded her head, shock jolting through her body. She never imagined Mulroney to be such a romantic. The knowledge made her a little dizzy. "I hope I can remember everything we talked about."

"Make some notes if you have to. It always helps me to refer back, and most of all, try to sound convincing." The genuine concern in his voice caught her off guard. Could she have been wrong about him? The question nagged at her. "Oh, and disregard what I said earlier about staying off social media. I permit you to tweet away. Let's see if it lures him out."

"I'll do my best."

She wasn't sure how she was supposed to concentrate on work at this point. Her heart tugged with worry over Brooke, and she was still heartsick over Salem. Now there was a pretend relationship to contend with and a smoking hot detective at her beck and call. She got to her feet, cut through the hallway, and up the staircase without looking back at Garrett. Why did it feel like she was getting in bed with the devil, an icy-blue eyed one at that?

CHAPTER 12

a fter Garrett walked Gillian through the doors of her shop, he'd made sure the place was secure and then crossed the street to the unmarked late model Sedan parked on the corner. An officer Garrett had seen around the station rolled down his window, and Garrett flashed his badge. "Detective Mulroney," he said and offered his hand.

"Scott Andrews. We've never met, but I've heard a lot about you, and Gillian Howe, of course." He cracked a smile. Garrett ignored the friendly ribbing. "I'll be your eyes and ears, Detective."

"Good. I'll be back at some point today after my meeting." Garrett handed Andrews his card. "My cell number is written on the back. Don't hesitate to reach out if anything looks suspicious." He hoped the officer didn't pick up on the protective note in his voice.

The officer's grin widened. "Don't worry. I'll keep an eye on your girlfriend." So much for being discreet.

The MBI offices were located twenty-five miles due north of Raven's Hollow. The building couldn't be found on a GPS or a map. Garrett had been here many times before since the two agencies worked together to solve a myriad of cases over the years.

And yet, coming here never got old. From the outside, the huge brick structure resembled a run-down factory, but inside, it was a high-tech mage facility. Wall-sized computer screens filled much of the space, along with life-size moving holograms of wanted criminals.

Denopoulos insisted they meet here, mainly because it was off the grid. There was too much at stake to risk talking at the station. Garrett hated the idea of dirty cops on the payroll. But like it or not, the investigation on the Shadow Cabal proved it was very much a reality. Going forward, there were few on the force he would trust these days.

"As far as we can tell, Lawrence has gone underground since he kidnapped Brooke Corey. He was last seen at a hotel in Clifton twenty-four hours ago; then, the trail goes cold." Garrett slid the file across the table to Alex Denopoulos, the only human on the MBI, and his demon partner, Cayden Teague, hoping they had something more to go on than he did. "We have the client list from the Cherry woman, which might be a place to start. We've contacted all the witnesses from the party, and no one's talking."

They were seated at a long conference table with Dubrosky on one side of him, Denopoulos and Teague on the other. As far as he could tell, they were the only creatures in the building. The staff consisted of robotic arms and artificial intelligence. Since the MBI had jurisdiction over the case, it had been decided that the RHPD would assist in an unofficial capacity during the investigation. For Gillian's sake—and Brooke's, of course—he would do everything in his power to help, even if it meant revealing his connection to Malcom and things from his past that he'd rather forget.

"Where do we go from here?" Dubrosky broke in, tapping her fingers on the conference table. She wore a navy suit and kept her dark hair pulled off her face in a tight ponytail. The only thing missing to her detective ensemble was a trench coat.

"First, I want to get the matter of the coven off the table. We've got uniforms parked outside." Garrett turned to his partner. "Dubrosky, can you stop by periodically to make sure those women are safe?"

"Got it covered, partner." Dubrosky smiled. "That should score some points with Gillian."

The three of them laughed. He ignored them and continued. "I've made some calls to check on Lawrence's alibi for the night of the murder. I'm still waiting to hear back." After Garrett filled them in on the captain's plan to use Gillian as bait, he exhaled, not sure how they'd react to this new information.

Teague nodded his approval, running a hand through his spikey, blond hair. "Let me get this straight, you and Gillian under the same roof, pretending to be a couple?" He burst into laughter. "Don't ever let me hear you complain about getting the shitty assignments, Mulroney."

Garrett muttered a curse. "Wait a minute. It's not like that—"

"Yeah, give it time. How's that working out so far?" Denopoulos chimed in, scratching his beard. "Does she know you've got the hots for her, Mulroney? I hope she's not walking around your place in those short little robes all the girls wear around the coven."

"Yeah, don't remind me." Garrett rubbed the back of his neck and tried not to groan. He'd already taken one cold shower this morning, which did nothing to fan the flames of his desire.

Everyone laughed, except Dubrosky. "Seriously, Mulroney, if you don't ask Gillian out on a real date when this case is wrapped, then you don't deserve her." She sat back in her chair and sighed, looking a little starry-eyed. When the room grew silent, she cleared her throat. "Moving on. We can take turns keeping an eye on her. I can stake out the shop, and pretend I'm a customer. But I think it's time to poke the tiger. What if we have Gillian go out in public to draw Lawrence's thugs to her with one of us hiding nearby?"

"Great idea, Dubrosky. Make it happen. In the meantime, we need to make a deal with someone from the party." After Denopoulos opened the Lawrence file and flipped through the pages, he pulled out his pen and began scanning the pictures inside. "We find one of them with a lot to lose, and see who's willing to make a deal. Hold on, what about this guy, David Jackson? If memory serves, he's an assistant to a local congressman by the name of Johnathan Stevens. I say we put pressure on him to talk. We make sure to offer him a deal to keep the congressman's good name from getting dragged into this. No formal charges have been made against Jackson, but that can change."

Teague mulled it over. "I think it's time for us to go have a long talk with Mr. Jackson before we go directly to his boss. In the meantime, we applied to the Council for an exigent warrant to get the credit card number Lawrence used at the hotel in Clinton. What about the connection between this dating website Lawrence and Malcolm Strauss are involved in?"

"We're still running some background checks on him to see how Malcom fits into all of this." Garrett rubbed his chin. It was still too early to reveal his hunch that Malcom Strauss and Malcom Von Scrivner were one and the same. That is his sire was back. No, he couldn't say anything until he had proof. "Any ideas where he may have gone and taken Brooke Corey?"

Denopoulos glanced at his tablet before looking up. A line appeared between his dark brows. "We sent a squad car over to Lawrence's residence. He's gone, and we checked two of his businesses here in the city. They're empty. It's like they never existed. I don't know how he managed to pull this off. I'm going to keep digging. I guarantee he may have closed up shop here, but he'll start up somewhere he has a connection."

"He's been mixing the proceeds from the blood ring in with the legitimate businesses," Garrett said, desperate for something to turn up soon. "He could be hiding Brooke in the basement of one of his bars or restaurants, but it's unlikely. Either way, I'll keep checking. Did forensics pick up any fingerprints at her apartment or on the box that was sent over to the coven?"

Dubrosky sighed. "Not a one. Whoever did it wore gloves. I checked the witness accounts and did a quick scan of the signed statements. There's nothing that leads us to Lawrence or where he could be hiding any of these women. As for his other operations, we could go over there to question his staff and get a warrant for his files."

"This is all going to take time," Garrett shot back. "We need to find a way to infiltrate his operation, and that's how we find him and Brooke Corey. He'll probably lie low for a while, and then reach out to his clients, maybe some from Rowena's Cherry's list. We come up with an op from that. We need to act fast. The longer Brooke Corey is with him, the harder it will be to break their bond."

"I've read his profile." Dubrosky took a sip from a mug and gestured with her hands. "He's a borderline sociopath. But the question remains, did he kill Serena Bensen on purpose, or by accident after he bit her?"

Garrett's phone pinged. He glanced at the text from Lawrence's office manager and shook his head in bewilderment. "Well, Lawrence might be guilty of a boatload of twisted shit, but he's not a killer. His alibi checks out for the night the Bensen woman was killed. We've got him on camera and it's time-stamped."

"That's the trouble with vampires," Teague muttered. "They stalk their prey and turn them into their personal feed bags." His gaze narrowed in Dubrosky's direction, before glancing over at Garrett with a sheepish expression. "Sorry, Mulroney, no offense."

Garrett cleared his throat. "None taken." Cayden Teague had roamed the Earth for centuries, but somehow never managed to let go of his distaste for vampires. Garrett could understand how any female, even a vampire, could get intimidated by the barrel-chested demon. He stood almost seven feet tall with a booming voice and gray horns curling along the sides of his head. Deep down the guy had a heart of gold. But he wouldn't get a pass for acting like a dick to his partner. His behavior was not okay. "Don't you think you're coming off rather gruff?"

Dubrosky glanced over at Garrett and held up her hand. "Thanks, Mulroney, but I've got this. Why don't you let us go over ideas for my cover at the shop?"

She glared across the table at Teague and hissed a curse in Russian, her fangs extending from her lips. "How dare you judge my kind? Who are you to talk? Demons are notorious for being egotistical male chauvinists, and you're no different."

"Have you been checking up on me?" Teague surged to his feet and leaned his enormous body over the table. "I'm flattered, but let's face it, sweetheart, it wouldn't matter anyway. I'm guessing you've already formed an opinion. Demons are third-class citizens outclassed by both vampires and witches. But hey, maybe being a male chauvinist is just in our brute nature."

"If you're third class citizens then you have no one else to blame but yourselves by holding onto grudges and lacking decorum." Dubrosky wrinkled her nose at the coffee stain on Teague's Metallica t-shirt, the one he wore under his suit jacket. "And stop calling me sweetheart."

Teague's horns elongated and flared red. "Do you prefer shrew? How about harpy?"

"I think this would be a good time for a coffee break. You in?" Denopoulos asked over the shouting.

"I'm right behind you." Garrett stood and followed him into the hallway.

"Did I miss something?" Denopoulos poured what looked like black sludge into two mugs and handed one to him. His mind immediately drifted to Gillian. Having her at his place, drinking coffee and eating breakfast, filled him with excitement, something he could get used to. And then he wondered if they'd ever get past the invisible barrier between them. She might be physically attracted to him, but he craved so much more from her. She may have accepted his apology, but he could tell from her body language, something still bothered her. Clearly, she still didn't trust him. He was determined to find out why. But he wouldn't let it detract from the case. She would never forgive him if he didn't find her cousin, and he would never forgive himself.

"Hey, we were talking about Teague and your new partner." Denopoulos prompted, breaking into his thoughts. "I like her by the way. She's whip-smart and not bad on the eyes."

Garrett never thought of Dubrosky in that way, but he supposed with her crisp white shirts and conservative pantsuits, she could be deemed attractive in a penal sort of way. Garrett inclined his head to where the shouting continued. "My guess is this all goes back over a thousand years to the battle of Ramayana."

"The battle of Ramayana?" Denopoulos shook his head, looking confused.

"All before my time. It took place on Arcadia, the demon plane." Vampire and demon relations were at an all-time high. Garrett refused to let a centuries-old rift between creatures get in the way of this investigation.

"Whoa, there's a demon plane? That's a new one." Denopoulos sipped his coffee, staring at him in disbelief.

Garrett's phone buzzed. "Excuse me for a moment." He walked off to the side and glanced at the text.

Hey Garrett, are you free tonight? Want to open a bottle of wine and hang out?

It was from Michelle, his interior designer, a woman he'd taken out and slept with recently. *Big mistake.* They hadn't spoken in weeks. He'd made it clear he wanted to keep things casual.

He'd explained to Michelle—along with every woman he took out— that he didn't do relationships. He kept things light. Being a vampire just made it complicated and painful all around if either party got attached. He made sure to always be upfront so no one got hurt. After she'd finished the job at his home, she seemed fine continuing a professional relationship. But he shouldn't have gone there in the first place. It was a lapse in judgment he wouldn't repeat.

And right now, he was focused on this case and Gillian. An image of her in that short robe she wore at breakfast flashed through his mind, but he shook it off. Eventually, when he didn't make plans with Michelle, she'd find someone who could offer her something real and long-term. He shot out a text and hit send.

Sorry, I'm working. But you go out, and have fun.

"Everything okay?" Denopoulos stood in front of him, angling his head at his phone.

"Yeah, all good."

"I believe you were telling me about this demon plane."

"Well, Arcadia doesn't exist anymore. This all took place long before I became a vampire. I'm surprised Teague never told you about that period in history." Garrett inclined his head in the direction of the conference room. "After losing the war, his people became enslaved by the Coterie, a cadre of ruthless vampires."

Denopoulos finished the last of his coffee and set his mug in the sink. "It certainly explains why he's giving your partner a hard time, but it's no excuse. He never talks much about his past. He's always been treated like a friggin' rock star for putting a bunch of vampires convicted of some heinous shit in Hellios, long before I came to work for the agency. You're saying you think it's related to this battle on Arcadia?"

"It's just a guess." Garrett hoped this wouldn't have any impact on their ongoing investigation. They had enough to deal with. There was no room for ancient rifts to get in the way. Talking about the past made him think of the similarities to his own.

"I'm curious, how come Teague's never given you a hard time?" Denopoulos asked, pushing Garrett back to the present. "You may not have been around back during this vampire-demon war, but you're one of them."

"I'm considered a young vampire in the grand scheme, especially in comparison to the Dubrosky family. They've been around for generations." Garrett took a sip of his coffee and made a face. The stuff really was awful. "She comes from an ancient line. Hell, they're practically royalty."

"In other words, she could've had family members who messed with his people?"

"It's certainly a possibility, but he's taking this a bit too far. Teague needs to find another outlet to work through his anger." Yeah, like Garrett was one to talk. He'd been searching for Malcom Von Scrivner for nearly a century to enact his revenge. Garrett shook his head, forcing his mind back to the present and set his mug on the counter.

"What do you say we break up *Grudge Match* in there?" Denopoulos pointed to the conference room.

Garrett chuckled. "My money would be on Dubrosky all the way. She might be petite, but she's a serious badass, not to mention she has a mean right hook."

When they walked back into the room, Teague and Dubrosky didn't exactly stand nose to nose, since Teague easily stood over seven feet and Dubrosky was five-two on a good day. But from the way they glared at each other, Garrett wasn't sure if they were going to kill each other or kiss.

"Break it up, you two and take a seat," Denopoulos commanded and shot a warning look at his partner. "Take it easy, Thor. Put the hammer down. Let's get back to the reason we're here today, the Lawrence case, remember?"

With a huff, Teague plopped down in his chair. "Of course. My apologies. You could always switch it up and take Gillian back to the coven. Who knows, it might draw Lawrence out. Either way, it's only a matter of time before he takes the bait and sends one of his minions after her."

Garrett would be ready when the vampire did. He wouldn't hesitate to rip him apart. "If I go to the coven, the other girls would intrude and put themselves in danger, which is why it makes sense for her to stay put for now. I'm sticking with the cover."

"As long as you're okay with the arrangement?" Denopoulos asked, giving him a sidelong glance. It was clear from the curious look on his face, and their conversation at the diner a few months back, he suspected Garrett's interest in Gillian wasn't purely professional.

"I'm making the best of the situation," Garrett muttered under his breath, trying not to draw attention to himself.

"I bet. I'm sure it's a real hardship playing house with a beautiful woman. All jokes aside, what are you planning to tell everyone?" Teague asked, folding his arms across his massive chest.

Garrett rubbed the back of his neck. "We've already come up with a cover. We stayed in touch after I finished the investigation on the coven and started dating recently. It made sense to keep our relationship a secret until we knew where it was going. Things moved quickly from there, and I asked her to move in with me. It might not be ideal, but this cover is for everyone's safety."

"What about the engagement party?" Dubrosky asked, glancing at Garrett with an expectant look on her face.

"It might raise suspicion if we both don't show." Garrett shot back, shifting in his seat. It would be one thing to pretend in front of a few people at Gillian's shop, but it was quite another to do it in front of a whole room full of friends and family. "It's your decision, Denopoulos."

"There will be questions if you both don't show. I'll tell Willow of course. She knows how to keep a secret. Besides, it will serve as a perfect time to convince everyone of your relationship," Denopoulos said with a wink. He'd met Willow while undercover, and their relationship had created quite a stir.

"The party's at Amanda's in Hoboken?" Teague glanced between them. "Don't you think it's a little too out in the open? It'll be one hell of a challenge to keep it secure."

"I'm friendly with the owners." Garrett smiled. "I eat at their other restaurant, the Elysian Café, every day for lunch."

Denopoulos pulled out his phone and began typing. "Funny, I heard the place was a speakeasy during prohibition."

Garrett nodded. "I used to go there when it was a speakeasy. It has an interesting history, not to mention the best sirloin steak salad in town." He grabbed his pad and pen and made a note to talk with them about security. "I'll make sure the entrances and exits are guarded at all times."

"I'm happy to help out," Dubrosky added, refusing to look in Teague's direction, which at this point was probably a blessing. They didn't need to go for round two. The conference table looked like it was made of solid mahogany. It would be a shame to see it turned into a pile of splintered wood.

"You'll have to make this fake relationship look convincing,"

Denopoulos insisted, getting to his feet. "Maybe you two should practice acting like you're in love."

The room erupted in fits of laughter.

He wasn't sure how Gillian would take the news. Garrett had a very strong suspicion this would be a major point of contention. "I guess this time the jokes on me." No question about it, this could quickly turn into a major shit show.

CHAPTER 13

*G*illian stretched out her hand to refill the mugwort and rosehip jars. They were arranged like glass soldiers on tall wooden shelves behind the shop's register. Glancing at the clock on the wall showed that it was almost nine, which meant she still had a few minutes to gather her wits before the other girls showed up for work.

How would she pull this off without cracking? She tried to recall the finer points that she'd gone over with Mulroney. "Garrett," she whispered, correcting herself. Saying his name out loud made her stomach flip. Getting used to calling him by anything but Mulroney would take time.

After Gillian rubbed her hands on her jeans, she examined her handiwork. Now pricked with black and orange lights, the ceiling of *Enchantments* gave off a starry effect to make browsing through the endless rows of tarot decks, ritual candles, crystal balls, runes, wands, and spellbooks a festive experience.

Once she climbed down from the step stool, she cleaned up the mess she'd left on the counter, booted up her laptop, and turned on the Spotify to R&B. Delilah had closed last night, so the store was in good shape.

Gillian loved to open, but not today. She relished the quiet before the store filled with customers. Mornings remained typically slow until about noon when people came in on their lunch breaks unless they had appointments. Today she had none, which was probably a blessing, considering her mind spun in a million different directions. Every few minutes she'd glance over her shoulder. Any little sound or creaking noise made her jump. Despite Officer Andrews popping in and out, she still couldn't shake the sense of dread in the pit of her stomach.

She exhaled, trying to focus, and glanced at the store schedule on the computer. On slow days, they accepted walk-ins, and if the customer liked their reading, they'd get booked for parties. She'd done her fair share of spa nights at private homes and the occasional bachelorette party. Brides, in particular, loved the novelty of having a tarot card reader there.

Always on the lookout for new customers, they started a mailing list for sales and promotions, which had grown considerably over time. Now they offered workshops and classes on Wicca, the use of essential oils, herbs in potions, and spellwork. She liked to think of the shop as Hogwarts for adults. None of them were growing rich by any stretch, but they were breaking even.

As much as Gillian enjoyed her job, her real love was doing her podcast. She still dreamed of being the host of a radio show someday. That dream would have to be on hold for now. Finding Brooke was her number one priority—her only priority.

She let out a ragged breath. Imagining what she was going to tell her friends about her new living situation made her break out in a cold sweat. No doubt she'd get bombarded with questions. Inevitably, the gossip would spread. If only she could go back in time when life was simpler, and she didn't have to lie to the people she loved, make up fake boyfriends, or be on the lookout for attacking vampires, which reminded her, she needed to go on the offensive.

She picked up her phone off the counter and typed a tweet.

#KurtLawrence #mediamogul or #monster? She posted it all over her social media and offered a silent prayer, hoping it would somehow lead them to Brooke.

The clack of heels forced Gillian to look up. Saje walked in with a steaming cup in her hands. She set it behind the register and stowed her purse under the counter. "What the hell's going on, Gillian? What happened to you last night that put you and the rest of us in danger?"

"I'll tell you everything, I promise. But first things first. Did you weave extra protections spells throughout the manor?"

"Yes. We are now the Fort Knox of covens, but you still haven't told me why that was necessary. I think I have a right to know," Saje said in an exasperated tone.

"You do. Where's Delilah? She's on the schedule today." Gillian's eyes darted to the back door. It had been her idea to open the shop and have all the women of the coven work together. She read tarot cards like Gillian but also created a line of soaps and lotions with magickal healing properties. She'd become a close friend. It would be hard to lie to her face about her fake relationship with Garrett.

"She's not coming in." Saje flicked on the neon open sign. "A slot opened up at a psychic fair in Secaucus. She thought it would be good for business, especially right before Samhain."

Gillian leaned over the counter to arrange the display of crystals before glancing back at Saje, trying to keep the gut-churning worry out of her eyes. After Gillian filled Saje in on all the gory details over the last twenty-four hours, she exhaled, not sure how she'd react. "Mulroney told me I could only tell one person, and it has been killing me not being able to confide in my best friend. But you have to swear not to tell anyone, for everyone's safety and especially for Brooke's. This won't work if we can't keep it a secret, and the fewer people who know, the easier it will be to pull this off."

"Don't worry, I won't say anything. I can't believe Lawrence kidnapped Brooke and killed your cat!" Saje shook her head. "It figures Nick hasn't mentioned a thing. Wait a minute, did I hear you right? You put a vampire in a coma?"

After that, it took Gillian a good ten minutes to calm Saje down. "Do you think between Mulroney and the agents, they'll be able to find Brooke?"

Anxiety coiled down her spine. "They have a few leads. Now that I'm a witness, and threatened to expose Lawrence on social media, Mulroney says I'm in danger, which is why I need to stay at his place. Naturally, we were forced to invent this charade about being a couple." Gillian reached for a stick of frankincense and a candle then lit both with a wave of her hand. "I can't go back to the coven."

"Who could've imagined that an invitation to the penthouse from a handsome, wealthy vampire would result in something so horrible?" Saje hands visibly shook as she dusted off the spines on the bookshelves.

"Trust me, living on the wild side isn't what it's cracked up to be." Ever since her mom's death, she'd tried to get out there and suck the lemon out of life, live every moment to the fullest. Death forces you to reassess your priorities. But at this point, she would give anything for a real connection with someone. She envied what Willow and Alex shared. What if that kind of love and passion just wasn't in the cards for her? Brooke's kidnapping made her painfully aware of all the things missing in her own life. At any moment, everything could be snatched away and drastically change.

Saje grabbed the keys and opened one of the glass cases to fill it with their pricier wands. "So you think Lawrence or one of his bodyguards will come after you?"

"If Lawrence comes after me, then there's a good chance he comes after all of you." Gillian would do everything in her power to make sure that didn't happen. "Which is why I have to keep him focused on me, keep him thinking the coven doesn't know anything. I plan to weave some protection spells of my own. If he does come for me, hopefully, Mulroney will be there, but I have to be prepared when he's not."

"What can I do?" Saje asked as she lit a pumpkin scented candle. The aroma swirled through the air.

"There must be a spell or a potion that can sever Brooke's blood bond without causing her any harm." Gillian bit her lip. "Can you bring some of the Grimoires from the coven here to the shop?"

"Sure. We can go through them together."

"Good. Why don't we try water scrying to see if it can lead us to Brooke before Delilah gets back?"

"Let's do it."

Saje got to work filling a cauldron with water while Gillian burned a bundle of sage in a copper bowl. Once Saje poured one of her truth potions into the cauldron, the water began to bubble. After they touched hands, magick pure and bright sparked through the air. A silhouette of Brooke rose from the surface of the water and billowed around like smoke.

"I can sense her will being compromised."

Gillian's heart squeezed. The next moment, another figure appeared and hovered above Brooke before the water turned blood red. "The dark prince. He represents Kurt Lawrence. I saw him when I read Brooke's cards. I didn't realize it at the time." Gillian moved her hands over the cauldron and whispered a spell.

"Let us see what can't be seen.

Give us a vision that allows magick to intervene

This is my will, so mote it be."

The two joined hands and repeated the spell a second and then a third time. Finally, a gate appeared like a hologram hovering in the air and coiled around Brooke like a rope. "A house with a gate?" Gillian whispered over her racing heart. "This could be anywhere."

"Hold on, there's some sort of symbol. Show yourself," Saje demanded. The slithering tail and wings of a dragon appeared encased in a shield. After the smoke dissipated, the water turned clear again. "It looks like a coat of arms. Not much to go on, but it's something."

"I'm calling Garrett." Gillian pulled out her phone and pressed a button. "Please be there," she whispered.

He answered on the first ring. "Gillian? Is everything okay?" Hearing him say her name made butterflies flutter in her belly.

"Yes, I'm fine. Look, I tried scrying for Brooke again, and this might sound crazy, but I saw a gated house with a dragon coat of arms. I believe she's being held there. It was very *Game of Thrones* like."

"*Game of Thrones?*" Garrett asked. "That's a book, right?"

"Yes, and probably the most popular TV show of all time. Do you think my vision could somehow lead us to Brooke?"

"I'll check the database and see what comes up. Good work, Gillian." Did he just compliment her? He cleared his throat, breaking the awkward silence. "I'll pick you up after your shift, and then, perhaps, we can order some take out. I think we should talk more and continue to get to know each other since we'll be attending the engagement party together. And it'll take your mind off of things."

Her foolish heart skipped a beat. "Yes, I agree." There was food and talking involved. Why did this sound an awful lot like a date? "I'll see you later," she said and ended the call.

"I still can't believe you're staying at Mulroney's." Saje's gaze narrowed. "I think hell may have frozen over for good this time. How's the whole fake couple thing going?"

"He's a lot different than you think." Gillian shrugged, hoping to sound nonchalant. "For starters, his home is like something straight out of Architectural Digest, and he can cook. But the clincher? He does the grocery shopping for the octogenarians on the block."

"Careful girl, you're sounding an awful lot like a Mulroney fan," Saje said with a mischievous gleam in her eye while she walked around the store, turning on every light. "Next thing I know you'll be telling me you're smitten."

"Oh please. I think you're reaching." She'd be lying through her teeth if she tried to deny his appeal. He was caring, charming, and took witty to a whole new level.

Saje turned back to face her. "Me thinks, the witch doth protest too much. When you talk about him, you get this dreamy look in your eyes."

Gillian couldn't deny the attraction. "Funny, Brooke said almost the same thing. But I don't think he's the relationship type. I found women's clothing in the guest room closet and a robe in the bathroom. All of those things scream player, and right now, it's the last thing I'm interested in."

"Maybe all this time he's been waiting for you to come into his life, and now you have. You can't fight that kind of chemistry." Saje said in a more serious tone and placed the cash drawer in the register. Gillian was still a teenager when her dad left, she struggled for years with abandonment issues. When her mom died, it took a long time to get over the blow. She couldn't take the pain of losing someone she loved again. Dating emotionally unavailable men simply became her default. Saje was one of the few people in this world who knew the truth about Gillian's past.

"In all the times he came by the coven, the girls and I used to take bets to gauge what would happen if you two ever got together." Saje pointed out. "It's pretty obvious the way you look at each other."

"Chemistry doesn't equal a relationship." And there was the little matter of him costing her the job of a lifetime. Gillian tried not to think too much about it and reached for her phone. Still nothing about Brooke.

"Fate's playing her hand here, my friend, and as a tarot card reader, you can't deny the signs." Saje handed her a deck of Love cards off the counter. "Well?"

"I'm not denying the signs. I'm simply not giving in to them. What good would it do? There's no future with a vampire." Gillian got paid to help people find love, and yet, she'd never experienced it for herself. Talk about irony.

"There's a legend that the springs in Sybil's Cave hold a powerful elixir. Vampires who routinely engage in sucking other people's blood use it to cleanse their own, but I came across a spell in one of the Grimoires that if used in conjunction with a series of potions, might be able to turn a vampire human again. Although, I can't say I know of anyone that it's worked on."

"Are you serious? I didn't know there was such a thing."

The bell dinged, keeping Saje from giving a further explanation. Lucas, one of their regulars, strolled in. With his long, shaggy blond hair and tattoos, he was the picture of the musician he aspired to be, rather than the Ace hardware employee he was.

"Hey, Lucas." Gillian waved and moved to the other side of the counter. She approached him, grateful for the distraction. "Are you here for a spell?"

"Yeah, that'd be great. Thanks." He gave her a lopsided grin. He came in all the time to buy carving candles for custom spells and incense before a show. "I thought you ladies might like to stop by Carpe Diem tonight. We're doing a gig." He handed her a flyer.

They'd been flirting for weeks now, but he'd never pulled the trigger and asked her out. Funny, a couple of days ago she would've jumped at the chance, but now she wasn't so sure. While part of her wanted to believe she was being more cautious after what happened with Lawrence, deep down she knew it had more to do with Garrett.

"I'm sorry, I have plans." Gillian snagged a white pillar candle off the shelf and then glanced up at Lucas with a smile. "Some other time."

Disappointment flashed in his eyes. "Yeah, some other time."

Gillian reached for a ritual knife off the counter and dug the tip into the candle. Once she carved a spell into the wax, she whispered an incantation, and then set the candle aside to let the magick take hold. She reached for her phone from the counter and once again frantically scrolled through her messages to see if there had been any word on Brooke. When she found nothing, her heart sank.

She tried to redirect the train of her thoughts and glanced over at Lucas, who browsed through the shelves. While he didn't necessarily give off an emotionally unavailable warning sign, he did have a passive vibe. Those kinds of males typically disappointed her in the end, leaving her bereft and unsatisfied. Maybe all the years of her father insinuating she wasn't good enough had taken their toll. She'd been plagued by insecurity ever since, too afraid to go after what she wanted, and settling for guys who weren't good for her.

While Lucas's demeanor was tentative and shy, Garrett was confident to the point of arrogance. He was pure alpha, the type to throw a woman over his shoulder and have his wicked way with her. The thought sent a ripple of awareness pulsing through her veins. Refocusing her attention, she placed the candle in a bag and rang Lucas up.

He walked back to the register and placed some cash on the counter. "It was good seeing you, Gillian."

"You too. Good luck tonight."

With a smile, he reached for the bag and walked out the door into the bright sunshine. Guilt slid in her belly. She hoped she hadn't led him on. Gillian felt a set of eyeballs burning a hole in her back and spun around.

"When are you planning to break the news to the other girls about your fake relationship with Mulroney?" Saje asked with a raised eyebrow.

"Maybe I'll just spring it on everyone at the engagement party, where we officially come out. In the meantime, I thought maybe you'd help me lay the groundwork." Gillian's eyes flicked to the door as it swung open. Every time a customer approached the counter, her pulse skyrocketed. Could Lawrence have sent one of them to kill her?

"Gillian? Hey, are you okay?" Saje whispered and walked over to where she stood. She gave her arm a reassuring squeeze.

"Yeah, my mind went someplace else." Gillian forced a smile and tried to calm her racing heartbeat.

"I'm happy to help smooth the rough edges with the other girls when it comes to you and Mulroney, but I'm guessing hearing the news from me will go over like a carrot stick in a trick-or-treat bag."

CHAPTER 14

*G*arrett stood outside Rowena Cherry's apartment building, hoping she could shed some light on her involvement with the Brotherhood. Before he could put his finger on her buzzer, his phone rang. He muttered a curse and held it to his ear. "Mulroney here."

"I'm glad I caught you," Denopoulos said in a clipped tone, which immediately put Garrett on alert.

"Why? What's up?"

"You need to get over to Elysian Park. I'm afraid there's been another murder."

The moment Garrett arrived at the crime scene, he instantly filled with rage. The body of a young female had been unceremoniously dumped in a bush, next to a kid's ball field. He couldn't get past the blatant display of evil and disregard for human life. Jesus, this case was turning into a ticking time bomb.

Garrett pulled out his badge and crossed through the yellow and purple crime scene tape while the blare of sirens rang in the distance. He kept his head down, trying to avoid the throng of reporters he recognized from *mage.com*.

Denopoulos and Teague were crouched next to the body, talking to a couple of uniformed officers.

"What do we have here?" Garrett asked, walking over to a box and pulling on latex gloves, paper booties, and a face mask from a cardboard kit marked *Biohazard*.

"We're still waiting for the coroner to make a positive ID," Teague said, scratching his horns. "But I'll give you my best guess: A female by the name of Kylie Macheo. She was reported missing by her roommate a couple of days ago and one of the women on the list from Rowena Cherry."

"Sonfabitch," Garrett muttered, shaking his head. "I just left the Cherry woman's place. I was about to ask her some questions about her boss when I got the call." He took out his phone and began snapping shots of the body. "Cause of death?"

Denopoulos shone a penlight and frowned. "Bite marks on her neck. Big surprise. From the width and placement, I'd say another vampire killing. From the rate of decomposition, it looks like she's been dead for more than twenty-four hours."

"Based on the position of the body and the dirt all over her clothing, I'd say she was killed somewhere else and dragged here. Any witnesses?" Garrett turned his head to glance at the people walking through the park going about their day, and his jaw clenched. This hit too close to home.

"Not so far," Teague muttered, pulling out a glass slide. "We could get lucky and find a passerby."

"It could be a copycat murder or one of Lawrence's thugs." Garrett's gaze roamed over the vic's clothing. She was dressed in a short skirt and a leather jacket. One high heel still dangled from her foot. "It looks like she was clubbing. The killer could've met her at a bar." He moved the light around to check for any clues on the body. He pushed his gloved hand inside her jacket pocket and removed a matchbook with the word *Birch* emblazoned across the front. He knew the nightclub on River Street well. "One of us needs to get over there and talk to the staff."

The only thing he could think about was making sure Gillian was safe. Anger and duty warred inside of him, forcing him to his feet. Garrett needed to get the hell out of there and see her in the flesh. "Keep me in the loop. I'm sorry, but I need to go." He removed his mask, booties, and gloves and threw them in a nearby trash can. God help him, there was only one place he wanted to be. *I need to warn Gillian.*

Between the steady flow of customers in the store and handling their online orders, the day should've flown by, but every few minutes Gillian nervously glanced at her phone, hoping to get some kind of update on Brooke. The moment someone would walk through the door, her heart would bang in her chest. And the churning in her gut never seemed to go away, no matter how many crystals she touched. She felt like she might be sick at any moment. By the time she managed to break free from a group of witches discussing the merits of essential oil in spells, she was a walking bundle of nervous energy. She grabbed her laptop and a few sets of tarot decks on her way to the storeroom. It was time for her podcast.

After she shut the door, she set her laptop on a card table, booted it up, and spread out her tarot decks. She grabbed three crystals from a shelf and set them around the cards. Then, she closed her eyes and tried to wipe the dark images from her mind. She took several deep breaths to calm her nerves and find her center. Scrolling through her email, she pulled up her questions for the podcast and pressed record on her computer. She hoped whatever she needed might unfold in the cards.

"Welcome to Eat, Tarot, Love. I'm psychic Gillian, and um, I'm here to, to chat on all things vegan, and I give advice on love and relationships." Her voice sounded shaky and hollow. She shook her head, trying to clear the agonizing fear and worry from her mind. But it was no use. She couldn't stay focused on anything for long. "Okay, let's get started. This email is from Nancy. I'm going to read it out loud.

"I've been doing online dating for a while now, but after a certain point, the guys I meet won't commit. It's almost like they're looking around the corner for the next best thing. I guess everyone figures they can just swipe right. What can I do to attract the kind of person who wants a real relationship?

"Thanks for your question, Nancy." When it came time to give her advice, her mind blanked. All she could think about was Brooke, and what she'd say if she were here. She'd probably tell Nancy something to help her move forward. Trying to channel strength from Brooke, Gillian sucked in a sharp breath and continued. "You bring up an excellent point. Some men develop narcissistic tendencies, always looking for that perfect person when it's actually a fear of intimacy. Let's see what the cards have to say."

Gillian cut the deck and shuffled the cards. Her hands shook as she pulled the next one. "The Death card. Don't be alarmed. This is good because it means the start of something new and letting go of what no longer serves you. In your case, it's all of those bad relationships. You seem to have no trouble attracting people into your life. Your job now is to recognize the ones who aren't worthy of your attention, and don't waste time on them."

Gillian flipped another one. "The Lovers card. I do see someone special coming into your life. This man is your twin flame, your soul mate. The exciting part is that you already know him. He might be a friend or an acquaintance. But first, you need to heal some things inside yourself before I see the relationship moving forward into love. Good luck, Nancy, and please let us know what happens."

There was no name attached to the next email.

What's the best way to silence a witch? Think about it and get back to me. Remember, the Devil makes work for idle hands. Stop the tweets, or you'll end up like your cat.

She felt the blood drain from her face in a rush, and her stomach threatened to revolt. Gillian put her hand over her mouth to swallow her scream. Thankfully, she hadn't read the email out loud. When she could string words together, she ended her podcast quickly. Her excuse, she was "having an off day." Tears clogged in her throat. The rush of adrenaline through her veins forced her to push her head between her legs. She took long, deep breaths to stop hyperventilating. Finally, after a few minutes, when her breathing became normal again, she picked up a crystal and held it to the center of her forehead and continued to breathe. With every breath, her focus became clearer. She could continue to fall apart or fight back. She decided on the latter, refusing to let a slimeball like Kurt Lawrence have power over her.

She dried her eyes on her sleeve and glanced at her watch. It was already after five, which meant Garrett was probably waiting for her in the shop. She remembered what he'd said about his heightened senses being able to pick up on a dozen conversations at once even from far away.

Had he heard her podcast? She seriously hoped not. The thought made her flush with embarrassment on top of everything else. She caught a glimpse of her reflection from the mirror on the wall. Today she wore a maroon fuzzy sweater that she'd picked up at a vintage shop, dark skinny jeans, and her favorite black, suede boots. The outfit was simple, but considering how distracted she felt, it seemed like a huge accomplishment.

Trying to smooth down her hair, which tended to frizz, she eventually gave up and pulled a hair tie from around her wrist. She twisted it back in a ponytail. After she cleaned up and gathered her things, she walked out of the storeroom. She spotted Garrett by the copper bowl section. It was hard not to with his tall, broad frame. His dark hair fell over one eye, and some delicious scruff darkened his jaw. He truly was sexy…a sight to behold. He must have sensed her in the room because he looked up, and their gazes locked and held. Her breath came out in a rush. Saje's words flashed through her mind. *You can't fight that kind of chemistry.*

He was exactly the type of male she avoided—the kind who would rip out her heart and crush it to smithereens. So why couldn't she ignore the attraction between them? If she was honest with herself, she'd admit what she felt for him was more than just attraction. She'd told him personal things—things she rarely told anyone. She'd even confided in him about her mom's death. The craziest part? He listened and seemed to genuinely care. Once again she wondered if she'd been wrong about him. Now everything seemed to point in that direction. She bit down on her lip, not sure what to believe anymore. Before she became overwhelmed, she crossed the room to where he stood.

Saje walked up to him at the same time with a huge, shit-eating grin plastered across her face. "Fancy seeing you here, Detective Mulroney. I hear it's not on official business for a change."

He cleared his throat, and if he was uncomfortable, he didn't let it show. "No. I'm here to pick up Gillian. Under the circumstances, I think you should call me Garrett."

"Well, Garrett, I hear you two are a thing. I'm happy for both of you, but if you do anything to hurt her, you'll have to answer to a coven full of angry witches," Saje said, playing along with the ruse. "And we're not above using magick on you."

"I'll keep that in mind." His blue eyes flicked back to Gillian, and he closed the distance between them. He shocked her by placing a kiss on her temple. "I missed you today, baby." Gillian's cheeks burned at the endearment. "I'm keeping up with appearances," he whispered close to her ear.

"No need. I told Saje everything," Gillian whispered back. "She swore not to say a word to the others for Brooke's safety. I think she was just having a little fun with you."

"Oh." He took a step back, shoved his hands in his pockets, and turned his attention on Saje. "Please don't say a word to anyone about this for the sake of Brooke and the investigation."

Saje nodded and placed her hand over her heart. "Witches' Honor."

Gillian waited for Saje to walk back across the store to help a customer. Then, Gillian's gaze darted to his. "What's going on? I'm picking up on your stress vibes."

"Let's go somewhere quiet. We need to talk." He pulled her off to the side and swallowed hard, his eyes glittering with unleashed fury. "I'm afraid there's been another murder."

Hearing the gory news became too much. Her whole body shook from head to toe, and before she could stop them, the flood gates opened up.

"Jesus, I'm sorry for just blurting it out." He stroked her arm and pulled her into a hug.

At first, the strength and heat from his body took her by surprise. Slowly, the tension began to drain, and when her tears finally subsided, she sighed, turning languid in his arms. The intoxicating scent of his cologne comforted and aroused her all at once. With his strong arms wrapped around her, she became painfully aware of the solid muscle beneath his shirt. He rubbed her back, his warmth surrounding her, and her senses went into overload. She wanted to stay wrapped in this cocoon for the rest of the day. But when Saje cleared her throat, she jolted in surprise.

Mulroney dropped his hands and took a step back. This time when he looked into her eyes, his features stretched tight with discomfort. "I'm sorry. I didn't mean to…"

"It's okay." Breathless from his touch, Gillian shivered, instantly feeling cold. "There's something else." After she filled him in on the threatening email Lawrence had sent to her, she shrugged, trying to unknot some of the tension in her shoulders.

"Make sure you forward me that email. We have reason to believe that the murders aren't being committed by Lawrence himself, but someone in his organization. Don't let the bastard scare you. That's what he wants. You have round the clock protection."

Gillian nodded her head, refusing to let the threat rub her raw. She needed to change the subject. "What does this mean for Brooke? Any luck finding a house with a dragon gate in your database? I know it's a serious long shot."

"I'm afraid not. I'm still checking." He stared at her long and hard. "We have people working day-and-night to find her. I know it's easier said than done, but you need to be patient."

She swallowed the lump in her throat. "Thank you. I appreciate you keeping me in the loop." The news gave her a glimmer hope. "I have a question. When we do find her, what am I supposed to tell everyone after our fake relationship comes to an abrupt end?"

He shrugged. "Simple, I freaked out over commitment issues. We got serious too fast and rushed into things." For reasons she couldn't explain, his words left a hollow feeling deep inside her chest. He angled his head to the door. "Are you ready to go?"

"Let me get my coat, and then, I'm all yours." Saying the words sent a ripple of cold fear coursing through Gillian's veins because the more time she spent with Garrett, the more she wished this relationship could be real.

CHAPTER 15

*G*arrett walked up to Gillian and handed her a glass of water. The second they'd walked through the doors of his apartment, she plopped down at the dining room table and spread out her crystals. She pivoted between her tarot cards and the pendulum trick in what he guessed was an attempt to tune into her cousin once again. By the anguished look on her face, she wasn't having much luck. He hated seeing her so tense and stressed. "Why don't you take a break?"

She nodded, looking exhausted. "I suppose you're right. I need to replenish my magick anyway." She got up to stretch, and her phone pinged. She picked it up and glanced at the screen, her eyes flaring wide. "One of my followers spotted Kurt Lawrence in a black Range Rover at a gas station in Darien, Connecticut. Somewhere off of Boston Post Road. She posted it on social media."

"I'm calling the captain." Garrett picked up his phone and relayed the message to his boss. He ended the call and turned his head to find Gillian pacing the room. "He's putting out an APB on the vehicle. For now, we do something to calm your nerves before you burn a hole into the rug."

A half-hour later, Gillian nodded toward the TV, looking visibly relaxed. "Let me get this straight, the plot of this movie revolves around a Romanian knight who curses his soul and becomes a vampire to reunite with his lost love? It seems rather extreme don't you think?" Gillian asked, taking a sip of her wine.

In pink PJ pants and a crème oversized sweatshirt—one side slipped off of her smooth bare shoulder showing a tantalizing glimpse of a black lace bra strap—she exuded softness and femininity. Even her damn feet were cute, encased in white fluffy slippers.

"It certainly runs contrary to the dating advice you give on your podcast," Garrett pointed out, setting the open bottle of Bâtard Montrachet on the table.

After he checked all the windows and doors in his apartment, they retreated to the basement. They reclined back in theater chairs, surrounded by the glow of candlelight, cartons of Chinese takeout, a half-eaten bowl of popcorn, and a couple of glasses of crisp chardonnay while the opening credits for Bram Stokers' *Dracula* rolled.

He couldn't remember the last time he'd enjoyed spending time with a woman more. "Some might even accuse you of being a hopeless romantic."

Her face flushed. "I guess you caught some of my podcast before I totally lost it?"

"I didn't know why at the time, but you acted like a pro. I'm sorry for listening in. I admit I was curious. I found your advice quite interesting." He wanted so much to tell her that despite the current trend to keep swiping right, any male who didn't spoil her or cater to her every whim was a complete moron. He took a long pull of his wine instead. "Back to the film, in terms of Dracula, much like other besotted males who came before him, he became tortured when the woman he loved perished. Taking his grief to the extreme, he cursed his soul to avenge her death."

Swirling the contents in her glass, Gillian motioned to the screen before her eyes latched onto his. "I'm guessing there's no happily ever after for those two."

"I'm afraid not. Their love ended in tragedy like most relationships between humans and the undead do." Saying it brought Garrett back to the moment he relinquished his humanity all those years ago. The memory would stay with him forever, burned into his soul like a brand. She needed to hear the truth because he was starting to like this woman, and no matter how much he wished it wasn't so, Garrett had nothing to offer her long term. But not now. He couldn't ruin this perfect mood, couldn't erase the smile from her lips. "I can't believe you've never seen this movie. I don't watch much TV. I favor the classics, and this is one of the best in my humble opinion," he said, trying to lighten the mood.

She pressed pause on the remote and swallowed. "There's a question I've been dying to ask. I feel like you know so much about me, and yet I know very little about your past. If we're going to pull off this charade successfully without raising suspicion, you should probably tell me how you became a vampire. I mean, it's not something we've talked about, and if you feel uncomfortable, or if the subject's too painful, I understand."

The question turned his mood dark. His shoulders slumped forward. Living an immortal life meant forever moving forward, and yet, there were some things he'd rather forget. "No, it's okay." If he ever hoped to forge any sort of relationship with her, even if it could only be ephemeral, he'd have to come clean about his past. After what she'd been through with Lawrence, she deserved the truth. Although once she heard it, she might be repulsed by his misdeeds, at least he'd know where things stood.

"I grew up in Viscri, a small village outside of Transylvania with my family. It was a simple life for the most part. My parents loved each other deeply and my younger sister, Sadie, was the apple of my eye. She was the kindest, gentlest soul I've ever known, and by the same token, she possessed this fire inside of her, a vivaciousness to live life. Nothing scared her. You remind me a lot of her." The words were out of his mouth before he could take them back. He only wished his voice didn't sound so pained.

"I remind you of her?" Gillian repeated, surprise lacing her voice.

He nodded. "It was a happy home filled with laughter and love."

Her face broke out into a beautiful smile. "You were lucky. Not all kids can say the same, myself included. It's the main reason I moved into the coven after my mom died. I never had any siblings and it was a chance to have a family." Her voice took on a wistful tone. "I'm sorry. Please go on."

His fingers brushed the back of her hand, and she drew in a breath. An ache of deep longing filled his chest. "Don't be sorry. Vlad Tepes was from Wachovia, a village not far from where I grew up. The year was 1850 and a disease known as Porphyria began to spread." He gulped the rest of his wine and set the glass on the table. "When a person became infected, they grew sensitive to sunlight, and their gums receded, making their teeth appear fang-like. There was no cure and many were found half dead with blood seeping from their mouths. Death was everywhere, and the villagers couldn't keep up with the bodies. They buried many in shallow graves.

When some would wake up, dig themselves out and come back to town, they were labeled *dracules,* or devils. Gruesome tales of vampirism began to spread, and people lived in fear."

"And that's when all the hysteria began?" she asked, taking another sip of her wine. The firelight caught a glint of red in her hair and a flush of pink on her cheeks from the wine. He wanted to look away but he couldn't, too captivated by her beauty.

He nodded. "When I turned twenty-six, I became ill with a condition known as Catalepsy, where a person lapses into a catatonic state. Their pulse and heartbeat become nonexistent, and they're believed to be dead." He picked up the wine bottle from the table and refilled their glasses. "My family had a funeral for me. You can imagine everyone's shock when I woke up and emerged from my coffin. I too was labeled a *dracule,* and the villagers wanted my head. Shortly thereafter, we were chased from our home. We lost everything." He never planned to open up to her, but all that changed the moment he held her in his arms.

She reached out and squeezed his knee, and a jolt of electricity shot up his leg. "Oh, Garrett, I'm so sorry. What a terrible thing for your family to go through. How did you escape?"

"We had to go into hiding."

The rush of memories forced him to swallow hard. He refocused his attention on his hot and sour soup instead. She didn't press him, and he was grateful.

After he finished his soup, he continued, "Our only hope was to get over the border to Hungary where we'd be safe, but the villagers followed us. We tried to hide in abandoned shacks and caves, but I grew weaker, and we were starving. I knew I was going to die. The only thing I cared about was saving my family."

Her chest rose and fell as though she needed to get something out.

"What is it? Gillian? Please, talk to me."

"We share a brutal history. My great-grandfather was Gilles Howe, the only male accused of witchcraft and later pressed to death back in Salem," she said in a soft voice. "Was there anyone who tried to help you, anyone who realized that you and your family were innocent victims in all of this?"

He stared into her beautiful face and wanted so much to be the kind of man she could see herself with, not the monster he had become. "A local blacksmith and his wife took mercy on us and let us sleep in their root cellar, but I knew deep down it would just be a matter of time before the villagers found us. They were out for blood and wouldn't rest until they chopped off my head and drove a stake through my coffin. The blacksmith and his wife devised a plan to get us safely to the border, but it was too risky. There was a very good chance we'd all end up dead. That's when Malcom showed up." A thick silence settled over them.

"Did you know he was a vampire?" Her brown eyes grew wide. He'd never been with a woman this easy to talk to. In all his years of courting, he'd never felt the need to until now.

"Not right away. I'd see him around the village—in and out of the pubs. I just knew there was something unusual about him. I never imagined that vampires could be real, let alone that he was one of the most powerful ones. The night before we were supposed to escape, I snuck out of the cellar. I was close to death. I wanted one last look at the stars and the feel of rain on my skin. That's when Malcom approached me. I didn't realize it at the time, but he was an Ancient traveling through Europe, trying to turn as many males as he could."

She stiffened beside him on the chair. "Why? What did he get out of turning men into vampires?"

"I discovered later he was an aristocrat who lost his title and all his money," he muttered. "It turns out he was a greedy bastard and needed a way to live the lifestyle he'd grown accustomed to. Malcom showed me what he was and made a deal with me, one I'd live to regret. He vowed to get my family safely over the border if I agreed to let him turn me."

The only sound came from the crackle of the fire and her soft, shallow breaths.

"After he turned you, what did he want from you?" She motioned with one of her chopsticks, digging into the veggie lo mein.

"He ran a business and wanted me to work for him as a kind of apprentice. I soon learned there were other vampires like him looking for women to bond with. Back then this kind of thing was quite lucrative, especially for women who didn't have good prospects for marriage or those who couldn't get work in other fields." When she grew silent, panic began to set in. "Say something, Gillian. I need to know what you're thinking." He half expected her to recoil in horror, but she surprised him when her expression changed from shock to compassion. Warmth filled his chest.

"I'm thinking you did what was needed to save your family." She set the carton on the coffee table and wiped her hands on a napkin. "No one could fault you. What choice did you have? Stop blaming yourself."

"You say that now, but you haven't heard the rest of the story." He let out a pent-up breath, amazed at how easily he could confide in her. Since the day she'd walked into his home, she turned his dark, dreary world into a place of light and beauty. "Malcom kept his promise and delivered my family safely to Hungary. I couldn't check on them right away because the first few months of the transition are very difficult. The fact is many end up dying from the toll it takes on the body. The thirst for blood is so consuming you can't see straight. I thought I'd go out of my mind from the craving."

Her brow creased in concern. "You've been through so much. I had no idea."

"When I could finally control my urge to bite anyone with a pulse, I held up my end of the bargain and found a willing young woman who'd fallen on desperate times. She was looking for a way to earn some fast money. I sent her to Malcom and prayed I wouldn't be damned for eternity." He lifted his glass to his lips and took another sip.

She paled. "What happened?"

"He blood bonded with her and offered her up as chattel to the highest bidder." He raked a hand through his hair. They'd just started to get to know each other. Now he risked whatever solid ground they'd gained. But he wouldn't lie to her. "In some cases, when a bond is broken, it can lead to madness. The selfish bastard tired of her, leaving her to go mad. I was sick with what I'd done and confronted him."

Her jaw dropped. "You confronted the most powerful vampire in the world?" Gillian whispered. "Weren't you afraid he might kill you?"

"No, not at that point. I think I wanted to die for what I'd done to an innocent woman," he said, shaking his head. "But Malcom did something far worse than kill me. He bragged that he'd done the same thing to my sister. It was all a sick game to him. I found out later that he'd turned entire families into blood slaves and took twisted pleasure in destroying them."

She gaped at him, opening her mouth and closing it again like she wanted to say something, but then thought better of it. Curiosity flickered in those warm eyes of hers. "Do all humans who blood bond with a vampire go mad if that bond is broken?"

"Not always. It happens with some. I can only compare it to the same predisposition of those who become addicted to alcohol or drugs. Once a blood bond takes hold, there's no denying an emotional connection, as well as a constant thirst for blood."

For several agonizing minutes, neither of them said a word. The air became thick, snapping with sexual tension.

A few bites of lo mein and then she asked, "What about Malcom? Did you ever go after him all those years ago for what he did to your sister?"

"I went to Hungary and found my family. My parents couldn't take the pain and shame of it all. They'd already endured my death and were still fragile. I wasn't thinking clearly and showed up at their door." Reliving that fateful night, even after all these years, made his gut clench with pain. "When they saw me, they realized what I'd become. The shock was too great. My father had a stroke and died, and my mother went shortly thereafter from a heart attack."

Gillian sucked in a breath. "What a horrible way to lose your family. You didn't deserve it, Garrett. No wonder you hate him. You can't blame yourself for what happened. It was all just a terrible tragedy."

"I hold Malcom responsible for killing them. I tried to find him to enact my revenge, but he was gone." Garrett rubbed a hand over his face. "I followed him through Europe for years, but I never found him. I moved around a lot. I lived in France, then Ireland, where I decided to finally change my name, hoping to put the past behind me. Around the turn of the century, I gave up searching for him and came to America to start fresh. I'm glad I did, or I would've never crossed paths with you."

The familiar tension thickened, heat creeping between them. Her cheeks flushed an even deeper shade of pink. "Is that when you became a cop?"

"No, not at first. I took odd jobs and moved around a lot, trying to blend into the background. Once people found out that vampires were real, I was able to stay in one place without raising suspicion."

When their eyes met, the pull grew stronger. "You turned your life around, Garrett. Isn't that the most important thing?" she asked, sounding so sincere it made emotion claw at his throat.

He loved her optimism. If only it could rub off on him. He'd become jaded living for all these years alone. "I wanted to do something to give back and protect the innocent, not corrupt them. I needed to make up for the deeds of my past. Rumors began to circulate that Malcom came here to the states because of Sybil's Cave."

Her fingers skimmed his cheek. He hissed out a breath. Her touch left a trail of need and raw heat in its wake. "Who you were in the past is not the person you are today."

"True," he said with a nod. "But it doesn't excuse what I've done."

His words did nothing to ease the crease around her mouth. "If you have reason to believe that Kurt Lawrence has been working for Malcom, I see now how this case has become personal for you, and not because of me or Brooke." There was a note of hurt in her voice.

Garrett decided to leave out the part about obliterating his sire to dust once he got his hands on the vampire. It was the only way to avenge his family's honor and stop the bastard from harming another woman. But Gillian wasn't in a state to hear that right now. "From the moment we met, it has always been personal for me."

Her eyes widened with a combination of wariness and heat. "Garrett," she murmured, and he moved closer and glanced at her lips. He needed to remind himself that no matter how much he wanted her, she was a witness and it wouldn't be right. So he counted to ten to keep from ravishing her.

"Immortality has been nothing short of hell. I'd give anything to be human again. Reliving the horrors of my past, and watching loved ones get sick and die while I go on without them, can be a fate far worse than death. There's no end to one's pain." He leaned back in the chair, drained from retelling the truth about his past.

"You're alive, Garrett, for a reason. By becoming a cop, you turned your life around and your karma. Whatever Malcom did to you and your family will come back to him times three. I didn't want to bring it up because I wasn't sure if it was my place, but Saje mentioned something about water from Sybil's Cave that can turn a vampire human again if combined with some ancient spells and potions."

The heartfelt words and passion in her voice stirred something deep in him that he hadn't realized was asleep. But he had lived too long and been through too much to put stock in such foolish notions. She tilted her head to the side, and her hair slid over her shoulder like a waterfall. He wanted to run his fingers through the silky strands and press his lips to hers, taste their sweetness.

"Have you ever heard of such a thing?" she asked, interrupting the train of his lust-fueled thoughts.

He chuckled and extended his arm to rest against the back of her chair. "Nothing against Saje, but I'm not overly confident there's any sort of elixir powerful enough to turn me human again. The Romani who traveled through Europe back in the day tried to peddle a cure with promises of potions that had transforming capabilities."

"Did you ever try one? What if it actually worked?"

"I assumed they would put some sort of curse on me that would be far worse than immortality." The pain of getting his hopes up only to have them crushed again wasn't something he was keen on.

This bearing of the soul wasn't his typical interaction. Sure, he dated his fair share of women...wining and dining them. Typically, by the time they'd make it back here for dessert, they both knew what they wanted. In the twenty-first century, women seemed to crave sex almost as much as men—or vampires for that matter. But being with Gillian felt different somehow. Having her here made him feel alive again.

His phone pinged. "Excuse me for a moment." He lifted it out of his pocket and glanced at the screen, shaking his head in frustration. Yet another dead end.

"What is it?" He looked up and Gillian's pulse pounded at her throat. "Did they find the car?"

"The bastard must've been tipped off and switched vehicles. They found one matching the description you gave in an abandoned lot. But if we've learned anything from this little exercise, it's that you might be onto something with the whole social media thing."

When her face fell, he resisted the urge to pull her onto his lap and wrap her in his arms. By far, she was the most alluring creature he'd ever laid eyes on. He wanted to get her mind off things. "I believe you were pointing out your friend's expertise with spells and potions."

"Yes. Willow is part Romani, and Saje is a genius with potions. I've been around my share of witches, and trust me, they are some of the most powerful I've ever known. Our coven is stocked with a library of Grimoires, ancient spell books from generations of witches. Whatever may lie in Sybil's Cave, I sense we could find a way to make you human again."

"I appreciate what you're trying to do, Gillian, and I'm not out to burst your bubble. But there's no cure, and if there was, I'd know. Witches and Romani have been searching for hundreds of years. Any vampire would pay a fortune or kill for such a thing." Her optimism was so genuine it almost stirred the beginnings of hope in him.

She sighed, looking crestfallen, and glanced over at their now empty cartons of Chinese food. Her hand moved to her stomach. "I'm stuffed. Thanks for dinner and for the distraction. I'm really glad you confided in me about your family."

Sharing secrets between men and women led to intimacy. By opening up to her he risked teetering on dangerous ground. "Gillian, I—" Before he could contemplate the situation any further, his phone buzzed on the table. He picked it up and glanced at the screen. It was a text from Denopoulos.

Meet me at the RH hospital. Greystone just woke up.

He got to his feet and shoved his phone in his pocket. "I'm sorry. We have to cut the evening short. I'm calling Dubrosky. She can stay with you. Once she gets here, I have to go."

"What's going on?" Gillian sat up on her knees. "Is it about Brooke?"

"No, but it's a lead, and let's hope it helps us find her. The vampire who attacked you is awake. I'm meeting Denopoulos and Teague at the hospital so we can question him."

"How will you get him to tell you about the Brotherhood?"

"Trust me, there are ways." And Garrett wasn't above using them.

Once Garrett got his hands on the vampire, he'd force him to cooperate. He'd make damn sure of it, for everyone's sake.

CHAPTER 16

*G*arrett walked down the dark, cavernous hallway that led to a subterranean area of the hospital where Damon Greystone was being held. It had been built back in the early eighties; right after vampires came out and about. The mage unit sat several feet below the main level.

After he crossed through a turnstile, he came to an enormous scanner and swiped his badge across the glass. A series of beeps echoed through the hall. Then, a gate opened, and he found himself enclosed in what felt like an enormous freezer. His breath fanned around him as he walked, the temperature dropping a few degrees with every step. The only way to revive the undead was to keep them on ice. Nowadays, most medical facilities housed extra blood and plasma for vampires in need of transfusions.

Once he made his way to an area of glass-paneled cubicles, he searched for room number seven. He pushed aside the cloth partition and found Denopoulos and Teague on either side of Greystone's bed. Teague reclined back in his chair with his feet up on the edge of the bed. He rested his horns against the wall for balance. They both turned when they saw him.

"Sorry, I'm late." Garrett decided to keep the part about sharing dinner and a movie with Gillian to himself. She occupied way too many of his thoughts as it was. He glanced at his phone, and his gut tightened. No service. It didn't surprise him down here. What if Gillian tried to call? At least he knew his partner would keep her safe. He could've sent her on this fact-finding mission, but he wanted to be the one to look the vampire responsible for trancing Gillian in the face.

"No worries. We were just getting started," Denopoulos said, rubbing his hands together. Bundled up in a black bomber jacket and a ski hat, at least he came dressed for the occasion. His heart went out to the guy. As a human, he felt the cold far more intensely than Garrett or Teague did.

Garrett glanced over at Greystone. The vampire appeared different than their first encounter at the hotel. For one, his dark blond hair stuck up in all directions, dirty and still caked with dried blood. And he looked leaner and far less cocky than he had the night of the bust. Garrett had to suppress a smile.

He supposed getting staked in the chest by a hundred-and-twenty-pound female could lower anyone's cocky meter a notch or two. Garrett set his briefcase down on the floor, pulled out the case file, and set it on the tray table. "Why don't you start by telling us why you were in the penthouse at the W hotel? Who put you in touch with Kurt Lawrence?" Garrett wanted to make him pay for attacking Gillian, but he needed some answers first. "Are you part of the Du Sang Brotherhood?"

Greystone remained silent, staring at the wall, while monitors beeped all around them.

"Let me remind you that it's in your best interest to talk," Denopoulos said, angling his head to the bag of blood intravenously being pumped into Greystone's veins. "I'm afraid the Council doesn't take kindly to vampires who try to bond with women against their will. They'll vote against you and send your ass straight to Hellios."

The mage prison for the criminally insane, and for those who'd committed heinous acts deemed a threat to society, sat at the ridge of a jagged precipice. The only way out was in a body bag. Such a fate seemed justified in Garrett's opinion.

Chair legs slammed on the concrete floor. Teague leaned in close; his horns elongated and flared red. "The Chimera guarding the perimeter eat pretty boys like you for lunch and grind up your bones into soup."

Greystone flinched. "I have no attorney here. I'm not answering your questions, and the petty threats are beneath you." His words belied the fear in his eyes.

"Why not let me try?" Garrett snatched a picture of one of the dead girls from his file and held it up. "Do you happen to know her, Mr. Greystone? Her name is Serena Benson. Her body was found two weeks ago on the seventh of October. I'm curious what you were doing on that chilly Sunday evening?"

"I've never seen her before. I was home alone finishing some work," Greystone muttered. "I'm a commercial real estate broker." Well, that explained how he could afford entry into the Brotherhood. From what Garrett had gleaned from his research, the fees were astronomical.

"This was someone's daughter or sister we're talking about, before her life was snuffed out and her body disposed of like a piece of trash." Garrett let out a pent-up breath and tried to keep the urge to punch the vampire square in the face in check. Every moment they wasted with this Neanderthal was a moment they could be searching for Brooke Corey.

"Why would I know who she is?" Greystone muttered, looking bored.

Denopoulos cursed under his breath, scratched his beard, and then shoved one of the more graphic photos under Greystone's nose. "Oh, I don't know, maybe because she was found with all the blood drained from her body in a way that only a vampire could manage, and then thrown in a ditch right off of Frank Sinatra Boulevard, not far from the W hotel." He flipped through the file before looking up. "Isn't that place one of your hangouts? Did you hit on Serena at the bar and then get a little rough, maybe do a little trancing when she told you to go to hell?"

"Can anyone verify your whereabouts that night? Perhaps a colleague could corroborate your alibi?" Garrett asked, moving to sit on the edge of his bed.

"I'm not answering any more questions without my attorney present." Greystone's hand hovered on the call button for the nurse. "If you'll excuse me, gentlemen, as much as I'd love to continue with this conversation, I tire easily and need my rest."

"We can place you at the scene at the time of the murder. Couple that with trancing, assault, and attempted blood bonding without consent, and you're looking at a life sentence, my friend." Garrett looked from Denopoulos to Teague, hoping one of them had an ace in their hip pocket because so far, they weren't getting jack from this piece of shit. Denopoulos shrugged and Teague only lifted his eyebrows. "It's in your best interest to start answering our questions. We're running out of patience, and if you don't start talking, we're prepared to transfer you to the infirmary in Hellios." Okay so maybe he was bluffing, but Greystone didn't need to know that. "And believe me, it's a lot different than the penthouse suite at the W."

Greystone sat up, suddenly looking alert. "I didn't murder anyone. I was just there to appreciate the company of a female for the night. No one was supposed to get hurt."

Teague stood and took a menacing step closer to Greystone until he was forced to look up at the demon's imposing frame. "Were you attempting to murder Gillian Howe? Or were you just trying to 'enjoy her company' against her will?" he demanded in a voice that grumbled like the bowels of hell.

"Gillian," Greystone repeated. His lip curled into a sneer. "The bitch who staked me?"

"Watch your mouth," Garrett warned, his fangs extending from his lips. "She can identify you, which puts you in a tight spot. Imagine how that scenario will play out to the Council with the case we have against you. I think it will go something like this, 'were you attempting to murder the young lady and throw her in a ditch after you turned her into a blood slave?'"

"No! None of it's true."

Denopoulos pulled a plastic bag containing a signet ring out of an envelope marked as evidence. "What about this little beauty? Does it belong to you?" Before Greystone could respond, Denopoulos turned it over, and his lips twisted into a smile. "What a coincidence, it looks like your initials are engraved."

"When your boss discovers that you were talking to us, he's going to take care of you in a big way." Teague ran his finger across his throat. "But we can help you by offering you a deal to keep you safe from him and out of Hellios. I'm going to ask you again, how did you get involved with the Brotherhood? And don't skip over even the smallest detail."

Greystone turned away from him. "It's arrogant to think that the three of you can protect me from *him*."

With a smile, Teague stepped aside and motioned to Garrett. "Why don't you tell him about the vampire protection program?"

"Oh, right." Fortunately, he'd been partnered with Teague on enough cases to pick up on his bluff. He turned to Greystone and made a point of shuffling some papers from his briefcase. "It's simple. You agree to our terms and we keep you alive, or we send you to Hellios, your choice. I'm personally hoping for Hellios."

Greystone glanced from Garrett to Teague and back again before sighing. "Fine, I'll tell you everything, but I want the offer in writing."

Teague gave him a nod. "Done."

Garrett removed a piece of paper and a pen from his briefcase, composed a quick affidavit, then signed and dated it. He slapped the paper on the dinner tray along with his pen and rolled both over to the vampire. They waited in tense silence while he read over the fake paperwork, and then signed it.

The moment Garrett put the papers back in his briefcase, Greystone started talking. "You must first be referred by someone already in the Brotherhood. Then, you get an access code to their website. Not much different than the more elite online dating services. After I make my selection, a phone number is provided to me. I'll call from a burner phone. A man answers, and a meeting is set up. After that, I wire twenty-five thousand dollars to a Swiss bank."

When he hesitated to go on, Garrett pressed him. "If you had women you paid to bond with for the evening then why attack Miss Howe?"

Greystone's eyes darted to the ring. "I may have gotten carried away. She was so sexy, and her scent made me crazy. Ah, the things I would've done to Gillian if given the chance."

A low growl emitted from the back of Garrett's throat. He lunged forward and grabbed the vampire by the neck. "Don't ever say her name. Don't even think it, or I will decimate you."

Denopoulos placed a hand on Garrett's shoulder "Easy there, big guy. He's not worth it. Let's go back to headquarters. We need to create a profile for you. I think we just found a way to infiltrate Lawrence's organization. I'm afraid it means turning you into one of them."

CHAPTER 17

*B*y noon the next day the foot traffic in the shop was slow. So in honor of Willow and Alex's engagement party, they decided to close early. From the moment Gillian had set foot inside the shop, she'd been trying to open a link to Brooke but without any luck. Trying hard not to scream with frustration, she downed a green drink to boost her energy and shoved a crystal in the front panel of her bra to replenish her magick. After Gillian shut everything down and emptied the register, she walked behind the counter and flicked the neon open sign off.

All morning long she kept checking her phone to see if there was any word on Brooke or any new sightings of her vampire captor, but nothing so far. She heaved a deep sigh, her whole body tensing with disappointment. She couldn't stop imagining what Greystone had said to Garrett and the other agents, wondering if any of it would assist them in their investigation.

Garrett made sure to text her a few times to check on her and let her know that a development had come up in the case. She prayed it led them one step closer to Brooke.

Today his partner, Natalya Dubrosky, had taken her to work. All morning long she'd browsed through the aisles, pretending to be a customer. As part of her cover, Natalya nixed the suit for jeans and a flowy blouse to blend in. Her witty manner and chilled vibe put Gillian at ease, along with the gun she kept holstered under a fringed suede jacket.

Saje walked to the counter and set a black overnight bag on the glass. "Everything you need for the party is inside, along with a gift I made just for you. See for yourself."

"You're the best." Gillian flushed, becoming overwhelmed with gratitude. "I don't know what I'd do without you." Saje had been her rock throughout this ordeal and the only one of her friends that knew the truth about her and Mulroney.

"You made me a gift? I think you have me confused with Willow. Last I checked she's the one getting married." Gillian unzipped the bag and removed a small hair spray bottle marked with a black x. "Extra hold?" Gillian asked, glancing at Saje with a smile.

"It's definitely not hairspray," Saje said, nodding at the small bottle in Gillian's hands. "What you're looking at is a potion I made from bat's blood, vervain, chocolate sprinkles, and a clove of garlic. It's a vampire repellent." Saje walked behind the counter and tallied the register receipts.

"Whoa, keep that stuff away from me." Natalya poked her head out from behind a bookshelf and made a face. "I can smell it from the other side of the store. It's making my eyes water."

"Sorry, Natalya. At least we know it works." Gillian shoved the spray bottle in her purse and walked over to Saje, pulling her into a hug. "Thank you for always looking out for me. You're the best friend a girl could have."

Tears swam in Gillian's eyes and Saje let out a small sniffle. Her best friend pulled away and gave her a watery smile. "Ditto. Are you ready to get out of here?"

"Yes. Let's go." After Gillian walked to the front door and clicked the locks in place, she turned on the alarm. She reached for the overnight bag and her purse off the counter, and when both Natalya and Saje made their way to the back, she flicked the lights. "Speaking of gifts, I already got one, but I still need to pick up some wine for the party. There's a liquor store right on the corner."

The three women made their way through the storeroom and out the back. The honk of taxi horns and the familiar smell of roasted peanuts from a nearby food cart soothed her frayed nerves.

"Okay, you two. I'm taking off. See you tonight." Saje gave Gillian another quick hug and headed in the other direction.

"I don't know about this, Gillian." Natalya jerked her head at the cop car parked across the street. "Garrett said I should take you straight home." They took a few steps to the flower shop next door. "What about a bouquet?"

Gillian glanced through the window at the long line. "It looks super busy in there."

"Okay then, wine it is." Natalya turned her head to the side and her gaze darted up and down the sidewalk. "The streets are crowded. We should drive over."

"It's right there." Gillian pointed to the end of the block. "Besides, you'll never find parking. C'mon, I promise I'll be quick."

They walked up the sidewalk through the throng of business people in suits and young moms wheeling strollers. She caught a whiff of vampires among them and tried not to flinch. Not every vampire was bad, she reminded herself, and thought of Garrett and Natalya. The loud chatter filled her ears and Gillian was grateful for the sound. A breeze blew a pile of leaves in every direction and she sighed, enjoying the crisp autumn air. The sizzling aroma of garlic bread from an Italian restaurant lingered in the air.

Natalya stopped in the middle of the street and touched her arm. "Hold on a minute. I'm getting a call." She moved off to the side and put her phone to her ear.

A delivery van screeched to the curb in front of them. A vampire in an arm sling climbed out of the back and attempted to unload a box onto the sidewalk without much luck. He glanced over his shoulder at Gillian with a pleading look in his eyes. "Excuse me, miss? Could you help me?"

Gillian hesitated for a moment, hating feeling like a scared little chicken. This was still her neighborhood and her peeps. "Sure, give me a minute." She slung the strap of her purse across her body and hoisted her bag onto her shoulder. Once her hands were free, she walked over to the box to lift it out of the van, and an arm wrapped around her waist in a vicelike grip. She let out a blood-curdling scream, and another hand closed over her mouth. She cried out and sank her teeth into his hand.

"Are you ready to go for a little ride?" he whispered close to her ear and lifted her off her feet. Her vision blurred as panic set in.

She kicked out with her feet, but it was like hitting a brick wall. He let go of her and shoved her into the back of the van.

"Stop right there and hold up your hands or I'll shoot you in the back." Natalya's voice cut through the crowd.

The asshole turned around, giving Gillian enough time to reach inside her purse and grab the potion bottle. She climbed out of the van, pressed her finger to the nozzle, and sprayed him on the side of his face.

He covered his eyes with his hands. "What the fuck? What did you spray me with? It burns."

"Get your hands up. You're under arrest." Natalya slapped a set of cuffs on his wrists and hauled him up against the side of the van while he continued to howl in pain.

"Did he hurt you? Gillian? Please, say something so I know you're okay."

Her chest heaved and her heart continued to thud against her ribcage. Gillian nodded slowly, trying to catch her breath. "You were right. I should've gone with the bouquet."

Gillian lifted the steaming mug to her lips and let out a deep breath. "What's in this? It's good." Her voice still sounded shaky, not to mention hoarse from all the screaming. She glanced over at Natalya, who was seated next to her on Brooke's couch. She'd agreed to take her to her apartment. It was the only place she'd wanted to go after the attack, hoping to pick up on her cousin's energy. Gillian leaned back in a cushion, trying to recover from adrenaline overload.

"It's brandy, hot water, nutmeg, and cinnamon. I found some liquor in a kitchen cabinet. You needed something to calm your nerves. I'm so sorry about what happened," Natalya's voice filled with guilt.

"Stop blaming yourself. It wasn't your fault. Except for a few scratches, I'm fine. Maybe Lawrence will think twice about sending one of his minions. You were a total boss back there."

Natalya cracked a smile. "You too. I'm quite sure that vampire is still trying to figure out what hit him."

After Gillian finished her brandy, she got to her feet and paced around the apartment, touching everything she could get her hands on, from the remote control to Brooke's favorite cookbook from the *Barefoot Contessa*. Nothing new came through, only fragmented images from the past.

"I think it might have the opposite effect. You've exposed him all over social media, which will cost him all of his high-power connections." Natalya fell silent when her phone pinged. "Hold on a sec." She glanced at the screen and pursed her lips. "Garrett just texted me. He's insisting on coming here to pick you up after the attack."

Her pathetic heart gave a little flutter. "Do you think Greystone told him anything that could lead us to Brooke?"

Natalya shrugged. "I'm sorry, Gillian. I can't say at this point."

Gillian did another sweep of the place, and finally, she gave up, feeling sad and emotionally drained. Suddenly, everything crashed over her all at once. She plopped back down on the couch and burst into tears. Her body shook with the force of her sobs. She reached for a tissue from a box on the end table and blew her nose. "I'm sorry. I've been trying to be strong."

"It's going to be okay. I promise." Natalya squeezed her shoulder. "You've been through hell and back. I think you're entitled to a good, hard cry."

When the tears finally subsided, she started to feel a bit better. She exhaled, and decided to try another way to create a psychic link with Brooke. She needed to channel her divination skills, and the best way to do that was to help someone else. "Have you ever had your cards read?"

Excitement flashed in Natalya's eyes. "Yes, but it was a long time ago. Do you have any here?"

"I keep a spare deck on me at all times." Gillian got up from the couch and reached for her purse off the table. She pulled out a velvet pouch and took a seat in a chair across from Natalya. The moment she held her cards and shuffled them, magick pure and bright pulsed beneath her fingertips.

"I've always been fascinated by the tarot. You have an amazing selection of decks at your shop. My Aunt Agatha was a witch. She read palms and used crystal balls. I remember going to visit her as a child, and you could always count on a line of people trying to get in to see her for a reading."

"How about you?" Gillian pushed the cards closer to Natalya, motioning for her to cut the deck. "Did you inherit her gift?"

"I'm not sure. I've never dabbled." Natalya tapped her fingers on the coffee table. "My family would've frowned heavily on the whole thing."

Gillian chuckled. "All the more reason you should give it a try. Let's see what the cards have to say." She flipped the Two of Pentacles, and the hairs on the back of her neck stood on end. Her mind filled with images of an older woman in a blue dress with grey hair. She sensed her spirit trying to come through. "I think your Aunt Agatha is trying to send you a message through me."

Natalya's eyes grew wide. "I can smell her." The room filled with the scents of leather and rose perfume.

"Can you get me a pad and something to write with?" Gillian's hands began to tingle.

"What are you doing?" Natalya passed over a small notebook and a pen from her bag.

"I'm going to automatically write the message she sends." Gillian closed her eyes, and her hand scribbled furiously across the page. After several minutes, she stopped and sagged forward, drained from the channeling. "Why don't you read the message? See if it rings any bells for you."

Gillian set the pad on the table while Natalya's eyes scanned over the words.

"The perfume bottles are tucked away in a blue hatbox at the top of your mother's closet. I can't believe this." Natalya inhaled sharply, and tears filled her eyes. "When my aunt died she left me her antique perfume bottles. I used to admire them as a child. We could never find them and looked for years. Thank you, Gillian. This means the world to me."

"You're welcome." Gillian squeezed her hand. "I'm glad I could help."

Natalya glanced at the rest of the message. A curious expression spread across her face. "Wait, there's more. I think this part is about Brooke. She still glows with health but longs to go home. The trees and the grass keep her magick flowing through her veins, but I fear not for long." Natalya ran her fingers over the words, and a line appeared between her brows. "The last piece at the end appears to be some sort of warning. Beware of the *odnoglazyy*."

"Beware of the odno-what?" Gillian asked, leaning forward to touch the paper.

"It's Russian. I'm not sure how to translate the word. Let me think, beware of the one-eyed man?" Natalya looked up at Gillian, shaking her head. "I'm not sure what it means."

"Sounds ominous," Gillian agreed. "I'll tell Garrett about it when I see him." She scooped up the cards and slipped them back in the pouch. With a sigh, she reclined in the chair and pulled her legs up to her chest. "Speaking of Garrett, how long have you known him?" she asked, trying to sound casual.

"We've been working together for a little over six months now, but it feels a lot longer." Natalya pulled a hairband off her wrist and swept her long, dark hair back in a ponytail.

Last night something had shifted between them, and Gillian couldn't help but wonder what it meant, if anything. Now that she understood what Garrett had been through, she saw him in a whole new light. But there was still the matter of him trying to ruin her reputation. She'd been avoiding bringing the subject up at every turn. There were far more important matters at hand, but at some point, they would need to clear the air. She couldn't put a label on what she felt for him exactly, but it filled her heart with a bittersweet tenderness.

"Garrett can come off a little menacing at times, but it's all an act." Natalya smiled wide and tilted her head to the side. "Inside, he's as soft and gooey as a marshmallow."

"Now there's a word I'd never use to describe him." And then Gillian recalled the way he'd interacted with his elderly neighbor Annette. She'd even called him "sweet boy."

Somewhere along the way she started to look forward to their interactions. He kept her on her toes. Did he do that with all the women in his life? She wanted to ask Natalya if their relationship had ever gotten personal, but it wasn't her place. Not that she could blame her if it had. Now that she knew him better, she couldn't imagine how any female wouldn't be drawn to him on some level.

"Gillian? What's going on in your head?" Natalya asked, bringing her back to the present. "I'm getting a strong vibe that you want to ask me something."

"I do want to ask you something, but I'm afraid it might offend you."

"It's okay. Please, go ahead."

"Well, it's really for the sake of the ruse. I just wondered in all of those months of you and Garrett working together, doing all those late-night stakes outs, did you ever, you know, get together in the carnal sense?" Gillian asked, holding her breath, waiting for Natalya's reply.

"Me and Garrett? God, no." Natalya shook her head. "I mean, don't get me wrong, you'd have to be half-dead not to notice how virile he is, but we've always had a professional relationship. I don't look at him romantically and vice versa."

Those few simple words filled her with relief. "Good to know."

"Believe me, you don't need to worry where I'm concerned. Of course for purposes of the ruse and all," Natalya said with a twist of her lips. "Anyway, I'm not savvy when it comes to matters of the heart." A faraway look appeared in her eyes.

Her aura turned from red to purple, and Gillian picked up on her sadness. She wanted to ask her about it, but she didn't want to probe since they didn't know each other that well yet.

Instead, she tried to backtrack. "Oh, you thought I was asking for me?" She placed her hand on her chest and then moved it lower to pull at a loose thread on her jeans. "I was curious, in case someone asked." Goddess, she was rambling now, making a complete ass of herself.

Natalya chuckled, putting her at ease. Gillian liked her, and under different circumstances, she could see them being friends. "If you say so. I can't speak for the other women in his life. I understand he has quite a reputation."

Her heart sank. "I can't say I'm shocked by the revelation." With a deep sigh, Gillian tried to process their conversation, and one thing became clear, there was a whole lot more to Garrett Mulroney than met the eye. And she was determined to unravel the mystery.

CHAPTER 18

"*I* should've been there. We need to talk about what happened." Garrett turned to Gillian as they veered out of the parking garage at full speed in a sleek, blue sports car that looked like something straight out of a Bond film.

"We will, but not now." Gillian cut him off. "Please, Garrett, if we get into what happened earlier I might lose my shit, and tonight is all about Willow and Alex. I want everything to be perfect for them." From the moment he'd picked her up at Brooke's, he couldn't stop apologizing. The message about Brooke had helped to ease the knot in the pit of her stomach. At least she knew she was safe, for the moment anyway. According to Natalya's aunt, it was only temporary. In the meantime, Gillian would work with Saje and pray they would find an ancient form of magick to break her bond.

He nodded. "Fine, let's talk about our cover."

She sighed, grateful for the change of subject. "Exactly how many fake relationships have you been in?"

"This would be a first for me." He chuckled and shifted gears, causing the engine to rev. "Try not to stress. If you do, everyone will pick up on it. We'll be fine." When he reached out to squeeze her knee in a gesture of reassurance, heat shot from her knee to the inside of her thighs. If the whole night went like this, then she was in serious trouble. His eyes flew to hers, the hard angles of his face caught in the shadows of the car. "You're going to have to get used to me touching you in public, Gillian."

When her eyes traveled back up to meet his, her pulse sped up. "Easier said than done."

She couldn't hide her body's reaction to him if she tried. Needing to cool off, she wrenched down the window. It was still relatively warm for the end of October, and she welcomed the rush of wind on her face. Streetlights and buildings zoomed by at a blurring speed. The car hugged the road like a second skin. She caught a whiff of Garrett's aftershave. The spicy scent lingered in the confined space and made her want to groan. Talk about adrenaline overload.

"What kind of car did you say this was?" she asked and turned back to face him, pushing her hair off her face.

"A Maserati Indy. I've owned this baby since the seventies, but I rarely get to drive her anymore. I always have a blast when I do." He flashed a gorgeous smile that made him look like a delighted little boy. This unrestrained side of him was sexy as sin.

"You talk about *her* like a person." She pulled her lip gloss from her black, beaded bag and swiped the wand across her lips. "Well, *she's* beautiful."

"So are you. You look lovely tonight, Gillian," he murmured. "There's nothing quite like a beautiful woman in a Maserati." The jade green cocktail dress and black bolero jacket she wore over it boosted her confidence.

She exhaled, wanting to bask in the compliment. *This is all for show*, she reminded herself. "You're laying it on pretty thick and no one's around. Are you practicing for later?" she joked.

"What if I told you I don't need to practice, it's simply the truth?" His eyes glittered in the darkness, full of sinful promises.

"Then I'll be sure to thank Saje again for bringing my things by the store." She smoothed down the front of her dress, which fell just above her knees, with a small slit up the side of her leg. By the time they got back to Garrett's place, she'd only had time for a quick shower and a blast of the hairdryer.

With her hair still damp, she had twisted it up in a clip. Then, she swiped on a little mascara and added bronzer across her cheeks. She'd been feeling self-conscious about her rushed appearance, but when

Garrett's heated gaze trailed over her, those insecurities were immediately laid to rest.

She picked up the silver-wrapped package at her feet. "This is Alex and Willow's engagement gift. I signed both our names on the card. It's a crystal water pitcher. You have excellent taste by the way."

He smiled wide, flashing a hint of fangs. "I appreciate the gesture, but as it happens I also picked something up a while back for the occasion." He took his hand off the wheel and patted the front pocket of his suit jacket. From the mischievous glint in his eyes, she sensed it was a surprise.

"It's okay. Any new developments?" she asked, hoping they had a solid lead on Brooke, and wondering if they had, was it in any way connected to her vision of the dragon shield.

"Greystone came clean about how he obtained membership into the Brotherhood. Since the bust, we've learned Lawrence has been forced to go underground. Now he's conducting his business from private residences. We should know more soon."

Gillian filled him in on the message from Natalya's aunt. "She said beware of the one-eyed man."

"I have no idea what it could mean. Maybe a fluke." Garrett took his hand off the wheel to rub his chin.

"Maybe, but I can't help but think there's something more to it." Gillian exhaled and pushed the nagging feeling of dread to the back of her mind. "Getting back to what you were saying about Lawrence conducting his business from a private home, how do you plan on finding this house?"

"It's going to take some time, but once we get confirmation I'm in with the Brotherhood, the plan is for me to go undercover as an interested party, and then, we wait." His expression turned serious, pensive even.

"It sounds risky. Do you think it'll work?"

"We don't have many other options at this point. The longer Brooke is with Lawrence, the harder it will be to break their bond. When we do find her, she may not go with us willingly."

Her stomach tightened with nerves. "Then how do you plan on rescuing her and breaking her blood bond with Lawrence?" She remembered what Garrett had said about the blood addiction taking place and his sister going mad when her bond was broken with his sire.

"I'm not sure yet. We're still trying to work out the details."

"I realize we've talked about this before, but I was thinking about asking the other girls to form a circle to see if we can use our collective magick and divine together to try and pick up on where Lawrence could be keeping Brooke. We could be discreet, maybe slip into one of the empty banquet rooms without anyone being the wiser?

Garrett shook his head. "Absolutely not. I'm sorry, Gillian. It's too risky, and it will raise too much suspicion. This is one instance where the ends don't justify the means. Besides, divination isn't an exact science. I'm afraid they'll only get in the way, and then, there will be six other women to protect around the clock besides you." He took one hand off the wheel to squeeze her hand. "I wish I had a different answer for you, but you need to trust me."

"I understand." She gave him a wooden nod and tried to hide her disappointment by glancing out the window. After that, neither of them said a word.

He pulled up to the restaurant and turned to her, his blues eyes filled with a mixture of concern and tenderness, chasing some of her anxiety away. When he brushed a stray lock of hair from her cheek, his fingers lingered on her chin, sending her pulse skyrocketing.

"Why don't we talk about it later? If you get too upset, it will be hard to pull this off. And you deserve a night off. Let's try and enjoy the evening." When he leaned over and brushed her cheek with his lips, a flare of emotion blazed through her chest. The scratch of his stubble made her whole body tingle.

He got out of the car, buttoned his jacket, and handed the valet the keys. He walked around to open her door and extended his hand. "Let's go."

Tonight he looked mouthwatering, and every inch the vampire dressed in a black, silk dress shirt with a matching suit jacket, slacks, and silver cuff links. He kept his dark hair slicked back off his face, accentuating cheekbones that looked like they'd been carved from stone, full, sensual lips, and a square jaw.

Gillian was so busy staring, she almost forgot the gift. She reached around for the box, then took his hand and stepped out of the car.

His gaze zeroed in on her legs and her stomach did a little flip. He rested his hand on the small of her back and guided her toward the restored brownstone. The heat from his touch sent licks of fire shooting across her skin.

"Are you ready for this?"

The concern in his voice warmed her almost as much his touch had. She took in a breath and let it out. She'd have to prepare herself for the endless amounts of questions. "No, not at all. I've already told Willow a fib, that Brooke had to go out of town on business." She felt a pang of guilt enjoying a party when Brooke still wasn't found.

"No need. By now Alex has probably given her a heads up. My guess is she'll mention it to you at some point."

A slice of moonlight lit up the sky, accentuating the dream-like quality of the night. They stopped on the curb, and she spotted a few familiar faces walking into the restaurant, but so far none of her friends yet. They tended to run fashionably late.

Garrett turned to face her. "There are a few things I wanted to go over with you before the party, but I didn't get the chance. I haven't seen much of you today," he whispered close to her ear.

Why did those few simple words sound so intimate? Could this be his way of saying he'd missed her? Then again, she could be reading too much into it, which tended to be her default. It was a hard habit to break, especially for a psychic.

"You don't think Saje said anything to the others?" he asked, looking tense.

"No, she understands how dangerous the situation is. I trust her with my life, and with Brooke's for that matter."

"Okay then. I know you hate to lie, just remember this is for everyone's safety. Now that we got that out of the way, I need to tell you something. Frankly, I'm not supposed to reveal the details of an op, but you've earned the right to know. I went to the mayor's office today to get his approval for a task force. With their help, we plan on rescuing all the victims who were subjugated into this blood ring once I get approved into the Brotherhood."

Hearing the words filled her with tears of joy. She tried to stop herself from getting carried away on a floating cloud of hope, but it was hard not to when he was confiding in her like this. "Thank you," she whispered, relief filling her chest.

"I couldn't wait to tell you." He sounded so sincere. Every nerve ending in her body was inclined to trust him, but then a pang of doubt reared up like an angry monster. Did he really give a shit about her or was he simply doing his job? The thought filled her with guilt.

"Gillian? What's going on?" The deep rasp of his voice made her breath catch.

"It's nothing." Damn, she was a terrible liar.

His jaw visibly clenched. "We need to talk." Garrett grabbed her hand and gently pulled her in the other direction.

"Hey, slow down." Gillian had a hard time keeping up in her peep-toe sandals. "Where are we going?"

Ignoring her, he stopped for a moment and gestured to the gift. "May I?" When she nodded, he took the gift out of her arms and the envelope from his jacket pocket and handed both to the nearest valet. "Please make sure these get on the gift table." Garrett pulled out a twenty and slipped it in his hand.

They headed in the opposite direction and ducked into the alley behind the restaurant. The smell of some kind of sizzling beef and freshly baked bread flared in her nostrils. Her stomach growled. She never did get a chance to eat today.

Garrett peered around the block to make sure they were alone and then waved to a hulking figure who stood guarding what looked like an employee entrance.

"Why aren't we going in?"

"I think there are a few things we need to clear up first." He stood inches away, his chest rising and falling with every breath, nearly touching hers.

"You want to do this now? Can't we talk about this later?" Gillian didn't relish the idea of being ordered around by him, but just in case it was some sort of safety issue, she was forced to agree.

He pressed his hand on the wall right above her head and bent closer. His warm breath fanned her cheek and sent her heart racing. "Clearly, this isn't only about Brooke. What else is bothering you? I've always wanted to know why you seemed to hate me."

"I don't think this is the time or the place." She looked away, refusing to meet his scrutinizing gaze. Somewhere along the way, the lines between fantasy and reality became blurred. She didn't want him to see how much he affected her.

His thumb caressed her chin, forcing her to look him in the eye. "Talk to me, Gillian." The way he said her name made her breaths come out in short, little puffs.

Gillian tapped her foot, not wanting to get into all of this right now. "You don't owe me anything, Garrett. This is a fake relationship. We barely tolerated each other up until a few days ago." The moment the words fell from her lips, she could practically feel the past rise up thick and heavy like a thunder cloud at a picnic. She motioned between them. "Is this some kind of interrogation technique?" He must've heard the sound of her heart. It pounded so hard and fast.

"Not one I typically use. Why? Is it working?" He pinned her with a gaze so dark, she felt it down to her toes.

Could he be using this whole fake relationship thing to get close to her? The thought made her chest ache. "Fine, you want the truth? A few months back, right after the investigation on the coven, I auditioned for a slot at a local radio station but I didn't get the job."

"I'm sorry. Whoever it was that didn't hire you is an idiot. I heard your podcast. It's fresh and entertaining." His eyes softened in the darkness. "But I'm not following. What does the radio job have to do with me?"

"Not long after the audition, I saw you at the bank talking to the mayor. His brother is the station manager." She shifted nervously on her feet. "When you both looked my way, I sensed that you were talking about me. Don't try and deny it, Garrett."

"You're right. We were talking about you, but not in the way you think." His gaze narrowed. "Let me get this straight, you assumed I told him that you were suspected of criminal activity? You think I'd ruin your chances at a job out of spite?"

When he put it like that, it sounded horrible, but at the time, she'd been so sure. "Garrett—"

"It explains your animosity toward me, but it's not true, never happened. For the record, I'd never do something like that to you." His face hardened a fraction, and his eyes flared with indignation. Goddess help her, he was telling the truth.

A moment passed and then another with neither of them saying a word. She'd been carrying around this misplaced grudge all this time when she could've been getting to know him better. Her sense of self-righteousness deflated faster than a pin popping a helium balloon. "I'm such an idiot. I misjudged you. I was wrong."

He ran a hand over his mouth. "Why didn't you say something all those months ago, right after it happened?"

"What was I supposed to do, march into the police station and accuse you of something I had no actual proof of, especially when I had at least five unpaid parking tickets stuffed in my glove box?" She cracked a smile. "I don't think it would've gone over very well."

His eyes twinkled with amusement. "True. Although I think I might be able to help you out with those tickets." He brushed a stray hair off her face, and every nerve ending in her body came to life. "The question remains, where does this leave us going forward?" His voice took on a husky tone, making it clear he wasn't only talking about the investigation.

"I can't think about anything until Brooke's found, but I do want to let the past go. I'm so sorry. Can you forgive me?" she asked in a soft voice.

"Apology accepted. I'm glad we finally cleared that up. I think we just had our first fight." He placed a hand on her hip, and goosebumps broke out along her skin. "I believe this is the part where we kiss and make up."

His gaze turned scorching hot. He moved his other hand from the wall to the nape of her neck and leaned closer, his lips a breath away. She closed her eyes in anticipation, ready to melt on the spot, when the thunder of a loud engine that could be heard halfway around the block made her jump, breaking the spell.

Garrett took a step back and cursed under his breath. "That would be Teague. His car has a very distinctive sound. We should probably go inside."

"Yeah, you're probably right." After their near kiss, Gillian needed a drink and a moment to compose herself before they faced their friends.

He motioned for her to walk ahead of him, and she wondered if he wanted to check out her ass. By the time they made it back to Amanda's, a bright orange car with black stripes sat idling at the curb.

Natalya stood at the front, guarding the door. "Good evening. You two look great together," she said with a wink. "I've been checking everyone's name to make sure they're on the guest list. Backup is meeting me here just in case."

"We should be in good shape," Garrett said, glancing over his shoulder before turning back around. "Lawrence would be foolish to send some of his thugs into a room full of supernaturals, but better to be prepared if he does."

A car door slammed. Gillian turned to see Cayden Teague step out of the noisy muscle car. She wondered how he managed to fit his enormous body into the front seat. Dressed in a navy suit jacket, torn jeans, a Metallica concert t-shirt, and black Converse, he held a bottle of Moet Chandon in his hand. His taste in clothing might be eclectic, but his champagne choice was classic.

He waved, and except for the short, spikey blond hair and gray horns, he looked like Chris Hemsworth's doppelganger. "Good night for a party, huh?" Cayden walked over and shook hands with Garrett and gave her a quick hug.

"Are you running a 340, 4-barrel under the hood?" Garrett gazed at the car in awe, a wide smile spread across his handsome face. Gillian immediately tuned out, not up on any sort of car lingo.

"I restored her a few years back," Cayden said with a note of pride.

Natalya turned to Gillian and rolled her eyes. "I've always wondered if men who drive fast cars are trying to overcompensate for something."

The two women burst into laughter.

Cayden walked over to where Natalya stood and scowled. "Funny, I've never had any complaints over the last few hundred years, but any time you want to find out for sure, you let me know, Detective Dubrosky."

"You really do have the most over-inflated ego." Natalya threw him a scornful glare.

"I think that's our cue to join the party." Garrett grabbed her hand and laced his fingers with hers. Gillian glanced down at their joined hands and a shiver slid through her.

"What's the deal with those two?" Gillian whispered to Garrett once they were out of earshot.

"Long story."

They walked through the door and right up to the bar. The restaurant gave off a classy, warm vibe. Instrumental jazz music played softly in the background. From the sounds of chatter and boisterous laughter, the party was in full swing. She wasn't sure who'd they run into first, and a stream of hot anticipation coursed through Gillian's veins as her gaze darted around the bar. She didn't recognize anyone, and it made her tense. Could one of these males be an attacker sent for her? She was still skittish from earlier. She reminded herself that the room was filled with cops and agents; she would be safe.

Tilting her head to the side, she took in her surroundings. Candlelight cast a glow in the dimly lit backdrop of silver and white balloons. Fairy lights twinkled from the ceiling, adding to the romantic ambiance.

Gillian placed her bag on a gleaming, mahogany bar and picked up a matchbook with Willow and Alex's name across the front. Her heart tugged. Willow had been through so much in her life and somehow managed to come through the other side, finding love and happiness with a great guy. Gillian wondered if the same would ever be true for her. This whole fake relationship made her head pound with overload, especially now that she knew the truth about Garrett. Did she screw up any chance at having something real with him? Her thoughts spun in a million directions.

"What would you like to drink?" Garrett asked, breaking into her musings. He rested a hand on the small of her back, and warmth seared through the fabric of her dress.

"I'd love a glass of Chardonnay." A few minutes later, the bartender poured her a glass and set it on a silver cocktail napkin.

"I see someone I need to have a word with about the op. I'll only be a few steps away, keeping a close eye on you and so will Teague. Excuse me," he whispered against her ear. After he pressed a kiss to her temple, he walked to the end of the bar with a glass of scotch in hand. The affectionate gesture shouldn't have made her flush, but somehow it did, even if this was all for show.

Glancing at the door, she was disappointed to find there was still no sign of her friends. It was time to go in search of them, and if nothing else, find the bride to be. Gillian took a long gulp of wine, hoping for some liquid courage, when someone tapped her on the shoulder.

"Gillian?"

She whirled around to find Ellen, the high priestess of her coven standing in front of her.

"You're back?" She pulled the petite woman into a giant hug, and after a few seconds, Gillian broke away, not able to believe she was here in the flesh. "I thought you were still on your cruise with Commander Smith."

"How many times have I told you to call him David? We flew back early. I wouldn't miss this day for the world." Ellen wore her flaming red hair in a pixie cut, accentuating enviable cheekbones. She was clad in a long, strapless black sheath dress that showed off her tan and some of her ink. Much like Alex and Willow, she and David had met last year when a serial killer targeted the coven. Despite the gruesome circumstances, they managed to fall head over heels in love.

The memory made Gillian long for a happily ever after. Why couldn't it have been that easy for her? Well, maybe because she tended to screw things up in that department.

"I'm so glad you're here. How was the Bahamas?"

"The Bahamas are beautiful, and very romantic, especially for new relationship beginnings. Is it true about you and Detective Mulroney? Where is he?"

"He's talking to David." Gillian pointed to the other end of the bar where Garrett stood amongst a sea of males, some even taller and broader than him. Cayden leaned on one side of the bar, and David, a distinguished-looking demon with reddish skin, jet black horns, and thick, grey hair, stood on the other.

"I can't say I blame you. Mulroney is a God. You two getting together doesn't surprise me one bit. I suspected as much the way he was always checking you out and sniffing around the coven."

Gillian tried to play it off, but the words made her skin flush. "On that note, I think I'm going to find the bride to be." She'd been wrong about Garrett on so many levels. Could she have missed his interest in her as well? "Do you want to come with me?"

"You go ahead." Ellen smiled. "I'll be along in a minute. There are some things I'd like to say to the handsome detective."

"Promise you'll go easy on him. Saje already took her shots when he stopped by the shop."

"I only want the best for you, Gillian. If anyone deserves happiness, it's you." Descended from a bloodline of hereditary born witches, Ellen knew how to create fire at will, which she used for divination and spell casting. But it also made her a force in high heels that few would mess with. "Besides, you're the closest thing I have to a daughter."

The words made Gillian blink back tears. Ellen had been a mother figure to her after her mom passed away. Despite their differences over the years, it was a relationship she treasured.

Before she smeared her freshly applied make-up, she headed into the dining room and bit back a gasp. Silver and white tablecloths, floating candles, and small vases of white roses adorned the tables. Crystal chandeliers glittered brightly overhead, their prisms picking up the glow from the fire sparking in an elegant brick fireplace.

Through the corner of her eye, Gillian spotted Willow and Alex talking to two men that were the spitting image of the striking special agent. Both stood over six feet tall with wavy, black hair, olive skin, and dark eyes. She'd heard about Alex's good-looking single brothers. Ordinarily, she would've gone over to flirt, but now all she could think about was Garrett and the possibility that this thing with him could lead to something real.

"Congratulations." Gillian walked up and kissed Willow on both cheeks. She went to do the same to Alex, and he pulled her into a bear hug.

Last year at this time, Willow had been fatally injured after a blast from a demon fireball. Gillian, along with the other witches from their coven, had used an ancient form of magick to bring her back from the other side. Now she was about to start her new life with the man she loved. Envious as she was, Gillian could think of no witch who deserved it more.

"You made it," Willow said with a wide, beaming smile.

She looked stunning with her reddish hair pulled back in a side-swept knot. She wore a cream-colored, figure-hugging dress, and a gleaming sapphire ring on her finger. Thankfully, she also looked distracted. Gillian hoped she didn't pick up on the churning worry in her gut.

Gillian motioned around the room. "I wouldn't miss this for anything. It's good to see you. I can't remember the last time we worked together."

While planning her dream wedding, Willow had taken some much needed time off from the store. Now she spent her days working with troubled teens at the youth organization she and Alex had founded, Hope House.

"Are you here with Garrett?" Willow asked, curiosity lacing her voice. "I hear you two are a thing."

She nodded. "We came together, but after Ellen gets done grilling him, I'm sure he'll be looking to make a hasty escape," she said, forcing a chuckle. Too bad it sounded fake. Once again those pangs of guilt came rushing back, only tenfold. Tonight she'd be forced to lie to her friends, but it was for their safety, she reasoned.

"So it's true?"

Gillian turned to the familiar-sounding female voice. Delilah, one of her coven mates, made a grand entrance in a short aquamarine cocktail dress that matched her eyes. She wore her blonde hair piled on top of her head.

"You've completely ghosted us, Gillian. Do you expect us to believe this thing between you and Mulroney is real?"

Moving on shaking legs, Gillian took a step closer, her lips twisted into a smile. She told her friends everything, especially when it came to men, which made the whole Garrett thing totally out of character for her. But she had to sound convincing, not just for the sake of the investigation and Brooke, but for their safety as well.

"Good evening to you too." Gillian squared her shoulders, put a hand on her hip, and pretended to be offended.

The overhead chandelier shook as sparks of magick lingered in the air, vibrating with the power of witches. The rest of her coven mates, Nadia, Arabella, and Belinda strode into the party like they owned the place. Dressed from head to toe in tight, black dresses, their eyes darted in her direction as they crossed the room.

She stole a glance over at Garrett, whose eyes warmed when they locked on hers. She only wished he could be at her side, helping her face them, but she understood the need to work on his cover for the Brotherhood. "I'm sorry for not telling all of you myself, but let's face it; you guys are a lot to take in. This relationship is still very new. I didn't want you scaring him off. And, what can I say? The line between love and hate is but a pendulum swing."

Delilah smirked. "I think the real question is how does Mulroney's pendulum swing?"

All the girls laughed.

"How's the sex?" asked Arabella with a wicked smile.

"What's it like to play house with a vampire?" Nadia chimed in. "Are his fangs sharp?"

Belinda crossed her arms over her chest. "You could've trusted us to have your back and not judge your decision."

Gillian supposed it was time to give up the goods, but she hated to lie. "We wanted to see where things went before we announced it to everyone."

Saje walked into the dining room looking dressed to kill in a black tuxedo jacket and matching pants. Her expression brimmed with confidence, draining some of the tension away. Backup had arrived.

"I can sense the conflict in the air," Saje said, gesturing around the room. "What gives? This is supposed to be a party."

Belinda held up a hand and her bracelets jingled together. "Hold on, we just wanted to hear about Gillian's new man."

A giggle came from Arabella. "And the sex! We're there's conflict, there's passion. "

Groaning, Gillian gave Saje a pleading look. "Can I talk to you for a second, like now?" She angled her head toward the exit.

Saje linked an arm through hers, and they walked out of the dining room and into an empty banquet room. Gillian shut the door and let out an exaggerated breath.

"It looked like the Colosseum in there and you were about to be devoured by a pack of lionesses." Saje sat down in a chair. "Nick refuses to tell me anything, but I sense something big is about to go down. He's glued to his computer, and he's always on the phone. I noticed a bag packed at the top of his closet in case he needs to go out of town in a hurry. It's either the case, or there's another woman."

Gillian shook her head. "Not a chance. Nick's crazy about you."

"Hopefully you're right," Saje said with a shrug of her shoulders. "I'm sorry I didn't mean to go off on a tangent. Any news on Brooke?"

"Funny you should ask." Gillian began to pace. "The vampire who attacked me talked, and now, Garrett's convinced he'll be able to find her. What I need to know from you is if you found anything in one of the Grimoires to break a blood bond."

"I think I may have found something. There's a potion that cleanses the blood. But it requires the water from Sybil's Cave."

"Sybil's Cave?" Gillian repeated. "I've heard those caves are seriously creepy. I thought that water only worked to cleanse a vampire's blood. Do you think it could work on a human?"

Saje placed a hand on her arm. "I think there's a good chance, but we'd need to ask a vampire first. I think that's a question for your fake boyfriend."

CHAPTER 19

*G*arrett stepped into a deserted corner of the bar with Teague on one side of him and Smith on the other. A glance over his shoulder ensured they were alone as much as they could be at a crowded restaurant.

"What did you come up with for my new identity?" he asked, relieved Kurt Lawrence had never gotten the chance to see his face in all the commotion at the penthouse. A part of him felt guilty for talking shop at his best friend's engagement party, and the other part of him feared time was running out for Brooke Corey.

Smith handed him an envelope. "You'll be going undercover as Sebastian Beam, a joint venture capitalist who travels all over the world and has lots of coin, but zero time for dating. You've been highly recommended by David Jackson, aid to Congressman Stevens, which gets your foot in the door. Once you make the formal inquiry about seeking a blood bond, using the intel we obtained from Greystone, we wire twenty-five thousand big ones to a Swiss bank. And if all goes according to plan, you should gain entrance into the Du Sang Brotherhood."

"What do we have here?" Garrett patted the envelope before tucking it into the empty pocket of his suit jacket.

"The usual: driver's license, passport, burner phone, and we even got you a black Amex card. Try to go easy." Teague smiled and reached for a handful of peanuts from a bowl on a table. "After we get confirmation on the bank wire, then we wait for you to get the go-ahead and get the location for the next house party. All we need is proof that Brooke is there. Once we get an exact location, we send an invisible drone over."

"That's where we come in, bust up the place, and save the girl. Well, that's the plan anyway." Smith glanced across the room at his date. "Now then, if you gentlemen will excuse me, I have a very attractive woman waiting for me."

"Don't let us stop you." Garrett gave Smith a playful slap on the back.

He searched the room for Gillian. Every so often, he'd tune in to her and pick up on her conversation. So far, she was nailing the whole charade. It impressed him how she managed to handle herself and the other women. Her friends regarded her with genuine respect and affection.

Garrett turned his attention to Teague and held up his glass. "This sure as hell better work. It sounds like a long shot, and Brooke's life is on the line, along with a lot of other women."

"Keep the faith, man." Teague took a swig from a pint glass. "I get that this has gotten personal for you, but you need to keep your perspective. How's the whole pretend love thing going with Gillian? You two look pretty convincing."

"So far so good." Garrett tried to play it cool. "She hasn't put any sort of hex on me, and we made it through the first few days without any bloodshed. I'd say that's progress."

"Yeah, I'm sure it's a real drag pretending to be in love with a beautiful woman." Teague smirked and angled his head in Gillian's direction.

An image of Gillian's long legs and shapely ass in her short, little cocktail dress flashed through his mind. A hot wave of lust crashed over him. "It's not as easy as you might think." Walking around his home in a constant state of arousal was a far cry from easy. And after their near kiss, he'd be forced to take another cold shower.

The lights dimmed and one of his favorite songs *At Last* began to play. Somehow Gillian must've sensed them talking about her because she turned, and those beautiful brown eyes found his in the crowd.

"Sorry, but duty calls," he murmured to Teague and smiled wide.

He finished the rest of his scotch and set his glass on an empty table. Garrett crossed the room, passing Alex and Willow on the dance floor. They swayed to the music as they gazed into each other's eyes. Seeing them, so clearly in love, warmed his heart and gave him hope for the world. It also made him more determined than ever to find Brooke and give her the same chance at happiness.

Once he made his way to where Gillian stood surrounded by her friends, he extended his hand to her. "May I have this dance?"

Color rose on her cheeks. "Of course." She let him take her hand and lead her out to the dance floor.

When they were a safe distance away from the other girls, she leaned in close to him. "I don't think this is such a great idea," she whispered. "We've never danced together before and there are just some things you can't fake."

"I can guarantee that I'd never, under any circumstance, make you fake it, Gillian." The quip made her blush even deeper, and he fought the urge to wrap her in his arms and kiss her right there. "Trust me, just follow my lead. Try and relax." He gripped her waist possessively, and something raw and primal rose within. Even if this was all for show, the vampire inside of him wanted to brand her as his own, let everyone know she was his. But she wasn't, not really. He had to remind himself of that simple fact.

"Do I have a choice in the matter?" Gillian asked with a grin and placed her hand on his shoulder.

Then he did what he'd been dying to all night long, he pressed her flush against his body. Her breasts crushed against him, and he wanted to groan, loving the feel of her curves. Amazed at how well they fit together, he glided them around the dance floor. Every eye in the room seemed to be watching them move to the soft beat of the music.

Her hips swayed, and from what he could glean from her body language, she wasn't immune to him, not at all. A combination of relief and satisfaction gripped him hard.

"I've been picking up on some of your conversations, and you were amazing out there," he whispered close to her ear, his lips brushing over her skin, earning him a shiver.

"I'm just trying to stick to the script. Did you hear the part about making a potion using the water from Sybil's Cave to bring Brooke out of her blood bond?"

"I must've missed that part. There's only one way I know of to break a blood bond and that's to go cold turkey. Nowadays, certain drugs can numb the effects, but there's nothing fool-proof I'm afraid."

"Look, I get what you're saying, but we need to try." Maybe it was the flicker of desperation in her eyes, or the subtle catch of her breath. Either way, he couldn't seem to say no to this woman.

"Vampires guard those caves twenty-four-seven. It's going to take some finagling. Gaining access to the springs will be no easy task, but I'll see what I can do."

Her smile made his chest swell. "Thank you." She glanced at their joined bodies. "You're incredibly graceful for a man of your size. Where did you learn to dance like this?"

"In Vienna, back in the late 1800s, when I was a much younger man. The world was a different place then. Everyone danced. If you wanted to touch a woman in public, you had to dance with her."

"I think it's safe to say we were doing very different things in our youth," she teased.

"I did hear something about you joyriding in Ellen's car when you were underage. It seems you were quite the lawbreaker."

Her lips curved into a genuine smile. "As I recall, some of the girls and I were playing Truth or Dare. It was a tradition of ours, and I never turn down a dare."

"I've never played the game, but I'm familiar with how it works." He ran his hand down her back.

The crowd began to tap their glasses to get the future bride and groom to kiss, pulling Gillian's attention from him. With a flourish, Alex dipped Willow low, bent over her, and planted a long, deep kiss on her lips that resulted in a round of cheers and whistles. The tapping resumed, and it seemed like every eye in the room became focused on them.

"Now this is a tradition I'm familiar with. Everyone's watching. I think they want us to follow suit—prove that we're a real couple. We should probably oblige the crowd." He leaned closer and wrapped his hand around the nape of her neck. "Think of this as a dare."

Shock crossed her face, and she pressed her hands to his chest. "You're not going to kiss me right here in front of everyone?"

"No," he said, angling his head closer to hers. "You're going to kiss me, and if I were you, I'd make it look good."

Gillian hesitated for a split second, then closed her eyes and pressed her mouth to his. At first, the kiss was soft and sweet, tentative, but when Garrett nipped at her bottom lip, a soft moan bubbled up from the back of her throat. It was like lighting a match to tinder. His hand tightened around her waist, and she molded against him. Her lips absorbed him like a drug. They tasted soft and sensual—purely male with a hint of scotch and mint. His tongue tangled with hers in slow, wicked laps. She met him stroke for stroke, losing herself in the kiss. She wrapped her arms around his neck, and his erection pressed against her thigh, hard and incessant. Considering where they were, and what they were doing, her first instinct was to pull away, but she couldn't. The kiss was just too good, and she'd been fantasizing about this for months. Her breasts grew heavy and aching, her nipples tight.

But then the voice in her head whispered, *this isn't real,* which meant this ridiculous sexual attraction could only lead to one thing—heartache. With a gasp, Gillian broke the kiss and pulled away, panting.

The whole room erupted in a chorus of loud whoops and claps. She laughed, embarrassed and aroused. "What have we done?" she murmured, trying to catch her breath.

When her eyes met Garrett's once more, she couldn't mistake the smoldering heat burning in his. "I think we've proved our point." He linked his fingers with hers. "Let's get out of here."

CHAPTER 20

*W*hen they got back to Garrett's apartment, he shoved the key into the lock, opened the door and let it slam shut. After he punched the numbers into the keypad on the wall, he made a beeline for the liquor cart. He poured half a glass of scotch into a sniffer and took a long swig. Sadly, it did nothing to tame the swirl of emotions raging inside of him. He held up the decanter. "Would you care for an after-dinner drink?"

Her expression grew weary. "No, and maybe you shouldn't either. Haven't you had enough to drink tonight?" A sudden heaviness filled the air, dampening the light mood from the party. Only a few hours ago he'd seen her laughing and smiling. He didn't want to be the one to cause the tightening around her eyes.

"Liquor doesn't affect vampires the same way it does humans."

He wanted to caress every inch of her body, taste her beautiful lips again, and steal every breath. He wanted to claim her over and over again, give her unimaginable pleasure until she could take no more.

But he simply stood there brooding instead.

Gillian set her evening bag on the chair and took a step closer, resting her hands on her slender hips. "Garrett? What's eating at you? I sensed something was wrong the moment we left the party. You didn't say a word to me in the car." Her beautiful brown eyes latched onto his and filled with hurt. "Is there something you're not telling me about this op?"

"It's nothing," he snapped, and immediately regretted his tone.

Now she thought he was angry with her. The truth was he was angry at himself for being weak. Why couldn't he leave well enough alone?

"I don't believe you. You're slamming doors and walking around here with a scowl on your face," she pointed out. "What's wrong?"

"All right, something is eating at me. I don't know how to say it without shocking you." He glanced down at his hands, and they now shook with lust. He imagined her lush flesh beneath his fingertips, learning every curve of her body. He looked up and concern flashed in those beautiful eyes, leaving him helpless to do anything but tell her the truth. Hell, he owed her that much. He left his glass on the cart and stalked closer to her.

"Try me," she whispered in a soft, feminine voice.

He moved closer still, until they breathed the same air. Her delicious lavender scent invaded his nostrils, adding further to his torment. "Fine, you want the truth? Here it is. I can't keep up this charade any longer. I know it hasn't been easy for either of us, but all this pretending is killing me. The truth is I want you, Gillian. So damn much it hurts." He exhaled and waited for what felt like an eternity for her to respond.

Her pulse pounded at her throat. She reached out to grip the arm of the barstool for support. The rush of her blood moving through her veins became music to his ears. Even if she couldn't say the words, she felt it too. "Garrett, please don't. What happened back there won't happen again. I can't do this with you."

"You can't? Or you won't? I realize what I'm saying goes beyond the limits of professionalism. You're a witness in a case involving family. But I just can't keep this to myself any longer," he said on a ragged breath. "I think about you all the time. When I hear your name or you walk into a room, I'm captivated. I have been since the very first moment we met."

She swallowed hard and her eyes filled with desire. "This is too much to take in right now."

"You need to hear this. In all my years on this planet, I've never met a woman with your strength or your courage. Your compassion and loyalty to your family and friends makes me want to be a better man." His gaze swept over her, taking in the freckles across the bridge of her nose and the sculpted angles of her face. If he admired her for an eternity it still wouldn't be enough. "You're so damn beautiful, you turn me inside out," he whispered, and pushed a silky strand of hair behind her ear, needing to touch some part of her.

"I don't know what to say. There's no denying your charms, Garrett." Her breaths came out in soft, little gasps. She bit down on her full lower lip, and he wanted to do the same, devour her...explore that lush mouth of hers when no one else was around.

"Whatever you're thinking I don't like it."

"I'd be lying if I said your reputation with women didn't make me cautious." She placed her hands on her temples and rubbed, looking torn.

"Gillian, there's something you need to hear, something I'm not proud of. I started dating a woman right after we met."

She turned away. "I don't think I want to hear about you having sex with another woman, Garrett."

He reached for her arm and turned her around to face him. "I slept with her thinking I could push you out of my mind. I knew immediately it was a huge mistake. It was your face I saw when I closed my eyes. All those times I came by the coven and poked around under the auspices of official police business, all I wanted was to see you. If that makes me the worst kind of bastard, then so be it. I'd do it again in a heartbeat."

Trading barbs with her was something he looked forward to and found far more intriguing than anything that came before her. Without trying, she'd blazed into his life like a fireworks display, and he was still reeling.

Her mouth fell open, and she gazed at him in confusion. "If that were true then why didn't you get my number from Alex or ask me out? Why wait all this time?"

The question gripped him like a hand around his throat. His entire body reacted, blood coursing through his veins like fire. "The truth...I'm a coward. I was too afraid you'd reject me and I couldn't take that chance. The first time I saw you, Gillian, you took my breath away. I've never had that kind of reaction to a woman in all of my many lifetimes. At first, it scared the hell out of me, but no matter how hard I tried, I couldn't get you out of my mind. Say you feel the same way. Don't try and deny that there's something between us." He stared at her in a silent challenge.

Her beautiful brown eyes lit with a mixture of caution and desire. "Yes, I feel it too. If I'm honest with myself, I've been aching for you for months now. I want you too, Garrett, more than I've ever wanted anything or anyone. But your past with women terrifies me. I've told you I have abandonment issues. Falling for a vampire would be like stoking the fire."

Her words gripped him like a vice, a savage hunger spread from his fangs to his groin. She wanted him more than anything. His cock throbbed against the front panel of his dress pants to the point of pain. If she only knew how much he wanted her, it might scare her away.

"I understand you're afraid, and you have every reason to be. I know what I'm asking and I have nothing to offer, no real future to speak of, but I can't deny this attraction, and neither can you."

"Garrett." Her voice came out like a plea.

"I want this to be real. I want you in my bed." He placed her hand on his chest, and she gasped. Her fingers burned a trail of heat through the thin silk of his dress shirt. "If I still had a heart it would be beating right now, only for you. Please tell me you want the same thing and put me out of my misery."

"I don't know if I can give you what you want," she whispered. "My track record with men..."

He cut her off by placing his hand on her hip and bunching her dress into his fist. A surge of possessiveness rose inside him. "There are some things you can deny, but your arousal isn't one of them. Jesus, I can smell you. I need to taste you. One kiss, Gillian, when no one's watching." He didn't wait for her to respond. His mouth swept over hers, and a blistering heat ignited inside him.

He licked at her bottom lip, and his fangs grazed the edge, making sure not to draw blood. When she wound her arms around his neck, he delved his tongue into the moist heat of her mouth. He wanted to exhaust all the passion he'd been restraining—that had been building and simmering for months now like a slow flame. He took in the sweetness of her lips, not able to get enough, and a wave of desire washed over him.

The soft little whimper that fell from her lips made him realize this was no whim she was giving into. She'd been suffering just as much, holding herself back, and it only made him want her all the more. He undid the clip that held all those lush waves in place and plunged his fingers into her hair. How many nights had he imagined her beautiful hair fanned out on his pillow and over his cock? He wrapped a handful around his fist and angled her head to deepen the kiss.

With a moan, her hands snuck under his shirt to explore, leaving fiery need and heat along his skin. His body soared to life like coming out of a deep slumber. He broke the kiss and moved his lips to nip at her ear, which elicited another sweet moan.

Not able to restrain himself any longer, his fangs extended fully from his lips. All he could think about was grazing them over every inch of her skin. "Gillian, you don't know what you're doing to me." He trailed kisses along the slim column of her neck.

She made these soft, sexy sounds, the kind that made him want to throw her over his shoulder like a damn caveman. He'd tie her to his bed and explore every inch of her body. He could spend hours kissing and touching her. He'd slowly slide the thin straps of her dress down and lick her breasts, suck on her nipples, and make her come, screaming his name until she begged him to stop.

But she wasn't ready...yet.

A voice inside his head told him not to scare her away, to take things slow and let her set the pace. "This is what I've been thinking about since the day I knocked on your door, but I won't push you, Gillian. The decision has to be yours."

She didn't answer him with words. She pressed her soft lips to his, and her tongue delved into his mouth. White-hot lust flamed to life inside of him like a wildfire burning hot and blazing out of control.

His cock throbbed. His control faltered.

He wanted this woman with every breath in his body. But he knew deep down, he couldn't push her to a place where she'd never return. She meant too much to him. With a sigh, he did something that just about killed him. He pulled away, carefully extricating his hands from her hair, leaving them both breathless and shaking.

Her chest heaved, and confusion flashed in those soft brown eyes of hers, which now looked drowsy with lust. Her lips parted, still red and swollen from his kisses. Her neck looked abraded from the scratch of his beard across her delicate skin. "What are you doing? Why are you stopping?"

"You're right. We can't do this unless you're all in, and right now you've got too much going on, too much to worry about. I have patience, Gillian. I will wait as long as it takes for you to be ready because if there's one thing I have, it's time." As for tonight, he'd take another ice-cold shower and pray that she'd come around sooner rather than later.

CHAPTER 21

*B*y eleven-o-clock the next morning the shop buzzed with customers, most of them women. Gillian walked around with a tray of Dixie cups filled with a variety of potions from love to prosperity and health. Pillar candles of just about every color flew off the shelves, faster than they could restock them, along with bunches of lavender from their solarium for love spells.

Saturday was typically busy under normal circumstances. Their customers liked to get their spellwork settled over the weekend, but with Samhain around the corner, they were slammed. Thanks to Belinda's wizardry on social media, *Enchantments* had grown quite a following. And based on the traffic in the store, their efforts seemed to be working.

Any time she caught a breather, Gillian checked her phone to see if Garrett had managed to come through with the water, but still no word so far. She couldn't bear to stand around and do nothing. She'd go out of her mind with worry. The only way she knew how to handle her stress was to keep her mind and her hands busy.

So she'd spent the better part of the morning, before anyone else had arrived, reading cards. The only vision that had come through was one of Brooke standing in what looked like a ballroom and wearing some white seventies looking dress. The Elvis classic, "Love Me Tender," played inside her vision. She wasn't sure what it meant but wrote it down in her journal nonetheless.

"Gillian?" Natalya walked up and took one of the love potion cups off her tray. Today she wore a long, flowy skirt and a peasant blouse. No one would ever guess she was a cop. "Are you okay?" she whispered with genuine concern in her voice.

"Who me?" Gillian forced a smile. "Yeah, I'm holding it together."

"Come with me for a minute." Natalya pulled her away to a quiet corner and made sure they were alone. "Try to act as natural as you can. We don't know who's watching. There are some extra uniforms parked outside for added security."

Gillian sighed. "Okay, got it." The news should've made her breathe easier, but somehow it didn't.

"This nightmare's going to end soon." Natalya held up the potion and swirled the pink liquid in the cup. "Does this stuff actually work?"

"It depends. Is there someone you're attracted to?"

Natalya's eyes grew wide and a furious blush spread across her cheeks. "Oh no. Hell no." She made a face and put the cup back on the tray. "I'll be in the reading area," she mumbled and walked away.

"Whatever you say." Gillian couldn't help but think there was a story behind that denial.

Saje broke away from a group of browsing customers and snuck behind the counter to reach for an oval mirror and dried flowers. "Hey, I wanted to talk to you." She glanced over at Gillian, and a gleam appeared in her eyes. "Talk about putting on one hell of a show last night," she whispered. "You two were giving off some serious pheromones. I went back to Nick's place after the party and banged the hell out of him."

Gillian gave a half-hearted laugh that felt as hollow as it sounded. "Glad I could help." After last night, talking about sex might just careen her senses into overload.

Lucky for her, they closed early today. She was running on fumes. Tossing and turning for hours, she hadn't slept a wink. She'd been restless and edgy, and now twelve hours later, her body was still on fire from something as simple as a kiss.

But that wasn't just any kiss. No. Garrett's kiss had been hot and sensual...and totally addicting. She'd replayed the scene in her mind, ruminating over every last detail, how he smelled, how he tasted, the softness of his lips. And she wondered if Garrett had ruined her. How could any male compare after that? It didn't help to have him so close, in the next room, only a breath away. It was making her lose her mind. But at least it helped her from obsessing over Brooke. She welcomed the distraction.

"Earth to Gillian? Mind telling me where you just went?" Saje's voice pulled her from a host of images, one more erotic than the next.

Gillian placed her hand on her chest. "Sorry, I zoned out for a minute. I guess I'm still a little sleep deprived. You know you were right, by the way, about Garrett having a thing for me."

"Well, I usually am, especially when it comes to sex and relationships." Saje grinned. "What happened? Did you two lovebirds finally have sex?"

"No, and I'm not going to for now." Not to say she wasn't tempted. "The truth is I'm just not sure where this could go. And I can't think of anything until Brooke's found. On that note, did you find a spell in one of the Grimoires?"

"I did, but it wasn't easy. I searched through the entire coven library and finally came across one. If it's invoked properly, it should do the trick. I brought the book with me so we could look at the spell together. It's in the back." Saje angled her head toward the storeroom.

Gillian glanced at the customers milling around the store. "It's too busy now. Let's try and sneak away when things calm down."

Between Gillian, Delilah, and Saje, the three spent the better part of the morning reading tarot cards and invoking a variety of incantations that ran the gamut from keeping a lover with a roving eye to succumbing to temptation, to bringing a couple back together after a separation.

They waited for a lull in the crowd and left Delilah to man the front. Gillian followed Saje into the storeroom and shut the door. Immediately, Gillian spotted the thick, leather-bound tome propped up on the desk. "I can't thank you enough for doing this. What did you find?"

"There's a spell along with a potion that acts as a kind of antidote to a blood blond." Saje waved her hand over the amethyst encrusted on the front cover. "Show me vampire curses." The brass buckles clicked and unlocked. The pages flipped to a section for Protection Spells against Otherworldly Forces. A picture of a symbol Gillian had never seen before appeared across the page. "This is the closest thing I could find. I'm afraid there's a catch." Saje glanced at the book, refusing to look Gillian in the eye.

Her stomach did a little flip. "What kind of catch?"

"The potion needs to be administered before the full moon or the bond can never be severed." Saje's shoulders sagged forward. "Hey, we still have time."

Gillian sucked in a harsh breath. "Then let's get to work." She ran a finger over the faded text. "It looks like we'll need dried garlic cloves, crushed henbane leaves, and vervain for the potion. The spell requires black candles and pagan beads."

"We're covered on the vervain and we have henbane leaves here. I'm sure Ellen has some beads lying around the coven. I can get started, even without the water." Saje pulled out her phone and took a picture of the page. "I'll forward you a copy. You'll need to memorize the spell."

Gillian read over the rest of the spell and froze. "Hold on, it says to add seven drops of familial blood at the end as the final ingredient."

Saje glanced at the page. "The way I understand it, you'll need to mix your blood with Brooke's and get it into the potion somehow." Saje went to one of the shelves of various magickal tools and picked up a small, sheathed ritual dagger. She walked back to where Gillian stood and passed the leather-bound handle to her. "You might want to hang onto this. Mixing your blood with hers is the only way to free her from the bond."

"How exactly am I supposed to do that?" Gillian reached for her purse off the back wall hook and shoved the dagger into the front pocket then zipped it shut.

"A small cut on both your hands should suffice. I think the hard part will be getting the potion down her throat if she resists. But Brooke needs to drink every drop or it won't take effect."

Gillian blew out a shaky breath. Assuming she could find a way to get Brooke alone once they did find her, how was she going to get seven drops of their blood into a potion and force her to drink it without puking? This wasn't going to be easy by any stretch. "I think we'd better go over this again."

The rest of the day went by in a whirlwind. Still no texts or calls from Garrett. She wondered if he managed to get his hands on the water. She tried to pass off the incessant checking of her phone by faking a smile and a positive attitude; although, in truth, it became harder by the minute.

When Gillian finished with her last reading of the day, which involved using a deck of Tarot Love Cards, along with rose petals and a green candle, she handed out the last of their potions. After she finished, she set the empty tray on the counter and started to clean up the mess from earlier.

Delilah walked up with her coat and purse in hand then touched her shoulder. "Are you okay? You look upset."

Remembering too late, Gillian put on a huge, fake smile. "Yeah, of course. Why? What's up?"

"Well, a certain someone is waiting for you in the essential oil section. A very cute, certain someone."

"Garrett's here?" A rush of excitement sparked low in her belly. Part of her hoped he had a lead on Brooke, but another part was just excited to see him again. She glanced at her watch. He wasn't due to arrive for another thirty minutes.

"Go see for yourself." Delilah tugged on a short, black leather jacket, and pulled her long, blonde hair out from the collar. "I'm going to head out. Don't forget about the Halloween Festival. Make sure to wear a costume."

"I will. Thanks, Dee. See you tomorrow." Gillian tried to smooth the loose hairs back into her ponytail, and then walked across the store, surprised to find Lucas sniffing some black pepper oil. She smiled. "How's life as a rock star? What are you here for today?"

Lucas turned, and his face lit up when he saw her. After he screwed the top of the oil back on, he set the bottle on the shelf. "I stopped by to thank you. The spell you did for me must've worked. My band's doing a gig at a private party. Who knows, it could be the start of something big."

"Way to go, Lucas. I'm happy for you." Gillian gave him a quick hug.

"I want to see what this will mean for my career. Do you have time for a quick reading?" Lucas gave her a flirty smile that did absolutely nothing for her.

"We were just about to close." She'd been a bundle of nervous energy all day. She couldn't wait to get out of there. Gillian stole a glance at Natalya, who stood nearby. The detective gave her a nod.

"Why not?" Gillian motioned for him to take a seat at a table in the reading section and walked behind the counter to get her decks. It wouldn't hurt to help a friend in need.

CHAPTER 22

*G*arrett parked his Jeep at the W hotel lot and cut across the pier. By the time he'd put a call into his captain to inform him of this unofficial solo op, he insisted Garrett go with backup after he finished screaming in his ear of course. He was about to infringe on the underbelly of vampire society, which, in his opinion, would only arouse suspicion and detract from the task at hand. His goal was to get in without any questions, and the only way to do that was to go it alone.

The entrance to Sybil's Cave sat at the base of Castle Place and Frank Sinatra Boulevard. Working in Raven's Hollow meant he'd passed by the caves many times before. If all went according to plan, today would be his first time inside.

Gothic stone arches rose above a black wrought iron gate surrounded by bramble. Dark, dreary energy emanated from the place even with the sun shining overhead.

Getting inside would be no easy task. Being a vampire gave him no special privileges for entry. Flashing a badge would probably only incite an attack, which was why he purposely left it, along with his Glock, in the car. The vampires in these caves had been left alone for years. To stroll in now in an official capacity could ruin his chances of getting the water and saving Brooke. He took a step closer and pressed a call button on the side of the gate.

Two hulking vampire guards appeared, one on either side of the arches with wooden stakes holstered across their massive shoulders. Dressed in long, black cloaks, dark sunglasses covered their eyes, and both wore earpieces. He needed to use his only trump card, his connection to his sire. "I'm the son of Malcom Von Scrivner."

The one closest to him pulled out a small needle and a collection tube from his pocket. "Prove it."

Before Garrett could stop him, he plunged the tip into the side of his neck, and he let out a hiss.

Once a few drops of blood splashed in, the guard secured the top with a stopper. "This should do," he muttered and walked to a built-in slab of stone with a lid next to the call button. He lifted the lid and placed the tube inside.

After several tense minutes, the guard nodded his head. "Go down the staircase and keep going. Someone will meet you in the clearing."

The gate opened and Garrett descended the stone staircase into darkness. He guessed the next step wouldn't be quite as easy. Once inside the caves, he passed stalagmites and large jagged rock formations. The scents of must and fresh earth flared in his nostrils. The constant drip of water echoed through the cavernous space, vibrating through his veins. Shadows danced across the walls, glistening in the darkness like ghosts. Vampire bats flew overhead. "How apropos," he muttered and kept on walking.

A loud growling made him reach for his Glock, and then he remembered he'd left it in the Jeep. When he got to the end of the cave, he found himself facing a pack of hellhounds with red eyes, pale skeletal bodies, and long fangs dripping with blood. Before they attempted to turn him into a snack, he gazed at them hard, using his best vampire glare, willing them to heel. Their slavering jaws snapped and sent blood droplets flying, but they didn't come any closer. One wined, then another. After a few minutes, they finally tucked their tails and dipped their heads in submission.

"Good dogs." Jesus, talk about security. Garrett walked past the hounds and came to a sanctuary filled with a deep, blue stream. More armed guards surrounded the perimeter. Flame torches lit his path to a clearing where a group of vampires stood beside a built-in wall filled with glass test tubes marked Sybilfina.

"Come forward." The vampire on the far right called to him. He was decked out in the same black cloak and dark glasses as all the others. "I don't believe we've met. But I certainly know your sire. We have multiple connections, sons and daughters of his all over the world." He got to his feet and lifted the tube of Garrett's blood to his nose. A satisfied smile spread across his face. "Your blood has quite a distinctive aroma with notes of an insatiable craving. How interesting. It almost makes me hungry."

Hell, what was he supposed to say except the truth? "I do crave a woman, night and day." He cleared his throat, wanting to get this over with. "I need water for someone close to her. You can think of it as a favor to Malcom." That statement would either get him a vial of water...or get him killed.

"Your honesty is refreshing. I will grant your request, but only on one condition."

He'd been prepared for this. Garrett pulled out a wad of cash from the front pocket of his pants. "I'm willing to pay whatever you ask."

The vampire laughed, but it came out more like a growl. "I don't want your money." He sniffed the air again and his fangs elongated from his lips. "I'll take payment one way—in blood."

After getting bitten for the first time in over a century, Garrett's stomach wanted to revolt. He held it together with one thought in mind—Gillian. By the time he parked his Jeep and walked the remaining block to Gillian's store, the last fleeting colors of daylight seemed to bleed away into the sky. The sun slowly dipped below the horizon in a burst of orange fire. People bustled through the streets, coming and going from work on this crisp, fall evening. Leaves swirled through the air and landed on the sidewalk.

If the spring water did as promised and severed the bond Lawrence had on Brooke Corey, then it was well worth the effort.

Now he'd just have to wait to hear back from the Brotherhood. He hoped it would be soon. They were running out of time, and the investigation kept leading to one dead end after another. The captain had lost all confidence in finding the rest of Lawrence's victims before one of his cronies killed again.

He'd never gotten the chance to talk to Gillian this morning and hoped his midnight confession hadn't scared her away. He found himself thinking about her all the damn time. His body tightened with need when he imagined finally taking her after all these months.

When he got to the front of the store, he peered through the window and caught a glimpse of Gillian walking around. She wore a purple, silk button-down shirt. Black jeans showed off her long legs. Raw desire gripped him just looking at her. He tracked her movements as she took a seat on a stool. Then, he caught sight and scent of a young vampire sitting across from her. He appeared tall with shoulder-length, sun-streaked blond hair and a sleeve of tats emblazoned across his arm. His look practically screamed artist or musician.

From the way the bastard unabashedly stared at Gillian, Garrett could almost guess the train of his thoughts—something along the lines of what she looked like naked. Jealousy and a powerful need to protect her rose up inside him like an angry monster. That was *his* fake girlfriend in there. He knew it was stupid and irrational, but he couldn't seem to keep the swirl of emotions raging inside him in check.

Gillian held up a tarot card to the encroaching piece of shit. He reached across the table and took it from her hand, his fingers closing over hers, and Garrett saw red. What if he was sent from the Brotherhood? Could he be checking up on her? Perhaps he'd been sent to scare her? Sure, his partner might be inside guarding her, but he couldn't forget what happened the last time.

With a curse, he marched through the front door and cased the store to make sure they were alone. He stormed up to the vampire and scowled down at him. "Hello, I'm Garrett, her boyfriend."

Natalya darted out from behind a bookshelf. "I believe that's my cue to go. Have a great night everyone."

"Garrett? I didn't hear you come in." Gillian got to her feet. "This is Lucas. He's one of my customers." She shot him a warning look for his rudeness.

"Nice to meet you, Lucas." He didn't want to pull the detective card, but he couldn't resist. Garrett flashed his badge. "The store's closed."

"Lucas, you don't need to go." Gillian's brows rose. Her eyes darted to Garrett's and fire burned in their depths. "We were just finishing a reading."

Garrett pointed to his watch. "It's past five. Time to go."

"I was just heading out anyway." Lucas grabbed his jacket and stood. "I didn't know you had a cop for a boyfriend." His voice brimmed with disdain. "If you two ever break up, let me know. I'll see you around, Gillian."

"I'm truly sorry about all this." Gillian led him to the front, and with one last look at her, Lucas exited the shop.

After she locked the door and closed the shade, Gillian spun around with her hands on her hips. "What the hell has gotten into you? I get that you have to be cautious, but he's a friend and a customer, not some stranger." When he simply stared at her, she sighed, looking drained. "Whatever, enough about him. I've been sitting on pins and needles all day waiting to hear back from you. Did you get the water?"

He tapped the front of his pocket. "I've got it right here." He decided to omit the gory details about exactly what it entailed.

"Oh, Garrett! I'm so grateful." Gillian approached him, and he held up his hand.

"This conversation isn't over." His tone came out harsher than he intended.

She sighed. "We're back to Lucas?"

"He's a vampire, Gillian. Do I need to remind you of what happened yesterday? How about the day before?" His hands clenched into fists at his sides, and he couldn't remember the last time he'd gotten this angry. "Innocent women are showing up dead. You need to be more careful."

She nodded. "I get it, but I can't shun every male that darkens the doorstep. He works next door at the hardware store for God's sake." She stared at him and crossed her arms over her chest. "I sense there's something else bothering you."

"Dammit, he was flirting with you. I could tell by his body language, and I didn't like it, okay?" Garrett growled, not able to keep the possessive tone out of his voice.

"Seriously?" Gillian shot back.

"Ahem." They both turned to find Saje standing behind them with a sheepish expression on her face. "I'm sorry to interrupt, but I overheard you managed to get the water. I'm going to finish the potion back at the greenhouse."

"You weren't interrupting. I was just having a lover's quarrel with my fake boyfriend," Gillian said with a lift of her chin before her gaze darted to Garrett. "The potion should act as a kind of antidote to Brooke's bond with Kurt. Can you please give Saje the water?"

"I hope like hell it works." Garrett took the small glass vial from the front pocket of his suit jacket and handed it to Saje with a nod. "Good luck. I appreciate all your help."

"It's my pleasure. I'd do anything for Gillian and Brooke. They're like family. I'll be in touch. I think you two need some alone time." Saje picked up a large, leather-bound book on the counter on her way out.

Once the back door slammed shut, Gillian reached for a large key ring and began locking the glass cases around the shop, refusing to look at him.

"I thought you understood that part of this cover entails us in an exclusive relationship. At least do your part to make it look believable." Saying the words made his nostrils flare.

She looked up at him and her expression might as well have said, "Screw off."

It took more than that to deter him. "Can we talk about this?" He shrugged out of his jacket and laid it on the stool she'd been sitting in. After he rolled up his shirt sleeves, he stepped closer to her. He wasn't going anywhere until they hashed this out.

"What's there left to say?" Gillian used a candle snuffer to extinguish the numerous candle flames around the room. She closed out the register and then turned to face him. "Except for maybe, 'you're being an asshat, and that was a crappy thing to do.'"

"Maybe we should start with why you're deliberately trying to blow this cover? Unless of course, you're interested in that guy?"

Hurt and anger flared in her eyes. "Are you really going to ask me that question after last night?" She walked to the brick wall and flicked off all but one light, casting the store in a dim glow. "I told you already, he's a customer."

Garrett followed her, closing the distance between them. "Maybe I am being an asshat, but it sure looked like something was going on, and I think I have a right to know."

"Now you're talking out of both sides of your mouth, Garrett. You want me to tell you if I'm interested in someone else when we've never talked about our respective love lives. Your reputation with the opposite sex is not a big secret. But do you think that's in any way my business? No, dammit!"

"Yeah? Well, that's where we disagree because I'm making this my business." He reached for her waist and hauled her up against his chest. He tilted his head to the side and his mouth clamped down on hers in a searing kiss. At first, she resisted, pressing her hands to his chest. But then, as he deepened the kiss, she moaned and wound her hands around his neck. Her tongue darted into his mouth and tangled with his. A fuse ignited inside him.

The kiss became rough and possessive. He wasn't gentle, and God help him, he didn't think he had it in him at this point. He wanted her so much and had for so long. Raw desire coiled down his spine and shot straight to his groin. He devoured her, taking her prisoner. To hell with what he'd said earlier about taking his time and going slow. All rational thought flew out the window when he saw her talking to another male. He needed to kiss her and touch her like he needed air. He wanted to wipe away any doubts from her mind and make her his.

Her fingers dug into his hair, and she kissed him back with hot, fiery lashes of her tongue. Her sweet taste exploded in his mouth like ripe fruit. He smelled her arousal, which only spurred his own.

He wanted to pleasure her, make her scream his name, but first, he needed her to be sure. With a gasp, he pulled back to gaze into her eyes. "Tell me you want this, Gillian, or tell me to stop." He rested his forehead against hers, breathing hard and fast, his body strung tight with need. He'd let her dictate how things would go, even if it killed him. After what she'd been through, she deserved to call the shots.

Her chest heaved and her lips parted. "Garrett, please don't stop."

Those few simple words were all the encouragement he needed. His lips trailed kisses along her neck. When he unbuttoned the first button on her blouse, her breath came out in short, little rasps. When he sucked on her shoulder and nipped at her collarbone, she moaned.

"I love how responsive you are. You drive me insane."

He unbuttoned the next button, and then the third, until her bra was exposed. And not just any bra, this one was black and lacy and pushed her breasts up to her chin. Staring at her, he licked his lips. He eased the cup down, exposing her areola and the rosy tip of her nipple. His erection throbbed and he pressed it against her thigh.

"Gillian, you're so fucking hot," he rasped and closed his mouth over her nipple.

She arched into him, whispering incoherent words of pleasure. He sucked on her breast and then moved to suck on the other one until she clawed at his back.

"Your mouth feels so good. Don't stop, Garrett."

His name on her lips made him wild. In the wake of his raging lust, relief washed over him. Despite her worries and distraction, she was right there with him.

He shifted his hips so they pinned her against the wall. Then his fingers trailed up her leg to her inner thigh. He cupped his hand over her crotch, and she let out another moan. He felt her heat, even through her jeans. His fingers went to her zipper, and then his cell buzzed.

The unfamiliar ringtone made him hesitate for a moment. "Shit, it's my burner phone. It's about the case." When his breathing became normal again, he pressed a button and put the call on speaker. "Sebastian Beam here."

"Good evening, Mr. Beam. This is Jason Massey. I wanted to let you know that we received your paperwork along with your wire transfer. Everything appears to be in order. I'd like to welcome you into the sanctity of the Du Sang Brotherhood. There's a party in Greenwich, Connecticut on Halloween that I'm sure you'll want to attend. It's a masquerade ball."

"I'll be there. I'm looking forward to it. Send me the address." Garrett ended the call and glanced over at Gillian. She watched him with weary eyes.

He cupped her cheek. "That was good news. We may have found a way to rescue Brooke and all the other victims. Once we get the address of the house, we can send an invisible drone and get a visual on the victims. Then, we get the task force in place."

A mixture of hope and gratitude flashed in her eyes. "I pray this works. I can't believe the party's on Halloween. It's when the veil between this world and the afterlife is at its thinnest and magick is at its strongest. This has to be a sign that we're on the right path." Squaring her shoulders, she gave him a hard look. "The potion Saje is helping me with requires my blood to break Brooke from her bond with Lawrence, and it must be done before the next full moon. I'll need to perform a spell at the same time. You may not get her away from him without making sure her bond is broken first. So like it or not, Garrett, I'm going with you."

CHAPTER 23

"This isn't open for discussion. You've already explained to me how both the spell and the potion works, countless times I might add, and I've told you we will get your blood beforehand. You're not going with me, and that's final," Garrett said in a raised voice and turned away from her.

He grabbed his cell off the breakfast bar. It had been beeping nonstop since the moment they left the shop. "Are there any new leads about Brooke? What aren't you telling me, Garrett?"

They'd both changed out of their work clothes, her into sweats and sneakers, Garrett into jeans and a t-shirt.

Moving from the dining room to the kitchen, their argument continued. "No one will see me. I'll be wearing a mask. I can find a way to sneak in." Gillian groaned and her eyes slid to the fridge. She got out a water pitcher, poured some into a glass and took a sip, hoping to calm down.

No matter how hard she tried to convince him she needed to go to that party, Garrett wouldn't budge. They couldn't seem to get past this one sticking point, but Gillian wasn't giving up.

The protective look on Garrett's face had ceased to be endearing an hour ago. "There's no way to keep one eye on you and attempt to get Brooke out of there safely. Do I need to remind you of what almost happened to you the last time? You could've been killed. The women at that party, outside of the victims, will all be law enforcement. It's no place for a civilian."

"I get it, but I'm not just a civilian. I'm Brooke's family and a powerful witch," Gillian shot back. "You said the agents will also be there to protect me. I'll be okay. I wouldn't take such a risk if I wasn't sure I could pull this off."

"Gillian, you'd be putting the entire op at risk. You need to let the police and the agents handle this. I'm done with this conversation. I'm sorry, but this is a critical time in the case. I've got work to do," he said and walked to the dining room where his computer sat chirping on the table.

He took a seat in an armchair and began typing. His body language became stiff and unyielding. No matter how hard she tried, she couldn't get through to him. Whatever progress they'd made over the past few days seemed to fly out the window. His guard was back up.

Gillian tugged at the collar of her sweatshirt, feeling like a caged animal. She needed to get outside and work off this anger. "I've been under fake light all day. I want to take a walk and stretch my legs. The fresh air and the trees will replenish my magick." If she could get close to water that would be even better.

"No, it's going to be dark soon," Garrett murmured, not bothering to look up. "It's too dangerous. You need to stay put for now."

Something in her snapped. "I'll tell you what's dangerous, me staring at these four walls for days. I'm tired of being told what to do by you." She was done with this whole, 'I'm in charge' detective routine. "You can't keep me here." She walked to the wall of windows and glanced at the gray, stormy sky and the first sign of the moon looming above the clouds.

"You're being unreasonable, Gillian." Garrett came up behind her and drew the blinds. Then, he glanced over at her with a sigh. "I understand this must be difficult for you. We're so close to getting Brooke back. You need to be patient a little while longer."

"You've been asking me to be patient, and I have, but it's not about having patience."

What if the potion or the spell didn't work and they couldn't bring Brooke back from the blood bond? Her stomach twisted into knots thinking about the story of his sister going mad. Gillian couldn't bear the thought of the same thing happening to Brooke. There were too many 'what if's' and risks to calculate. Her mind blurred with all the things that could possibly go wrong.

"This is about me not following your rules."

"You need to stop right there." His gaze bore into hers as he took a step closer.

She crossed her arms over her chest. "Why? What are you going to do? Don't pretend you understand what I'm going through. This case doesn't touch you personally. There's nothing at stake for you, Garrett. No one for you to lose." The moment she said the words, she regretted them. Her hand flew to her mouth. "I'm so sorry. I didn't mean to be so callous. I'm not thinking clearly."

"You're right. I have no family to speak of anymore." His voice sounded hoarse. "And while I did experience something similar many years ago with Sadie, I don't know what I'd do, or how I'd feel in your shoes. All I can offer you is my word. You need to trust me." His phone buzzed. He lifted it up and glanced at the screen. "I'm sorry. I need to take this in private. Stay put." He put the phone to his ear and headed downstairs into the basement.

Her skin burned under the thick cotton of her sweatshirt. The sensation of being caged in became overwhelming and sent her in a tailspin. Before she said something else she regretted, she decided to go for a run and clear her head. She stalked to the barstool and grabbed her phone, along with her earbuds out of her purse. With a deep breath, she headed for the front door, risking the chance of a vampire lying in wait, ready to pounce on her. But she desperately needed to do something with the blazing anger and uncertainty boiling up inside of her.

She jogged down Garden Street at a steady pace with Snow Patrol blaring in her ears. Her heart pounded in her chest. But if she didn't work off some of this angst, she'd lose her mind.

After a few blocks of pulling fresh air into her lungs, she started to feel better. With every step, some of her anger and frustration melted away. Her head began to clear as she edged closer to the river. When she slowed down and took deep, steadying breaths, her mind drifted to Garrett. She didn't know why he had managed to get under her skin more than any other person. The pragmatic voice in her head seemed to know the reason. A sense of love radiated from her chest, the kind she'd never felt before. The feeling enveloped her entire body and scared the living hell out of her.

A sharp pang cut through her and made her ache. Now looking back, she'd been the one who'd been unreasonable.

Darkness fell over the sky, lifting the protective cover of twilight. Coming out here had been a really bad idea; in fact, probably one of her worst yet. She'd been so caught up thinking about her argument with Garrett, that she'd lost track of time. Her gaze darted around the deserted park right off Frank Sinatra Boulevard. From what she overheard Garrett say to Natalya, this wasn't far from the area where the police had found the body of Serena Bensen. The thought sent a surge of adrenaline rushing through her veins. She fought the panic rising from her throat.

Her music suddenly stopped, and her fear spiked. She glanced down at her phone. Crap, the battery was dead. With everything going on today, she'd forgotten to charge it. Dark clouds hovered overhead. A loud clap of thunder boomed in the sky and she jumped. A sense of dread twisted in her gut. The next moment, rain came crashing down in big, fat drops, soaking her straight to the bone. She ran for cover under a tree.

Through the corner of her eye, a shadow passed and then disappeared from view. She tried to sense if it was a mage, human, or animal, but the rain made it impossible to detect. She crouched into a ball to stay hidden, wishing she hadn't been so careless and foolish.

The wind picked up, rustling the leaves and her heart began to pound. She wished like hell she could call Garrett. An image of him catching her in his arms at the hotel, and then another of him rushing through the door of Starbucks in search of her, flashed through her mind in a colorful montage. All he ever tried to do was protect her, even from the very beginning. The realization brought tears to her eyes.

Even though she'd only been gone for a short time, she already missed him. If he was willing to try, then so was she. She was done with being scared. And she realized, as she got to her feet, she was running away from him when she should be running toward him. She'd been trying to avoid this very thing her whole life. But she didn't want to run away anymore. Another shadow passed and the wind began to howl, making her whole body tremble. She willed herself to get it together and figured she had two choices, stay here and cower, or face her fear head-on. So she turned around and headed back to Garrett's apartment, running as fast she could.

Garrett paced back and forth across his basement. "We need to get a layout of the house."

"The moment you gave us the address to the party, we sent the Bat out to do surveillance of the outside."

The Bat was a fully operational, invisible drone that came with microphones. It could take photos and record video, yet was only the size of a matchbook. One of the many perks of going to work for MBI was that Alex got to play with all the cool gadgets. Once the bat was in place, they could get a feed of the other victims, and then they'd make their bust. He hoped it would be enough to put all of these bastards deep in the bowels of Hellios forever.

"What's the plan for covers? How will you get the rest of the agents inside the party?" Garrett asked, hoping like hell this worked because there was too much at stake for something to go wrong now.

"Smith did some digging and found the name of the security firm contracted for the night of the ball. He had a little chat with them, and they were more than willing to cooperate. He posed as one of their guards, which allowed him access to the house. He managed to get in and discreetly lay surveillance equipment and microphones, so we can listen to all of Lawrence's conversations. He cased the property, but sadly none of the women are there yet, or we'd send our guys in."

"Does Smith know where the women are being held now?"

"No, but he overheard one of the guards say all the women will be brought in at some point before the party. Teague's calling the builder to get the blueprints. After everything's in place, we'll have a better idea as to the rest of our covers."

"Speaking of covers, Sebastian Beam's going to need a costume for the occasion."

"I'll have one of our guys set you up with something. I wanted to give you a heads up on the credit card Lawrence used to pay for his hotel room. It's linked to an LLC, some shell corporation operated by Malcom Von Scrivner. He has quite a laundry list of felonies, including money laundering and kidnap. He's your sire?"

Garrett gritted his teeth. "One and the same I'm afraid."

"There's something else you should know. Joe Tate sent me the coroner's report. He found traces of paint and wood chips under the nails of the last vic."

"It sounds like our killer could be a handyman." Garrett pulled his notebook from his pocket. "I'll check the address of the Macheo girl and see if there was any remodeling going on in her building."

"Good idea. Hold on a sec." Alex swore under his breath. "I need to pull over, visibility's shit. I'm driving and it's coming down hard."

Garrett used the interruption to tune into the sounds coming from upstairs. He could only hear the storm raging outside. He couldn't detect Gillian's heartbeat anywhere in the house. "I have to go. I think Gillian took off. I need to find her."

"Call me back when you do," Alex said, ending the call.

Taking the stairs two at a time, Garrett called her name over and over again, but it was useless. He could tell by the icy sensation filling his chest, he was too late. She was already gone.

Garrett searched the neighborhood, but Gillian was nowhere to be found. He tried to pick up on her scent, but it was lost in the rain. She'd stopped answering her phone. God, if something happened to her he would never forgive himself. Shaking his head, he refused to let his mind go there.

Between the agents and his partner, they'd called all of the witches from the coven to see if they'd heard from Gillian, and so far, no one knew of her whereabouts. He reached for his cell out of his pocket and dialed Alex's number again. He answered on the first ring. "Garrett? Nothing on this end. Any word?"

"I still haven't found her. She was angry when she left," Garrett said, making his way back up his street, praying she'd turn up.

"What happened?" Alex asked, sounding concerned. "Did you two get into a fight?"

"Gillian said I didn't understand her cabin fever, and perhaps that's true. She's insisting on coming with us to the party to sever Brooke from her blood bond. According to her, the potion only works using her blood, and Gillian must perform the spell at the same time, but it's one hell of a risk. And it doesn't excuse the way she's behaving, taking off and acting reckless, putting herself in danger—worrying me sick." Garrett picked up his pace, his fear mounting with every step.

"Gillian is a ballsy witch. Look what she did to Greystone? And what about the flunky who came after her outside her shop? She messed him up with her hairspray trick. Like it or not, she can handle herself, Mulroney. We need to consider her help if there's even a chance she can break Brooke from her blood bond. We can find a way to get Gillian into that party and keep her safe. I'm not about breaking the rules, man, but this time, we can make an exception. Take it from me, if you care about this girl at all, and I know that you do, stop acting like a prick. Put your pride aside and let her in. I made the same mistake with Willow and I almost lost her."

His words struck a chord. Panic gripped Garrett like a vice around his throat. "I've got to go. I need to find her." He couldn't let his mind contemplate the alternative. After he shoved his phone back in his pocket, his gaze darted up the block in search of her, but with the storm raging on, the streets were empty.

When his phone remained silent, he started to imagine the worst. He decided to drive around the neighborhood to cover more ground and headed to his Jeep. With his keys in hand, he jogged up the block and spotted Gillian sitting on his front stoop.

With his heart in his throat, he wanted to run to her—crush her in his arms. But he stopped in his tracks and stared, hoping she was real.

She got to her feet when she saw him. Regret and desire burned in those gorgeous brown eyes of hers. "Garrett?"

"Where did you go? I've been looking all over for you, calling you every five minutes and you don't pick up." Did she know he'd been going out of his mind? If she had any idea just how much he cared, she'd probably run again in the other direction.

"I needed some time alone, and then I came back to talk." She pushed her soaking hair off her face. "I'm sorry about not answering my phone. I didn't mean to worry you. I guess it would suck if something happened to your star witness," she joked, looking miserable.

"You think I was worried about you because you're my witness?" Saying the words out loud filled him with pain.

She shook her head. "No, that's not what I meant. I'm sorry for running away. It was selfish and childish of me. And I'm sorry for those things I said to you earlier. I didn't mean to hurt you. My words were spoken in anger, and a whole lot of fear. I got frustrated. I realize now that you're only trying to protect me and Brooke, but that's not the only reason I ran."

He took a tentative step closer and remained on the sidewalk while the rain continued to pound down on them. "Why did you run?" he asked in a choked voice. "What was the other reason?"

"I want to get close to you, and you won't let me in. I've been trying to fight this thing between us." She swallowed hard, and his gaze darted to the pulse point pounding at her throat. "And the truth is I'm not sure I want to fight it anymore."

Without conscious thought, his feet seemed to move through the gate to the bottom step. He gazed up at her wet, tear-streaked face, and guilt surged in his veins. For the first time in over a century, he felt alive again, and all because of her. Even if she didn't know it yet, she was the one in control. She held all the cards in her hands. And it killed him that he'd hurt her enough to make her cry.

"What are you saying, Gillian?"

"When I close my eyes, it's your face I see, your kiss I crave, even in my dreams. No matter how hard I try, I can't stop."

Was he hearing all the things he'd been dreaming about for months? He continued to stare at her, and her gaze filled with such longing, it made his chest tight. "Do you understand what you're getting yourself into?"

"Nothing will keep me from wanting you, Garrett. I—"

He didn't let her finish. He climbed the steps, bent his head, and sealed his lips over hers. The taste of her was like a balm to his soul. Her tongue tangled with his in deep, velvety strokes, leaving him breathless. The kiss became demanding and possessive, filled with all the passion he'd been restraining for months now. She moaned softly and wrapped her arms around his neck. Shaking with lust, he pulled out his keys and reached past her hips, fumbling with the lock, his lips never leaving hers. The door slowly creaked open.

With a curse, he broke the kiss, and alarm set in. "What the hell..."

"Shh," she soothed. "It was me. I forgot my key and used magick to open the door. I only came out here when I sensed you near. I needed to see your face."

"Gillian," he whispered, breathing her in.

His lips found hers once more. They tumbled into the apartment, and he kicked the door shut with his sneaker. After engaging both the deadbolt and flipping the doorknob lock, Garrett pinned her up against the wall. They tore at each other's clothing. First, her soaked sweatshirt, and then his rain slicker hit the floor. He flicked the clasp on her bra and slid the straps down her shoulders. She shivered. The scrap of lace landed on the floor with the rest of the discarded, wet clothing.

In the light from the hallway, he got a better look at her. The sight of her breasts, full and lush with dark areoles and rosy tipped nipples, made his chest swell. "You're so fucking beautiful."

If he was gentleman, he'd run a hot bath for her, make her a brandy, but right now nothing in the world could keep him from touching her, tasting her, making her come.

"Garrett," she breathed and looked at him with naked desire burning in those brown eyes.

"It drives me crazy when you say my name like that."

He cupped her cheek and pressed his erection against her thigh to emphasize the point. Panting, he fought the need to take her right there against the wall like a rutting animal, but he couldn't. He wanted their first time to be something special—something they'd both remember.

"Baby, you don't know how many times I've dreamed about doing this, of having you look at me the way you are right now. But I'm afraid I won't be able to take it slow and sweet the first time." Later, he'd cherish her for hours if she let him.

"I hear slow and sweet can be highly overrated," she said, breathing hard. "We've had six months of foreplay. I'm ready and I don't want you to be gentle. I need you, Garrett, every part of you." Her voice sounded raw like broken glass.

She slipped off her sneakers and her soaking socks. He removed the last of her clothing, and she kicked them to the side. She stood before him naked, except for a black, lace thong. Not able to control himself any longer, his fangs descended fully from his lips, and he let out a growl. He tugged at the thong, and the sound of the rip echoed through the hallway.

"I'll buy you another one," he promised between kisses.

She curled her hand around his cock and rubbed him through the denim. He let out a low hiss. "It's okay. If you recall, I have plenty."

"How could I forget? I haven't stopped thinking about what you might be wearing under your clothing ever since." He slid off his wet sneakers and rid himself of his jeans, pushing them down, and tossing them into the pile. Only his boxers remained.

"I can't believe we're actually doing this." She shook her head as though coming out of a dream.

He could barely catch his breath to tell her all the things he wanted to say for months now. "Gillian, I vowed that if I ever got the chance to finally make love to you, I'd cherish your body and worship you for hours, but right now that's not happening. I need to be inside you. Are you sure you're ready for this?" He could barely restrain himself any longer. He rubbed his cock against her moist heat, wanting to explore every inch of her luscious body.

"Please, Garrett. Don't make me wait." When her voice filled with need, something primal and possessive clawed at him. He captured her mouth with his in a long, deep kiss. With a playful nibble to the corner of her bottom lip, he curled a finger into her wet folds and groaned at finally being able to touch her naked flesh.

When a sweet moan fell from her lips, he added another finger until her head fell back in ecstasy. His cock damn near ached and his tongue had gone fuzzy. She was so wet and ready, so perfect for him in every way. He rubbed and flicked his thumb over her tight little nub, taking her to the brink and back again, drawing out every breath and moan from her lips. All he wanted to do was give her pleasure.

"Yes, yes, don't stop, right there! She dug her nails into his back. "Garrett," she whimpered. He gave her another open-mouthed kiss, savoring the taste of her.

Her hips started to shake, so he increased the motion with his fingers. When she began to pulsate and tighten, he knew she was close. Her body shuddered, and then she went off like a rocket. Breathing hard, her head fell back against the wall. "Oh, God."

"Fuck, you're beautiful to watch."

He kissed her temple and then pressed his forehead to hers. His erection throbbed to the point of pain. He rubbed it against her thigh, barely hanging on by a thread.

"You need to say what you want, Gillian. Are you sure? Do you trust me?"

"I do trust you, so much."

She wrapped her arms around his neck and tugged him down in a passionate kiss. A fire spread from his fangs to his groin, threatening to overtake him. She moaned and clawed at his back, her urgency matching his own.

She slid her mouth down to bite his ear and murmured, "I know what I want, and I want you, Garrett. Your turn to get naked, Detective."

He ran his hands up and down her arms. The heat from her skin whispered through his veins and seeped into his blood. "I think for once we can agree, Miss Howe."

A smile spread across her beautiful face. "It's about time." She tugged at his boxers, and his cock sprang free. Her brilliant eyes widened with appreciation. "Wow, just wow," she murmured and continued to stare at him in awe, humbling him beyond words.

He wanted this woman like no other.

He lifted her into his arms, and she wrapped her long legs around his waist. In a tangle of limbs, he headed to the living room with her lips fastened to his and their breaths mingled together. His fingers brushed over her nipples and covered her breast. She let out the most exquisite sounds of pleasure. They didn't even make it to the couch. He practically fell onto the floor, taking her with him, his body absorbing the fall. They laughed, and the sound became sweet music to his ears. Damp strands of her hair brushed over his skin, tickling his chest.

"Garrett, we don't have protection."

Her slender fingers reached down and traced a line from his forehead to his temples and then moved to his jaw.

He silenced her with another long, wet kiss. "There's no need to worry about a condom. Vampires can't procreate, nor catch diseases." His need for her frightened and exhilarated him all at once, and to know he could be inside her without barriers made it even hotter.

A beautiful smile spread across her face. "Then we're in business."

Desire, warm and wanton, flashed in her eyes, filling the emptiness inside his chest.

In one quick move, he switched their positions so he was on top and planted his hands on either side of her head. He lifted her hips and nudged the tip of his cock inside her entrance. He moved, slowly at first, taking his time, wanting to bring her to new heights. But when she pushed her hips up, the last bit of his control slipped. He couldn't hold back; he thrust hard and deep.

Heaven was the only word that came to mind. He filled her, and at that moment, he never felt so alive.

"You're so wet for me. You feel so damn good, so tight. This won't last long," he murmured in a voice thick with lust. God, it was better than he imagined.

She arched into him, her body molded to his. She met him stroke for stroke, grasping at his shoulders, digging her fingers into his skin.

The sound of their bodies slapping together, their heavy breathing piercing the air, became too much.

"Jesus, Gillian."

He drove into her over and over. She moved with him, driving him to the brink of insanity. Her legs spread wider, and she was right there with him. Finally, he got to claim her, after months of fantasizing. She was real, and his.

"Oh Garrett, I need—"

He slid his fingers between them to rub her clit. He tried to prolong his orgasm. His body stretched to the breaking point. Her cry went off and rang sharply through the room. The expression on her face and the sound of her climax set him off. He stroked into her again and then when he could take no more, his hips jerked once, twice.

"I'm going to...ah!" He growled her name and crushed her body to his while he exploded into her. Wave after wave of pleasure consumed him.

When he finally caught his breath and his ability to form coherent words again, he pressed his forehead to hers, praying he didn't hurt her. "I'm so sorry if I was rough with you." He reached up and stroked her cheek. When she remained silent, his gut tightened. He brushed her hair off her face. "Talk to me, baby."

Her eyes turned smoky and filled with unmistakable lust. "Take me to your bedroom."

CHAPTER 24

*B*utterflies fluttered in Gillian's belly. She wanted to curl against Garrett and melt into a puddle on the mattress, but right now she could barely move. She sighed with contentment and ran her hands up and down his muscled back. She was rewarded with his sharp intake of breath. She smiled, reveling in the moment. She continued to stroke him, loving the feel of his skin. It was like touching silk over steel. His naked body was a thing to behold. She'd never felt like this before. He was unlike any guy she'd ever been with. He knew how to rile her, piss her off, and leave her breathless with passion. All of which screamed disaster in red blinking lights. Brooke would say she was overthinking things.

Brooke.

She tensed, fretting what would happen when they did find her. No matter what, she'd never lose sight of hope.

"Gillian? What are you thinking? I can see the tension come over you." He brushed a finger between her brows. "Right here." Garrett murmured in a throaty voice and then buried his face in her neck. He turned onto his back, taking her with him. "No regrets, I hope."

"It's nothing. I'm here with you and just experienced the best sex of my life," she said and touched her lips. Still basking in the afterglow of postcoital bliss, she moved to tuck in the nook of Garrett's arm. Normally, she would've been self-conscious lying beside him naked, but the undisguised lust in his gaze was all the assurance she needed.

"Why do I detect a 'but' in there?" He moved onto his elbow and reached over to push her hair behind her ear.

"I can't help but feeling guilty enjoying myself, when Brooke's still out there with Lawrence."

"I understand." He caressed her arms, and she shivered. "You care very deeply for the ones you love. I've seen you with your friends. You go out of your way to care for the people in your life. It's what makes you the warm, wonderful person that you are. For now, we know Brooke's alive. You've seen her in your visions, and you got a message from Natalya's aunt. If we could rescue her any faster, we would. In a few days, she'll be back here with you. I give you my word."

They lounged on his king-sized bed with their legs entwined. Decorated in navy and taupe with dark wood furniture, this room gave off a more masculine vibe. After round two on the couch, they'd made their way up here to his master suite on the third floor. She'd snuck into the bathroom for a quick shower and let her hair air-dry.

"I'm still blown away by all of this, but in a very good way." Being here with him was the best adrenaline rush of her life, like walking on a tight rope from twenty stories up. "This sure beats all those times we were at each other's throats. I'm still not letting you off the hook about going to the party." Great sex or not, she wasn't giving in on the matter. His scent invaded her senses, a combination of sandalwood, sweat, and clean laundry. She breathed him in and closed her eyes. She stretched like a cat, loving the feel of his arms wrapped around her.

"Breaking the rules seems to be a thing for you. I wonder how far back this rebellious streak of yours goes." A mischievous sparkle flashed in his eyes.

He turned her so she lay flat on her back and tickled her sides. His fingers moved to caress her breast then danced across her nipple, making her shiver.

"I talked to Alex by the way, and he agrees with you." His hand moved to her stomach. He drew lazy circles across her skin with his finger. "We're letting you go with us to the ball, but you must do exactly what we tell you, understood?"

She sighed with relief. "I promise you won't regret it. Don't worry. I already have a costume. Thank you."

Once Brooke was found and Lawrence was behind bars, she wasn't sure what would happen to this pseudo-relationship of theirs. Would she be another notch on his belt when all was said and done? She pushed the unpleasant thought to the back of her mind.

"You're welcome."

He pulled her toward him so they faced each other and placed a tender kiss on her lips. They'd made love twice already in the span of hours, and yet, his erection still prodded her. Her finger traced a line from the center of his chest to his heart. The image of a Mallowmar cookie came to mind. Somewhere under the hard shell lay a marshmallow.

"I do have a question." Cuddling together like this, skin to skin, made all the barriers between them melt away.

"You can ask me anything, Gillian."

He stroked her hair and massaged her scalp. She sighed with contentment, loving his sensual touch.

"When we were making love, did you think about biting me? I was just curious if that's a major turn-on for you."

His hand stilled mid-stroke and untangled from her hair. He stretched his arms over his head, and his chest flexed with the movement. She couldn't stop staring at all the lean, sinewy muscle in front of her. His torso and stomach looked to be carved from stone. Her gaze roamed lower to his dark "happy trail". She licked her lips in appreciation. Ellen was right, he was a God.

"You know how to get right to the point, don't you?" From the edge to his voice, the question seemed to weigh heavily on him.

"I'm sorry. I just think we should be honest with each other from now on. I want to get to know all of you. No more playing pretend," she said and sunk deeper into the pillows.

"Okay, I suppose you do have a point." He sat up and ran a hand through his hair, making it stand on end. "My urge to bite you is the same intense, sexual urge I have to lick inside your core, and suck on your breasts, taste the sweetness of your release. But biting into the flesh and tasting your blood, getting aroused from the act itself is purely a vampiric tendency, not a human one."

"When you say it like that I get warm all over," she whispered. His sultry words made her body flame to life, ready to combust. "You told me that I could never get addicted to your blood. If that's not your concern, then what is?"

He gazed at her with raw hunger in his eyes. "There are those vampires that can get carried away in the throes of passion. They drink too much and drain all the blood from the body. I'd never bite you no matter how tempted I was because biting you could bring up memories of what you witnessed with Brooke, and what Lawrence did to her. Are you bringing this up because you saw my fangs? Did they frighten you?"

"No, I found them sexy. I just want to get to know you better, Garrett, every part of you. It would be totally different with you. It would be incredibly sensual. Don't ever compare yourself to Lawrence. You're nothing like him. You're kind and loving...generous. You're a man of honor."

He took a deep breath. "I don't know about that last part. I'm supposed to be protecting you, not seducing you. I never intended for this to happen. I suppose it was inevitable. I couldn't fight my attraction to you no matter how hard I tried. It only grew the more I got to know you." A fierce expression came over his handsome face. "I've already crossed a dozen lines. Don't ask me to cross anymore."

He leaned over and pressed his lips to her mouth, kissing her deeply. He rubbed a finger between her legs. His touch made her melt. Her body liquefied on the spot.

She pulled away, breathless. "I understand why you won't bite me, but I want to feel your fangs on me." She touched his cheek, running her hand over a day's worth of delicious scruff. "Please."

"Gillian, sweet, sweet Gillian. What are you doing to me?" His blue eyes stayed latched on hers, turning molten with desire, and her heart fluttered in response. "The moment I pushed inside your warm, wet heat I went over to the dark side, and loved every minute of it, I might add. There's no going back for me." He spread her legs, and climbed on top of her, forcing her breath out in a rush.

His hardness beckoned her and made her wild for him.

His dark head moved down her body, and the sight aroused her beyond belief. He cupped her breast and his fangs scraped her nipple. The sensation of the two made her wet and needy, desperate for more. He moved lower still, and his fangs grazed her inner thigh.

"Garrett, don't stop," she whispered on a moan.

His tongue darted inside her core. He licked and sucked, over and over in the same sensitive spot. And just when she thought she'd explode into a million pieces and scatter to the wind, he reared up, guided his thick erection into her core, and pushed inside her to the root. She whimpered from the tingling heat shooting up her spine.

"I need to feel you. You feel so tight, so good. You drive me crazy."

He filled every part of her, stretching her until she swore she could take no more. Pleasure and pain collided together in a sensation of pure bliss. When he looked at her this time, his expression radiated with desire, and if she stared at him long enough, she swore she could get lost forever.

He lifted her arms over her head and laced their fingers together. She wanted to stay this way until the sun came up—their two bodies joined together as one without a care in the world, but then reality would set in and pull them from their bubble.

With every part of their bodies touching, he moved at a slower pace, unlike the frantic lovemaking of earlier. This time his paced slowed and became more intimate in every way. She loved the weight and the heat from his body on hers.

"Oh, God…Garrett." Her body began to shudder with each deep stroke. She moaned and lifted her hips, and he increased the pace. Waves of pleasure curled up her spine, making every nerve ending tingle. Sensations moved through her with each roll of her hips. When it became too much, she turned her head.

"Gillian, stay with me," he said in a commanding voice, touching her chin. "I need to see your face when you come." He reared up, altering the angle without slowing his pace, and they both let out a groan.

He kept his gaze locked on hers. The edge of her climax raced through her. Her body began to undulate from the heat and the friction. Her nerve endings sparked with pleasure and pain. "I'm close. I'm going to—" She gripped his broad shoulders for dear life.

"Come with baby, that's it." His words elicited another gasp from her lips.

A rainbow of light and color filled her vision and she broke apart.

He repeated her name and lifted her hips, driving into her with one last thrust. His face twisted into an expression of pure bliss. With a roar, he spilled inside her. After a few minutes, he continued to breathe hard with his face buried in her neck. He eventually lifted his head and kissed her softly on the lips, then rolled off her.

"You undo me, Gillian." His words made her heart flutter.

Sated and happy, she turned and touched his jaw. "I've always secretly wondered if the legends about vampires are true, the ones about being able to go all night long?"

In one quick movement, he pinned her to the mattress with the weight of his body. A sinful gleam flared in his blue eyes. "Baby, I'm only just getting started."

Hours later, after ravishing each other God knew how many times, they sat tangled together, soaking in his clawfoot tub. Candlelight flickered from just about every surface of his bathroom. Enveloped in steam, he glanced up at the skylight and the view of the night sky.

"I could get used to this," Garrett whispered close to Gillian's ear. His gaze moved to her neck. He brushed the hair off her nape and massaged her shoulders.

In response, Gillian lifted her leg, and one pink, painted toenail darted out to crank on the faucet to add a little hot water. "Me too. Except for the part where we get all pruney." She lifted her hand to show him and rested her head against his shoulder. He had no intention of going anywhere.

The scent of shampoo and body wash lingered in the air, along with the intoxicating fragrance of her sweet musk. Her lovely ass stayed nestled against the ridge of his erection. Needless to say, he'd been hard from the moment they got into the bath. He wrapped his arms around her body, loving the silky texture of her skin. As long as he lived he could honestly admit without hesitation that nothing compared to this. Every minute he spent with Gillian moved him beyond words.

"I think I like getting pruney with you." He smoothed her hair back and kissed her temple. "Tell me a secret about yourself. I want to know you, Gillian, for real this time." There was no sense in holding back anymore.

"Tonight when I was out there all alone, I couldn't stop thinking if something happened to me, I'd never see you again." Her words made his chest tight.

She somehow managed to scoop out all the ugliness and death he'd seen over his lifetime and fill it with lightness and beauty. And the thought of anything happening to her threatened to let it all back in. But nothing would, nothing could, as long as she stayed in his arms. A warm, fuzziness spread from his head to his toes.

"I'm here now and I'm not going anywhere." The statement felt completely out of character for him, considering his pattern with women. Never getting too close meant that no one got hurt, and yet, the idea of losing Gillian made panic settle into his limbs like wet concrete.

He reached his hand between her thighs, gliding his fingers in her moist flesh. She opened for him on a sigh, splashing water over the sides of the tub. He loved making her squirm. "There will be puddles leaking into the basement if we keep this up," he said with a chuckle.

"Is this how you persuade all your witnesses to talk?" she asked, sliding her hand out to poke him in the ribs.

"Only the gorgeous ones." He moved his hands to rest on either side of the tub and stared over her head to the window, wondering what repercussions he'd face for getting involved with a witness. "I'm kidding. Overall my lifetimes, I've never done something like this before. I plan to email my boss and take full responsibility. I value my professional life."

"I didn't plan on this happening either, Garrett." After a tense moment, she sat up and hugged her knees to her chest.

"No, baby, I didn't mean it to come out sounding harsh. For the past hundred or so years, my career was all I had. I value it, but I value you more." He rubbed her back. "Okay, back to my question, I believe you were about to tell me a secret that you've never told anyone."

She relaxed against his chest. "After everything you've been through, I'm afraid it may sound insensitive."

"Hey, you should never be afraid to speak your truth, no matter what." He stroked her wet hair. "In this scenario, how about we assume I'm a flesh and blood man."

"Well, in that case, I do have a secret I've never told anyone. Ever since my mom died, I've dreamed about having a large family of my own. Growing up without any siblings was lonely, especially on holidays. I always imagined my children would resemble my mom in some way. Everyone told us we looked so much alike. For me, it would be like getting a piece of her back to treasure every day. Does that sound cheesy to you?"

He remained silent. Her words cut through him like a knife. No matter how much he cared about her, it would never be enough. He couldn't give her what she wanted, what she deserved. Whatever foolish hopes he held onto evaporated like mist. He swallowed the lump now clogging his throat. "Not at all. I think it's a beautiful sentiment."

"Your turn for a secret. Have you ever been in love?" she asked in a tentative voice. The question filled him with regret.

He rubbed his hand along the nape of her neck. "There was a woman once, Lilly. She lived in the village I grew up in. We fell in love, but it didn't work out in the end. What about you?"

"No. I've kissed a lot of frogs in my day." Her slender shoulders slumped forward. "But sadly, none of them turned out to be princes."

"I find that hard to believe unless you're simply meeting the wrong ones. You're smart, caring, not to mention incredibly beautiful. I bet men would be lining up for you in droves if they thought they had a chance. What about what you do with your cards or one of Saje's love potions for that matter? You've never put either to good use?"

She angled her body to face him and reached up to trace a finger over his lips. In the candlelight, her eyes glowed like topaz. "I know it might sound hypocritical considering what I do for a living, but no. Helping others find love is my destiny and makes me happy beyond words, but when it comes to falling in love, I suspect it will happen for me the old fashioned way, when I'm not looking."

"Gillian," he murmured and caressed her cheek. In a different time and place, if he let himself, he could fall hard for her. Hell, any male would be a fool not to.

"Hey, with everything going on, I wanted to remind you about the Halloween festival tomorrow afternoon. You haven't forgotten about it, have you?"

He'd been wrong when he listed her attributes. By far, her heart was what made her so beautiful. "I need to do a debriefing with Dubrosky and the other agents before the op, but don't worry. That's one place you'll be safe. The park will be teeming with cops for the event. I'll drop you off and meet you there after I'm done. Sebastian Beam has a ball to get to."

Unsure of what would happen when he faced off with his enemy, Garrett chose to stay present and enjoy the wonderful woman in his arms.

CHAPTER 25

"You're sure this is going to work?" Gillian whispered to Saje, who stood next to her at a long, wooden table. They'd set it up with a big, black cauldron filled with candy. Brochures and business cards from the shop were scattered over a fringed, purple tapestry, along with donation cups for her charity in honor of the festival.

The other girls from the coven stayed behind to man the store. They needed all hands on deck. Halloween was their busiest day of the year. She should be there to help, but this event meant too much for her to miss. Gillian's stomach tightened into knots as she glanced up at the sky. By this evening the moon would be full, which meant time was running out for Brooke. They had to give her the potion tonight.

"I added all the ingredients and went back and rechecked the spell at least a dozen times. You've got the hard part, forcing Brooke to drink this sludge," Saje said, breaking into her thoughts. She held her nose as she handed over the small glass vile. "It smells like rotten eggs."

"As long as it does what it's supposed to, I don't care what it smells like." All she could think about was seeing Brooke again and bringing her home. Gillian placed the potion vile in her purse and set it on a metal chair at their table.

To best represent *Enchantments*, and in the full spirit of Halloween, they both wore witch costumes. Clad in a layered, baby blue, taffeta dress with a crown and a sparkly wand, Gillian came as Glinda. Saje knocked it out of the park in a long, black dress, tall pointed hat, and a green face. She looked like the spitting image of Elphaba from *Wicked*.

Gillian turned her face up to the sky, basking in the warmth from the sun, a welcome reprieve from yesterday's storm. But she wouldn't dare complain. Last night was one of the best of her life.

An enormous pumpkin sat on a bed of hay off to the side of their table. Anyone who guessed the weight won the cash prize. All the proceeds went to her charity, Hope Club.

She turned to find Saje staring at her with a curious expression across her green face. "What?"

"You look different today. You're glowing." Saje said with a smile. "My psychic sense tells me it has nothing to do with the glitter, and everything to do with the sex."

Gillian's whole face flushed. "Watch what you say, there could be children present." She tried to play it off by straightening the brochures on the table. No use lying, Saje would find out eventually. She always did. Besides, they didn't keep secrets from each other. "Okay fine, things might've taken a turn on the hot and steamy side. But let's face it, where could this lead? I'll grow old and wrinkled, while Garrett stays young and vibrant forever. I could never expect him to stick around." Even if they found a way to be together, how long would their relationship last? His track record didn't bode well for anything long term.

"Hey, all jokes aside, this isn't just about sex," Saje said in a softer tone and squeezed her arm. "I can tell by the way you say his name and the dreamy look in your eyes when you talk about Garrett that you're in love."

"What? Are you nuts?" Gillian's heart began to pound in rhythm to Saje's words. No, she couldn't be in love. It was too soon. It was ridiculous. But when her mind drifted to Garrett, she got these warm tingles that pulsated throughout her whole body. Gillian could spend hours talking to him and never get bored. When he looked at her, she could see the tenderness in his eyes, and feel it in his touch.

And there was the sex—it was passionate and intense—simply out of this world. She knew deep down, no male could ever compare to him as a lover. Now after living with him, she could honestly say he was the first person she wanted to see in the morning and the last person before going to bed.

"How did this happen?" Gillian murmured, still in a daze from the sudden realization. The whole thing made no sense, but Goddess help her, it was true.

"I never thought I'd see the day, but oh, how the mighty have fallen. Head over peep-toe sandals it seems."

"Yeah, well, it won't last long." Gillian shrugged and tried to play it off. She turned her head away, embarrassed.

"While I was making the potion for Brooke, I came across the spell to make a vampire human again using the water from Sybil's Cave, along with a regimen of herbs. I can't say whether or not it would work." Saje tilted her head to the side. "The girls and I would have to do some more research first. The only way to know for sure would be to have Mulroney try it out."

"I'm not sure he'd agree to be a guinea pig. He seemed pretty closeminded about the subject the last time I brought it up. He's a total skeptic," Gillian said, not able to keep the hurt from her voice.

"He's probably afraid because he has too much to lose if it doesn't take. Talk to him, Gillian, what do you have to lose, except for a chance at happiness?"

The summation of the situation filled her with warmth. "I know it's coming from a good place, but has anyone ever told that you're a meddler?" Gillian asked with a smile.

Saje considered this and shrugged. "At least twenty times a day."

"I appreciate all the trouble you went to. You're the most amazing friend a girl could have. Thank you." Gillian pulled her into a hug.

"Someone needs to give you both a good, swift kick in the ass. I figured if not me, then who else would?" Saje said in a voice thick with tears. She pulled away and sniffed the air. "No offense, but you smell like Eau de vampire. They will smell you from twenty paces away." Saje tapped her foot. "Hold on." She picked up a packet of herbs from the table and pulled off the gleaming, silver, heart-shaped amulet from around her neck. She opened it, sprinkled some herbs inside, and waved her hands over the locket. "This will mask your scent and your heartbeat."

"Way to think on the fly. Thank you. I don't know what to say."

"You don't need to say anything, just go get our girl back." She walked to the end of their table and stopped to chat with a group of women who wanted to buy raffle tickets.

Could Garrett be human again? The question reverberated inside her head like a mantra.

Once the parade got started, families with kids filled the park and gravitated toward their table. Shrieks and laughter rang through the air. The sweet smells of Carmel apples, funnel cake, and popcorn drifted closer, making her stomach rumble. Uniformed officers patrolled the area. Every now and then one would stop at the table to hand out stickers to the kids, and let her know they were keeping a close eye on her.

Gillian and Saje gave out packets of dried herbs from their garden and incense cones to the adults. The kids got candy and wooden wands. A donation can for Hope Club sat on the table. Children from the local hospital, many of them leukemia patients in remission, took part in the festivities and got the chance to march in the parade. This was a fundraiser to help pay for their treatments. When she tried to imagine the ordeal of having a sick child, and the astronomical medical expenses not covered by insurance, her heart squeezed.

A little girl who looked around six or seven, wearing a black and red witch costume, broke away from her mother and skipped toward Gillian. She stopped at the table, eyeing the candy in the cauldron before her big, green eyes darted to Gillian's costume. "You're Glinda, the pretty witch."

"Well, thank you." Gillian bent down so they were at eye level.

In the bright light of day, the girl's pale skin and dark smears under her eyes became apparent. But her spirit shone through from her soul. No doubt about it—this kid was a fighter.

"You're a pretty witch too. What's your name?"

"Sienna. We both have on witch's costumes."

Gillian smiled. "Yes, and do you know what every witch needs? Some real magick." Before Sienna could respond, Gillian waved her hand at the cauldron. It slid from the other side of the table and stopped in front of the little girl.

Her eyes widened. "You can do magic. You're a real witch." She reached toward the cauldron and pulled out a candy bar.

"Are you here with a parent, Sienna? We'd better ask first to make sure it's okay." Gillian gestured to the chocolate in her small hand.

Sienna turned her head and a tall woman with short, brown hair hurried over to the table to stand beside her. "Mom, can I have some candy? This is Gillian and she said I could."

"Go ahead." The woman smiled at Gillian. "Thank you. Hi, I'm Jacqui. I hope she's not bothering you?"

"No, not at all. I'd like to sprinkle a little fairy dust on her if it's okay. It's great for making wishes."

"Can I please have some fairy dust, Mommy?" Sienna jumped up and down with excitement. "Pretty please."

Jacqui nodded. "Sure."

Gillian picked up the pink sparkle dust from a cup on the table and poured some in her hand. "Can you take off your hat for a moment, honey? The dust works better if we place it on your forehead."

When Sienna took off her hat, Gillian tried not to stare. All of her hair was gone, only peach fuzz remained. "My hair was brown before my chemo treatments, and when it grows back, I wish for it to be purple. My favorite color."

Her mother touched her arm and pulled her close. "Sienna, your hair can't grow back purple. Only hair dye can change the color. How about you wish for something else, sweetheart?"

"Okay, I wish for my hair to grow back again, no matter what color, so people stop asking if I'm a boy."

Gillian tried her best not to cry, but tears clogged in the back of her throat. Sienna's courage blew her away. When she gathered her composure, she whispered, "I think that's a perfect wish." She gently pressed the dust to Siannas's forehead. "I want you to close your eyes and imagine the place where you keep all your dreams. Think of the wish in your mind over and over again until it becomes real to you. How about I add a spell for some extra magick?"

With her eyes squeezed shut, Sienna nodded her head.

May all good things come to thee.

Your beautiful hair will grow back for all to see.

And this is my will, so mote it be.

Sienna opened her eyes and smiled, revealing a missing front tooth. "Thanks for the fairy dust."

"It was truly my pleasure." Gillian wrapped her in a hug and held on tight, wishing with all her heart for Sienna's health to be restored.

"Thank you," Jacqui said with tears in her eyes. Smiling back at Gillian, she led Sienna over to the candy apple stand.

At that moment, Gillian's heart filled with so much love, she thought it might burst. Maybe meeting this sweet, little girl was a sign from the powers that be of good things to come, to teach Gillian to embrace the future without expecting the other shoe to drop. If Sienna could hold onto hope after everything she'd been through, then Gillian could too. Maybe there was a chance at a future with Garrett after all.

Garrett stood outside the fence of the park with his mouth hanging open. He had been unable to keep from staring in stunned silence when the little girl took off her hat. He'd tuned into her conversation with Gillian, listening to every word and getting choked up.

Watching Gillian interact with Sienna made one thing clear—she was a natural with children, a born nurturer. He'd been standing there for several minutes, checking out the scene to make sure Gillian was okay. Turning his head, he glanced at the uniforms trolling the park. They should've made him feel safe, but they didn't, not really. There was no way to know who Lawrence would send after her, especially now that they were closing in. The Council had the bank put a freeze on all affiliated assets and accounts linked to Malcom's credit cards.

His eyes, of their own accord, flew back to Gillian, and his chest grew tight. No matter how much he wanted her, if he stuck around, he'd take her dream of a family away. He'd give anything to be human again, and be able to make all of those dreams come true. But it was only a fantasy. He'd heard the wives' tales and myths about witches creating elixirs and spells to turn a vampire human again, but none had unlocked the mystery of a true cure. If they did, he'd know. There was only one thing he could do to save Gillian from heartache in the long run.

When he tried to take a step, it felt as though his shoes had been filled with lead. He glanced over at the kids marching in the parade, some hobbling on crutches, others in wheelchairs, with pallor complexions. Life had never seemed more unfair. He could only imagine what these families would do to find a cure for their child's illness. What they wouldn't give for a guarantee of more time with their loved ones, while he stayed cursed, frozen in immortality.

With a heavy sigh, he walked past the gate and into the festival area. Garrett approached Gillian's table and whistled. He admired how the blue, flowing dress hugged her curves. The sight of her lightened his dark mood.

"Let me guess, there's no place like home? You're the most beautiful witch I've ever seen."

"Garrett? When did you get here?" The way Gillian said his name, breathless and excited, warmed a part of his soul. She came around the table to brush a kiss on his cheek. "How was the debriefing? Is everything set for tonight?"

"We have a lot to go over, but we can discuss all the details and your role on the drive over. There's one thing I need to tell you, and I know you'll be happy about it. The MBI sent a drone to do surveillance of the house. We got footage of Brooke. She's there and she's all right, Gillian."

"Thank God." Gillian burst into tears. She wrapped her arms around his neck and crushed her face to his chest. Sobs of relief shook her body while he rubbed her back. "Thank you."

"Hey, it's okay. Let it all out, baby," he whispered. When her sobs began to subside, she pulled away, and he handed her a handkerchief.

"I see you came prepared for the occasion." She dried her eyes, rubbing off her smeared mascara.

"I'd rather see you smile, than cry." He grabbed his wallet and pointed to the raffle tickets. "How many will these buy?" he asked, handing her three, crisp hundred dollar bills.

"All of them with some cash to spare. Thank you. It's very generous of you." She walked to the table and stuffed the money in the raffle can, picking up a few books of tickets and handing them to him. "Hold onto these. Who knows, you could get lucky," she whispered in a breathy voice.

Hell, he could still taste her on his lips—hear the rush of her blood through her veins. He couldn't make love to her again in good conscience, not when he planned to break things off. "On second thought, we should go," he said, resisting the urge to return the quip.

He'd never been so connected to another woman in his life, not even with Lilly. But this time he wouldn't be selfish. He'd wait until after tonight to end things. She would be reunited with Brooke and happy. It would hurt less then. He refused to let anything get in the way of the op. He had to stay focused on saving Brooke and those women. In the end, he'd bring Lawrence down for good.

"There's still a lot to discuss for tonight, and I'm not planning to stick around." Such prophetic words were never spoken. Guilt twisted his gut, but it was misplaced. Breaking it off with her was the best thing he could do for her in the long run.

"We're just finishing up here. Let's wait for the raffle to be called, and then, we can head home." The moment she said the words, she froze. "I meant your home of course, not mine."

He could never give her the kind of home she wanted—one with a family. What kind of self-centered bastard would he be if tried to take her dream away from her? "I know what you meant." He shot back in a voice laced with anger, not at her, but the situation.

"What's wrong? There's a strong, negative vibe coming off you all of a sudden." She studied him like a puzzle piece that didn't fit anywhere.

"It's nothing." He ran a hand through his hair. "I have a lot on my mind, and I just want to get out of here."

Her gaze narrowed, looking him over. "Don't say it's nothing when clearly something's bothering you. I can tell by your breathing and the change in your voice. I thought we got past this, Garrett, and we could be honest with each other. Did I freak you out when I said let's go home? Is this part of your commitment phobia?"

His anger flared. "I thought you were a psychic, not a therapist." He didn't want to do this here.

Hurt flashed in her eyes and made him feel like something he wiped off the bottom of his shoe on the way over. "Can we go somewhere and talk about this in private?"

With a nod, he led her by the elbow to a quiet corner of the park, away from the crowd, but where officers patrolled the perimeter. Once he made sure they were alone, he exhaled. "I'm sorry. I didn't mean what I said. It was cruel and effusive of me."

Her chest rose and fell with heavy breaths. "What's going on? Does this have to do with Brooke? Is there something you're not telling me?"

He shook his head. "No. Everything's in place." If he was attached to her now, what would he be like in a month or a year? How could he just walk away when being with her made him feel alive? She brought light and color into his dark, dreary world. Ever since she fell into his arms, his heart seemed to beat again.

"Then what's going on? Don't try and deny you're upset about something," she insisted, not letting up.

"Let's talk about this later. Can we head out?" This wasn't the time and certainly not the place.

"Why, so you can sit and stew on the drive to Greenwich?" She crossed her arms over her chest. "I don't think so."

"Look, Gillian, I'm not used to discussing my feelings with someone. I've lived for over a century alone. I'm not going to change. I don't do relationships." Granted, he sounded like a bastard, but it might be the only way to make a clean break without prolonging her pain.

"I didn't think you'd cave so quickly." Her voice sounded shaky. "This must be some kind of record, even for you." Her eyes filled with tears, and it made his chest ache.

"We don't need to do this right now. There's a big night ahead. Let's dispense with the drama." He wished he could backtrack and tell her everything would be okay, but he couldn't find it in him to lie. Better to hear it now. He should've never gotten involved with her in the first place. She was young and beautiful with her whole life ahead of her. She deserved a real flesh and blood man, not a monster.

"Is that what this is to you, drama? After last night, and all the time we spent together? I thought I meant something to you. I guess I was wrong. I didn't realize you only have sex with no strings attached. Why not just say the words, Garrett?" Tears streamed down her cheeks, and she let out a hiccup.

"Gillian," he whispered, her name clogging in his throat.

He wanted to take her in his arms and pull her to his chest, swallow every tear with a kiss, and make love to her for hours on end. Wipe all doubts from her mind. But what would be the point? She'd only resent him in the end. He'd rather live with her anger than her disappointment.

"You're a god damn coward," she railed, swiping at her tears.

He couldn't imagine another day without her, let alone a lifetime. He couldn't bear the pain. How would he get over this...over her? "You're right. I am a coward. Whatever we shared was well, unexpected, and I'm afraid it has to end."

She was crying hard now, deep sobs from the soul. "It was unexpected? Is that the best you've got?"

A young, uniformed officer walked over, one that Garrett didn't recognize. His scrutinizing gaze roamed over Garrett before he turned to

Gillian, a look of concern etched on his face. "Is this vampire bothering you, miss?"

"I think we got it covered. You can get lost," Garrett muttered, his anger getting the best of him.

The cop rounded on him and took a step closer. "Excuse me? I need to see some ID."

Garrett cursed under his breath and flashed his badge. "This is a private matter, Officer."

"My apologies, Detective. If you need anything, miss, you let me know."

After the cop walked away, Gillian looked up at him with tears still in her eyes. "I'm not driving over to the party with you. I'm calling Natalya to see if I can ride with her."

Garrett took a step closer to her and let out a ragged breath. It wasn't supposed to happen like this. "You can't change the plan, Gillian. You're supposed to be driving to the party with me. Even if you're upset and angry, you're not in a position to make that call."

"Try and stop me. I already have on my costume and I have the potion. I refuse to sit in a confined space with you." She started to walk away and he stopped her by reaching for her hand.

"Gillian, please don't walk away, not like this." If only Garrett could go back in time when he held her in his arms, for that sliver of time, everything seemed right in the world.

"You're just trying to push me away, afraid to make a real commitment, to see where this takes us. I don't care if you're a vampire, or if our time together is short. It doesn't matter to me."

Her words flayed him open. This need for her was growing into an all-out obsession, which was why he needed to let her go. "You say that now, but I couldn't have you wasting precious years on me."

"You're giving up on us because of some misplaced moral code?" She shook her head in confusion, and he felt her pain, a feeling of deep sorrow that tore through the center of his chest.

"Don't you see? I have nothing to offer you. I couldn't give you what you want. It would be selfish. The woman I told you about, Lilly, the one from my village, what I didn't tell you last night was that she still wanted to be with me, even when she realized I became a vampire. She said nothing could keep us apart."

"Why do you make it sound like a bad thing?" she said in a soft voice.

"Trust me, it was. After I watched my family die, I clung to the last shreds of my humanity, and part of that was holding onto Lilly. Eventually, she grew concerned about how people would perceive our relationship. I was weak and still devastated from losing the people I loved most in the world. I looked forward to those few stolen moments I shared with Lilly. I agreed to live and love her for the time we had."

Gillian glanced down at the handkerchief, still gripped tightly in her hands, before her eyes met his once more. "What tore you apart?"

"She became consumed with finding a way for us to be together forever. She needed an Ancient to turn her, so she went to Malcom. Of course, he was happy to oblige. It became a conquest for him, and another way to destroy me. Very few people can take the pain during the transition. Most humans die, which is why there are so few of us in the grand scheme of things. Lilly succumbed to the toll it took on her body. Don't you see? Her blood is on my hands."

"You can't blame yourself, Garrett," she whispered and placed a hand on his cheek. "It's not like you forced her. She made the choice herself."

"Yes, but I should've never gotten involved with a flesh and blood woman. This is why I don't do relationships. They can only end one way, in tragedy."

"Saje found a spell using the water from Sybil's Cave in one of the Grimoires. What if a cure exists?" The soft lilt of her voice became clogged with fresh tears. "You need to have faith."

"Nothing can turn a vampire human again. Believe me, if there was such a thing, I would've tried it by now." There's no sense believing in fairy tales. It would only lead to sorrow.

"You're not even going to let us try?" she whispered in a shaky voice.

When he remained silent, Gillian took a step back with a horror-struck look on her face. "I guess that's all the answer I need."

At that moment, an announcer's voice broke through the deafening silence from a megaphone. He called a number over and over again. To Garrett, his voice sounded muffled as he could only focus on his gut-wrenching pain.

Gillian glanced over at the books of tickets stuffed into his front jacket pocket and waved her hand. One of the books soared up in the air and flipped to the number that the guy kept calling. "It looks like you're a winner. You better go collect your prize." With that, she turned her back on him and walked away, leaving him staring at the spot, long after she was gone.

Garrett couldn't imagine how he could be a winner when it felt like he'd just lost the most important thing in his life.

CHAPTER 26

$\mathscr{G}$arrett maneuvered the silver Lotus Evora, courtesy of the MBI, down a narrow, winding road, and past what looked like centuries-old oak trees until he came to a clearing. The vehicle was registered to Sebastian Beam in case someone from the Brotherhood traced the license plate.

When he spotted the black MBI van parked behind a delivery truck, he pulled over. They chose this point on the map, a stretch of ten miles from the actual house, to meet. The plan involved Gillian jumping into his back seat and staying hidden until he got through the gate.

He wasn't sure how she'd act once she saw him or what they'd say to each other after the scene earlier at the park. But he couldn't think about that now. This was about rescuing Brooke Corey and the other victims and finally getting enough evidence to bust up the Du Sang Brotherhood once and for all, not the state of his ill-fated love life.

Once he turned off the engine and got out of the car, careful not to get his Victorian waistcoat caught in the door, he undid the middle button and let out a deep sigh. The coat stretched tight over his shoulders and back, restricting his air supply.

His knee-high, buckled boots kicked over the gravel as he approached the van. The side door slid open with a hiss. Nick Hastings, a demon special agent he'd worked with on occasion, and from what Garrett now knew, Saje's beau, stepped out to greet him. Like most of his kind, he stood close to seven feet tall with an imposing, muscular frame. "Hey man, you look the part," said Hastings, shaking Garrett's hand with an appraising glance at his costume. "I'm sure you'll blend right in."

"That's the plan. What's going on? Any updates?" Garrett craned his neck to see over Hasting's horned head into the van. Still no sign of Gillian. But he knew nothing in this world could keep her away from her cousin, not even the way things had been left between them.

"We've got a full tech team inside this baby. Commander Smith connected small antennae to the AC units, allowing us to pick up on everything through surveillance cameras. The receiver can transmit a signal, which allowed us to park further away to reduce visibility. But the signal doesn't cover the whole property. All of you will be connected by microphones, so you can hear each other's conversations. From here we'll be able to hack into Malcom's private computer and get the goods." Hastings handed him a mic.

"And that's when we have a chat with Mr. Lawrence."

They'd already had enough to lock him up and throw away the key before, but now that he jumped bail and crossed state lines, he had no more get-out-of-jail-free cards. He'd have no choice but to make a deal, one that involved giving up his boss. Garrett placed his ear pierce, untied the jabot around his neck, and buried the mic inside the white, flowy shirt that came with the costume.

After a series of beeps and static, he did a soundcheck. "Can anyone hear me?"

All three agents, Denopoulos, Smith, and Teague, responded immediately. The only one who didn't respond was his partner. "Have you seen Dubrosky?" His words caught in his throat when Gillian stepped out of the van.

She looked like a vision, a beautiful angel that would never be his to cherish again. The realization left him numb. The good witch costume from earlier was gone, replaced with a sexy cop costume. She no longer wore a long, flowing skirt, but a skin-tight mini dress cut up to mid-thigh, showing an indecent amount of her long legs. She'd replaced the low-heeled boots with high heels. An oversized cop hat covered most of her face, and a small purse dangled from her hip.

The idea of putting herself in harm's way, dressed like that in a room full of blood-thirsty vampires, made his gut burn. He swallowed hard and tried to focus on the plan. "You're to stay put in the back seat of my car until the valet pulls into the garage. Once you get the go-ahead, you go in through the side patio door at the west entrance of the estate. Big Red, one of the agents at the party disguised as a waiter, will leave it open for you. You walk in and blend with the other women in costume until you get the signal. There's no way the guards could keep track of what everyone's wearing. If anyone stops you…"

"I'll pretend I'm lost. Natalya went over everything with me several times," Gillian said and stared at the long, blond wig on his head now pulled into a black ribbon. It dug into his scalp and made his head itch. "Lestat from *Interview With A Vampire*? Clever choice. No one will ever recognize you."

"I told you I favor the classics."

Her eyes darted to his shoulder holster. "Is the gun real?"

He nodded. "Not only is it real, but it's also loaded with silver bullets for the occasion."

"Then you might want to use this." Gillian reached inside her purse and pulled out a spray bottle. His eyes instantly burned, forcing him to take a step back. "Let me guess, vampire repellant?"

"Try spraying it on the gun. It won't affect you once it gets absorbed into the metal, but it should mask the scent of the bullets."

The plan was for Smith to meet him at the security checkpoint, but Garrett supposed a little extra protection couldn't hurt. "Why don't I let you do the honors?"

After Gillian sprayed the gun, she shoved the bottle back into her purse. "All set."

"We just need to fit you with an earpiece and a mic."

At that moment, Dubrosky poked her head out of the van. "Hey, partner. We'll be your eyes and ears from here on out." She angled her head in Gillian's general direction. "Try not to worry, she's been briefed. It was my idea to pick up a shorter costume so her dress wouldn't stick out from under your cloak. At least now she doesn't look like a character from a children's movie."

"Right. It makes sense." Garrett said through gritted teeth. He took a tentative step closer to Gillian and her lavender scent perfumed the crisp night air. She wore her hair up in the cap with tendrils falling around a glittery, black mask. He'd give anything to know what she was thinking right now.

"You need to place this in your bra," he said and handed Gillian the mic. Their fingers touched and a shock of electricity zinged up his arm. His chest filled with longing and deep regret. "The transmitter can pick up all of our conversations."

Hastings cleared his throat, breaking some of the tension. "On that note, I think I'll leave you to it. See you on the other side." He got back into the van presumably to give Gillian some privacy.

"I'll use magick to conceal the mics." She waved her hands and closed her eyes.

"Stars and moons, sand and sea.

Mother Earth let her cover thee.

This is my will, so mote it be."

She opened her eyes and tilted her head to the side. Gillian bent forward, and he noticed a silver heart necklace now hanging from her slender neck. Their eyes met. "This will mask my scent and my heartbeat."

"Frankly, that slipped my mind. Good thinking, Gillian."

She ignored his praise and lifted the front panel of her dress. "I just need a minute." Garrett caught a glimpse of a silver bra, and the outline of her pert, rosy nipples. Blood, fast and hot, rushed straight to his groin. If she was trying to torture him, she was doing one hell of a job.

"All set," she announced after she adjusted herself. They did another soundcheck.

"Remember, Alex will be in a waiter uniform working with the catering staff, and Smith will be part of the security detail."

"I'll be the one driving the kick-ass delivery truck after you rescue Brooke," Teague piped up into the mic.

"There will be other agents throughout the party, undercover as bartenders and waitstaff. They'll be keeping an eye on you should you run into any trouble. Any questions?" Garrett asked, ready to get back on the road.

She shook her head and let out a deep breath, looking tense. "I don't think so."

"I'm parked close by, but I imagine the gravel will be treacherous in heels. Let me help you." He reached for her hand, but she waved him off.

"I don't need your help." She hobbled along and managed not to twist an ankle.

She dropped the crystal in her hands. When she bent down to pick it up, Garrett caught the glint of the blade she planned to use on Brooke, strapped in a thigh holster. His mouth went dry. After they reached his car, he opened the door to let her duck into the back seat. She curled up in a ball and covered herself with his long, black cloak.

"Are you okay under there? Can you breathe?"

"I'm fine," she muttered in a muffled voice. "Let's get this over with." He got the distinct impression she wasn't only talking about getting to Brooke, more like she couldn't wait to get away from him. He couldn't blame her, not after the way he treated her.

"Fair enough." He got into the car, turned on the GPS, and floored the gas. He peeled out of the clearing in the direction of the house. With one hand on the wheel, he reached for the mask on his passenger seat and covered his eyes. *Showtime.*

Once they reached the enormous wrought iron gate, he gasped. "You were right all along about the dragon shield. The satellite images from the drone didn't pick it up. We're nearing the security box. Remember to stay ducked down." He pulled up and lowered his window. "The name's Sebastian Beam."

"Wait a moment, please," said a voice on the other end. After a series of buzzing noises, the gate lifted. "You may enter, Mr. Beam." He drove down a long, stone driveway to an enormous courtyard flush with grand, sweeping lawns.

When the sprawling, multi-level French country estate appeared, Gillian's head popped up, visible in the rearview mirror. Greeted by Rockefeller era stone walls, ivy-clad pillars, and a slate roof, he now knew where all the blood money had gone. Incandescent lights lit up the house and made quite the visual against the backdrop of an inky sky. "Business must be good," Garrett muttered in disgust.

"Holy shit, can you say *Wolf of Wall Street?* This is place is huge. It's where I had the vision of Brooke. She's here. I can feel it in my bones. Does this place belong to Kurt Lawrence?" Gillian asked in a sickened voice.

"No. It took some digging, but it's linked to a credit card number used by Lawrence. It's an entity owned investment property, and wouldn't you know, the entity's controlling principal is Malcom Von Scrivner. I see the valets. Stay down."

Garrett pulled the Lotus behind a row of Ferraris, Lamborghinis, Aston Martins, and stretch limos. He hopped out of the car and stretched, his gaze darting to the back seat. He caught a glimpse of Gillian's leg and tugged at the edge of the cloak, making sure every part of her stayed covered. When the valet approached, he turned and slipped a twenty in his hand. "Take good care of her."

He managed to walk about five steps when a vampire, dressed in all black with a wire dangling from his ear and a gleaming, silver stake holstered to his hip, stopped him. The guard blocked his path and held up his hand. "Arms straight out and legs apart, sir."

"I expected to be on a first-name basis before we got to this point in the evening," Garrett said with a twist of his lips. Smith was supposed to be guarding the front. He'd been hoping to bypass the security check. Instead, Garrett picked up part of his conversation, something about getting held up at the outdoor Loggia attached to the library.

Before he could fathom what a Loggia entailed, the guard patted him down. He motioned to the nineteenth-century pistol from Garrett's private collection, the one he kept holstered in a shoulder strap loaded with real silver-tipped bullets for the occasion. "I'll take that for you, sir. You may retrieve it after the party."

Garrett let out a low chuckle. "It's part of the costume, but if your boss deems it necessary to confiscate a prop, then knock yourself out. I'm sure the old guy who rented it to me will have a good laugh over the whole thing."

"Smith will meet you inside in a few minutes. Try and play nice. The goal is to get you inside," Dubrosky said in his ear.

The guard pursed his lips in annoyance. Someone called his name and the vampire turned, allowing Garrett to slip past him and blend in with the crowd.

"Quick thinking, Detective," Denopoulos said into his mic over the crash of pots and pans in the background. We're looking for Malcom, but so far no one's found him yet. I suspect the bastard knows how to stay hidden. As soon as we get Lawrence, he'll be forced to lead us to his boss."

Garrett couldn't respond without giving away the wire in his ear, so he simply smiled and kept on walking to the main entrance of the house.

Lush, green shrubs and tall arborvitaes greeted him. He snuck a peek through the arches of the courtyard to the lawns, and Versailles came to mind. Golf carts filled with guests zoomed past.

Taking the stone steps that led to the main entrance, Garrett glanced over at the sea of costumes, from a couple dressed as Marilyn Monroe and his all-time favorite baseball player, Joe DiMaggio, to a provocative Snow White with her Prince Charming, all of whom wore masks to cover their faces. But he could sense how uncomfortable the women seemed from their body language.

Everyone came in costume, and Garrett wondered if Malcom was somewhere among them. Would he be able to recognize the bastard after all these years? A cluster of women clad in vampire costumes, complete with crimson lips and plastic fangs, walked up the staircase, teetering on stilettos with glazed looks in their eyes. He could smell their perfume, along with their fear.

An attractive female dressed as Marie Antoinette stood at the open doors. A high back stool with an ornate crystal bowl on top sat to her right, filled with red, velvet boxes. "Good evening and welcome." With a glance at his costume, she checked her iPad. He'd been required to include how he'd be dressed via text.

"We have you right here, Mr. Beam. My name's Joanna. Please let me know if you need anything. Enjoy." She reached into the bowl and handed him a small box, which he placed in the top pocket of his waistcoat.

"Thank you, Joanna." Once Garrett stepped through the threshold, he glanced at the enormous hallway. The over the top display of wealth and opulence bought from the blood of the innocent made him want to hurl the box at one of the gold filigree mirrors hanging on the wall. Between the winding staircase that appeared to go as far up as the heavens, to the high vaulted ceilings and enormous brick fireplace, he deemed the place fit for a king. Or in this case, the head of a blood ring. He reluctantly admired the architecture and imagined Malcom had the place custom-built to his specs.

"What's with the gift?" Dubrosky asked, breaking into his musings.

"One way to find out," he whispered back. When he opened the box, a red signet ring stared back at him. Trying to hide his revulsion, Garrett slipped the gold band on his finger, and crossed into what he knew from the layout was the formal great room where most of the guests now congregated. "We need to confirm Malcom's here."

"Hang on, Mulroney. We're searching the crowd, trying to do face recognition scans, but with the masks, it's almost impossible."

White-gloved waiters and waitresses walked by carrying trays of flutes filled with champagne. A waiter brushed past him with a tray of hors d'oeuvres and Garrett caught the scent of the strawberry blond demon agent from the Greenwich field office. They called him Big Red.

Set up in the corner with stools and loveseats, an enormous bar seemed the place to congregate. The MBI had sent in their agents to pose as bartenders.

At first glance, the room appeared to be at capacity, buzzing with chatter. Despite having studied the blueprints, Garrett wasn't prepared for the sheer size of the house and the number of creatures and humans inside. It made their jobs more difficult.

There was a task force nearby, prepared to bust up the place and rescue all the women as soon as they got the okay. If they went in too soon, they'd have a blood bath on their hands. Once they got Brooke Corey and the rest of the vics out of there, they'd seize whatever they could from Malcom's computers, and hopefully, put him and Lawrence away for the rest of their miserable lives.

Garrett wasn't sure how Lawrence had managed to pull off something this elaborate as a fugitive. He tuned into the multitude of conversations around him, hoping to pick up on something that would lead him to Brooke and the sleezebag host for the evening.

"Does anyone want to venture a guess as to how Lawrence will be dressed tonight?" he whispered into his mic." In all the surveillance video the agents managed to listen to, nothing had given them any clue on his choice for a costume.

"Do you see anyone dressed as Attila the Hun or Lucifer? Any giant douchebag costumes?" Teague said into his mic.

Garrett tried hard not to laugh. Leave it to Teague to always provide comic relief under duress.

"You're not helping matters," Dubrosky shot back.

Turning his head, Garrett searched the room again for Lawrence, and his attention became diverted to an area next to a wall of windows where an eight-piece band played. Something about the bass guitar player, who was dressed as a pirate, looked familiar, but he couldn't figure out from where.

Frustrated, Garrett exhaled, his tension mounting by the second. Shit, they could be anywhere. The song ended and a vampire dressed as Elvis walked up to talk to the band.

"We'd like to do a request from Mr. Lawrence." The guitar player announced to the crowd. The song, *Love Me Tender* began to play.

Searching for "The King," Garrett crossed the room and cut through the crowd, when a vampire dressed in a Danny costume from the movie *Grease* approached him with a wide, beaming smile. "Good evening, you must be Mr. Beam. I spotted you from across the room. Lestat, right? Excellent costume by the way. I'm Jason Massey. We spoke on the phone." He shook Garrett's hand.

"Yes, of course. Please, call me Sebastian. Thank you for coming over to introduce yourself. I just arrived and I'm still getting my feet wet, so to speak." Garrett glanced over at the group of young women he'd seen walking into the party and pretended to check them out, playing his part to the hilt.

"I could tell by the way you've been gazing around the room that you're searching for that special someone. Let me explain how things work at these kinds of gatherings. You may choose someone on your own to be your companion for the evening, as long as they're not currently with another vampire, of course. Or we can choose for you. But remember, as a member of the Brotherhood, you have unlimited access to all of our companions from now on."

"So is that what the twenty-five thousand bucks gets you?" Now speak into the mic loud and clear, you piece of shit.

Massey smiled. "Exactly. We can arrange to have a companion come over to you immediately based on your personal preferences."

Once they received the MBI wire transfer, he'd been required to fill out a Scantron for Sebastian Beam's personal preferences for a blood bond. The whole exercise had made his stomach turn. "I'd like to have a drink first." That was Denopoulos's cue to come and find him.

"The choice is yours. Whatever you choose, Sebastian, you won't be disappointed."

"I haven't had a chance to meet with Kurt yet. I'd like to speak with him about a new venture. I'm sure he'll find it quite interesting. Business before pleasure I'm afraid. I thought I saw him walk by."

"Not to worry. I'll bring you right over to him."

"We're in luck. I just got a facial scan match to your sire, Mulroney," Dubrosky said in his ear. "He's in an Aro costume."

Not sure who Aro was, Garrett exhaled with relief. Now all they needed to do was create a diversion to allow Gillian to get Brooke away from Lawrence, take her to an empty powder room, administer the potion, and then get the hell out of there. At least he hoped it would go down that smooth. As soon as she gave the signal, Teague would meet them at the rear of the house.

"We have a visual on Gillian," Hastings said in his ear.

Garrett tried not to show any reaction as he followed Massey through the crowd. He stopped when he smelled Kurt Lawrence. The vampire was clad in a white and gold jumpsuit with his dark hair gelled to within an inch of his life. Pasted-on mutton chops covered the sides of his face.

His Priscilla stood nearby wearing a long-sleeved, white mini-dress and tall, white go-go boot. The black wig teased into a Beehive, and the heavy makeup made Brooke Corey almost unrecognizable. Her eyes narrowed in recognition when she glanced over at Garrett and then glazed over.

"Kurt Lawrence, I presume? I've been waiting a long time for this moment. We finally get to meet in person." Garrett slapped Lawrence on the back—hard.

Before the vampire could respond, Denopoulos walked up holding a tray of red wine goblets and purposely bumped into Garrett, spilling the contents of the tray all over his rented Victorian waistcoat. Glasses crashed onto the marble floor and scattered everywhere. "I'm sorry, sir, let me help you."

"This jacket has been in my family for generations," Garrett snarled. "What kind of people do you have working for you, Lawrence?"

"Are you insulting me?" Denopoulos shouted, getting right up in Garrett's face.

"I think that's obvious. You're a blundering disaster," Garrett growled. "Now step aside."

"I'd rather be a blundering disaster than an insufferable fop like you." Denopoulos glared at his waistcoat now soaking wet and stinking of red wine.

"You don't know who you're addressing. Plan on getting ripped apart." Heads turned in their direction. and the women got out of the way in anticipation of a fight.

"Mr. Beam, you need to calm down. You're causing a scene," Lawrence admonished, trying to hold Garrett back. The vampire turned and waved his hand in the air. "Security!"

Smith, along with three guards, rushed over and stood between Garrett and Denopoulos. "Is there a problem here?"

Dubrosky's voice came into his ear. "Gillian, you're up. Mulroney and Denopoulos, you need to make this look good."

Denopoulos grabbed Garrett by the collar and jabbed his fist into his face. Garrett made a show of stumbling backward. He rubbed his jaw and then rushed him, tackling him to the marble floor. They rolled around in a heap of limbs. A crackling noise pierced his ear, followed by dead silence. Son of a bitch, he'd just crushed his mic.

The room erupted in shouts and screams.

Through the corner of his eye, he saw Smith approach. The demon ducked out of the way at the last second, coming close to getting kicked in the face. He grabbed Garrett by the back of his waistcoat and hoisted him to his feet. "You'll need to come with me, Mr. Beam." He held him in a chokehold. "I'll personally escort you out of the party."

CHAPTER 27

The moment the fight broke out, security guards scattered throughout the room. Before one of them could grab Brooke and whisk her away, Gillian slipped out from behind a marble column and scanned the crowd for Brooke. She spotted a woman across the room in a white mini dress and a black wig. Then she remembered her vision, so she cut across the ballroom, praying no one would notice. Seeing her in the flesh after all this time made her want to hug her cousin until her ribs ached. But there was simply no time. She grabbed Brooke's hand and whispered in her ear. "Brooke, it's me, Gillian. We need to go. Now."

"Gillian? What are you doing here?" Her voice sounded haunted, and her words were slurred. When she tried to take a step, she wobbled in her boots. "Where are we going? I can't leave Kurt."

"We just need a moment to talk, and then we'll be right back. Hang onto me, sweetie." Gillian tugged her along, heading toward a set of doors. "Talk to me, Natalya, which way?"

"Who's Natalya?" Brooke murmured, looking over her shoulder.

"There are twelve bathrooms in this house. I'm trying to get a visual on all of them to find an empty one. Hang on." A few tense minutes passed. Then, Natalya finally said, "Okay, head out of the great room and make a right, then continue down the hall. It's the third door on your left. Make sure to lock it when you get inside. I'll send someone to put an 'out of order' sign on the door."

"Let's go." Gillian did her best to look nonchalant while she practically dragged Brooke from the great room and down the length of the hall, hoping and praying no one would stop them. Luckily, the hallway was empty. All of the security guards seemed to have rushed to the area where the fight had broken out.

Gillian hurried her pace with her arm linked through Brooke's. Once she found the door, she turned the glass knob and slammed it shut with a wave of her hand. After Gillian locked it behind her, she turned and let out a gasp. Paneled in red lacquer with white vanities, crystal chandeliers, and huge, silver mirrors, she'd never seen a bathroom this fancy in her life.

"C'mon there must be a make-up area with some chairs." They pushed through red and gold draperies and entered a sitting area filled with red cushioned benches.

"I don't feel so good all of a sudden," Brooke whispered as Gillian sat her down in one of the benches. "I need to go to Kurt. He'll find me, and neither of us will ever get out of here. I can't live without his blood. I won't." Her head slumped to the side and rested against the wall.

Rushing to the sink, Gillian filled a cup of water, came back, and placed it in her hands. "Drink this, and listen to me, Brooke. Garrett and a group of special agents are going to help us. I'm wearing a mic. They can hear us. They're going get us out of here and away from Kurt. I will break your blood bond. You just need to listen to me and do what I say."

Brooke lifted her head and the color drained from her face. Her skin looked as pale as death. Tears streamed down her cheeks. "I thought I'd never see you again, Gillian. I know what you're trying to do, but it's no use. Leave me while you still can."

"I'm not leaving you, no matter what." Gillian fought the rush of tears and took a seat next to Brooke. Wasting no time, she reached for the potion vile, tucked safely in the silk pouch in the pocket of her dress, and set it on the vanity. Once she unsheathed the dagger from her thigh holster, she plunged the tip of the blade into the center of her hand. She winced as blood seeped from the cut and began to flow.

"What are you doing?" Brooke sniffed the air and a savage hunger spread across her face. She leaned into Gillian, her eyes focused on the drops of blood like someone about to savor a tasty meal.

Gillian stopped her by plunging the tip of the blade into her hand and Brooke flinched in pain. "Saje made a potion that will free you from your bond with Kurt forever, but you have to do exactly as I say." Gillian closed her eyes and focused her mind, willing her magick to call to Brooke's. Sparks flew from her fingertips and circled above Brooke, surrounding her body in a glowing, white light.

After a few minutes, Brooke jerked upright, becoming more alert. Some of the haze lifted from her eyes. "Help me, Gillie."

"Brooke."

"You need to hurry, Gillian. The guards are searching for Brooke. They'll stop you when you try to escape," Natalya said in her ear. "We're trying to send an agent to you now, but we're outnumbered by Lawrence's thugs. We're waiting for the task force to close in. They should be coming through any minute now. Teague will take it from here."

Without a second to waste, Gillian slapped their hands together and held tight. "Your blood and my blood. We are family, and it's our blood that's bonded together." She opened the top of the potion vial with her free hand and let a few drops of their blood spill inside.

Now came the hard part, getting Brooke to drink every last drop. Gillian racked her brain, trying to figure out a way to get her to open her mouth. She'd have to be quick. She tried not to panic. Then, an idea came to her. Brooke had always been terrified of spiders.

"Don't move." Gillian looked up. "There's a spider web right above your head."

Brooke opened her mouth to scream and Gillian poured the potion into the back of her throat. Before she could spit it out, Gillian held her cheeks together. "I'm sorry, but this is for your own good." When she finally swallowed, Gillian chanted the spell.

Everlasting truth, love, and harmony,
I ask the Goddess to break what should no longer be,
Restore the blood from this innocent and set her free,
This is my will, so mote it be.

Gillian chanted the spell over and over again. She pulled Brooke into a hug and waited, hoping and praying for the magick to take hold. After a few minutes, Gillian leaned back and glanced at Brooke, who sat up straight.

"How did you find me?" Brooke blinked as though awakening from a deep sleep.

"I'll tell you all about it later. Right now we need to find a way to get the hell out of here." Gillian searched the bathroom and her heart skipped a beat. *No window.* She paced back and forth, trying to come up with a plan. Her gaze caught on the gold tassels wrapped around the draperies. "I have an idea, but we need to hurry."

By the time Gillian and Brooke made their way from the bathroom, they looked totally different than when they'd walked in. Switching costumes, Gillian had tossed the black wig in the trash and used her dagger to cut the sleeves and the front of Brooke's white dress into something resembling a mini toga. She'd taken the gold tassels off the draperies and wrapped them between her boobs and around her waist like a sash. Then, she performed one last bit of magick, weaving a spell to change Brooke's appearance and her scent.

They headed down the hallway and chaos exploded all around them. Shrieks and screams tore through the air. Cops dressed in riot gear cut through the crowd, pointing what looked like high-powered rifles and silver stakes at the vampires throughout the house. Gillian stole a glance at Brooke, who looked like she'd pass out at any moment. "Don't make eye contact with anyone."

They continued toward the back of the house. "We're out," she said into her mic and tried to hurry their pace.

Brooke stopped walking and began to shake. "I'm not going to make it, Gillie. You go without me."

"No. We're almost there. I've got you. Hold onto me."

"Walk to the terrace and down the steps. Past the lawns, you'll see a white delivery truck," Cayden replied. "You're doing great."

When they got to the doors to the terrace, the chaos continued there. Police helped the women out of the fray and escorted them into black vans. Gillian and Brooke stayed clear and walked across the long expanse of the patio, past the outdoor couches and Chinese lanterns. Blazing fire pits lit their path to the stone steps.

"Keep coming," Cayden murmured. "I can see you."

They cut across a grassy knoll until Gillian finally heard the rumble of an engine. When they got to the delivery truck, she slid the door open and practically shoved Brooke into the back. "Thank God."

Gillian collapsed into the seat and took off her mask, shaking from head to toe.

Cayden turned to face them and concern flashed in his eyes as he looked over at Brooke. "Are you okay?" He flicked on the interior lights inside the van.

Her head slumped forward on her chest, her breathing now labored. Gillian touched her hand. "She's ice cold. Brooke? What's wrong?"

"It looks like she's suffering from blood loss. A medivac should be on the way. We anticipated something like this, but they won't have enough blood for all these victims. We had no way of knowing there were so many." Cayden said with a shake of his head. "I can't risk it. We could lose her. I'm taking her straight to a hospital." He handed her an enormous jacket from the passenger seat. "Here, put this on her."

Gillian wrapped the jacket over Brooke's shoulders and held her hand, praying they'd get there in time. "Drive, please."

"Let's bounce." Cayden turned to face the front. He shifted the truck into gear and sped away, leaving the squeal of tires and the smell of burnt rubber in his wake. They drove down a dark, winding road that headed away from the estate.

"When will this nightmare end?" Gillian asked, and then glanced over her shoulder to see if they were being followed.

"We're not out of the clear yet. The task force has their hands full. They're still at the front of the house. We need to make it past the rear gate. The guards won't be inclined to let anyone leave the property." Cayden pressed buttons on his phone, which sat in a holder on his dashboard.

When they reached the wrought iron gate, it was closed. Cayden stopped at the security box at the guard shack. "Quick, put the jacket over you. They're looking for Brooke, which means trying to get away from this house of horrors is going to be a bitch. The other agents have no visual on us here. We have to wing it." Cayden wrenched on his window. "I'm from Haven Catering. I'm just leaving. We need this truck for the next job."

"No one gets through the gate," a male voice said from the other side. A light shone into the car and Gillian prayed he didn't see them. There was a crackling noise as the guard spoke into a radio.

After a few minutes, Cayden cursed. "He's not opening the gate. I think they're onto us. Time for plan B." The van lurched into reverse and backed up. The wheels spun in the gravel. "I can try and crash through the gate, but it looks too high. There's no way." He glanced in the rear-view mirror. "Shit, the station guard is headed this way. Listen to me, Gillian, the gate only opens by the swipe of a card. The moment he gets here, I'll knock him out and hand you the card. You go out the back of the van, swipe the card, and come right back. "Got it?"

"Promise me one thing. If something goes wrong, you head straight to the hospital with Brooke. Don't waste time coming back for me. Garrett will find a way to get me out of here."

"C'mon, Gillian, you can't ask me to make that kind of promise," Cayden shot back.

"Promise me, Cayden!"

He sighed. "Fine, I promise."

With no time to hesitate, Gillian stood on wobbly legs, trying not to throw up from nerves, and moved to the rear door of the truck. She glanced over her shoulder. The guard approached Cayden's door, and he got out of the van, grumbling about getting to his next job. Then, he grabbed the guard by the throat and slammed his head into the side of the truck. The guard crumbled to the ground in a heap.

Cayden took the card from the lanyard around his neck and passed it over to Gillian. "Go now. I'll stay here with Brooke."

Gillian jumped from the back and ran to the guard station, trying not to trip in her heels. Once inside, she glanced at the blinking green panel and swiped the card across the board. Turning her head, she exhaled when the gate opened. She ran back toward the van and stumbled when a giant hand wrapped around her throat, cutting off her air supply. She choked and gasped as he turned her around to face him, lifting her halfway off the ground. Dangling in midair, she tried to kick him in the groin, but she missed and only managed to hit his shin.

"Don't even think about going anywhere." Finally, he put her down, releasing his hold on her throat.

Coughing, she lay on the ground, gasping for air. She glanced over at a second guard, now racing toward the driver's door, but before he could reach it, the van zoomed through the open gate and onto the main road.

She sighed with relief. At least Brooke would be safe.

A golf cart pulled up and the guard pushed Gillian into the rear seat. "You're too much trouble for your own good."

They sped back toward the house and came to an abrupt stop at an enormous garden set up like a maze. "There's police up ahead," he muttered. "Get out." He grabbed her by the arm and nudged her along, beyond the topiary bushes, fountains, and trees set in huge terra cotta pots.

Before she could try and make a run for it through the maze, the guard pushed her past a row of hedges and tall shrubs to a clearing. "We'll wait here until I decide what to do with you."

A rustling in the bushes made Gillian glance over her shoulder. A vampire, dressed as a pirate with a patch over his eye, walked toward them. He carried an unconscious woman whose head lolled to the side.

"What the hell are you doing here?" The guard demanded, flashing a light on the pirate. "You've been warned about this kind of thing. You're not supposed to kill any of them. You stupid sonofabitch. This place is crawling with special agents and cops. You're not taking the rest of us down for murder." The guard reached for his walkie-talkie "I'm calling the boss."

Adrenaline coursed through Gillian's veins, making her tremble from head to toe. Her stomach roiled. She breathed in and out, willing herself not to puke in a bush.

"Hey, there's no need to call anyone. At least come over here and help me hide the body before the cops get here."

All the hairs on the back of her neck stood on end. Gillian recognized his voice immediately. She should, he'd been coming into the shop every day for the past three months. *Lucas?*

The guard walked over to Lucas and took the woman from his arms. "Let's get this over with."

"I couldn't agree more." In one quick movement, Lucas picked up a shovel off the ground and slammed the guard in the head with a loud thwack. They both dropped with a sickening thud.

Gillian screamed, now finally understanding the message from Natalya's aunt. It rang in her ears like a raven's call. *Beware of the one-eyed man.*

CHAPTER 28

*G*arrett and Smith tore from the great room and into the main hall while all around them cops and special agents fought with Lawrence's guards.

"Denopoulos and I are going to get Lawrence out of here," Smith said, his gaze darting wildly around the hall. "You need to go after Gillian. I'm not sure if you heard what happened in the scuffle."

Garrett froze. "No. My mic got crushed. What's going on?" He couldn't live with himself if anything happened to her.

"They ran into a snag. Teague managed to get Brooke out safely, but one of the guards grabbed Gillian. Thankfully, we still have contact with her, but we don't know where he's taken her. We estimate she's somewhere on the grounds…"

Garrett didn't let him finish, he was already heading out the side door to the patio. He cut across the stone path and ran down the steps to the gardens, when a blood-curdling scream pierced the air. "Gillian?"

He raced to the sound of her voice, passing a maze and a row of hedges. He found her in a clearing with the pirate from the band holding her around the waist.

"Get your hands off her," he demanded.

"Garrett? Oh my god." Tears filled her eyes. "She's dead." Gillian pointed to a young woman dressed as a vampire. He'd seen her walking into the party. She lay still on the ground, next to a shovel, along with an unconscious bodyguard. "L-lucas killed her."

Lucas? The encroaching-piece-of-shit-musician? He was the killer? The headscarf covered most of his long blond hair. "How the hell are you involved in all of this?" Reality hit him like a punch to the gut. He remembered the matchbook. "Let me guess, you play at a club called Birch?" He must be part of the Brotherhood. "You need to let Gillian go. This has nothing to do with her," Garrett said, trying to reason with him.

"I didn't expect to see either of you here tonight. Now you've gone and ruined my plans. She knows too much. You both do. I can't let you leave here." Lucas twisted Gillian's arms behind her back, and she winced in pain.

"I'm not going to ask you again. I thought I told you before, get your hands off my girlfriend." Garrett took a predatory step closer to Lucas, his fingers curling into fists, ready to rip the bastard's head off.

"Don't come any closer, or I'm afraid I'll have to silence her for good," Lucas warned. extending his fangs.

Time to try a different tactic. He needed to do his good cop routine. What would he do if the bastard hurt Gillian? Garrett swallowed hard. "Do you know the penalty for killing a cop? I'll tell you, automatic execution. I don't think you want to hurt us, Lucas. Why don't we talk about this? If you turn yourself in now, the Council will take it into consideration. You have options."

Gillian tried to wriggle free, but Lucas kept one arm around her waist, holding her in a death grip. Garrett wanted to pounce on him and tear him to shreds, but he was still too far away. In a matter of seconds, Lucas could sink his fangs into her neck and drain all the blood from her body. He couldn't take a chance with her life.

Lucas must've guessed what he'd been thinking because he glared at Garrett and snarled. "If you take one step closer, I'll kill her." He pulled out his cell and pressed a button. "I'm in the maze."

When Garrett's eyes met Gillian's in the darkness, he wished he could comfort her in some way, let her know that he'd find a way to get them out of this.

"Why are you doing this, Lucas?" Gillian asked in a voice laced with fear, still trying to flinch away. "You're talented. How did you end up down this road of death and debauchery?"

Lucas frowned and seemed to take Gillian's words to heart. "Talent doesn't get you shit without connections. My band played at a restaurant owned by Lawrence. He told me after my set that he could help my career. The dude knows people in just about every industry. He introduced me to Malcom, and he offered me a deal I couldn't pass up."

The revelation forced Garrett to gnash his teeth. "In other words, you agreed to let Malcom turn you for a chance at fame and fortune?"

"Who the fuck are you to judge me? People do all kinds of crazy shit for their careers. In exchange, I went to work for the Brotherhood and did whatever they needed."

"What I don't get is how these women ended up dead, Lucas." Garrett had never suspected Lawrence killed the two other vics from the start. He might be the worst kind of scumbag, but he wasn't a killer.

"It was an accident. I couldn't help myself." Lucas shook his head, a note of remorse in his voice. "The bloodlust became too much. I never meant to kill Serena. I just couldn't stop. I liked Serena, just like I liked you, Gillian. This whole situation sucks because now I have no choice but to kill both of you to keep you quiet."

"Wait, Lucas. You need to stop right there." Garrett held up his hands.

Garrett's words caught in his throat when Malcom Von Scrivner strolled into the clearing. A black suit cut perfectly to his tall frame made him blend into the night, but the light caught on a silver dragon necklace hung around his neck. His dark hair hung past his shoulders, and framed his face, revealing a widow's peak, and skin so translucent, it looked like chalk. He stood in front of him with the same soulless, evil glint in his eyes.

"Let me guess, you came as yourself—a bloodthirsty monster."

"No, he's dressed as Aro from the *Twilight* movies," Gillian whispered and tried to kick Lucas in the shin. He muttered a curse and wrapped her in a chokehold.

Rage boiled up inside Garrett. He had to force himself to stay rooted to the spot and not lunge for Lucas's throat. He needed to stall. *"Twilight?"* he repeated, not sure who or what she was referring to.

"You should try to familiarize yourself with pop culture, Garrett, so you don't sound like such a dinosaur. I bet you could learn a thing or two from this beautiful young lady." The Ancient turned his full attention on Gillian and stalked closer to her. He sniffed the air. "Who might you be?"

"Stay the fuck away from her," Garrett shouted, not able to hold back.

"Touchy aren't we? Is she your girl?" Malcom taunted, skimming a finger down Gillian's arm. She tried to turn away, but Lucas held her still. His sire's eyes focused on the pulse point at her throat. "I can see why. She's quite fetching."

"She's got to be silenced, and so does her boyfriend." Lucas broke in and glanced over at Garrett. "They know what's going on. I, um, made another mistake. But I promise it won't happen again."

Malcom glanced at the body of the girl on the ground. His lip curled into a sneer. "You're right, it won't. It was you who exposed this operation to the police by killing those two women and not disposing of their bodies properly. You'll pay for being so careless." His trained gaze zeroed in on Lucas. He smiled and whispered, "Pins."

Lucas let go of Gillian and fell to his knees, writhing on the ground in pain.

"Garrett." Gillian ran to him, and he wrapped her in his arms.

"I promise I'm getting us out of here." Garrett tried to think of an escape plan. If he moved too quickly, Malcom could be on Gillian in a heartbeat.

"Now then, I hope you've learned your lesson." Malcom raised his hand and Lucas rose to his feet like an invisible string controlled his body. "I'm afraid your services with the Brotherhood have been terminated." His sire pulled a silver stake from his hip and stabbed Lucas square in the chest. Blood spurted from his mouth. When he sank to the ground, a gurgling sound erupted from his lips.

Malcom turned his attention on them and sneered. "A man in love loses his edge. Wouldn't you agree, Garrett? I don't think your Gillian will want to watch as I stake you and all the blood drains from your body. I promise it will be quick, but I'll drink her slowly, savor her like a fine cabernet."

With a roar, Garrett let go of Gillian and charged Malcom, shoving him to the ground. He caught the Ancient by surprise, knocking the stake from his hand. He punched and kicked him over and over again, bloodying his face and nose. Malcom reared up and headbutted him, knocking him back. The Ancient dove on top of him and twisted his hands around his throat. Garrett gasped and drew his weapon from his shoulder holster. He smashed the butt of the pistol into the back of his sire's head. Malcom groaned and rolled away, gasping in pain.

Garrett pressed the barrel to Malcom's head. "Turn around, Gillian. I don't want you to see this. I should've done this a long time ago. This is for Sadie."

"Ah Sadie, I'll never forget the taste of your dear, departed sister...so sweet," Malcom taunted and spit blood onto the ground.

"I can't tell you how good it's going to feel when I blow your brains out all over this garden. It'll take the groundskeepers a week to clean up the mess." Garrett pulled back the trigger to cock the hammer.

"Garrett, no!" Gillian's voice made his hands still. "Not like this. You can't kill him execution-style no matter what he did. You'll be kicked off the force. Don't sink to his level. You're a great cop and a great man. Don't let him take what you've worked your whole life for."

Malcom's sinister laugh rang through the trees. "How touching. I think I'd rather be dead than listen to this dribble. I beg of you, do it already, and put me out of my misery."

"Shut up," Garrett muttered, his finger pulsed on the trigger. "I lost my humanity a long time ago, the moment you sank your fangs into me."

"It's not true," she said, her voice thick with tears. "I know the honorable man that you are, the kind, caring friend and neighbor. If you do this, you'll never forgive yourself. You'll live with it every day for the rest of our lives. Be the man you were meant to be, Garrett, the man I fell in love with."

She loves me? Gillian loves me? She believed in him, no matter how much he tried to push her away. His chest swelled with an emotion he couldn't identify. She was right. He couldn't do this.

His hand wavered, and Malcom used it to his advantage. Malcom's gaze locked on his and he couldn't seem to look away. "Needles."

Garrett dropped the gun, his whole body contorting in pain. The sensation of needles digging into his skin burned like a thousand bolts of electricity.

"Stop it! You sick, bastard," Gillian screamed. The next moment Garrett's gun rose in the air and smashed Malcom in the back of the head, knocking him to the ground. The sensation of pain fell away.

"Garrett got to his feet, dragging Malcom with him. He caught movement in the bushes and tightened his hold on Malcom. "You can thank her for sparing your miserable life. Perhaps, you'd be better off rotting in Hellios. I can assure you, they don't serve cabernet."

Smith ran over to them pointing a high-powered laser gun. "Hands up,

Malcom Von Scrivner. You're under arrest for crimes against mages and humanity." Garrett let go of Malcom and took a step back while Smith placed his sire in cuffs.

"Took you long enough," Garrett muttered. He ran over to Gillian and pulled her into his arms. He wanted to breathe her in and never let her go.

"What did I miss?" Denopoulos ran over, sporting a giant red mark across the right side of his face, and an even larger laser gun. "You wouldn't believe me if I told you." He helped Smith get Malcom out of the clearing.

Garrett turned to Gillian and tilted her chin up. He eyed her body, checking for injuries. "Did he hurt you? Are you okay?"

"I'm fine, just a few bumps and bruises."

"What do you say? Are you ready to get out of here?"

"You have no idea." Even in the dim light, Garrett could see her face soften into a sad smile. "But I'm afraid nothing's changed between us, Garrett. I'll never stop loving you, but it's like you said, this relationship was never meant to be."

CHAPTER 29

"**W**hat's your position on man caves, for or against?" Saje posed the question to Gillian and Brooke.

Resting her head against the couch cushion in the parlor, Gillian finished the last of her dinner and set the container on the coffee table. The three women had been binge-watching HGTV for the past few hours in an attempt to recapture what used to be a typical Friday night. After living at Garrett's for the past week, being back at the coven felt strange and oddly comforting at the same time. They had the whole place to themselves while the rest of the girls manned the shop.

"Nick's been talking about using the spare room in his condo as one," Saje said, curling up in an oversized chair under a throw. "I said that if we're doing this there's no "man cave" or "my cave" but we can do an "our cave". Funny, he hasn't brought the subject up since."

All three women laughed.

"You will keep that demon on his toes twenty-four-seven," Gillian teased.

If one good thing came from the whole ordeal, it was Nick asking Saje to move in with him. After all the murder and mayhem—witnessing what could happen in the blink of an eye—he declared his undying love to Saje, insisting he couldn't go another day without waking up to her in his bed. Despite Saje claiming this was Nick's over-the-top way of making sure he got laid regularly, Gillian knew Saje was secretly thrilled. And the fact that Nick was a hymera, part human and part demon, meant he'd die eventually and could procreate.

Gillian had to admit, the whole declaration thing was kind of sweet. Even she couldn't have predicted such a happy ending coming from this nightmare. Too bad she couldn't say the same.

"Any word from Garrett?" Saje asked, lowering the volume on the remote.

"We broke up." Gillian tried to keep the hurt out of her voice and failed. If he truly loved her, he would have come after her, and he didn't. Maybe this was his pattern, or maybe he simply didn't feel the same way. At this point, she didn't know what to think anymore.

It had been three days since the night of the masquerade ball, and there'd been no texts or calls from him. At first, when she still hadn't heard from him, she imagined the worst, but when Natalya had called to check in on her and Brooke, confirming that he'd shown up for work, she'd lost all hope of him coming after her. Too hurt to face him, Gillian went to his place later that morning to pick up her things and had left the key with his neighbor.

"Don't give, up, Gillian. Everyone reacts to extreme stress in different ways. Give him time," Saje urged in her best eternal optimist voice.

Gillian picked up a deck of tarot cards off the table and began shuffling them. She looked up at Saje and forced a smile. "And sometimes you have to know when to fold your hand." When she'd gone and declared her undying love to Garrett, her feelings hadn't been reciprocated. The sooner she accepted the fact he'd remain a vampire and she a human, the easier it would be to get over him. If only her heart could believe it.

Brooke, who remained silent this whole time, seemed content to flip through decorator magazines and listen to their conversation. It reminded Gillian of old times, a girl's night in front of the TV, eating take out from Bareburger, their favorite vegan place, and bitching about men. But no one could deny the change in Brooke after her kidnapping. No one seemed to want to talk about the giant, pink signet ring in the room.

Fortunately, Brooke had agreed to go see a therapist starting next week, and Gillian planned to go with her. Maybe she'd even make an appointment for herself. She needed to stop this pattern of going after emotionally unavailable men once and for all.

"I've talked to the other girls," Gillian said, touching her arm. "We're all in agreement. We think you should move in here with us. You don't have to give me an answer right now." She set the deck down and reached for her tea. She put the mug to her lips, enjoying the taste of cinnamon, lemon, and ginger. The last thing she wanted for Brooke was to have the memory of that awful night come rushing back. She'd taken the weekend off to regroup.

"What we lack in privacy around here we make up for in comradery. There's always someone to talk to, no matter what," Saje chimed in. "Don't forget the rituals we go to as a group and movie night. We even host teas with those cute little sandwiches for the other covens in the area. You should consider it, Brooke. It really can be a blast around here, and you could have my old room."

Brooke gave a tentative smile. "I think I'd like that. It would be nice to be with friends and family right now. I'm not ready to go back to my apartment. But what about my lease? It's not up for another few months."

"I'm sure we can find someone to sublet your place in the short term. You can decide what you want to do after that." Gillian placed her mug on a coaster. "We can advertise it. I know a ton of reputable sites."

"You seem well versed on the subject. Have you been looking for yourself?" Saje asked and got to her feet. She started to clean up their mess.

Gillian shrugged. "I guess a part of me couldn't wait to leave here, to prove I could live on my own, but I realize now that was a waste of time." If she'd learned anything from this whole mess, it was that Glinda was on to something. Maybe there really was no place like home. "At the end of the day, it doesn't matter where you live. It's about the feeling you get when you're there. Nothing beats coming home and feeling love."

Her mind automatically drifted to Garrett. He'd broken her heart, and now she wondered if it would ever mend. But that didn't mean she couldn't enjoy a different kind of love, one that revolved around Brooke and her friends. She wanted to move on and put the whole thing behind her.

"That, right there, is why I do what I do." Brooke sat up and some of the haze seemed to clear from her eyes. "Thanks, Gillie, for reminding me. It's going to take some time, but I'm still here."

Gillian leaned over to hug her, relieved she'd started to sound more like herself. She pulled away and got to her feet.

"How about we call it a night?" Gillian said as she clicked off the TV.

Together, the three of them took the empty containers into the kitchen. She started to put the leftovers in the fridge when her phone buzzed in her back pocket.

She reached for it and glanced at the unfamiliar number. Maybe it was an out of town client. She hit accept. "This is Gillian."

"Gillian, this is Max Williams calling from WESX radio in Salem, Massachusetts. I'm sorry for calling so late. I've been in meetings all day and this is my first free moment. Is this a good time to talk?"

"Yes, absolutely." Gillian walked to the center island and sat down on a wooden stool, excitement inflating her chest.

"I listened to your demo tape and loved it. I'd like to invite you to come here to Salem for an interview. We have a slot that just opened up and would like to talk to you about filling it with a weekly show. Unfortunately, I'm going out of town for a stretch. But I have some free time this week if you're free. I'm sorry for the last minute notice."

She swallowed and tried to find her voice. "No, it's okay." She glanced over at Brooke and grinned. She couldn't leave at a time like this. "Thanks for the offer, but I'm not sure I could break away right now. I appreciate the call. I need to check my schedule. Can I get back to you?"

"How about I text you all the details? It was great speaking to you, Gillian. I hope to meet you in person. I think you'd be a great addition to the station."

"Thanks, Max. Talk to you soon." She ended the call and glanced up to find Saje and Brooke staring at her with curious expressions across their faces. "I guess you heard that?"

"Yes, and you've got to go, Gillian," Saje insisted, tying up the garbage bag. "This could be your big break."

"Even if I took the time to do this, I can't just leave. I need to help find someone to sublet Brooke's place."

"I agree with Saje, you need to do this, Gillian. If you don't, you'll spend the rest of your life wondering, 'what if'." Brooke walked over to her and held both her hands in hers. "And you know, this would be the best way for me to heal. If you do this you'll show me that no matter how bad things suck, they'll always get better. Between you and Saje, there's still a silver lining that came out of all this."

"The silver lining is a reality for Saje. As for me, well, that's still debatable." Gillian exhaled and tried to mull Max's words over in her head.

"Brooke can help me pack up and drop off my stuff at Nick's place." Saje carried the bag to the back kitchen door. "Then, we can go get the rest of her stuff and move it into my room. I can stay in yours while you're away."

A combination of excitement and warmth filled her chest. "What do I have to lose at this point?" Gillian used her phone to google the airlines.

When Garrett got back to his apartment, he went straight to the liquor cart and poured himself a brandy. Taking a swig from his glass, he sighed, but it did nothing to ease the knot in his gut. He loosened his tie and flicked on the TV to ESPN.

He glanced around his empty apartment. Over the past week, he'd gotten used to seeing Gillian's beautiful face. Everywhere he looked reminded him of her. If he closed his eyes, he swore he could hear her laughter and still smell her perfume. Now only emptiness greeted him. Going back to his solitary routine would no doubt get old real quick.

He'd made the choice to let her go, and now he'd have to live with that choice. Even her brush with death couldn't convince him otherwise. Gillian deserved a normal life, something he could never give her.

His doorbell rang, and for a split second, he wondered if it could be her. He rushed to the door, breathing hard in anticipation. His eyes focused past the window to find his neighbor on the other side. Flooded with disappointment, he opened the door. "It's good to see you, Annette. I'm sorry, but I'm not really in the mood for company."

"Even more reason for us to talk. You look awful."

Tell me something I don't know.

She stepped inside and shut the door, then pointed to his table. "May I come in and sit down?"

He nodded. "Why not?"

The older woman glanced around at the empty take-out cartons and newspapers piled in a corner and shook her head. He hadn't been in the mood to clean up. She set his spare keys on the table and took a seat in a dining room chair. "Gillian left these with me. What happened between you two?"

"We broke up." The words tasted bitter on his tongue. He kept thinking he'd wake up, and somehow, things would be different. "I could never be what she needed in the long run." He slumped into a chair across from her and sighed. Exhaustion pressed down on him like a heavyweight.

"Nonsense. I saw the way you looked at each other. People live a lifetime to find that kind of connection with someone." Annette patted his hand. "Do you love her?"

"I don't see how that's the point, but yes, deeply. She's everything to me. But it doesn't matter. The one thing she's always wanted is the one thing I can never give her—a family." Garrett set his glass on the table and realized he was the only guest at this little pity party. Drinking alone did nothing but put him in an even deeper fog. "I had to let her go. It wouldn't be fair to her."

"Fair?" Annette said with a laugh. "For someone who's lived longer than me, you sure have a lot to learn about life and women. Stop being a martyr and talk to her, Garrett. FYI, there's something called adoption. People do it every day."

"I appreciate what you're trying to do." He got up from the table and shoved a hand through his hair. "But it's not the same as your own blood."

"Is that so?" Her green eyes sparkled with wisdom. "You've heard me gush about my son, Henry. He's not my biological child, but I love him with all my heart. I'd take a bullet for him. How's that for blood?"

Garrett swallowed the lump suddenly clogging his throat. "I didn't know Henry was adopted."

"That's the point. It doesn't matter." She lifted the key ring off the table and dangled it in her small fingers. "Love goes beyond what runs through your veins. It's the choices we make that turn us into the people we become. Let Gillian make the choice. I always say a little bit of wonderful is better than a lifetime of ordinary. If you truly love her, then you should do what will make her happy."

"I let her down when she needed me the most." She'd told him she loved him and he said nothing back. "She'll probably never speak to me again." Thinking about how he treated her made his stomach twist into knots.

"It's never too late. Go to her and find a way to make things work. If you don't, you'll regret it for the rest of your days. Tell her how you feel and show her that you'll be there. Maybe make a grand gesture to show her you care."

"A grand gesture?" he repeated and hope blossomed in his chest. Annette's words rang in his ears with the force of a drum. *A little bit of wonderful is better than a lifetime of ordinary.* God, he'd been such an idiot. He needed to go to her and tell her he couldn't live without her for another minute, let alone another day. He'd do anything in this world to get her back.

"I'm sure something will come to mind." She handed him back the keys with a knowing smile. "You might want to clean up the mess first."

Garrett bent to kiss her on the cheek. "Thank you, neighbor."

He'd wasted enough time; he refused to waste anymore.

CHAPTER 30

*G*arrett walked to the back of the manor and into the greenhouse. He found Saje, Delilah, Brooke, and Ellen, the high priestess of the coven, toiling away at a butcher block table. Herbs and candles, along with mortars and pestles, covered almost every available surface.

Saje looked up when she saw him, and he was shocked when she gave him a friendly wave, especially after her warning about hurting Gillian in the shop. It all seemed like a lifetime ago.

"I'm sorry for just dropping in like this, but I've been trying to reach Gillian, and she's not taking my calls. I know I don't have a right to ask, but please, tell me she's okay."

She must've picked up on the desperation in his voice because she took pity on him with a reassuring smile. "She's fine. Let's talk." After she wiped her hands on her jeans, she led him to the corner of the greenhouse, away from prying eyes, which were currently shooting daggers at him. He couldn't blame them. Not after the way he'd behaved.

"I'm sorry about the other girls. They're just being protective of Gillian. She's been through so much," Saje whispered, shooting a glance at the other women, who got back to work cutting herbs and stirring cauldrons.

He huffed out a breath. "I know. And I never meant to cause her more pain. I'm grateful she has people in her life who care about her. I've driven by the shop but she's not there, nor here. I'm going out of my mind. Where is she?"

"She went out of town on a job interview."

I've lost her for good. His whole body tensed. "Do you know when she'll be back? I need to talk to her."

"Look, Garrett, I'm trying not to get in the way and respect your wishes. Gillian told me you're not too hopeful about a cure for vampirism, but you should know that we've completed the final elements of the potion with the help of Brook's magick, and the remaining water from Sybil's Cave. I have every reason to believe it will work."

"We're back to that, are we?" Getting his hopes up only to have them crushed would lead to more anguish.

"You have every reason to be skeptical. This potion is untested and comes with serious risks, but it's real, Garrett."

He rubbed his chin, contemplating the possibilities. "What sort of risks?" If he didn't at least consider it, he'd never know for sure if he could be human and have a life, a future with Gillian. Annette was right. He'd live to regret it for the rest of his days.

Saje exhaled, refusing to look him in the eye. "There's a good chance you could age back to when you were turned."

"In other words, turn into a pile of ash?"

She nodded. "I'm afraid so, but we'd know right away. If you do decide to give it a go you should understand one thing, it won't happen overnight, but eventually, you will turn human again."

Garrett couldn't go on without Gillian, living day and night wondering, 'what if.' He refused to live a half-life. He needed to take a chance, no matter what. "Tell me what I need to do."

By the time Gillian walked through the doors of the coven, it was noon on Sunday morning. She wheeled her suitcase into the hall and glanced around. The place appeared to be empty.

"Anybody home?" she called.

When no one responded, she took off her leather jacket and hung it on a hook by the door. Bright morning sunlight poured in from the bay window, bathing the hall in a soft, warm glow. She lifted her arms in the air and stretched her muscles, still tight from sitting on a plane for all those hours. She couldn't wait to get outside in the fresh air and go for a run.

She walked down the hall, past the kitchen. When she got to the ritual room, she found Brooke, Saje, and Ellen practicing spells and drinking coffee. A Grimoire sat open on a book stand. Magick pure and bright sizzled in the air, along with sparks of fire that shot from Ellen's fingertips, which she used to light the candles on the fireplace mantle.

Not used to seeing all the women practicing magick together, a flutter of excitement sparked in Gillian's belly. "What going on?"

Ellen turned to her and waved her hand around the room. "Have a look for yourself."

The wall of unfinished sheetrock had been primed and painted a soft taupe to match the rest of the room. All of the moldings and baseboards had been replaced and also painted.

"Wow, the room looks amazing. Who did all this?" Gillian asked with a sinking suspicion she already knew the answer to her question.

"Garrett. Who else? He did a great job and cleaned up after himself. By the way, he looks incredibly hot in coveralls, just saying." Saje walked up and pulled her into a quick hug. "He's so lost without you, Gillian. You should call him and put him out of his misery."

Gillian tugged free and tried not to think too much into the gesture. "Throwing some paint on the wall doesn't change anything." She hadn't bothered to return the sudden barrage of calls and texts from him. What was the point?

"He's a keeper for sure," Brooke agreed. "And not just because of the coveralls, although that doesn't hurt." Her cousin's laughter sounded more and more like her old self. Color warmed her cheeks, and her posture wasn't as stiff and withdrawn as it had been a few days back.

One step at a time, Gillian supposed. Being here with the girls would make all the difference for Brooke.

"He found someone to sublet my apartment."

"What? How? I've been gone for a few days," Gillian said, surprised by this new revelation.

"He said his partner needed a place." Brooke sipped her coffee. "It's all set. Natalya stopped by to pick up the keys and hung out for a while with everyone. She's awesome. She's moving into my place as we speak."

"I don't know what to say." Gillian shook her head, still in shock by the sudden news.

"I want to hear all about your interview, but you need to reach out to Garrett first. He's been calling nonstop to see if you're back. He wanted to pick you up from the airport, but I figured you needed some space and you'd want to do this on your terms." Saje lifted her fingers. "Three, two one." The doorbell chimed. "Go get him, tiger."

"Crap, nothing like an advanced warning." Gillian glanced down at her sweats and oversized sweatshirt. She imagined looking her best the next time she ran into him. Of course, she looked like a mess.

Pushing her shoulders back, she walked to the door and swung it open. Her whole body swayed when she came face to face with Garrett after six long, agonizing days. She missed him so much she ached. His face looked drawn, and he smelled different. Dark smears appeared under his light blue eyes, but to her, he looked just as handsome as ever. Her heart gave a little flutter. He wore a navy flannel shirt and jeans. She'd never seen him dressed so casually and reluctantly she had to admit, the look worked for him.

"Garrett, what are you doing here?"

"Gillian, God, you don't know how good it is to see you. I've been calling but you don't pick up your phone. Can I come in? Or better yet, can we go somewhere and talk? There are some things I need to stay to you, starting with I've been such a fool." Garrett reached up to touch her cheek, and she flinched away. Hurt flashed in his eyes.

"I'm sorry," she whispered, not intending to hurt him. "But you're giving me all these mixed signals, and I don't know if I'm ready to do this again. I just got in a little while ago. I need to go for a run and clear my head."

"Let me take you to dinner tonight. There's something important I need to tell you. Gillian, sweet, sweet, Gillian," he murmured, and the endearment made her throat tight with tears. He leaned closer, and she caught a whiff of his clean laundry scent. Every part of her body responded to his smell, and it was all she could do not to fling herself into his arms.

She took a step back, holding her ground. "I'm not ready to go to dinner with you, Garrett. You hurt me too deeply."

"I need to explain. Please, meet me at my place. Where we can have some privacy. Give me that much," he pleaded.

Maybe it would be good closure for both of them. "How about I stop by after my run, in say, an hour?"

A wide smile lit up his face. "It's a date."

When Gillian got to Garrett's apartment, he stood at the door. His face lit up when he saw her, and her pathetic heart somersaulted.

He stepped aside as she walked past him into the hallway. "Why don't we sit down in the living room?" He gestured for her to go in front of him and rested a warm hand at the small of her back. A wave of heat and longing washed over her.

"Please come in and make yourself comfortable." She took a seat on the couch. He sat across from in her in a winged back chair. A myriad of emotions flashed in his eyes: relief, regret, and maybe even love. "Thanks for meeting me here. Can I offer you something to eat or drink?" Sitting here with him like this gave her a strange sense of déjà vu.

"I'm fine. I want to thank you for doing the renovations at the coven and for getting Natalya to sublet Brooke's place. It was kind of you."

"My pleasure. Anything for you." She tried to ignore the conviction in his voice and swallowed hard.

"What happened with your job interview?" He pinned her with his intense blue gaze. "Please tell me you're not moving."

She shook her head. "As much as I loved what they were offering, I could never leave. My home is here. What did you want to talk to me about?" she asked, getting right to the point. There was no sense dragging this out.

"Where do I start? I've been foolish and stubborn."

"Don't forget pigheaded," she said, trying to break some of the tension.

His lips twitched. "Yes, pigheaded, but it was my fear of loss that kept me away. There's something you need to know," Garrett continued. "Right after we met, I stumbled upon this apartment and had this compelling urge to buy it. At the time, I wasn't quite sure why I needed such a big place, but somewhere in the back of my mind, I knew it was to build a life with you." He reached across the table and took her fingers in his, rubbing his thumb across her skin. "Not calling you after everything you'd been through was foolish, but people do foolish things when they're in love." He reached behind him and handed her a beautifully wrapped package. "This is for you."

"Garrett, I...Wait, what did you say?" Her heart began to pound wildly in her chest.

"You heard me. I love you, Gillian. God so much, with all my heart and soul, and every last breath in this hundred-and-fifty-year-old body. I got freaked about not being able to give you a family."

"We can adapt," she said, laughing and crying at the same time.

"I'm sorry for being an old-fashioned ass. But if you give me another chance, I promise to make it up to you for the rest of our lives. I vow to be the man you need when things get tough. I'll be there to dry your tears." He reached out, caught one with his thumb, and brought it to his lips. "Sweet. I'll protect you against anything and anyone. You're the most loving, caring, beautiful woman I've ever known."

"Garrett, I love you so much. I forgive you." She leaned across the table and gave him a deep kiss. He pulled away and sighed then motioned to the box. "You still haven't opened it."

"You didn't need to get me a present." She lifted the box and shook it. "Whoa, it's heavy." Ripping off the paper, she opened the top to find a set of worn leather books inside. The first edition copies of *Pride and Prejudice.* "I couldn't. These belonged to Sadie."

"I want you to have them, and so would she. I remember you told me that when you moved after your parents' divorce, the only thing that made the place feel like home were your books. I want you to feel at home with me, Gillian. Always. No matter where you are, you're my home. Now lift the ribbon."

"What are you saying?" She glanced down at the book. There was a red ribbon enclosed in the front cover. When she lifted it, a lock of hair was wrapped around it. "You're giving me your hair? Is this some kind of vampire thing?"

He smiled, his blue eyes crinkling at the corners. "Take a closer look, Gillian."

When she did, she saw dark hair and a tinge of gray. "What's this?"

"It's my hair. I took the potion while you were away. I'm not completely human yet, but the change is taking place and I'm aging, even as we speak."

"Oh, Garrett." She leapt up from the couch, and he pulled her into his arms. A flood of happy tears clogged her throat.

He leaned back. Love and passion burned in his eyes. "I want you to move in with me. I moved half of my things out of my closet to make space for you. It's your home now, if you want it to be. I've never lived with a woman before, and you're the only woman in the world I could ever dream about living with. Please, say yes," he murmured and placed a soft kiss on her lips.

"Yes! But not right now. I can't leave Brooke, not after everything she's been through. Please understand," Gillian said, lacing their fingers together. "We take it day by day, and in the meantime, I'm available for dates. Do you think you can live with that for the time being?"

He kissed her again more urgently this time, delving his tongue into her mouth with deep, velvet strokes. Butterflies fluttered in her belly. He pulled away, leaving her breathless and happier than she'd ever been in her life. "I can live with that for now. We've got a whole lifetime together and it starts now. Remember, baby, I'm not going anywhere."

Midnight Craving

Arcadia, the demon plane
   1324

The air swirled with sand, gritty blasts that caught in Cayden's throat and stung his eyes. He loathed the desert—loathed the sight of dead grass and tumbleweeds. Trudging through the dunes with two enormous water jugs balanced on his shoulders, he could think of much better ways to pass the time. But this was his job, his *officium*...he was a slave.

This land had once been a Shangri-La, overflowing with lush vegetation and natural springs, but not anymore. Water was now a commodity around here, rationed for their new ruling class, the Coterie. If someone had told him a cadre of vampires would win the war and eventually take over his people, he would've laughed in their face.

Fate could be one twisted bitch.

An acrid blast of sweltering heat hit him square in the chest and made it hard to breathe. Sweat trickled down his back, soaking through to his linen kilt. A former general in the army, he'd been stripped of his uniform and his post. The navy sash around his waist remained, the only marker that delineated him as a former officer. Now cracked lips and an insatiable thirst were his only spoils of war. He'd do just about anything to have a raindrop touch his skin or witness a desert bloom.

War eviscerated hope and any chance of a better future for his people. He tried to tamp down his fury when his nostrils flared with the tang of blood. It was everywhere, winding its way through the canyons turning their once crystal blue lakes to red.

Cayden followed the path from the reservoir to the royal tent. Pushing through the gossamer netting, he walked into a makeshift kitchen set up behind a silkscreen. The tent buzzed with voices and the faint strum of a harp. He settled the jugs on the dirt floor and let out a groan.

"Where have you been? You know better than to keep the queen waiting."

The soft, female voice made his heart bang against his chest. He turned to find Abigail, one of the slave girls behind him with a teasing smile on her face. Her golden hair wrapped around her small pink horns in long plaits and hung down her back. Blue eyes the color of the sea remained locked on his. He closed the distance between them and scooped her up in his arms. When he lifted her in the air and swung her around, she let out a squeal of pure joy.

"What else can she do to me at this point?" he murmured and set Abigail on her feet. He'd gotten into enough tussles with the royal guard to finally figure out what he could get away with. Maybe that's why his back looked like a road map of welts and red scars, some of the perils of living under a court filled with ruthless bloodsuckers he supposed.

"Behave yourself. Someone will see us," Abigail said with a laugh, craning her neck to look him in the eyes. Their relationship remained chaste, never getting the opportunity to do much more than hold hands and kiss, but that would change soon. He planned to make her his for all eternity.

"You go out first and blend. No one will be the wiser." He winked and tugged on one of her braids.

"Says you, demon." She blew him a kiss and then ducked out.

With one last smile at her fleeting form, Cayden turned his head and poured the water into smaller bottles. He placed them on one of the adorned silver trays engraved with the ruling class coat of arms and walked through the curtain.

He found Lilith, their new queen, lounged on her throne with other members of the undead royal court. Slave men and women fluttered all around her like a swarm of bees at a picnic. A royal crown of thorns adorned her head of long, jet black hair. She wore a sheer silver gown with glittering jewels that had once belonged to his people. Her dark eyes were flat...soulless. She was as beautiful as she was ruthless, a viper to the core, one that could strike at any moment. Nothing could stifle her hair-trigger temper. If you so much as looked at her the wrong way, you were toast. Hundreds of his former soldiers had perished at her command.

"You may step forward, half-breed," Lilith commanded in a bored voice.

Half-human and half-demon, his Hymera status didn't bode well in court. He tried not to drag his sandaled feet as he made his way to her throne. He set the tray on a table in offering and bowed low, averting his eyes. Conversations drifted over the music. His head jerked up when he caught the ramblings of "expanding the royal line" and "conquering new realms." The Coterie would stop at nothing to gain power.

Searching through the crowd, his gaze landed on Abigail. A silent promise of love and splendor passed between them. Catching the interest of the queen, Abigail quickly looked away and poured wine into her goblet.

"Am I interrupting something, demon?" Lilith's question forced the royal guard into stunned silence. She glanced from Abigail to him and back again.

"No, my queen. Forgive me for my insolence." His gaze latched onto the purple and green Coterie banner emblazoned with their symbol. "I was simply admiring the royal colors," he lied, praying she didn't pick up on his interest. Slaves were forbidden to be together. Their job was to serve the kingdom, period. He'd never seen the king, but he was known to be a fearsome warrior. It was rumored he'd left his queen to fight wars and conquer other thrones.

"You're a dreadful liar." Her dark eyes flared with interest as they performed a slow sweep from his bare chest down his torso to his sash. He tried his best not to flinch, but her flagrant perusal made his skin crawl. "You're filthy." Lilith titled her crowned head to the side. "Do you ever bathe?" Snickers rang through the tent.

"I fancy a soak and a full canteen, your highness, but it's difficult for those who have no access to water," Cayden quipped, not able to hold back.

"Someone who's not afraid to speak his mind is a rare treat around here. Permission granted. As a former officer, you'll use my chamber to bathe." The queen pointed to an area of shimmering curtains behind the throne.

"Many thanks to a just and kind ruler." Cayden bowed again, not sure why she chose to make such an allowance for a half-breed demon, but he wasn't about to complain.

After Cayden finished his duties, he made his way to the queen's private bath and filled the makeshift tub using a bucket. Once he removed his cloth, he inched himself into the water, but only half his body fit. His limbs hung out the sides of the tub, but bloody hell...the moment the water touched his skin he hissed out a breath.

He reached for a cake of soap and the sickly, sweet scent of Lilith's perfume filled the air. The vampire slithered to the tub. "My queen." He bowed his head and did his best to cover his nakedness. *Too late.*

"No need to avert your gaze. The marks on your back prove you're either very brave or very foolish. I'm determined to find out which." When he glanced up, her eyes widened with unmistakable lust. She took another step closer and her fangs jutted out from her lips. "I see the way you look at the slave girl, demon. Your allegiance should only be for me. I want you to prove your loyalty to the crown."

There was no mistaking her meaning. For fuck's sake, how was he supposed to get out of this with his balls intact? He swallowed hard. The moment she loosened the tie at her neck, he stopped her by holding up his hand. "Please don't."

Shock lit her features. "You refuse me?" She might be his queen, but there were some things he refused to do, and this was one of them. Even if his heart didn't belong to Abigail, her proposition repulsed him to the core. This was a calculated move to enforce her will over his, to shame and disgrace him. This wasn't about desire—it was about control.

"As you wish. Just remember, there's always a consequence to the choices we make, and I believe you just made yours, demon." And then in a blur, she was gone.

That was no veiled threat. She'd make him pay, which left him with only once choice, to escape with Abagail tonight.

"Cayden? What's going on?" Abigail whispered. "Your message said it was urgent." They stood in a clearing of ancient stones and barren trees lit by a sliver of pale moonlight.

He reached for her shoulders and drew her close. "We have to leave immediately. The queen's going to send her guards after me. Frankly, I'm surprised I'm not already dead and rotting in the ground for spurring her wrath."

Abigail's eyes filled with tears. "Don't say such things. What happened?"

"I disobeyed an order. It's a long story. Do you trust me?" Cayden caressed her cheek, gazing into the face of his beloved. He'd find a way for them to be together, forever.

"Of course I trust you…with all my heart. But I can't leave, not without saying goodbye to my family."

"No," he said in a gruff voice. "It's too dangerous."

"They're my people, Cayden. Besides, I know the path better than anyone, even in the dark. No one will see me."

"I'm coming with you—"

She pressed a finger to his lips to silence him. "It's safer if you stay here if the guards are after you. Wait for me. I promise I'll be right back." She kissed his lips and disappeared into the night.

Cayden ran his hand through his hair and paced, his heart pounding in his throat with every step. After several agonizing minutes, when a cold chill filled the air and left him sick with dread, he knew something was wrong. Abigail had been gone too long. He should've never let her go alone.

Taking off at a sprint, he ran in the direction of the village. A deafening cry pierced the air. *Abigail?* Once he reached the slave huts, he found a trail of blood in the sand. His chest twisted with gut-wrenching pain when he came upon Abigail's mangled body lying in a ditch. Blood dripped from the bite marks in her neck. Blood everywhere…so much blood. *No!*

He scooped her up in his arms and tore a piece of her kilt, pressing it to the wound to try and stop the bleeding. He cradled her to his chest, whispering soothing words. "Don't leave me…don't…don't." A wild sorrow gripped him and made his chest ache and his throat burn.

Her eyes welled with tears. "Cayden," she said through ragged breaths. "I'm…so sorry." Blood seeped from her lips. "I-I didn't keep my promise. Tried to… get away." She reached up and pressed a bloodied finger to his lips. "You…must go on. We will find each other on another plane. I…will love you…forever."

When he pressed his face to her chest, it became wet with tears. At first, he thought they were Abigail's, but then he realized as his heart broke and shattered, they were his own. One way or another, he vowed revenge.

THE END

Thank you for reading! Did you enjoy?

Please Add Your Review! You can sign up for Shari's newsletter for more here.

And don't miss more paranormal novels like, TIDES OF TIME by City Owl Author, Luna Joya. Turn the page for a sneak peek!

SNEAK PEEK OF TIDES OF TIME

Magic and family drama sucked Cami in the same as riptides. Sometimes, she could spot them coming on the horizon. Other mornings, like today, they swept her away without warning. Such was life in a legacy witch lineage with all its rules and expectations.

She pushed through the staff door of the emergency animal hospital and blinked against the blinding Southern California sun after another all-night shift. She scanned her surroundings as she'd done everywhere for the last year, balancing her backpack on her hip so she could fumble through it. Had she forgotten her sunglasses? She jumped at the approaching squeal of tires, her scattered nerves fraying. Her older sister's Mini Cooper skidded to a halt less than three feet away from where she stood.

She scrubbed her hand over her face. Why was Delia here? Shouldn't she be at work? Her courthouse was an hour away in Los Angeles traffic. So why was she here shoving open the passenger door?

"What the heck, Deals?"

Delia met her gaze. "Mina's missing."

Just like that–*riptide*.

Cami jumped into the car and dumped her bag on the floorboard.

"More like she's temporarily lost." Swinging her sleek blonde ponytail over her shoulder, Delia slammed the car in reverse and shot out of the parking lot. "She slipped unsupervised."

Cami sucked in a breath. Their youngest sister's power was slipping through time. Mina's body would move in the location as it was today, but her mind traveled to see a different time through another person in the same geographic space. Scenery changes after the psychic impression made for perilous slips. "Where? When?"

"She toured a historical mansion last night courtesy of a USC alum." Delia spat the last words.

"Focus." They didn't have time for sibling or college rivalries. "Mina's slip?"

"Right." Delia shifted gears and raced down side streets toward the ocean. "She followed a woman named Sunny Sol out of the mansion. I ran a search on the name. It came back to an actress from the 1920s and '30s. Mina trailed Sol along the bluffs down to the beach."

"The bluffs?" Panic shot through Cami, and her own powers thrummed in response to the strong emotion. Mina had chased an actress from old Hollywood along steep cliffs? Mudslides and falling rocks could've easily changed the landscape over the decades. Mina wouldn't have been able to distinguish the past surroundings from her present ones.

"Don't get me started." Delia switched lanes. She barely squeezed between a bus and a truck.

Cami grabbed the handle above her head. "We can't find Mina if you get us killed with your crazy driving." Her older half-sister might be the ultimate protector, but Delia drove as though her little race car had its own force field.

"Mina sent a 911 text fifteen minutes ago. Luckily, I was already in Santa Monica interviewing a witness for a trial next week." Delia slid a look her way. "I knew your ringer would be off so I called her back."

Cami spent every hour either at the animal hospital, cramming for board certification, in the ocean, or sleeping. She'd graduated with honors from the top veterinary medicine program in the country last year. Her psychic affinity for communicating with animals helped, but she still had to put in the work. Her vet residency didn't leave much free time. As a deputy district attorney, Delia understood long hours.

"I figured I could catch you before you left work." Delia streaked through a yellow light. "Mina's phone died before she told me where she was. She forgot to charge it."

Typical. Mina could be flighty handling the basics of life.

Delia swung a hard left onto the downhill ramp for the Pacific Coast Highway, locally known as the PCH. "You'll have to use your call to find her."

No. Cami's chest tightened. She didn't tap into her elemental magic, and there was no way she could tell her sisters why. She—the quintessential "good girl" Donovan sister—had broken the first rule of magic. There'd be no coming back if others discovered why she'd really walked away from her element.

"I wouldn't ask if it wasn't the only way without spending hours driving up and down the coast hoping to find her." Delia's stone-faced glare gave nothing away, but her voice had softened. "You and I don't know spell craft. There's only one person who could whip up a locator spell in an instant, and I didn't think you'd want me to call her."

"Ama." Cami sighed. She couldn't call Ama. Her mother, a powerful spellcaster, would ask too many questions if she discovered Mina had chased a historical psychic vision alone. Mina didn't need a one-way ticket to magical mommy guilt trips. It was bad enough Delia knew. "We're not telling Ama."

She fingered the pendant at her neck, similar to the one all four sisters wore. Ama had spelled the charms to warn them of danger. Hopefully, Mina had hers on.

"She called from the shore. I could hear waves and seagulls." Delia swerved into the turning lane and pulled into a beachfront parking lot. She stopped the car. "I know you and your element had some kind of a falling out a year ago."

Each of the four sisters had a call to an element. Cami's was water. She could manipulate it, communicate with it, cause damage with it.

It hadn't been a simple breakup with her element. She had nearly killed a man with her connection to water. So much for *harm none* with magic. While she'd gone to the beach daily since then and surrounded herself with its comfort, she hadn't let herself give in to her power. Not when she'd abused and then refused it.

But her sister needed her. She swallowed back the fear of what might come if she tapped into that big source again.

She unbuckled the seatbelt and tugged her stained scrubs off, stripping down to a threadbare graphic T-shirt and undies. She wadded the work clothes into her backpack, slid a pair of shorts on, and switched Crocs for flip flops.

Delia opened her door.

Cami stopped her. "Why don't you keep your couture, 'dry clean only' self in the car?" She didn't want anyone witnessing her return to her element, because what if it all went wrong?

Delia paused with her hand on the door. "Want some privacy?"

She bobbed her head, checked her necklace, and climbed out. The ocean breeze snagged her short curls. "Give me five minutes."

"Hey, Cams?"

She ducked into the open car window.

"If you can't do this, it's okay." Delia unlocked her phone screen. "I'll keep trying in case Mina finds a way to charge her phone."

Cami took a deep breath. "I've got it." If only her voice hadn't wavered.

Stepping onto the sand, she slipped off her shoes and strode toward the water's edge. She wouldn't risk this but for her sisters.

While she longed for her elemental magic to soothe and guide her, the very same source could rebuke her for misusing her power. She feared its condemnation. It'd be too much, but Mina needed her help. She leaned down, sweeping her fingers into foam on the wet sand.

Fighting doubt and worry, she reached for her magic and sent a tentative call to her element. The ocean responded in warm welcome without judgment, and she forced back the urge to tap fully into her power.

Oh, how she'd missed this.

She wanted to walk into the waves and savor each precious lap against her skin, to let the water bathe away the fear and darkness she'd carried. The need to link to that tidal power pulled her in, promising absolution she didn't deserve. She had to focus on Mina before she lost herself to the water's beckoning homecoming.

She pushed past the water's thrum of longing and expectation until her power conjured images of Mina waiting at the water's edge further north. Cami breathed a sigh of relief and gratitude along the connection.

"Thank you," she whispered and said a reluctant goodbye. With a single glance over her shoulder, she hurried back to the car and jumped inside. "Found her. Head north."

Delia tore out of the lot and zipped across three lanes of traffic. She smacked the steering wheel with her palms when they got stuck at another red light at the busiest intersection on the PCH in Pacific Palisades.

Gas stations, grocery stores, and a restaurant jammed together in the precious real estate across the street from the shore. Cami craned her neck to check the signs as they passed through the intersection and accelerated. Corraza's Restaurant.

"If Mina has slipped, she'll be starving." Each sister's magic had a price. Mina's had always been hunger. "We can head back here if they're open."

"I'll check once we find her."

They passed beneath a pedestrian bridge next to a steep set of stairs cut into the bluff.

"Here," Cami said. "She's close by, near the water's edge."

Delia flipped a U-turn in the parking area of a large Spanish-style building with arched entrances and windows below a hexagon-shaped center. "Go. I'll catch up with you."

Cami jumped out of the car and sprinted for the water. Her power called to her, directing her. She hopped the concrete barrier and raced across the sand, searching for her sister. Perched on a rock jetty, Mina stared over the waves.

Cami called out, relieved when her sister turned with clear eyes, not the dazed obsidian dilation of magic.

Mina ran a shaky hand through her hair. "You came for me."

"Always." Cami stooped to pick up her sister's hooded sweatshirt and sandals tossed nearby. She studied the strain in Mina's eyes, the dark smudges beneath. "Were you out here all night trailing Sunny Sol?"

Mina took her hoodie and gave a weak smile. "Hazards of slipping. I should've known better than to be curious."

"When I think of what could've happened to you." Cami slid her eyes closed.

"I couldn't resist, and then I got pulled in too deep."

She knew all about the overload when magic overwhelmed logic.

Mina's lips twisted. "Do you ever want to be normal? No elemental powers? No psychic ability?"

Cami wanted a lot of things: to stop looking over her shoulder; to have a good man adore her without going crazy stalker abusive on her; to have her hard work correct the bad choices she'd made so she wouldn't doubt every new one; to not have to worry about their family's magic.

She nudged Mina. "Come on. Let's go save Delia from ruining whatever designer shoes she's wearing. We spotted a place to eat a mile back. Maybe they've got pancakes."

Minutes later, Cami half-dragged her younger sister through the glass doors into Corraza's Restaurant to find a table while Delia parked the car. The swift change from bright sunlight to the darker interior had Cami blinking behind sunglasses she'd borrowed from Delia.

If only the dimmed lighting and dark glasses could excuse her gawking at the man behind the front podium. All muscles and tanned skin, he looked up from his notes, and his gaze locked on her face.

The exhaustion of back-to-back shifts must have caught up to her. Or the cost of her magic decided to crash into her as it did for Delia, who'd black out from using too much.

Cami bit back a groan. She'd drawn so hard on her psychic ability to connect with animals last night and then her elemental magic this morning, she should've expected her powers would demand replenishment. Her magic craved fulfillment from a hot guy. *This* hot guy. She'd probably leaked the desire all over him. She swallowed, shoving down the need as best she could with the powers calling for collection of a debt owed.

With one hand bracing her sister, Cami tugged her sunglasses into her tangle of curls and blew out a breath. Feeding Mina was top priority. No more sexy daydreams about a handsome guy.

The fleeting second she'd given in to the fluttering in her belly had been the best part of her week. Time to return to the reality of her witchy family.

Don't stop now. Keep reading with your copy of TIDES OF TIME , by City Owl Author, Luna Joya, available now.

And sign up for the City Owl Press newsletter to receive notice of all book releases!

Want even more paranormal books? Try TIDES OF TIME by City Owl Author, Luna Joya, and find more from Shari Nichols at sharinicholsauthor.com

She had a very good reason for breaking the first rule of magic ... and the second one ...

Cami Donovan has secrets. Big ones that no one can ever know.

All she can do now is try to forget the past and focus on the future. But as it turns out, her future—her *family's* future—might not be shiny and bright unless she can help her sister resolve the cold case murder that's been plaguing her psychic visions.

Falling for the sexy history expert who holds the keys to it all? That was *never* part of the plan.

The last thing on Sam Corraza's mind is romance. Emotional entanglements bring nothing but pain. His past certainly taught him that. But when he's presented with an old Hollywood mystery to solve, he can't stay away—from the case, or the enchanting witch who brought it to him.

As they unravel the evidence—and their feelings for each other—it becomes clear that the past is coming back to haunt them in a big way.

With danger closing in, can Cami and Sam overcome all that stands between them—or is history destined to repeat itself?

Please sign up for the City Owl Press newsletter for chances to win special subscriber-only contests and giveaways as well as receiving information on upcoming releases and special excerpts.

All reviews are **welcome** and **appreciated**. Please consider leaving one on your favorite social media and book buying sites.

For books in the world of romance and speculative fiction that embody Innovation, Creativity, and Affordability, check out City Owl Press at www.cityowlpress.com.

ACKNOWLEDGMENTS

There are several people who contribute to an author's work and I've been blessed to work with some of the best! This book was made possible thanks to my incredible critique partner, award winning author M.Kate Quinn; my brilliant daughter, Jacqueline, my fabulous editor, Heather McCorkle and the rest of the crew at City Owl Press, many thanks to Yelena Casale and Tina Moss.

I'd like to thank my dear friend Tanya for giving me the grand tour of Hoboken, the inspiration for the fictional town of Raven's Hollow. I'd also like to thank psychic, Amanda, for her knowledge and patience in helping me bring the character of Gillian to life on the page. To my husband and my kids— you're my world!

Thank you readers! Your kindness humbles me beyond words.

xoxo

Would you like to stay up on all the latest news? Sign up for my newsletter here.

ABOUT THE AUTHOR

Shari Nichols grew up in a small town in Connecticut where haunted houses, ghosts and Ouija boards were common place, spurring her fascination with all things paranormal. Ever since she read her first Barbara Cartland novel, her life-long dream has been to write sexy, romantic stories. When she's not writing, she's reading, going to the gym, or hanging out with family and friends.

She lives in New Jersey with her husband, two children, and her golden retriever. Shari's a member of Romance Writers of America, New Jersey Romance Writers, Liberty States Fiction Writers and Fantasy, Futuristic, and Paranormal Romance Writers. Sign up for her newsletter here.

Awards: Golden Leaf Finalist, NJ Author Best Book Finalist, The Beverley Award, HOLT Medallion Finalist, Literary Titan Silver Medal Winner.

sharinicholsauthor.com

facebook.com/sharinicholsauthor

twitter.com/Shari_Nich

instagram.com/shari_nichols

ABOUT THE PUBLISHER

City Owl Press is a cutting edge indie publishing company, bringing the world of romance and speculative fiction to discerning readers.

www.cityowlpress.com

www.ingramcontent.com/pod-product-compliance
Lightning Source LLC
Chambersburg PA
CBHW031215020726
47499CB00002B/596